Stealing Second:
Sam's Story

ALSO BY BARBARA L. CLANTON

THE CLARKSONVILLE SERIES
Out of Left Field: Marlee's Story (Book One)
Tools of Ignorance: Lisa's Story (Book Two)
Going, Going, Gone: Susie's Story (Book Three)
Stealing Second: Sam's Story (Book Four)
Out at Home (Book Five)
Tools of the Devil (Book Six)
Going Under (Book Seven)
Stealing Hope (Book Eight)

THE WHICKETT SERIES
Art for Art's Sake: Meredith's Story (Book One)
Dani's Story (Book Two) … <Coming Soon>

THE GRASSE RIVER SERIES
Quite an Undertaking: Devon's Story (Book One)
Rebecca's Story (Book Two) … <Coming Soon>

THE GIRLS' SPORTS SERIES
(Children's Books Ages 9-12)
Bases Loaded
Side Out
Live, Love, Lacrosse

.

STEALING SECOND
Sam's Story

BOOK FOUR IN THE CLARKSONVILLE SERIES

BARBARA L. CLANTON

eBook ISBN   978-1-953734-19-8

Revised First Edition 2022

9 8 7 6 5 4 3 2 1

Cover design by Sarah (Forcoverservice)

Published by:
Bibi Books Publishing Company, LLC

Dedication

For Patricia Gengo, whose love of music and life
has inspired me throughout my lifetime.

Acknowledgments

I'd like to thank Sheri Milburn and J Robin Whitley for taking time from their own writing to help me with mine. I'd also like to thank Maureen May and her Strings classes for letting me observe and absorb. Thanks, once again, go out to my Regal Crest family – Cathy Bryerose, Mary Phillips, and Donna Pawlowski. I am also ever grateful to my friends and family, who give me continual inspiration and support. And thanks, finally, to Jackie Weathers, my life partner in all aspects of being.

Author's Note to the Revised Edition

I have been given the amazing opportunity to go back and re-edit my earlier work, and I have taken up that opportunity gladly. "Stealing Second: Sam's Story" is Book Four in the Clarksonville Series, initially published in 2013. It was the fourth novel in the Clarksonville series and written from Samantha Rose (Sam) Payton's point of view. I hadn't originally intended each of the main characters to have their own stories told, but they rose up and rebelled until I promised to do it. Oh, main characters can be so persistent. Now, about nine years after the first publishing, I am grateful for the chance to revisit this original story.

And just a note that this is a *revised* edition, not a second edition. Nothing major has changed in the story plot. Only the grammar, punctuation, and awkward stuff (to my current ears and eyes) have been changed, updated, or eliminated.

I'm confident that the emotions and situations will stand the test of time and that you, dear reader, will enjoy Sam's coming-out story.

Cheers,
Barb
Central Florida (June 2022)

Table of Contents

Chapter 1
Falling in Love

Samantha Rose Payton sat in the East Valley dugout next to her best friend, Susie Torres. They were ultra-early for their summer softball game, and except for them, the field and dugouts were empty. Even though she should have been getting ready for the game, Sam leaned back against the cement block wall and sighed.

Susie shot Sam a sidelong glance. "*¿Que pasó, chica?*"

"Nothing." Sam sighed again.

"*Aay,*" Susie spoke to the field as if Sam wasn't there, "she says, 'nothing,' but drags me out here early, sighing every two minutes. Dizzy blonde." She got a whack on the arm for her comment. "Hey!" She rubbed her arm where Sam had hit her.

"I'm not dizzy."

"But you *are* blonde."

"So's your girlfriend," Sam teased back.

"But Marlee's not dizzy."

Sam crossed her eyes at her best friend. Susie had always been a true friend, her only friend until recently, ever since ninth grade.

"C'mon, what's wrong?" Susie's tone was more serious. She pulled her cleats out of her bag.

"Nothing. Everything." Sam had been restless at home, waiting around to go to the game. Her parents were due home later that evening after a long weekend of political schmoozing downstate in

1

Albany. Politicians were constantly trying to woo her parents into making generous contributions to their campaigns. Sam could care less about that sort of thing. Her nanny, Helene, had left early that morning for a shopping trip to meet her sister just over the border in Cornwall, Canada for the day and wouldn't be back until late that evening. That left Sam bouncing around the mansion all by herself. Even practicing the violin for her mother's luncheon in two days couldn't hold her interest. Thank God Susie didn't mind heading to the field super early.

"Did your parents find out you were a big ole lesbian?" Susie teased.

"Shhh." Sam's eyes grew big. Thank God no one was around to hear. "That is never going to happen, and you know it."

"You're so far in the closet you've decorated." Susie rolled her eyes.

"I like the curtains in there, okay?" Sam growled.

"Okay, okay." Susie put her hands up in defense. "So, what's wrong? Your black eye got you down?"

Sam reached up and touched her eye. It wasn't sore anymore, and the swelling had gone down days before. She knew from a last look in the mirror before leaving the house that it wasn't black; it was more greenish-yellow. Sam swirled a finger around her ear. "Bree was one screwed-up chick, wasn't she?"

"I can't believe she took a swing at you," Susie said, shaking her head.

"And connected." Sam touched her eye again.

"You should have hit her back, but enough stalling. What's up with you?"

Sam looked down, not sure how to talk to her best friend about her girlfriend or even if she should. Some things should remain private. And there was that other thing. Susie was her ex.

As if reading Sam's mind, Susie pressed on. "Are you and Lisa okay?"

"Yeah." Sam's heart clenched at the lie. "Well, no. I don't know. I'm not sure." Sam felt her cheeks heat up as she watched confusion and compassion mix on Susie's face.

"Spill it."

"Spill what?"

Sam and Susie both jumped at the sound of Coach Gellar's voice.

"You two are here early." Coach Gellar looked at her watch. "It's not even close to five o'clock." She put her coach's bag down on the bench.

"I wanted to stretch and throw early." Sam gestured to her eye. That wasn't the real reason, but she figured her coach would buy it since it was her first game back after getting punched by an opposing player.

"Understandable," Coach Gellar said and then went about her business getting ready for the game.

Susie stood up. "C'mon, let's go stretch."

"Okay." Sam grabbed her cleats and glove and followed Susie to left field.

Once they plopped on the ground, Sam tossed off her sandals, put her socks on, and then her right shoe.

Susie tightened the laces on her cleats and then put her feet together for a butterfly stretch. "So? What's the problem?"

Sam lay back on the grass and stared at the late afternoon sky so she wouldn't have to look directly at Susie. It was a brilliant mid-

August blue with a few lazy clouds dallying overhead. She took a deep breath for courage and went for it. "I know I keep bugging you about this, and you can tell me to shuddup, but—"

"Yes, we did," Susie answered the unasked question.

Sam's head whipped around. "You did? When?" She sat up.

Susie scowled at her friend.

Sam put her hands up. "Okay, sorry. TMI. I know. Are you, like, on cloud nine?"

A blush crept up Susie's neck to her face tingeing her dark cheeks even darker. Susie was Puerto Rican and seemed to have a perpetual tan that got darker during the summer, but the blush was more than evident. She hid her face in her hands and then pushed them up on her head, mussing her usually perfect auburn hair. "You're so nosy, Sam."

"Sorry." Sam felt her face flush. "But, c'mon, I have no one to talk to about this stuff. I can't talk to Helene about sex."

"Most people don't have nannies after age five, you know."

"Shuddup." Sam felt her blush intensifying. Susie was right, though. Most people she knew didn't have nannies at all. Her family, the East Valley Paytons, had an image to uphold and servants were part of that image. Changing diapers, potty training, and general child-rearing were beneath her parents, of course, so that's why they had obtained Helene's services when Sam was born. Sam frowned. Susie was right. No one had a nanny when they were seventeen. She wondered, not for the first time, when Helene would leave.

Susie cleared her throat. "So?" The one word held an interesting mixture of sympathy and curiosity.

Sam wasn't sure how to phrase what she wanted to say. She found courage when Susie sat quietly waiting. Sam whispered, "Lisa

4

and I are stuck at second base if you know what I mean. Shouldn't Lisa and I have already, you know, moved on?" Sam waved her hands around, desperately not wanting to say the words, hoping Susie would figure out what she meant.

"Are you shy about it?"

"No, I don't think so. I mean, you remember how you and I almost—" Sam gestured with her hands again.

"Yep, and then Helene walked in on us." Susie laughed. "*Aay*, it was probably better that she did, 'cuz we both know we make better friends than girlfriends. I think we got together last summer because we were both lonely."

Sam nodded.

"You know," Susie said, "Lisa's a whole year younger than you are."

"I know."

"Maybe she's not ready. I shouldn't be saying this, but," Susie looked around, presumably to make sure no one was within earshot, "I was ready to—" Susie gestured with her hands the same way Sam had done, "way before Marlee was. I had to be patient and take things at her speed."

"Yeah? Maybe that's all it is then. So, I shouldn't worry?"

"Nah. Lisa will let you know when she's ready. And believe me, when she's ready, you'll know."

Sam blew out a long sigh. "God, I feel so much better. I thought there was something wrong with me."

"I think Lisa needs to feel safe and secure. That way, she can relax. So, *both* of you can relax."

Sam nodded in agreement. Hopefully, Susie was right. Movement behind her caught her attention, and she looked toward the parking lot. A few of her teammates were trickling in, but so far, there was no sign of Lisa with her catcher's gear slung over one shoulder. "Maybe I kept sensing that she wasn't quite ready or something, and I didn't want to push. I mean, we got to second base fast. Too fast, probably." She chuckled. "I think it's the only time I've stolen second on Lisa Brown."

"*Aay, Santo.* It's probably the only time Lisa has ever let anybody steal second."

"Oh, God. Don't say anything to Marlee. Okay? I'd be mortified if she knew we were talking about this."

"I won't."

"Cool."

Susie cleared her throat. "So, after you stole second, why didn't you go for third?"

Sam burst out laughing and buried her face in her hands. "I don't know."

Susie smiled sympathetically. "Just relax, *chica.* It'll happen when she's ready. When you're *both* ready."

Sam hadn't even considered that maybe she wasn't ready either. She vowed not to put any more pressure on herself. She had been getting herself worked up over nothing. It would happen when it happened.

Susie gestured toward the parking lot. Lisa and Marlee were walking up to the fields and were laughing about something. Lisa's happy face and sexy dimples sent a shiver through Sam. She watched her tall girlfriend open the gate to let Marlee in first. That was so like Lisa, to put other people first. That probably came from being the big sister to three much younger siblings.

Lisa pushed her long black braid behind her back, and Sam

immediately wanted to unbraid it and run her fingers through the long tresses. Sam was turning to mush as she watched.

"What's that sound?" Susie asked as she stood up.

"What sound?"

"You. Planning to steal third." Susie grinned and then smacked her friend on the shoulder before running toward the dugout.

Sam leaped up to chase her friend but fell back down with a laugh. She only had one shoe on. She quickly threw the other one on, grabbed her sandals and glove, and headed toward the dugout on the run.

"Hey, slowpoke," Lisa said, the twinkle in her eye melting Sam's heart. She gave Sam a quick nudge with her shoulder.

Sam nudged back and drank in Lisa's smile. She tore herself away to greet Marlee. "Hey, Marlee."

"Hey, Sam." Marlee grinned. "Lisa's got news."

"Oh, yeah?" Sam raised her eyebrows. "What?"

Lisa blushed and shot daggers with her eyes at Marlee. "You weren't supposed to say anything yet. I was going to break it to her gently."

"Oh, man." Marlee put a hand over her mouth and mumbled, "Sorry."

Susie laughed. "Now you have to tell."

"Okay." Lisa grimaced and looked at Sam apologetically.

Sam's stomach flipped. She had no idea what Lisa's news could be. A thousand thoughts flashed through her mind. Lisa wouldn't break up with her right there in front of everybody, would she?

Lisa put a gentle hand on her arm. "It's not that bad. Relax, okay?"

Sam hadn't realized how tense she'd become. "Okay."

"I got my physical for school this morning."

"What's wrong?"

"Nothing. I promise. It's just that I'm not five-nine anymore."

Susie burst out laughing.

Sam's mouth dropped open.

Marlee laughed. "Sam, you're catching flies."

Sam snapped her mouth shut. "Okay, so how tall are you now?"

Lisa grimaced before she said, "Five ten and a half. I grew an inch and a half since last summer."

Susie laughed again. "The basketball team's gonna recruit you, Lisa."

"Oh, believe me, they try every year."

Sam leaned close to Lisa's ear and whispered, "There's more of you to love this way."

When Lisa's blush reached the roots of her dark hair, a wave of tingles flushed through Sam. She rubbed her face, hoping no one saw her blush.

Susie reached for a softball from the bucket. "C'mon, Sam, let's get this team stretched. We're supposed to be the leaders or something."

Sam and Susie led the team in their warmups and later led the charge onto the field to start the game against the Northwood Sharks. The Nor'easters quickly ran up the score against them, so Coach Gellar took Sam, Lisa, and Marlee out of the game early to give the substitutes playing time. That was okay with Sam because she winced when a Northwood runner slid into second base. She'd had a weird flashback about Bree sliding into second and then attacking her.

"C'mon, Nor'easters," Sam called from the dugout bench, "just one more out."

"C'mon, Mary," Marlee called to the second-string pitcher, "show 'em what you've got."

Back on the field, the Northwood batter swung hard at the ball but missed for the third strike and the last out of the game.

Sam leaped up. "Way to go, Nor'easters!" She, Lisa, and Marlee ran onto the field to congratulate their teammates.

After the high-five line, Coach Gellar called them together. "Good job, girls," she said. "Nice pitching, McAllister." She nodded her approval at Marlee. "Great job, too, Walker." She nodded at Mary. "We've got fifteen wins and no losses. On Thursday, I expect us to stay undefeated after we play Little Bend. That'll make us the first-place team going into Saturday's tournament."

Sam nodded along with the rest of her teammates. Thursday's game would be a cakewalk.

"The Elmhurst Rage is our closest competitor," Coach Gellar continued. "They only have two losses so far. Both from us."

Sam and her Nor'easter teammates hooted at that news, but Coach Gellar threw in a cautionary note. "Don't let them fool you. They are a very good team, and I fully expect to meet them in the finals." She looked each of them in the eye to get her point across.

Sam understood how important winning was to their coach. When their high school team, the East Valley Panthers, lost to Marlee and Lisa's Clarksonville team during the spring season, Coach Gellar had given them so much grief that Sam was almost glad her team hadn't gone any further. And, since Clarksonville went on to beat everybody on their way to win the State Championship title, losing to them seemed okay somehow.

After reminding the team that they would have batting practice before Thursday's game, Coach Gellar dismissed them. Sam and her friends changed into street shoes and headed out to the parking lot together. Sam opened the trunk to her Sebring convertible and threw her gear inside.

She gestured for Lisa to throw her gear next to hers. "I'll drive you home later after we visit the yacht."

"Cool." Lisa shot her a suggestive look that made Sam's insides shake.

Marlee and Susie walked up after storing their gear in Marlee's van. Susie leaned back against Sam's car.

"My wonderful girlfriend is going to drive me home after our trip to the marina," Lisa said to Marlee, "so you're off the hook."

"Cool. Call me if anything changes."

"I will," Lisa said. "Let me get my wallet and phone from your car."

Marlee spun on her heels, and they headed back toward her van.

Sam watched Lisa walk away, admiring her strong athletic gait and the swing of her dark braid. Lisa looked back over her shoulder as if feeling Sam's eyes on her. She raised one eyebrow and smiled suggestively. Sam almost dissolved.

"Hey, Sus?" Sam said to her friend.

"Yeah?"

"Can you keep falling in love with the same person?"

"I think maybe you can," Susie said. "I do it every day."

Sam nodded in agreement. "Me, too."

Chapter 2
With You, I'm Sam

Sam pulled the Sebring into the marina parking lot and angled the car toward the sunset. She wanted Lisa to have the best view through the convertible's open top of the sky glowing orange, tinting the few remaining clouds and trees on the Canadian side of the St. Lawrence River.

"It's so beautiful tonight." Lisa leaned her head back against the headrest.

"Mmm. So are you." Sam smiled at Lisa. She knew it was cheesy, but it was true. Her stomach clenched as a wave of desire spread through her. She cleared her throat. "C'mon. Let's sit on the deck and watch the summer sky for a while."

Lisa nodded and opened the passenger door.

Sam desperately wanted to hold Lisa's hand as they walked to the yacht, but she couldn't risk being seen. Word would get around that the daughter of Gerald and Mimi Payton was seen holding hands with a girl. Not that people spied on her, it was just that being Samantha Rose Payton in Clarksonville County meant that everybody knew who she was.

Sam led the way past fishing boats and pleasure boats on their way to the tri-level Marquis-720 motor yacht. Sam stepped on board and held her hand out to help Lisa step from the dock onto the deck.

"Thank you," Lisa said with a nod as she stepped on board.

"You're welcome." Sam unlocked the door to the main cabin, and they headed toward the lounge area in the stern. They had come to the yacht before, but Sam hadn't felt comfortable going beyond kissing Lisa below decks. Maybe this time would be different.

Lisa stopped and picked up a formal photograph of Sam and her parents. "Look at you. So formal with your pearls."

In the picture, Sam and her father were standing stiffly behind Sam's mother who was seated in a high winged back chair, and if it were possible to sit stiffly, her mother was doing it. Sam grimaced. She hated that picture. With her pearls, mother's diamonds, and father's tailored suit, the pretentious picture wreaked of money and the fact that her family had plenty of it.

Sam snorted and pointed to her image in the photograph. "That girl? The one with the pearls is Samantha Rose Payton, the perfect princess and heiress to the Payton family fortune."

Lisa put the photo back and turned toward Sam. "So, who are you?"

"I don't know." Sam grunted. "All I know is that I'm Sam when I'm with you."

"I like Sam a lot." Lisa grinned. "But I'm still not sure who Samantha Rose is." Her hand gestured to the surrounding yacht.

"That makes two of us." Sam shrugged and led the way to the head cabinet so they could freshen up.

They each took a moment to wash their hands and use the bathroom, and after grabbing two Sprites from the refrigerator in the galley, Sam led them to the leather couch on the upper deck.

"Here you go." Sam handed Lisa a can and then plopped next to her on the couch. She left plenty of space between them since it was still light enough for anyone to see.

"Thanks." Lisa popped open the top and took a sip. "Mmm, this is so amazing."

"Mmm," Sam agreed, knowing Lisa wasn't talking about the soda.

They watched the orange sky fade to red and then a mixture of grays. The seagulls squawking overhead at the incoming fishermen completed the scene.

Sam lowered her voice. "I wish I could cuddle with you out here."

"Me, too." Lisa smiled sympathetically. "Someday."

"That would be nice, but…"

"I know," Lisa said. "You can't."

Sam nodded and looked back at the twilight sky. They sat in silence for a while, drinking their sodas and enjoying the end of a beautiful August summer day.

Sam set her soda down on a side table and turned her head slightly to take in Lisa's profile. Lisa had the cutest little nose and high solid cheekbones. Her long dark braid was pulled in front of her shoulders, making her look like a Native American princess. Her eyes were a delicious light brown that melted Sam with every glance. Her lips were pouty and oh-so-kissable. A low-grade hum settled across Sam's body. She silently reached for Lisa's soda and placed it next to hers on the table. Lisa turned toward her and sent a silent message of yearning with her eyes.

"Let's go inside," Sam said huskily.

"To your cabin?"

Sam nodded.

"Okay." Lisa stood up.

They made their way inside the yacht. They'd gone to Sam's cabin before, but things felt different this time. Sam's body hummed as she led the way down the spiral staircase to the lower deck and headed for the bow. Before they even made it to the cabin, Sam turned and flew into Lisa's arms. Their lips met in a fury of passion. Sam moaned as a wave of desire shot through her. She lived for Lisa's sensuous kisses.

Sam pulled back, her breathing heavy. Forehead to forehead, her lips barely touched Lisa's.

"Sam," Lisa whispered, "you're killing me."

Sam answered by pressing herself against Lisa and searing her with another kiss. After a moment, Sam led the way into her cabin. She remembered what Susie said about Lisa needing to feel safe and secure, so she locked the door behind them. She turned and wordlessly pulled Lisa's uniform jersey off. She ran her fingers along the outline of Lisa's sports bra. Lips replaced fingers until Lisa tugged at Sam's jersey, demanding equal time. Sam pulled her own jersey off and threw it on the floor. They fell together on the bed.

Sam trailed slow and tender kisses from Lisa's neck to her delicious cleavage.

Lisa sat up and gently pulled Sam's bra off. Reaching for Sam's waist, she rolled Sam onto her back. She removed her bra with a quick tug before lowering herself on top.

Sam's body hummed its pleasure at Lisa's kisses. When the sensations threatened to overwhelm her, she rolled Lisa to her side, and they lay face to face. Lisa kept her eyes closed while Sam softly trailed a finger across her sensual lips. Lisa kissed the finger and then opened her eyes, her lustful gaze making Sam whimper.

Lisa whispered, "I love you." She leaned closer and nibbled on

Sam's earlobe.

"Same," Sam squeaked as shivers ran down her body.

A creak in the floorboards overhead sent Sam sitting bolt upright.

"Did you hear that?" Sam whispered.

Before Lisa could answer, they heard another footstep above them.

"Oh, shit." Sam leaped off the bed. "Someone's on the yacht." She frantically searched for their shirts and found them on the floor near the door. She tossed Lisa hers. Sam tugged her uniform jersey over her head without bothering to put on her bra.

"Geez, geez, geez," Lisa mumbled in panic as she fumbled with her clothes.

"Shhh," Sam motioned at Lisa to remain quiet and still. She wanted to hear where the intruder was.

"Samantha Rose?" came a booming voice from just outside her cabin door.

Sam and Lisa squealed in panic.

"Daddy?" Sam dislodged her heart from her throat. "Is that you?" She thanked her lucky stars she had locked the cabin door. A glance told her that Lisa was now fully dressed.

"Yes. Are you all right?"

"Yes, Daddy. I'll be right out, okay?"

"What's going on in there?" His voice was all business. He jostled the locked doorknob. He was trying to get in.

"Nothing. I was just giving my friend a tour of the yacht."

The doorknob rattled again. "Why is this door locked?"

"Oh, is it?" Sam said innocently.

"Open this door immediately."

"Hang on." Sam mentally thanked Lisa for smoothing the bedspread, so it didn't look rumpled. She kicked her bra out of sight and then unlocked the door. "Hi, Daddy." Her heart was pounding.

He burst into the room. His eyes scoured the small room as if looking for something or somebody. "Oh," he said after taking one look at Lisa. The disappointment in his voice was unmistakable. That's when it dawned on Sam. Her father thought she was in the cabin with a guy. She bit her bottom lip to stop a laugh. If he only knew.

"Daddy, this is Lisa. She plays on my summer softball team." She kept her arms folded across her chest because she didn't want her father to notice that she wasn't wearing a bra.

"It's a pleasure to meet one of Sam's friends." He cleared his throat, obviously embarrassed by his presumption.

"It's nice to meet you, sir," Lisa said. "Sorry about the locked door. I think I locked it by mistake. I don't know much about boats."

"That's all right, young lady."

"And this yacht is absolutely gorgeous. Sam was giving me the nickel tour."

"Indeed. Carry on then."

"Daddy?" Sam said.

"Yes, Kitten?"

Sam cringed at the pet name he used for her. "I thought you and Mother were still in Albany."

"We got home a little while ago."

"It's okay that I'm on the yacht, isn't it? I mean, you said I could." She pretended to be ignorant about why he had burst in on them.

"Of course, it's okay. As long as you don't take her out to sea, that is."

"Not on your life," Sam said with a laugh. "You're the captain of this ship."

Her father beamed, his blue eyes twinkling in the dim light. His boyish sandy blond hair made him look younger than his actual fifty-three years. "Don't stay out too late." He headed out of the cabin.

"I won't," Sam said. "Thanks for making sure we were all right." Of course, she wondered how he knew they were even there, but she didn't dare ask. Someone from the marina office must have called him and said Sam was on the yacht with someone tall. Did they think Lisa was a guy? Far from it.

Sam turned to Lisa and mouthed, "Sorry." She retrieved her bra and quickly put it back on. Out loud, she said, "So, this is my cabin. Let's go back up to the main deck and get our sodas, okay?"

"Sure." Lisa fell into step behind Sam.

Once on the main deck, Sam spotted her father on the dock. "Bye, Daddy."

"Bye, Kitten. Be safe, okay?"

"I will."

He headed toward the chauffeured Lincoln Town Car idling in the parking lot.

Sam watched until the Town Car was well out of sight. She turned, not sure what she'd see in Lisa's face. Lisa smiled back at her with so much gentleness that Sam melted. "I am so sorry."

"Don't be. It's okay." Lisa blew out a sigh. "Thank God he didn't catch us. My nerves are shot."

"Mine, too."

"But you know what?" Lisa said.

"What?"

"My father would have done the same thing."

Sam laughed. "Which father?"

Lisa chuckled. "Both."

"C'mon," Sam pulled her keys out. "Let's go to our usual spot on Raymond Road."

Lisa nodded. "I don't think I'll ever be able to look at this yacht in quite the same way ever again."

"Same," Sam said with a laugh. "I guess it's no longer an option for us."

They headed back to the upper deck to get their sodas, turn out lights, and lock doors.

Once in the Sebring, Sam put the top up, and they headed back toward the secluded farm road in East Valley. It was dark when she pulled the car far up the deserted road.

Sam undid her seatbelt. Lisa did the same.

"You were quiet on the drive over," Lisa said. "Are you okay?"

Sam wondered how she was going to explain her father's paranoia about protecting her. "We almost got caught."

"I know. That was close," Lisa said. "How did your father even know we were there?"

"Someone from the marina must have ratted on us." Sam shrugged and then snuggled into the softness of Lisa's shirt. She chuckled.

"Why are you laughing?" Lisa asked softly.

"Me." Sam gestured to her front. "I was standing there braless in front of my father."

"At least it wasn't topless."

"No kidding." Sensing that things had cooled off considerably after her father's intrusion, Sam kissed Lisa on the forehead. "Baby, I know we were about to, you know, but…"

"Yeah, we should try another time," Lisa said. "I'm still freaking out a little."

"You look so calm and cool."

"Not a chance." Lisa shook her head. "My heart is pounding."

Sam laid her ear on Lisa's chest. The familiar heartbeat was smooth and rhythmic. "I think you'll live."

"Oh, thank God." Lisa stroked Sam's head.

"Hey," Sam sat up, "do you want to get some ice cream instead?"

"I thought you'd never ask."

"I hope you're not too disappointed." Sam started the engine, turned on the headlights, and headed back toward Raymond Road.

Lisa took a long time responding. "I *am* disappointed, but not with you, Sam. Just with the circumstances, I guess."

"One of these days, we'll find a place of our own where no one will interrupt us. Do you still love me?" Sam asked playfully.

"Of course, I do, doofus." A light-hearted smack on the arm accompanied Lisa's answer.

Sam beamed. It was the best smack in the world.

Chapter 3
The Puppet Show

Sam touched her eye. The bruise was now a spectacularly faded yellow and just looked weird instead of cool.

"You look like you've been playing hockey," Helene said.

"Watching it on TV is as close as I'll ever get to playing hockey," Sam said to her nanny.

Helene smoothed in the cover-up makeup under Sam's eye. "Good as new." She stood back to admire her handy work. "The ladies who lunch will never know that Miss Samantha Rose was in a fistfight."

"I was not in a fistfight," Sam protested. She groaned at Helene's teasing smile. "Bree hit me, and then I fell down. End of story. A fighter I am not." She chuckled. "If Susie hadn't held everybody back, I think Lisa would have killed Bree."

"You really like her, don't you?"

"Lisa?"

Helene nodded.

"Yeah. Did you know we've been together for three months and a week already?"

"You're counting the weeks, eh?"

Sam felt her cheeks flush. Talking to Helene about Lisa was cool, but Sam had to make sure her parents didn't overhear. They didn't know their only child was gay, and there was no way in hell she was going to let them find out. The thought made her head hurt, so she changed the subject. "Are the *ladies* here yet?"

Helene checked her watch. "Not yet. In about fifteen minutes."

Sam stood up, linked arms with her nanny, and together they walked through Sam's bedroom into the living room of her suite. Not many seventeen-year-olds had their own bedroom suites with private living rooms, but Sam wasn't like most seventeen-year-olds. Sam lived in a mansion surrounded by rolling lawns, a tennis court, a swimming pool, and myriad gardens, all taken care of by servants and hired staff.

"C'mon," Sam said, "let's get this puppet show over."

"Duty calls." Helene grinned as they headed down the hallway toward the main staircase leading to the first floor.

Sam's mother's gardening committee was having its August meeting, and Sam, of course, would be playing her violin to entertain them. She'd played for her mother's guests since she was three years old. That was over fourteen years' worth of dog-and-pony shows.

Helene groaned when they got to the bottom of the stairs. Sam's mother was talking with one of the women from the committee who had arrived early. "She's going to have my head for not being down here to answer the door."

"Sorry, Helene." Sam reached up to touch her eye. "You go on. I'm going to say hello to Daddy first."

"Oh, sure, throw me to the wolves," Helene said with a fake frown.

"I want to ask him about the lake house again."

"Good luck with that one." Helene patted Sam on the arm and

headed toward the music room.

Sam went in the opposite direction down the first-floor hallway and was about to knock on the closed door to her father's study when she heard him on the phone.

"Remember, David," her father was saying, "I reward people that are faithful to me and my family. I reward people who keep their word." Her father didn't speak for a moment. David, whoever he was, must have been talking. Groveling, probably. "I'm glad we've come to this understanding." Sam's father added, "Just get it done."

Sam heard her father place the phone back into its cradle. She waited twenty more seconds and then knocked lightly.

"Come," he said.

Sam opened the heavy door and stepped into the room. Her father sat in his leather chair behind the mahogany desk, reading what looked like legal papers. The two-toned desk commanded the center of the room like a judge's bench in a courtroom. The dark paneling and manly décor of the room made it abundantly clear this was her father's space. Sam always felt small in there.

Sam stopped two feet from the edge of the desk and waited for him to acknowledge her.

After several long minutes, he looked up, and his face brightened. "Hello, Kitten."

"Daddy," Sam groaned, "I'm seventeen."

"You're still my good little girl, aren't you?" His chiseled chin gave him an air of distinction, but Sam knew not to cross him because behind those kind blue eyes was a man used to getting what he wanted. Their family didn't own most of the real estate in Clarksonville County because her father was a softy.

Sam folded her arms across her chest. "How was your trip to

Albany?"

"Ahh, politicians," he flicked his hand dismissively and leaned back in the chair, "pompous fools, every last one of them."

"So why do you give them money?"

He smiled at her with a twinkle in his eye. "Kitten, let Daddy worry about those things. Go play your violin for your mother's company." Clearly having dismissed her, he turned his attention back to the papers on his desk.

"Okay, Daddy." She turned to go, feeling slighted. Her father thought she couldn't possibly understand politics or the family finances. *He still thinks I'm his* good *little girl.* He'd never give his little *kitten* permission to stay at the lake house with her friends. Not when he thought she was still nine years old. And he would positively freak if he suspected his perfect little kitten was a lesbian. Defeated, she reached for the doorknob. Just as she touched it, she remembered Lisa's Aunt Fran told her once that she and Lisa looked grown up. Maybe it was time for her father to see it, too.

She spun on her heels, adrenaline pumping. "Daddy, I know I asked you before," she hesitated for a moment, trying to find the right words. She forced herself to look up at him. "I'd like to take some friends to the lake house. The weekend after next."

"No," he said without hesitation. "It's not a good idea for you girls to be alone on the lake. It's not secure." He shook his head. "And I don't know these new friends of yours."

"You know Susie, and you met Lisa on the yacht."

"Samantha Rose," he glared at her over the top of his reading glasses, "I said no."

"Okay, fine." She cursed herself for giving in so quickly. God, how she wished she had a backbone. She slunk out of his study, tail between her legs.

Once in the hallway, she smoothed down her bright yellow sundress and made sure her hair was still securely tacked on top of her head. She took a deep breath and steeled herself to greet the ladies who lunch.

Stepping into the music room, she wasn't surprised that Mrs. Worthington was among the first few guests. Mrs. Worthington was probably in her fifties, like Sam's mother, but had her nose so far up her mother's butt, it wasn't funny.

"Samantha Rose, darling." Mrs. Worthington leaned in for a two-cheek kiss.

Sam obliged, kissing the air on either side of the woman's cheeks, desperately trying not to inhale her hairspray.

Sam stepped as far back as protocol allowed. "It's nice to see you again, Mrs. Worthington."

"You look lovely, dear. How is school?"

Sam didn't bat an eye. The first rule of entertaining was to put guests at ease. So, what if Mrs. Worthington didn't know that school was still out for summer. It was Sam's duty as Mimi and Gerald Payton's only child to play junior hostess and make guests feel comfortable.

"Senior year starts in about a week and a half, but I expect it to be a good experience." Sam stifled a laugh. *A good experience? Oh my God, that was so cheesy.*

"Well, that's nice, dear," Mrs. Worthington said with a smile.

"Thank you for coming today." Sam nodded and then stepped back, releasing Mrs. Worthington to join the entourage building around her mother.

Helene scurried around like a pro answering the door and

serving tea to the steady stream of women arriving for the committee meeting. Several years before, Sam had helped Helene answer the door, but her mother reamed them both out afterward. It wasn't Sam's place, her mother had told her. Let the servants take care of those things. Since when was Helene a servant? Sam always thought of Helene as a member of the family.

Sam shot Helene a sympathetic smile, which was returned. Sam wished she could have stayed in her room that afternoon to get ready for her six o'clock game, but she remembered her role as debutante and approached a group of women who had been watching her. All of her life, people had stared at her. It had been unnerving when she was younger, but, over time, she learned to ignore the unwanted attention. Still, she always wondered what people wanted from her. A smile or a word from Samantha Rose made them happy for whatever reason. Sometimes she wanted to shout at them to leave her alone, that there was more to her than the debutante puppet Samantha Rose Payton—the princess of Clarksonville County. She hated every minute of it but put on her practiced smile and greeted her mother's guests warmly.

She steadily worked her way through the guests and, after what seemed like forever, stood next to her mother. Her mother's designer dress was an acquisition from a recent shopping trip to New York. Her freshly colored platinum blonde hair from a recent visit to her hairdresser was neatly pulled up into a tight bun. Yes, her mother did know how to dress to impress.

"Samantha Rose, dear," her mother said as if surprised to see her. "Would you favor us by playing a few selections?" She gestured toward the Stradivarius displayed on the closed grand piano. Apparently, all the guests had arrived, and it was time for the puppet show to begin.

"Of course, Mother." Sam went to her violin and placed it delicately under her chin. She quietly tuned the strings.

"Is everyone here?" Sam's mother said.

Mrs. Worthington did a quick count and nodded.

Sam's mother clapped her hands twice to get the women's attention. "If everyone has their tea, please be seated."

One thin woman held up her empty hands and frowned as if to say she had rudely not been offered tea. Sam couldn't get over how emaciated the woman was. She looked like a walking skeleton. Maybe the woman thought you could never be too rich or too thin. Unfortunately, Sam's mother adhered to the same philosophy. Sam chided herself for her negative thoughts. She hoped the woman wasn't ill.

Sam's mother gestured toward Helene to wheel the silver tea service cart over. Helene obliged and poured hot water into a china cup. She offered the woman a selection of teabags.

Sam methodically applied rosin to the bow giving the thin woman enough time to fix her tea. Sam waited for her mother's introduction.

"Thank you for playing for us this morning, Samantha Rose." Her mother turned toward her seated guests. "Samantha has been playing the violin since she was three. Isn't that right, dear?"

Sam smiled graciously and nodded. The puppet was designed to please.

"Whenever you're ready." Her mother sat down.

Sam lifted her head high in performance mode. She played the opening measures of *Spring* from Vivaldi's *The Four Seasons* and heard murmurs of approval. She'd learned over the years to play music her mother's guests would recognize, otherwise, they got bored. She'd learned that lesson the hard way when she was in middle school. At one of her mother's luncheons, she had played a particularly challenging piece and overheard one of the women later complaining about how the music went on and on and on.

Through many trials, she found familiar music and strung them together in medleys, not staying with one piece for too long, in case the music went "on and on and on." She wanted to throw *Turkey in the Straw* into the mix, but her mother admonished her by saying redneck fiddle music would never be played under her roof. Sam laughed privately at her mother's ignorance. She hoped one day to be as good as some of those "redneck" fiddle players she'd heard.

After the Vivaldi, she switched to Brahms and played a sampling from the *Hungarian Dance Numbers Six* and *Seven*. When she saw some of the women's smiles fade, she turned it up a notch with Rossini's *William Tell Overture*. Of course, most of the women probably knew it as *The Theme from the Lone Ranger*, but who cared? It was a fun piece to play.

Her hair came loose from its tight bun as she flung the bow frantically over the strings. She was working up a sweat, but that couldn't be helped. She hoped her eye cover hadn't run. *Mustn't ruin Mother's luncheon no matter what.*

Sam pulled her bow across the strings one last frantic time and ended the piece abruptly. After a surprised silence, the women erupted with applause. Sam lowered her bow and violin and bowed politely.

Sam's mother stood up. "I know I'm biased, but isn't she wonderful?"

The group clapped again, Mrs. Worthington the loudest.

"Mother," Sam said, "you should play something for us." She gestured toward the piano as she put her violin back in its case as if she were done playing for the day. They both knew she was not.

"Oh, I don't know." Her mother put a hand on the pearls hanging from her neck.

"Yes, please do." There was Mrs. Worthington right on cue. She didn't even know she was part of the script. The other women added their voices and encouraged Sam's mother to play for them.

"Well, all right," Sam's mother agreed and headed toward the piano, "but you should play with me, Samantha Rose."

Sam had moved off to the side of the room out of the spotlight. "Very well, Mother. Shall we play *Forgotten Dreams*?"

"Yes, that would be lovely."

Of course, they had practiced the piece several times earlier that morning, but the guests didn't need to know that. Sam pulled the violin back out of its case and took a moment to retune while her mother settled in behind the piano. Sam placed the violin under her chin and lifted her head, indicating she was ready. Her mother played the first note, and Sam joined in softly behind the piano lead. Eventually, Sam took over the piece as planned. Her mother continued to play underneath the violin for most of the song until the end, when Sam pulled back and let her mother have the grand finale moment. When they finished, the guests leaped to their feet and clapped. Sam's mother shot Sam a grateful smile, and Sam's heart swelled because her mother's genuine smiles were very few and far between.

Sam reached for her mother's hand. They bowed together to more clapping and cheering. Her mother gave her a stiff hug and then invited the women into the dining room for lunch.

Sam sighed, happy because that part in the puppet show was over. Now all she had to do was make it through the luncheon. She placed her violin and bow back in the case. She needed to hustle and lock it in her room for safekeeping.

Sam headed up the stairs as quickly as she could without running. Mustn't keep the ladies waiting. Once in her room, she locked the violin in its cupboard and smoothed her eye cover. Satisfied she wouldn't embarrass her mother, she scurried down the hall and then down the stairs. She slowed her pace as she neared the dining room and did an invisible happy dance when she saw she had been placed at the last seat on the left side of the table with no one in front of her. Her mother sat at the head with the thin woman on one side and Mrs. Worthington on the other. Sam introduced herself to the woman she would be sitting next to throughout the luncheon. Mrs. Smyth was a relative newcomer to the committee, and her grin gave away the fact she was excited to be sitting next to the princess. *And the puppet show continues.*

Helene and their part-time cook, Mrs. Tardelli, brought out bowls of cold dill soup for the first course. Mrs. Tardelli wore cooking whites, and Helene wore a full-sized apron over her usual dark skirt and white blouse. Sam felt bad that Helene had to play so many different roles at the luncheon. It would be nice if Helene could sit down and eat with them just once instead of serving them.

Sam bit down her irritation and took a hefty spoonful of the soup. She was absolutely starving. Playing the violin always did that to her. Well, that and not eating breakfast. She dug in for another spoonful but caught her mother's disapproving glare. Sam nodded once and put her spoon down. "One must eat like a bird," her mother had drilled into her. "Especially around guests." Helene would, hopefully, bring her a sandwich later like she usually did.

Sam made it through the luncheon, eating enough chicken Caesar salad to curb her hunger but not enough for her mother to shoot her another disapproving glare. Sam was envious of the women, like Mrs. Smyth, who didn't realize they were supposed to demurely pick at their food instead of eating it. After forever, her mother announced that coffee and dessert would be served in the music room with the committee meeting after that. Sam held her breath, hoping she wouldn't hear the words, "Join us, Samantha Rose."

Sam's mother finally nodded; it was their private signal for Sam to excuse herself. Sam almost sighed out loud in relief. She said her goodbyes and walked out of the dining room calmly instead of fleeing the way she wanted to. She didn't even care that she had to hide in her room for a couple of hours until it was time to leave for her game against the Little Bend Black Widows. The ladies who lunch would be long gone by then, which was good because it would have been a big no-no to be seen in her softball uniform. Such a tomboy activity was most definitely not befitting Samantha Rose, the debutante. Her mother hated that she played softball, but Dr. Boyle had convinced Sam's mother it was okay for Sam to participate in the "rough-and-tumble" sport, as her mother called it. He'd said it would be a good way for Sam to make friends since she'd had none when she first started ninth grade. They hoped it would relieve Sam's stress and reduce the frequency of migraines. It had helped, not completely, but some.

Sam was about to bolt up the stairs to her room when the front door opened. Rolando, her father's driver, stepped into the foyer. His black suit and white shirt were neatly pressed as always. He was an older Italian man with graying dark hair and a pencil-thin mustache that made him look distinctly European. He had been her father's driver ever since she could remember.

Sam practically skipped back to the foyer to greet him. Even though she was trying to convince everyone that she was a mature young woman, she always felt nine years old around Rolando.

"How are you today, Miss Samantha Rose?" Rolando gave her a quick hug.

"Fine." She looked up at him expectantly.

His eyes twinkled as he deliberately avoided her gaze by looking up at the chandelier.

Sam cleared her throat.

"Was there something you needed, Miss?" His face broke into a grin.

She pushed out her lower lip in a boo-boo face.

"Don't cry, *mia bella ragazza.*" He reached into his pocket and pulled out a butterscotch candy.

Her boo-boo face shot into a smile as she took the candy from his hand. "Thanks, Rolando."

He bowed slightly and chuckled.

"I'll tell Daddy you're here."

"Thank you, Miss."

She coughed as she neared her father's study, so he would know she was approaching. She knocked, waited for him to say, "Come," and then opened the door.

"Rolando's here, Daddy."

"Thank you, Kitten." He didn't look up.

She turned to go but hesitated, hoping he'd changed his mind about the lake house. She glanced back at him, but he was so absorbed in his work that he didn't even notice her. With a sigh, she walked out and headed to the stairs. Maybe she'd go back to bed and dream about Lisa until it was time to pick up Susie for the game.

Chapter 4
Never Let Them See You Cry

Sam pulled the convertible into Susie's driveway and popped the trunk. Susie leaped off the hood of her rusty Toyota and tossed her softball bag in the open trunk.

"Top down. Nice." Susie gave an approving nod as she hopped into the passenger seat. "Hey, guess what?"

"What?" Sam backed the car out of the driveway and headed toward Sandstoner Fields. And toward Lisa. She grinned; she couldn't help it.

"*Aay*, wait a second. You're grinning like *un gato*. Are there new development in the, uh, *amor* department?"

"No." Sam felt her face flush. "Just shuddup, okay? I'm working on it."

"Touchy, touchy." Susie grabbed Sam by the arm. "Guess who got a job in the Science Center at the college?"

"Marlee?" Sam teased.

Susie shook Sam's arm. "No."

"Your angel of a brother, Miguel?"

"No!"

Sam couldn't keep a straight face and laughed. "That's awesome, Sus. When do you start?"

"Tomorrow."

33

"On a Friday?"

Susie nodded. "Yep. Orientation. They'll show me around, and I'll meet the professors and some students. It's going to be so cool."

"You're such a science geek." Sam smiled at her friend, hoping that Susie's new job would work out better than the last one had. "No more babysitting?"

"*Dios,* never again." Susie rolled her eyes. "Anyway, let me tell you what I'll be doing." Susie rambled on excitedly about setting up labs and helping the professors. She rambled on so long it took up the entire drive to the field. Sam had contributed three, maybe four, words to the whole conversation.

Sam pulled the car into the Sandstoner Fields parking lot. Her heart quickened when she spotted Lisa and Marlee waiting for them near Marlee's van. A delicious tingling overtook her at the sight of Lisa. Her Nor'easter uniform pulled deliciously across her chest. And her shoulders, they were so strong.

Sam put the convertible's top up and popped the trunk. She checked her eyeliner in the rear-view mirror one last time. Lisa once said Sam looked sexy wearing eyeliner, so Sam made sure she wore it all the time. Satisfied it hadn't smudged, she bolted out of the car and grabbed her gear from the trunk. She shouldered her bag and ran toward Lisa and Marlee, not waiting for Susie.

Lisa put her arms out, and Sam flew into them. After a moment, she reluctantly let go.

Susie walked up calmly and coolly and gave her own girlfriend a quick hug.

Marlee turned to Sam. "Any news about the lake house?"

"Sus," Sam glared at Susie, "you weren't supposed to say anything yet."

"You know I can't keep anything from her." Susie made puppy dog eyes at Marlee.

"Gag me." Sam rolled her eyes. "It's not looking good for the lake house, you guys. I have an idea, though." She'd have to run the idea past her parents first, but it shouldn't be a problem.

"What's that, baby?" Lisa asked.

"I thought Daddy might change his mind if he got to know you guys, so I thought maybe if you wanted to, uh…" Sam couldn't help the vulnerability she felt as she tried to invite her friends to the mansion. She hadn't invited friends over since her eighth birthday party. Her parents had started a tradition of giving out lavish and expensive party favors every year, and after a while, it became clear to Sam that her *friends* weren't there to celebrate her birthday. They were there for the expensive stuff they would go home with—Barbie Dream Houses or iPads. Sam refused to have any friends at the house after that. Things changed when she met Susie in ninth grade, though, and Sam took a chance and invited her over. Susie had been the only one since then. And Lisa. Once.

"Do you guys want to come back to the house after the playoff games on Saturday, go swimming, have lunch, and meet my parents?"

"Absolutely yes." Lisa gave Sam a tight hug.

"That sounds like fun," Marlee said. "I've never been to your house."

"Marlee," Susie said, "Sam's house isn't exactly a house."

"It's not?"

"Nope." Susie chuckled. "It's a tent." Sam's mouth flew open at the lie. Susie put up a defensive hand as Sam tried to smack her on the arm. "It's a cardboard box. They live under the highway."

"You lie like a rug." Sam pushed Susie playfully. At Marlee's confused expression, Sam said, "It's a big house."

"It's a mansion," Lisa clarified.

"Cool," Marlee said. "I've never been in a mansion before."

Abby, the Nor'easters' lanky shortstop, strode by. "Hey, it's the Clarksonville clique." She patted Sam on the back. "You guys better get it in gear. Coach already has the pitching machine fired up."

"Crap," Sam said. "We're right behind you."

Marlee shut the back door to the van, and they followed the trail Abby blazed through the parking lot.

Sam frowned as they walked. What did Abby mean by 'the Clarksonville clique?' Did the four of them always keep to themselves? Did people notice? Did they know she and Lisa were together? Sam groaned. She didn't want people to know, mainly because she couldn't risk her parents finding out.

Sam blurted, "You guys will have to be on your best behavior. No touching. No looking at each other, either."

"We should wear blindfolds?" Lisa asked with a chuckle.

"No, c'mon. You know what I mean." Sam smiled when Lisa grinned at her. Sam hated that she was so easy to tease. As she melted under Lisa's smile, she realized that she would see Lisa in a bathing suit. A familiar tingle of desire ran through her. Lisa held open the gate to the field for everyone to pass through and gave Sam a bump with her hip as she went by.

The pre-game batting practice went quickly, and Sam felt good about her swings at the plate. As the Black Widow team trickled into the visitors' dugout, Sam and her teammates hustled to put the pitching machine and practice balls away in the dugout storage room.

Coach Gellar read the starting lineup and reminded them that she expected nothing to stand in the way of their undefeated season. Speech over, she turned and headed toward home plate with a bat. "Infield, let's go," she said, her back to the team. Lisa picked up the bucket of balls and hurried toward the plate. Sam, Abby, and the other infielders scurried to their positions for their infield warmup.

Sam scraped her cleats across the infield dirt, smoothing out her second base territory. Coach Gellar took a ball from Lisa and hit a sizzling grounder to Keisha at third base. Keisha fielded the ball cleanly and threw a rocket to Mae at first, but Sam's eyes were wide open. Coach had hit the ball harder than usual. Another sizzling grounder went to Abby at shortstop, who scooped it up and threw it on target to first. Sam's heart was racing. She was next. She crouched low, ready to move in any direction. Coach Gellar swung her bat and smashed the ball toward Sam. Sam put her glove down and waited for the ball to bounce into it. Instead, it smashed into her shin. She muffled a cry, even though it hurt like hell. She shuffled to the ball, scooped it up, and tossed it to Mae. How the hell had she missed it? She was watching it the whole way.

"I'm sorry?" Coach Gellar bellowed toward her. "What was that you said, Payton?" She cupped a hand behind her ear.

Oh, God. Coach is in one of her moods. If Sam didn't ask for another grounder right away, the entire infield would end up doing a million laps or pushups or whatever else Coach felt like torturing them with. "I said, 'Can I have another one, Coach?'"

"Ahh, that's what I thought." Coach Gellar put her hand out for another ball. Lisa dutifully handed it to her. Sam hated that Lisa not only had to see her humiliation but sort of had a hand in it, too.

Coach Gellar smashed another grounder at her. This time the

ball bounced off her glove instead of her shin. She scrambled after it and finished the play.

"What was that—"

"Can I have another one, Coach?" Sam interrupted before her coach could finish.

Unfortunately, that pissed off Coach Gellar even more because, without a word, she hit a grounder to Sam's right, just out of reach, then another to her left. Sam pounded her glove against her leg in frustration but asked for another each time. Grounder after grounder after grounder came rocketing her way until Coach Gellar bellowed, "Outfield, take your positions."

Sam turned toward right field, blinking away the sting of tears. She hadn't fielded a single ball cleanly. What was the matter with her? She couldn't wipe at her eyes because Coach Gellar would know she'd gotten to her. She fixated on a tall pine tree behind the outfield fence and took a long slow breath. "Never let them see you cry," she murmured, repeating the mantra she had learned as a child. She had been trained to hide anger, sadness, frustration—basically any emotion that showed weakness.

After an eternity, their pregame warmups were finished, and the Black Widows took the field for their turn.

Lisa motioned for Sam to meet her at the far end of the dugout. "You kept pulling your head out."

"I did?" Sam had been wracking her brain trying to figure out how she'd missed every ball.

Lisa nodded. "Are you afraid?"

Sam shrugged.

"I think you are because of your black eye."

Sam sat down hard on the bench. Maybe she was afraid. At least once a day, she remembered the exploding pain of Bree's fist against her face. Sam turned to face her girlfriend. "How do you always know what's bothering me, even before I do?"

"I don't. Not really." Lisa smiled. "I could see you from my vantage point behind the plate. It looked like you kept tensing up."

"I guess." Sam chuckled. "But being afraid didn't help, did it? The balls kept hitting me anyway."

"You've gotta be fearless around here." Lisa tapped Sam once on the thigh and then turned to watch the Black Widows warm up.

When the umpire called for the Nor'easters to take the field to start the game, Sam raced Susie onto the field.

Susie patted Sam on the back. "Keep your head in there, okay?" She didn't wait for Sam to respond and veered off for left field.

"I'll try," Sam called after her.

Sam pounded her glove and got in her ready position, determined to keep her head down and watch every ball squarely into her glove. Marlee stood with the ball in the pitcher's circle and gave Sam a thumbs-up. Sam nodded back. It was nice to have support, even if it was only from her Clarksonville clique. The rest of her teammates, her shortstop Abby included, hadn't said a word to her.

The first batter for the Black Widows stepped into the batter's box. Sam rolled her eyes. Every part of the batter's uniform was black. Her cleats, jersey, shorts, visor, and even her socks were black. The eye-black underneath each eye was the icing on the cake. Did the Black Widows think they would scare the undefeated Nor'easters into losing? Not a chance.

Marlee whipped her arm around and threw the first pitch of the game. The batter swung and hit a hard grounder right at Sam. Sam took a step back and tried to keep her head down, but the ball took a weird hop and bounced into right field. The batter ran to first base safely. Sam blew out a frustrated sigh.

The next Black Widow batter swung at Marlee's first pitch and smacked a foul ball just outside the left field line. Susie chased it down and tossed it in. Abby shifted to her right and motioned for Sam to cover if the runner tried to steal second. Sam nodded and crouched in her ready position.

Sure enough, the runner took off for second base. Lisa came up throwing, and Sam got to the base in plenty of time. She snatched Lisa's line drive out of the air and put the tag on. The runner slid hard into Sam's glove, jarring the ball loose. It trickled toward center field.

"Safe," the umpire in the field yelled, throwing both arms out to the side.

"Shit," Sam muttered and smacked the ground.

Abby picked up the loose ball and called for time.

"Time," the umpire granted.

"Payton," Coach Gellar boomed as she paced the dugout, "get your ever-loving head in this game."

Sam knew better than to answer back. She simply nodded and then leaped to her feet. She dusted herself off with a couple of agitated swipes.

Abby ran over. "You okay, Sam?"

Sam nodded once briskly and trotted back to her position. She pounded a fist into her glove and stared at home plate. She had to get her 'ever-loving' act together.

With a runner now on second base, the batter stepped back into the box and smashed a line drive up the middle to center field.

Rachel, the center fielder, grabbed the ball and threw it to Sam in the infield. The runner that had been on second was rounding third and heading home. Sam heard Lisa call for the ball at the plate. Sam vowed not to mess up and pivoted. She threw the ball with all her might toward home, only to send an airmail throw clear over Lisa's head. Sam threw her hands up and groaned as the runner scored.

The play wasn't over, though, because the batter, who had run safely to first base, took off for second on the error. Lisa picked up the ball behind the plate and rifled it back to Sam at second. Determined to prove herself, Sam caught the ball and threw herself at the runner, who was now sliding into second.

"Safe!" the umpire yelled.

"What?" Sam flew to her feet with the ball in her glove. The umpire turned his back and walked away as if daring Sam to question his call any further. Out of the corner of her ear, she heard Lisa call, "It's okay, Sam. We'll get her at third."

Sam, grounded by the sound of Lisa's voice, nodded and tossed the ball back to Marlee as calmly as she could.

"Time," Coach Gellar barked to the home plate umpire.

"Time," the home plate umpire granted and took off her face mask.

"Bring it in," Coach Gellar growled at the infielders as she headed toward the pitcher's circle. She glared at Sam. "Not you. You're done for the day." She pointed toward the dugout. "Miller, get in here. Maybe somebody on this team can play second base today."

Sam groaned in frustration, but remembered she was a Payton and held her head high. She didn't dare look any of her teammates in the eye, afraid they'd see the sheen of tears in her eyes.

Sam opened the dugout gate and calmly stopped to get a sip of water from the water fountain. She needed a second to clear her head. What she really wanted to do was fling her glove at the dugout wall and then kick it down. But she didn't. She couldn't. She was a Payton. Always calm, cool, and collected. Instead, she walked to the far end of the bench and sat down. No one in the dugout said a word to her, which was good because she wouldn't have been able to answer them past the lump in her throat. No one was going to see her cry. Not then, not ever.

Chapter 5
Pride

Sam sat with Lisa, Susie, and Marlee at a picnic table at the far end of the Stewart's parking lot. It had gotten dark after the game against the Little Bend Black Widows, but luckily their table sat strategically underneath a lamp post. Sam's friends devoured their ice cream as if they were starving, but Sam stirred her Crumbs Along the Mohawk sundae without much thought.

"What's the matter, baby?" Lisa said.

Sam shrugged. "I almost cost us the game today."

"No, you didn't," Lisa said and put a reassuring hand on Sam's wrist.

"That's all Coach Gellar thinks about, isn't it?" Marlee asked. "Winning?"

Susie nodded. "She was in one of her moods again. You know how she zeroes in on one person and harasses them until they're ready to commit suicide?" Susie rolled her eyes. "I guess that's you now, *muchacha*. Used to be Christy, then me, and now you."

"I guess." Sam shrugged. "But why do I suck so bad?"

Her friends laughed, and Marlee said, "Two, you don't suck."

"*Aay*, you'll be okay, Sam," Susie said. "You had a bad day. That's all."

"She's right." Lisa nodded. "You're gonna be a rock star against

43

Milford on Saturday."

"I don't want to be a rock star. I want to be a second baseman. One that..." Sam looked down as her eyes welled up with tears.

Lisa's strong hand rubbed her back. She leaned closer and whispered, "It's okay, baby. It's okay."

"*Aay, mierda.*" Susie groaned.

Sam sucked back her misery. "What?"

"Ronnie Alesi." Susie pointed to a charcoal gray Toyota Camry pulling into the parking lot.

"Oh, God." Sam wiped at her eyes. "Please don't see us, Ronnie. Please don't see us."

"Who's Ronnie Alesi?" Lisa whispered.

"He's only East Valley High School's biggest drama queen." Sam tried to look everywhere except at Ronnie.

"Blows things out of proportion, eh?"

"That too," Susie said with a laugh. "Actually, he's big into theater at school, and he really is a queen. He doesn't care who knows he's gay. Coming out for him was like a party."

"A coming-out party." Marlee laughed. She snuck a peek and said, "He looks like Adam Lambert."

"Yeah," Sam said, "I think that's the look he's going for."

"He's kind of cute," Marlee added. "If you go for that sort of thing."

Everyone laughed, and out of the corner of her eye, Sam snuck a peek at Ronnie and his theater geek friends getting out of the car. She agreed with Marlee. He was cute with his short, spiked hair, groomed meticulously to look like he'd just gotten out of bed. "Shit, he's coming over."

"Samantha! Samantha Ro-ose," Ronnie sing-songed. "You can't

hide from me, girlfriend." He sashayed over with his friends trailing behind. He stopped in his tracks and threw both arms out to the sides holding his friends back. "Girl, what happened to your eye?" He shot a glance at Lisa.

"Softball, Ronnie. What else?" Sam nodded to Ronnie's friends, Alivia and Karl, who had followed him over. "Hi, you guys."

"What? No 'hi' for me?"

"Hi, Ronnie," Sam said, resigned.

"It's Ronald now."

"Ronald?" Sam held back a laugh when Karl rolled his eyes behind him.

"Yes, honey. I'm trying for an air of sophistication. It's going to go something like this." Ronnie held a fist toward his mouth as if holding a microphone. "The Tony Award for best actor goes to…" he threw his shoulders back and stood up taller, "Ronald Alesi!"

Alivia and Karl clapped behind him, but it was a slow bored clap as if they'd heard the story a hundred times.

"See? See?" Ronnie turned to bow to his admiring fans. "They know."

Sam smiled in spite of herself. She had to admit that Ronnie was entertaining. He even made strings class fun with his jokes and teasing. "Okay, *Ronald*. I want tickets to opening night when you hit Broadway."

"Oh, he's gonna hit something all right," Karl muttered under his breath.

Ronnie whirled around dramatically. "*Et tu, Brute?*" He wagged a finger at Karl and then spun back to face Sam. To Lisa, he said, "Scooch over, dearie. I need to speak to Miss Samantha Rose privately."

Lisa shrugged and moved over, giving him room on the bench. He sat down and leaned toward Sam, his face inches from hers. Sam wanted to poke him between the eyes to make him move back, but she knew he was simply creating a dramatic moment.

"So, darling," he said, "will you do it?"

"Do what, Ronnie?"

"Ronald."

Sam exchanged an exasperated glance with Lisa. "Do what, *Ronald*?"

"*Fiddler on the Roof.* Mrs. Dickens said you have to do it." He sat back, but Sam still had the urge to poke him.

"What are you talking about?"

"Mrs. Dickens picked this year's musical because of you."

"Ronnie, c'mon. You know I'm not into acting. I tell you that every time you try to recruit me for a play." Sam crossed her eyes at Lisa, who seemed to be trying not to laugh. "I'm fine in the pit."

"We've got to get you out of that orchestra pit, dearie. But I'm not talking about acting. We want you for your fiddling skills. We want you to be the fiddler."

"On a roof?"

"Exactly. Right guys?" Ronnie appealed to his friends.

They nodded, and Alivia said, "I hope you'll do it, Samantha Rose. All you have to do is play your violin."

"And dance," Karl added.

Alivia smacked him in the chest, her eyes wide as if he wasn't supposed to mention that part.

"Just a little dancing?" Karl added meekly, red tingeing his cheeks.

"Dancing?" Sam frowned.

"One scene. Maybe two," Ronnie said.

"I don't know." Sam shook her head. "Where? On top of the set? Mother and Daddy will never let me do it. Anyway, isn't the fiddler supposed to be a guy?"

Ronnie laughed. "Honey, this is theater. We'll dress you up in black, tie your hair back and stash it under a hat." He waved a hand. "It'll be fabulous. You'll be so butch."

Susie burst out laughing, and Sam threw her a friendly shut-the-hell-up glare.

"Ronnie, I can't promise you anything." All Sam wanted to do at that moment was go back to being miserable.

"Okay, girlfriend. Just think about it. *Capisce*?"

"No promises."

"Yay." Ronnie clapped like a giddy schoolgirl and leaped off the bench dramatically. He glanced at Lisa, leaned close to Sam's ear, and whispered, "She's gorgeous."

Before Sam could react, he spun around on his heels, entourage in tow, and headed toward the Stewart's entrance. He started singing a chorus of *If I Were a Rich Man*. Sam shook her head in disbelief when Alivia and Karl joined him in full voice.

"Geez," Lisa said once Ronnie and his friends had gone inside, "what was that all about?"

Sam laughed. "That was Ronnie Alesi, East Valley High School's drama queen."

"Now you know our pain," Susie added.

"What do you know about it, Sus?" Sam groaned. "You've never had a class with him. Last year I had three with him." She counted on her fingers as she said, "Math, English, and Strings."

"What instrument does he play?" Lisa asked.

"Double bass." At Lisa's perplexed look, Sam amended, "Upright bass. The big stand-up instrument."

"Oh, yeah. I know what that is."

"He's really good," Sam said. "Mr. Auerbach will probably put us in the same quintet again this year."

"Were any of the others, you know, members of the church?" Lisa asked.

Sam shrugged. "I have no idea. I don't think Alivia is. She had a boyfriend last year. I don't know about Karl."

"So," Marlee asked, "are you gonna do the play?"

"Who knows? I doubt Daddy would ever let me stand up on those rickety sets they build, let alone dress up in guys' clothes."

"Oh, c'mon." Lisa slid closer. "I want to see you dressed up all butch."

Sam felt her cheeks get warm. "I'm not butch enough for you already?"

Before Lisa could answer, Susie blurted, "We should enter you in one of those drag king shows."

"What, pray tell," Sam asked, "is a drag king show?"

"It's like a drag *queen* show, but women dress up like guys and lip-sync to songs. They put on fake beards and mustaches and wrap ace bandages around their, you know," Susie gestured to her chest, "boobage to flatten them down."

"Sus? How the hell do you know all this?"

Susie smiled. "I watch that LOGO channel on cable. I caught my mom watching it once. I think she was doing research, trying to figure me out. They were running a RuPaul marathon, though, so I'm sure she's more confused than ever."

Sam laughed along with her friends.

"You know what I think?" Lisa said.

"What?"

"I think you like Ronnie. Not as a boyfriend, but as a friend. You know what I mean?"

"Ronnie's okay. I just can't hang out with him. He's so out, you know? I can't risk it."

"We're all in the same boat," Susie said. "Even though the three of us are out to our parents," she waved her hand to include Marlee and Lisa, "we're not out at school or the rest of the world."

"You're still not out to your parents yet, Sam?" Marlee asked.

Sam shook her head. And it's not going to happen in a million years. "Helene knows."

"Nannies don't count," Susie said.

"I've told you guys a million times that I'm not coming out to my parents," Sam blurted. "I'm just not."

"My mom guessed about me," Lisa said, "but I finally told my dad. The one I live with. It wasn't that hard. He said he already knew and supported me no matter what."

"How could he *not* know?" Marlee said. "You spend all your time with Sam. It's funny how parents know these things. My mom hinted around until I got the nerve to tell her."

"*Dios mio*," Susie said. "Marlee's mom has been incredible about it, about us. She treats me like her future daughter-in-law. It's awesome."

"She really likes you." Marlee smiled coquettishly at Susie. They had celebrated their four-month anniversary three days before, and it was obvious they were crazy about each other. Marlee turned toward Susie and said, "She said you were good for me or something insane like that."

Susie stuck her tongue out at Marlee and then laughed.

"So, anyway," Lisa said, "everybody here's had a good experience coming out. Three for three. Collectively, we're batting a thousand."

Sam picked up her plastic spoon and swirled her now-melted ice cream. She jammed the spoon in the paper cup and pushed it away as if to finalize her statement. "Look, you're all coming over on Saturday to go in the pool, right? That will be a baby step toward me coming out, okay? If Mother and Daddy meet you guys and feel comfortable that I'm not hanging out with creeps, then when I do tell them, maybe they'll picture you guys and not scary lesbian psycho killers with crew cuts."

Once they recovered from laughing, Susie leaned in close. "You know, *muchachas*, the college has this gay group. When I go there tomorrow—"

"To start your new job," Marlee interrupted.

"*Aay*, I'm so excited," Susie gushed. "Anyway, when I go to the college tomorrow, I'm going to check them out. They're called the Rainbow Council. Hey, do you guys know how a rainbow is made?"

Sam groaned. Another one of Susie's impromptu science lessons was about to begin.

Susie continued without waiting for anyone to answer. "The sun shines on raindrops in the atmosphere. Each raindrop is a tiny prism that bends the light. Colors bend at different angles, so that's why you get a rainbow full of different colors."

"You're such a science geek." Sam rolled her eyes dramatically, in total Ronnie fashion.

"I know. And my mother wants me to be a nurse. Go figure. Anyway, the Rainbow Council has meetings every month, and they have this big gay pride festival in October. Maybe we can go."

"Pride?" Sam wondered out loud. "Where's the pride in being gay? Everybody hates you. People want to kill you. You have to hide all the time. I'm happy that you guys got lucky coming out to your parents, but mine aren't going to take this well." *Understatement.*

"She may be right, guys," Marlee said. "We're lucky our parents are okay with us, but that might not be the case for everybody. Think about it. Like Susie said before, we're all still hiding from other people, aren't we?"

Sam's thoughts tripped all over themselves. Ever since getting yanked out of the game earlier that day, she had been bumming about Coach Gellar and softball, and now that her friends were pressuring her to come out of the closet, she had new worries; worries that made softball and Coach Gellar seem minuscule.

Sam desperately needed a change in subject. "Hey Sus, let us know how your new job goes at the college tomorrow."

"*Si, claro.* What are you guys doing tomorrow?"

"I'm going to Lisa's to help babysit the three musketeers. I don't think they've seen my glorious black eye yet." Sam faced Lisa. "Have they?"

"Nope," Lisa said. "Lawrence Jr. and Bridget will love it, but Lynnie might faint."

"We have to toughen that girl up," Sam said.

"And you're just the butch to do it," Susie teased.

Sam couldn't find anything decent to throw at Susie, so she stuck her tongue out instead.

"C'mon, you guys." Lisa stood and tossed her cup and spoon into the trash barrel. The others did the same. "We don't have much time before Marlee and I have to head back to Clarksonville."

51

"I guess we'll meet back here in an hour and a half to exchange passengers," Marlee said to Sam. "Sound good?"

Sam nodded. "Okay."

They said their goodbyes, and Susie and Marlee headed toward the van.

Sam and Lisa headed toward the Sebring, and Lisa folded her five-foot-ten-and-a-half-inch frame into the passenger seat. "I can't believe summer softball's over on Saturday."

"Time marches on, I guess," Sam said. Before getting in the car, she called to Susie and Marlee, "Have a good evening, you guys. And, uh, don't do anything we wouldn't do."

"*Aay, muchacha*, that means the sky's the limit." Susie laughed.

"Shuddup," Sam said with a laugh and slid into the driver's seat.

"Hey," Susie said to Marlee, "do you know what color's on the top of the rainbow?"

"Either blue or red," Marlee answered. "I don't remember which."

"Red. East Valley red."

"No way. It's Clarksonville blue," Marlee countered. "I remember now."

Sam and Lisa chuckled at the overheard conversation. Sam backed the car out and pulled onto County Road 62. She glanced at Lisa, whose dark braid was pulled over her shoulder, exposing her neck. Sam couldn't wait to plant kisses on that gorgeous neck. She cleared her throat. "Let's go someplace where we don't have to talk science, softball, or fiddlers on rooftops."

"I've got a better idea," Lisa said and reached for Sam's hand. "Let's go someplace where we don't have to talk at all."

Sam pressed harder on the gas pedal. "I knew this day had to get

better." They headed for their favorite secluded farm road to be
alone.

Chapter 6
Perfect Samantha Rose

Sam stood in her room, violin tucked under her chin, eyes closed. She didn't need the sheet music in front of her. She knew the piece by heart. She pulled the bow slowly across the strings and, taking a slow breath, stretched her fingers up the neck to play the higher notes. The piece wasn't too hard, and it wasn't one she needed to practice for her mother's luncheons. She needed it for herself. Being an only child and growing up without any friends, she had often turned to music for solace. At long last, she pulled the bow gently across the strings and stretched out the last note. Tears flowed from closed eyes. She let the final note linger in her mind as she swam in sadness. She lowered the bow first and then the violin.

A gentle clearing of a throat from the hallway told her she wasn't alone. "May I come in?" Helene asked softly.

Sam opened her eyes and rubbed at them with the hand that still held the bow. "Sure." She turned her back to the door and gently placed the Stradivarius and bow in the case on her desk. She wiped at her eyes with both hands before turning around. She hoped Helene wouldn't notice she'd been crying.

"Chantal says hello." Helene's face held a sweet, concerned smile. Sam knew she'd been caught.

"That's sweet. How is she?" Sam asked.

"She's fine. From what she told me on the phone this morning, she's going overboard buying clothes for the new baby, but it's her first, so I can't blame her."

Sam sat down on the couch in the living room of her suite. Along one wall sat a home theater with a big-screen TV, surround sound, a six-stack DVD player, and a Blu-ray player. A cabinet held her myriad gaming equipment – equipment she rarely used. The floor-to-ceiling bookshelves lining another wall were crammed with books. The desk near the door to her bedroom held her laptop, iPad, and a color laser printer.

Sam pulled her feet up under her on the couch. "When is Chantal due?"

"I should have a niece by New Year's." Helene grinned and sat on the other end of the couch.

"That's nice." Sam was genuinely happy for Helene and her sister.

"So, what's up?" Helene asked gently.

"What do you mean?"

"Samantha Rose, you were playing the *Theme from Schindler's List*." Helene frowned in a way that told Sam she wasn't getting out of it.

Sam stared at her hands folded in her lap but didn't respond.

"I think this dreary rainy day has gotten you down." Helene sighed. "That piece makes me want to go back to bed and try again another day." The silence grew between them until Helene said, "C'mon. What's up, *mon petit hibou*?"

Sam relaxed a little when she heard Helene's French pet name for her. Helene was French Canadian and had been born in the province of Québec. Sam let out a long sigh. It was a good thing

Helene had interrupted her when she did because *Chaconne* was next on the song list. Helene might have called Dr. Boyle if she'd heard that.

Sam glanced at her nanny and shrugged. Helene couldn't fix the fact that Sam was on Coach Gellar's hit list or that her father had almost caught her on the yacht with Lisa the way Helene had caught her with Susie. Sam's parents would disown her or send her to a boarding school in Switzerland if they ever found out she was gay. The princess would never do anything to shame the Payton family name. She would never do anything horrible like be a lesbian.

"You look tired." Concern was obvious in Helene's voice.

"I didn't sleep well last night." *Serious understatement.* Every time she drifted off, she pictured her parents catching her and Lisa together. Her adrenaline had pumped, and her heart had pounded so hard that it took forever to calm down enough to sleep.

"Did you have a fight with Lisa?" Helene asked gently.

Sam shook her head. "No, we're great." *Except we can't seem to get past second base.*

"Are you nervous about the pool party tomorrow?"

Sam smiled at the thought. "No. Well, yes, but I'm not freaking out about it." *Not yet anyway.* "It better stop raining by tomorrow."

"The forecast is for sun."

"Thank God." Sam blew out a sigh.

"I'm glad your parents gave you permission to have the party."

"Oh, God, me, too." Sam chuckled.

"Your mother is supervising the maids downstairs as we speak."

"Weren't they just here?" The maids, pool and maintenance staff, and the landscapers usually came to work at the mansion Monday through Thursday. Never on Fridays or weekends.

"She called the maids back today to get ready for your party. I think your mother is more excited about the gathering than you are."

"I haven't brought friends over in a while."

"Since elementary school, if you don't count Susie," Helene said gently.

"That's true."

"So, what's bothering you, honey? Growing pains?"

Sam grunted and rolled her eyes. "Why does everything have to be growing pains?" She instantly regretted her flippant tone. "I'm sorry, Helene. I didn't mean that the way it came out. I'm—" She sighed. "I don't know. I'm anxious to get on with my life and be my own person."

"Everyone has growing pains, Samantha Rose. It's not reserved for the young. Ever hear of a mid-life crisis?"

"Why? Are you having one?" Sam grinned so Helene would know she was teasing. She and Helene always had an easy way of talking with each other.

"No." Helene chuckled. "I'm illustrating a point. Everybody's unsure or unhappy at different points in their lives."

"Maybe that's what it is then. Growing pains." Sam knew it was so much more, though, and simply smiled at her nanny. Helene's blond hair had a few hints of gray. When did that happen? Helene was thirty-seven, or maybe she was thirty-eight. Sam couldn't remember, but she knew that Helene had lived with them since the first day baby Samantha Rose had been brought home from the hospital. There was no smooth way to ask Helene how much longer she would continue to live with them and be her nanny, but the question hung heavy on her mind. She stuck to her more immediate troubles.

"I love Lisa so much, but I can't..." *tell anyone.* She couldn't finish the sentence out loud. "There's so much hiding. We never have time to be alone with each other. There's no privacy." Sam felt her chest tighten up again and couldn't stop the tears.

Helene slid over on the couch and pulled Sam into a tight hug. "Shh." Helene rocked her like she'd done steadily for the last eighteen years. "Shh, *mon petit hibou.*"

Sam let her misery flow, safe in Helene's arms. When her well of tears ran dry, she let Helene hold her tight.

Helene spoke softly. "I remember when you were, oh, six years old, and you told me matter-of-factly you were going to marry your classmate, Janet."

Sam laughed quietly. "I remember that. First grade. Janet Baker."

"Mm hmm. You never announced these things to your parents, though."

"I guess I knew better, even then."

Helene nodded. "And then third grade, remember your crush on that cute little redhead?"

"McKenzie." Sam sat up. "That didn't last long. She borrowed some books from me and never gave them back."

"I forgot about that. I've lost track of the others since then. And I'm sure there were a few you never told me about."

Sam shrugged but smiled sheepishly, admitting that she'd held back some crushes from her nanny over the years.

"And then you turned sixteen and developed a crush on a tall, dark-haired girl from Clarksonville that, as far as I can tell, hasn't gone away," Helene teased.

Sam felt her cheeks get warm thinking about Lisa. Her chest tightened again, but she willed herself not to cry.

"This one's not a simple childhood crush, is it?"

"No," Sam said. "It's so unfair that I can't tell anyone about her, about us."

"You mean your parents."

Sam nodded. "I mean, I'd like to have the basic freedom of holding her hand. You know, like, anywhere. Everywhere."

"Is your father letting you take your friends to the lake house?"

"I wish." Sam shook her head. "That's never going to happen in a million years." Labor Day weekend was only a week and a half away, and then her senior year of high school was going to start after that. If she had any guts, she'd ask again, but when it came to pushing Gerald Payton, only fools tried it.

"And all of this has you playing the *Theme from Schindler's List*?"

Sam nodded. "That and I seem to have forgotten how to play softball, and Coach Gellar's on my case about it." She blinked back the tears brimming in her eyes, amazed that she had any more to shed. "I want to tell Mother and Daddy about Lisa and me, but I can't. You know I can't. They'll never ever understand. They'll send me away to get reprogrammed or something." She smacked the armrest of the couch, but it didn't make her feel any better.

"You'll be eighteen in a few months. Tell them then."

"I can't," Sam spat. "They're so into their high-society image—"

"Samantha Rose, don't be disrespectful. They're your parents."

"I know, but you're the one who raised me, Helene."

Helene looked away from Sam as if she couldn't deny the fact that whenever Sam was hurting, she'd run to her nanny. If Sam needed advice, she didn't go to her parents. She went directly to Helene.

"If I told them about Lisa and me," Sam continued, "they'd never let me see her again. They're never going to let me be who I am." Sam rubbed her temple at the start of a tension headache. "They want the perfect blond-haired blue-eyed Junior League debutante they can parade out for people. They don't want a dyke for a daughter."

Helene inhaled sharply but didn't respond to Sam's harsh words. Instead, she pointed to Sam rubbing her temple. "Migraine?"

"No, thank God. Just lack of sleep." Sam stood up. "Listen, I have to get ready to go to Lisa's. Who knows how long they'll let me keep going to Clarksonville." She heard the resigned tone in her own voice.

Helene stood up and pulled Sam into a quick hug. "Promise me you won't play *Schindler's List* anymore today, especially because you were about to play *Chaconne* or *Vocalise* next. Am I right?"

Sam nodded. She never could hide anything from her nanny. "I thought you liked Rachmaninov."

"I do, but you need to pick cheerier songs. Don't wallow."

"Oh, and you don't wallow?" Sam playfully accused. "I heard Beethoven's *Moonlight Sonata* coming out of your fingers on that piano downstairs the other day. Or how about Chopin? Which *prélude* is it you don't wallow in?" Sam raised both eyebrows in an accusing but playful expression.

"Touché," Helene admitted. "*Prélude Number Four.*"

"Hey, let's play *Vocalise* for Mother's next luncheon. Accompany me on piano."

Helene didn't smile. "You know your mother doesn't want me

to play when the ladies are here. I'm too busy serving tea or helping Mrs. Tardelli in the kitchen." Helene cupped Sam's face in a nurturing gesture. "You're a good girl."

As Helene turned to leave, Sam said, "Don't forget, I'm having dinner at Lisa's bio-dad's house tonight, so I'll be home late."

A frown flickered across Helene's face. It was gone so quickly that Sam wasn't sure she'd actually seen it. "That'll be nice. Say hello to Lisa for me."

"I will. Her aunts are visiting from Massachusetts."

"Sounds like a family reunion. Drive carefully, okay?"

"I always do."

Sam listened as Helene's soft footsteps faded away on the carpeted hallway outside her suite. She locked up her violin and, on her way to the bathroom, paused in her bedroom to look out the rain-splattered windows. Hopefully, Helene's weather prediction was right, and it would be a sunny day for the pool party. She sighed and threw her hair into a ponytail and wondered if she and Lisa would be able to find alone time. It was hard with Lisa's three younger siblings underfoot. Maybe they could bribe nine-year-old Lynnie to watch the kids while they snuck into Lisa's bedroom for a few minutes.

Satisfied with her hair, she laughed at her black eye. The kids were going to love it. Her mother had a fit the day she came home with it. Sam let her parents think she'd gotten hurt in the softball game. Actually, that part was kind of true, but it wasn't a softball that hit her. Sam's mother wanted to yank her off the team immediately, but her father talked her out of it. Her mother placed a panicked call to Dr. Boyle to make sure. Sam laughed at the memory. What in the world did a psychiatrist know about black eyes?

Sam wondered if she should make an appointment with him to talk over her troubles. "Now that I have friends, why do things feel more hopeless than ever?" she said to her reflection as if talking to her psychiatrist directly.

Dr. Boyle would say it was because the stakes were higher, and she had more to lose. It might make sense to have an unbiased listener hear her problems. But how in the world could she tell him that she was gay? That the perfect princess was a dyke?

Dr. Boyle would probably say it was a phase. He'd say Sam was confused, and she'd grow out of her crush on her friend Lisa. Was that all it was? A crush? Sam shook her head. No. She'd had crushes on girls her entire life. What she felt for Lisa was so much more than that.

"Screw Dr. Boyle." Sam shoved her car keys and wallet in her pockets and headed out her bedroom door. *Psychiatrists don't know everything!* And who was she kidding, anyway? Dr. Boyle would tell her parents she was gay. And that, above all else, was the thing to be avoided.

Sam yanked the box of books she'd collected for Lisa's brother and sisters off her desk and stomped out of her suite, mad at herself for thinking Dr. Boyle could help her. Her parents paid him to keep perfect Samantha Rose perfect.

Chapter 7
The Best Sound I've Ever Heard

After what seemed like two hours instead of forty-five minutes, Sam pulled the Sebring into Lisa's driveway. Maybe the trip felt longer because of the rain. Her dull headache hadn't helped, either. At Lisa's, she didn't have to be in the closet or be wealthy debutante Samantha Rose Payton. At Lisa's, she could be herself.

With a growing smile, she popped the trunk and pulled out the box of books she'd brought for the kids. She dashed between raindrops to the front landing and rang the bell. When she heard the door open, she lifted the box to cover her face.

"I know it's you, Sam," Lynnie said with a laugh.

Sam lowered the box. "Wow. I can't fool anybody in this Brown household anymore."

Lynnie smiled and opened the screen door wide enough for Sam and the box to squeeze by. Lynnie, at age nine, was the closest to Lisa's age but seven years younger.

"Samtha!" A mop-haired blur raced toward her. Sam had just enough time to set the box on the floor and brace for impact from Lisa's three-year-old sister Bridget.

Bridget slammed into Sam, forcing her to take a step back. "Weesa said you were coming."

63

Sam reached down and picked her up. "I wouldn't miss a visit with my best girls and best guy for anything in the world." Sam smiled at Lisa's six-year-old brother Lawrence Jr. "How're you today, buddy?"

"Fine," Lawrence Jr. said shyly. He grabbed the hem of Sam's shirt since both of her hands were occupied holding Bridget.

"Excellent. Now, where's my—" Sam was about to say, "other best girl," but then Lisa stepped out from the back room. Sam's knees went weak the way they always did when she first saw Lisa. She had to put Bridget down when her muscles turned to jelly. Lisa's siblings blathered on to Sam about oatmeal with raisins that looked like dead flies, but she heard little of it. Her whole being was focused on Lisa in her tight shorts and long tanned legs, her shapely shirt, and long black braid. Lisa smiled. Sam's eyes locked onto Lisa's pouting lips and red cheeks. Lisa must have been doing something physical because her face was flushed.

Sam swallowed around the lump growing in her throat. "Hi."

Lisa's smile broadened. "Hi." She gestured at the box of books on the floor. "Books?"

Sam nodded.

"For the three musketeers?"

Sam nodded again.

"Hey, you guys?" Lisa said to her brother and sisters. "Sam brought you some books. Pull them out while she and I make lunch."

They cheered and flew at the box. Even Lynnie, usually reserved, wasn't shy around Sam anymore. Sam followed Lisa's beckoning finger into the kitchen. The Brown family kitchen didn't have a door on it, but if they snuck off to the side near the sink, they couldn't be seen from the living room. Lynnie knew about them and was a willing accomplice keeping Bridget and Lawrence Jr. occupied to give Sam and Lisa a few minutes alone together.

Lisa leaned back against the sink and opened her arms wide. Sam flew into them in much the same way Bridget had flown at her. Sam snuggled under Lisa's chin. Lisa was so tall, and yet their fit was perfect. Sam wanted to stay locked in the embrace forever, but then again, what was she thinking? Lisa's lips waited to be kissed.

"I couldn't wait for you to get here," Lisa whispered.

Sam picked her head up and looked into Lisa's deep brown eyes, the eyes that weakened her to the core every time. She tilted her head back, and their lips met. A surge of desire flashed through her. Lisa's lips never failed to turn up the volume on Sam's yearning. Lisa put her hand on the back of Sam's head and pulled her impossibly closer. When Lisa moaned, Sam knew they would be in trouble if they didn't slow down. The kids were in the next room.

"Bridget, no! Come back here," Lynnie yelled.

Sam bolted away from Lisa as the three-year-old ran into the kitchen and grabbed Sam's hand.

Lynnie hesitated at the threshold. "I'm sorry. She got away from me."

Lisa nodded. "It's okay, Lynnie."

Bridget pulled Sam into the living room.

"Sorry," Sam called back over her shoulder as the three-year-old led her through the living room to the makeshift salon Lisa's mother used to cut and style hair. During the summers, Lisa's mother worked at a salon in Clarksonville while Lisa stayed home to look after the kids. Lisa's father, her stepfather to be more accurate, was a roofer by trade and a general handyman during the winter when roofing was out of season.

The Brown Family house was small, so small that Lisa shared one of the three bedrooms with Bridget, and Lynnie shared a room with her six-year-old brother Lawrence Jr.

"What's up, Bridget?" Sam sat down in one of the salon chairs. "Are you going to give me a haircut?" Sam kicked herself for even suggesting it because Bridget's eyes grew wide.

"Wet's be twins."

Sam raised her eyebrows. Bridget's hair was a mop of dark brown curls, but her mother, or more likely Lisa, had managed to pull the hair into two tiny pigtails. Sam knew there was no refusing the three-year-old.

"Go for it, Sweetpea." Sam took the hairband out of her hair. "Go get a clean brush from the drawer." Bridget ran to the drawer, and Sam got the step stool Bridget used to reach her "customers." Sam's hair had often been used as amusement for the kids, but she didn't mind since it had so far only involved washing or styling it in weird ways.

Several minutes later, Sam and Bridget emerged from the back salon. Lisa, Lynnie, and Lawrence Jr. cracked up when they saw the new style.

"What?" Sam put a hand on her hair. "What's wrong with four pigtails?"

Lisa grimaced. "I especially like the one sticking straight up on top of your head."

"Bridget's special touch. Right, Sweetpea?"

Bridget giggled as Sam grabbed the three-year-old and twirled her around a few times. She plopped her into her booster seat at the kitchen table, where chicken and stars soup and peanut butter sandwiches were laid out for lunch.

"I think you should keep those in when we go to William and Evelyn's later," Lisa said.

"I think that would be no."

After lunch, they cleaned up the dishes and settled in the living room to watch "Spy Kids 3," a movie Sam had brought over. Sam let Lisa think she'd already had the movie and was letting them borrow it, but truth be told, she'd bought it on the way over.

Sam's heart swelled as Bridget climbed into her lap when the movie started. Lisa flashed Sam one of her melting smiles, and all was right with the world. Sam snuggled into the cushions and let her head fall back against the high-backed couch. She hadn't felt this relaxed in weeks. She fought to keep her eyes open but knew it was futile. The filling lunch, the rainy day, Bridget in her lap, and Lisa nearby sent her to a warm and happy place. A place she hadn't been in a while. She drifted off to sleep, not caring if she got teased about it later.

"I'm home," a voice announced loudly. The front screen door banged shut.

Sam woke up and struggled to open her eyes. She looked toward the television screen only to find that it had been turned off. Bridget was nowhere to be seen, either. She sat up to see a grinning Lisa on the other side of the couch.

Sam stretched her arms up. "Mmm, did I fall asleep?"

Lisa nodded. "For three hours."

Sam's eyes grew wide. "Three?" She brushed several Lego blocks off her lap that had somehow ended up there, probably from Bridget. She shook her head to loosen up the cobwebs of her fuzzy mind. Something felt weird, but as she reached up to touch her head, she remembered Bridget's hair makeover and the unglamorous pigtails sticking out all over her head.

"Samantha Rose," Lisa's mother said, "that is such a special look." She chuckled and put her bag down by the front door. "The hair is a Bridget creation, I presume?"

Sam nodded and then yawned.

"Oh, my. Are we keeping you up?"

"Apparently." Sam felt her cheeks get warm. She was a little embarrassed about letting her guard down so completely.

"And we have the pictures to prove it." Lisa laughed and held up her father's digital camera.

"Oh, no," Sam cried and felt her pigtails again. By this time, Lisa's brother and sisters had come back into the living room. "C'mon, let me see."

Lisa slid next to Sam on the couch, and everyone gathered around them. Lisa turned on the camera and selected view mode. The first picture that came up was of Sam and Bridget. Both of their mouths had fallen open in sleep.

"Oh, my God," Sam said. "My black eye completes the picture. Yeesh." She looked up at Lisa. "Do not, I repeat, do not post these on the internet."

Lisa grinned mischievously. "Too late."

Sam knew her face must have shown the horror she felt. Samantha Rose would never let herself be seen that way.

"Sam, Sam, Sam," Lisa said quickly and put a hand on her arm. "I'm kidding, but Lynnie printed out a copy for your personal collection."

Lynnie stepped forward and handed Sam a four-by-six-inch copy of the photograph. She must have used the printer and paper that Sam had "loaned" their father.

"Thanks, Lynnie," Sam said. A warm feeling spread across her chest. She wanted to bottle it to keep forever.

"Ahh, but there are more." Lisa scrolled to the next one.

Sam burst out laughing when she saw her body and head covered with Lego blocks. "How did I not wake up?"

"Lawrence Jr. was quiet for once."

Sam faked a gasp. "Lawrence Jr., you did this to me? You're the Lego maniac?"

His grin was so big it almost split his face.

"Ooh, I'll get even with you, buddy. Watch out." Sam wagged a finger at him.

"You were sleeping so hard," Lisa continued, "I think the Clarksonville marching band could have come through here, and you wouldn't have woken up."

Lisa's mother patted Sam gently on the shoulder. "I'm glad you feel comfortable here with this motley crew."

Sam's heart swelled again. This was a family. This was what family life should be, silly brothers and sisters you could goof around with and caring parents who didn't mind if you weren't always perfect.

Lisa scrolled through the rest of the pictures, and when she came to the last, Sam gasped. "What?" She touched above her lip. "You guys drew a mustache on me?"

The entire family laughed as Sam bolted off the couch, Lego blocks flying, and ran to the bathroom. Sam took one look at her ridiculous image in the mirror and burst out laughing. She laughed so hard that she doubled over. The audience of Brown children giggling in the bathroom doorway made her laugh even harder.

When Sam finally caught her breath, she said. "You guys suck. I can't believe you did this to me." She reached out and grabbed for Bridget, but Bridget squealed and jumped out of Sam's grasp.

Lisa blocked the doorway as if protecting her younger siblings now hiding behind her. "You almost woke up when Lynnie drew it on you."

Sam gasped. "Lynnie did this to me?" She looked behind Lisa at the now-grinning Lynnie. "Sweet, shy, innocent Lynnie?" She lunged toward Lisa, who, at the last minute, moved to the side and let Sam through.

Lynnie squealed as she bolted away. Sam caught her easily and playfully tackled her in the living room. A tickle fest ensued, which naturally attracted Lawrence Jr. and Bridget, who both leaped on top of Sam.

After several minutes, Lisa's mother cleared her throat. "Uh, you two had better get going. Aren't you due at William's in an hour?"

Sam sat up and caught her breath. "Yeah, I'd better do something about my new makeover." She gestured to her face and hair. She bugged out her eyes in a comical way, and Lisa's mother laughed.

"C'mon," Lisa held out a hand to help her up. "You can use the bathroom first."

"Thanks." Sam got up. "You know what?"

"What?"

"That was the best sound I've ever heard."

Lisa looked at her questioningly.

Sam pointed to the kids who were still on the floor recovering. "Kids laughing."

Lisa smiled so big it made Sam's heart swell. She vowed to dedicate her life to making Lisa smile.

Chapter 8
Samantha Rose Can't

Sam and Lisa cleaned up from their day of babysitting and jumped into Sam's car to head to East Valley for dinner with Lisa's bio-dad William and his wife, Evelyn.

"You're so good with them," Lisa said, taking Sam's hand.

"Who? The three musketeers?"

"Mm hmm."

"I like your family," Sam said.

"And I like *you*." Lisa brought Sam's hand to her lips and kissed the back of it. Sam had all she could do to concentrate on driving as Lisa kissed each knuckle in turn. Lisa turned Sam's hand over and kissed the palm gently.

Sam sighed as delightful tingles ran through her. "Uh, Lisa?"

"Mm hmm?" Lisa kissed her way up Sam's wrist.

"We're going to crash."

"Sorry." Lisa stopped her trail of kisses and pulled Sam's hand tight to her chest.

"Uh, not better."

"Sorry." Lisa grinned. She let both of their hands fall between them on the center console—the same console that was the bane of their existence whenever they tried to get close.

They made a quick stop at Price Chopper and bought fresh-cut flowers for their hosts. Forty-five minutes later, they pulled into the driveway of William and Evelyn's one-story Cape Cod house in East Valley.

"Your aunts are here already." Sam gestured to the Honda Civic with Massachusetts plates in the driveway. One of the many bumper stickers on their car read, "COEXIST." Different religious symbols made up the letters of the word. Another bumper sticker read, "BE CAREFUL WHO YOU HATE – it could be someone you love." Sam pointed it out to Lisa. "I need to get that one for my parents."

"C'mon, don't be so pessimistic. You don't know that they'll hate you."

"You're right. Hate might be the wrong word. How about abhor, detest, loathe, revile?"

Lisa frowned. "That's harsh, don't you think?" The concerned look that passed over Lisa's face made Sam regret she'd brought it up.

"I'm just kidding," Sam said. But she wasn't. Lisa didn't know Gerald and Mimi Payton. They would protect what was theirs at all costs. And that included Sam. She plastered what she hoped looked like a genuine smile on her face and followed Lisa to the front door.

"Knock, knock," Lisa said as she opened the door to her bio-dad's house.

Evelyn, William's wife of barely a month, greeted them. "Hello, girls. C'mon in. We're glad you could make it."

"Sorry, we're late." Lisa gestured at Sam. "Someone had to remove her mustache."

"Mustache?" William asked from behind his wife.

Sam rolled her eyes as she stepped inside. "Some little delinquents drew a mustache on me while I was vulnerable."

"She made the mistake of falling asleep with the kids around," Lisa added.

"Ho ho," William said with a laugh. "Apparently, that was not a wise thing to do?"

"No, it wasn't." Sam shot an accusing glance at Lisa, but Lisa looked up at the ceiling innocently as if she'd had nothing to do with it.

Lisa handed the bouquet of lilies to Evelyn. "Thanks for having us over."

Evelyn lifted the flowers to her nose and breathed in the fresh fragrance. "Mmm, these are lovely, girls. Thank you." She led them to the kitchen.

Traces of William's bachelor days were evident. His Buffalo Bills glasses sat on the counter, but Evelyn's more feminine influences were also evident. White lace curtains covered the windows, and flowers sat in a vase on the table. Both Evelyn and William were in their mid-thirties, and it was the first marriage for both of them. Lisa had always known she had a different father than her siblings and had finally met him for the first time two months earlier. Her mother and William had been high school sweethearts, but when she found herself pregnant at the end of their senior year, William wasn't quite ready to be a father and ended the relationship. Sam was glad he wanted Lisa back in his life, especially because William's younger sister Fran was gay. Aunt Fran and her wife Margaret had become instant role models for Sam and Lisa.

Aunt Fran leaped from her seat when she saw them. She crushed them both with hugs. She was tall, like her brother, and had the same jet-black hair. It wasn't hard to see that Lisa got her height and dark hair from that branch of the family.

"It's so nice to see my nieces." Aunt Fran's smile beamed. "And look at your tans. It must be all that softball."

Aunt Margaret moved in for her hugs. "This one would be outside playing ball all day, too, if we didn't have a mortgage to pay. She plays in a women's rec league during the summer."

"That's cool," Lisa said. "It's in the genes, I guess."

"Hey, everybody," William gestured toward the kitchen table set for six, "go sit down. Dinner's almost ready."

"Can I help?" Lisa asked. Sam stood next to her, ready to pitch in too.

"No, dears." Evelyn waved them toward the table. "Go on and visit with your aunts."

"If you're sure."

Evelyn nodded. "I've got the big guy here to help me."

They laughed and sat at the kitchen table as instructed. Sam turned toward Aunt Fran. "So, what position do you play?"

"Shortstop."

"Cool. I play second base." *I think.*

"Middle infielders rule!" Aunt Fran high-fived Sam across the table. "We're coming to your tournament tomorrow."

"You are?"

Both Aunt Fran and Aunt Margaret nodded.

"All of you?"

Evelyn and William added their own nods.

"Geez, a real family reunion," Lisa said. "My folks, sisters, and brother are coming, too."

"East Valley still plays at Sandstoner Fields, right?" The question was directed at Sam.

Sam nodded.

"Go Panthers!" Aunt Fran put up a hand for another high-five.

Sam slapped her palm. "Did you play for East Valley?"

"I sure did." Aunt Fran nodded. "Let's see, you're about Lisa's age, right?"

"A year older."

"You were probably in preschool when I played."

Sam and Lisa laughed, and then Sam narrowed her eyes. "You didn't play for Coach Gellar, did you?"

"No, Coach Morrison. He was one of the social studies teachers."

"Phew." Sam blew out a sigh. "I was about to trade war stories with you."

"She's a tough one?"

"Understatement. Right, Lisa?"

Lisa nodded and rolled her eyes in response.

"Ooh," Aunt Fran gushed, "I can't wait to meet her tomorrow."

"Honey," Aunt Margaret put a warning hand on her wife's arm, "don't stir up a hornet's nest, okay?" The gesture looked like one Aunt Margaret employed often.

"Who me?" Aunt Fran asked innocently.

"By the way," Lisa said, "my brother and sisters don't know that William is my biological father."

"They think he and Evelyn are Lisa's *friends*." Sam put air quotes around the word friends.

"Which we are," William said and put an enticing platter of sliced pot roast on the center of the table. Evelyn added bowls of mashed potatoes, gravy, green beans, and a tossed salad to the mix. William reached behind him and grabbed a basket of rolls from the countertop.

"It smells amazing." Aunt Fran inhaled deeply. "I love comfort food."

William smiled. "Evelyn's an awesome cook. I got lucky."

"Yes, you did, big brudder. And speaking of getting lucky—did a vampire get your neck, Sam, or was Lisa a little too enthusiastic?"

Sam's eyebrows shot straight up, causing everybody to laugh. She put a hand to her neck.

"It freaked me out, too, the first time I saw it," Lisa said. "I thought she had another girl on the side."

Aunt Fran howled. "So? Sam? Are you giving yourself hickeys?"

By then, Sam realized what they were talking about, but Lisa answered for her. "It's from her violin. The chin rest or something?" She looked at Sam for confirmation.

Sam nodded. "It's called a violin hickey."

Lisa sighed dramatically. "Someday, I'll get to hear her play."

Sam's face got hot. She was going to be a nervous wreck if she ever played in front of Lisa. "Someday," she agreed. She had no idea when that would be, though.

William took beverage requests and then filled glasses. Once he and Evelyn sat down, he raised his wine glass. "A toast to my growing family."

Sam, Lisa, and Fran raised glasses filled with sparkling water, while Margaret and Evelyn raised their wine glasses.

"I became a husband for the first time a month ago. I hope she won't get tired of me too soon." He raised his glass to Evelyn, who smiled sweetly back at him. It was easy to see the honeymoon period hadn't worn off yet. "I finally got to meet my beautiful daughter and her equally beautiful girlfriend." He smiled at Lisa and Sam and raised his glass higher. They raised theirs in response. "And I hope to spoil my new niece rotten when she gets here in December." He looked at his sister.

"Oh, geez," Lisa said to Aunt Fran. "That's a baby bump, isn't it?"

Aunt Fran's grin answered the question. Lisa leaped out of her chair to give her aunts a big double hug. "I'm so happy for both of you."

"Congratulations," Sam said. "You'll be wonderful parents."

"Thank you, Sam." Aunt Fran's face flushed from the attention. "So, what do you think? Do you girls want kids?"

"Someday," Sam answered way too quickly. What if Lisa didn't want children?

"Someday," Lisa echoed. She reached under the table and squeezed Sam's hand.

"Guess you should get married first, now that New York made it legal," Aunt Fran added. "We had to move to Massachusetts." There was no mistaking the disgruntled tone in her voice.

"Leave the kids alone, Fran. They have plenty of time to think about that." William winked at Lisa. "Let me be a dad for a while before I become a grand-paw." He passed the basket of rolls to Sam. "Or a father-in-law, for that matter."

Sam was grateful for William's intervention. She took a roll and passed the basket to Lisa. Sam imagined how her parents would react if she told them she and Lisa were getting married. Sam's heart rate quickened at the thoughts swirling in her head. Oh, God, who would have the baby?

"So, wait one second, Aunt Fran," Lisa said. "At William and Evelyn's wedding last month, you knew you were pregnant, didn't you?"

Her aunts exchanged a glance. "We wanted to be sure everything was okay before telling anybody," Aunt Margaret said.

"And we didn't want to steal the spotlight from my big brudder," Aunt Fran added.

"I knew about it, though," William boasted.

"I didn't." Evelyn laughed. "He's good at keeping secrets." She glanced at Lisa, but what could have been an extremely awkward moment somehow wasn't. William had managed to keep the fact that he had fathered a child when he was a teenager a secret from Evelyn but eventually fessed up a month or so before their wedding. Evelyn seemed to take the news well because she had asked Lisa to be one of her bridesmaids.

During dinner, they discussed everything from Sam's glorious black eye to Aunt Fran and Aunt Margaret's new venture into parenthood. Sam learned more than she ever wanted to know about artificial insemination, sperm donors, and fertility clinics. Once Aunt Fran knew she was pregnant, she and Aunt Margaret got busy turning one of their spare bedrooms into a nursery. Aunt Fran went on to describe her weird hormonal cravings in way too much detail. Sam wasn't sure she wanted to hear about it, but she wouldn't have changed where she was for the world. She was with family. Family who accepted her for who she was.

Sam was pleased when everyone ate heartily and didn't simply move the food around on their plates pretending to eat. She even followed Lisa's lead and asked for seconds. Helping to clean up after dinner was kind of fun, too. She never got to do anything like that at home. Usually, Helene, Mrs. Tardelli, or one of the hired maids cleaned up.

Once the dishes were in the dishwasher, and the pots were

Barbara L. Clanton

soaking in the sink, they headed into the living room. William brought in two kitchen chairs so everyone would have a place to sit.

"Fran," William said, "you should do what I did. Get your kid when she's sixteen. No diapers, no terrible twos."

Aunt Fran howled with laughter and slapped her thigh a couple of times. Sam and the others couldn't help joining in.

"So, what about you two?" Sam said to William and Evelyn once she recovered from laughing. "Is Lisa going to get another sister or brother any time soon?"

"We're trying." Evelyn smiled at William.

Aunt Fran covered her ears with both hands. "I do *not* want to hear about my brother's sex life."

"Oh, and I didn't have to sit through an entire meal listening to the joys of artificial insemination?" William teased back good-naturedly.

"Time out." Evelyn made a T with her hands. "We need a subject change immediately." She picked up a stack of CDs from a side table. "The DJ made copies of the songs played at our wedding." She handed a CD to each of them.

"Ooh," Aunt Fran ran her finger along the top of the jewel case, "these are some good tunes. C'mon, put it on. Let's dance." She stood up and moved the coffee table to one side.

"Excellent idea." Sam leaped up and helped Aunt Margaret move the kitchen chairs back into the kitchen to make room.

Once enough furniture had been moved out of the way, Evelyn put the CD in the player. The first song was a fast Beatles tune. Sam and Lisa danced with wild and silly movements. Sam remembered the first time she'd ever danced with Lisa. It was at an East Valley softball party at their pitcher Christy's house. Susie had invited a few

Clarksonville players, and Sam remembered how her heart soared when Lisa walked into the recreation room where the team was playing ping pong. Sam's hands sweated so much that night she could barely hold the ping pong paddle. After the tournament, someone put on club music, and they moved the furniture out of the way, like they had just done in William and Evelyn's living room.

After the first song, Aunt Fran sat down. Apparently, she and the baby were ready to sit out for a while. After checking to make sure she was all right, Aunt Margaret rejoined the dancing on the impromptu dance floor. Sam and Lisa laughed when Aunt Margaret cut in on William and twirled Evelyn around. Not to be outdone, William cut in on Sam and twirled his daughter. Sam, left out in the cold, good naturedly sat down next to Aunt Fran to keep her company.

A few minutes later, though, Sam jumped up when Sarah McLachlan's song *Ice Cream* came on. She cut in on William and said to Lisa, "Let's waltz."

"Waltz? To Sarah McLachlan?"

Sam waggled her eyebrows. "It's three-four time. Perfect for waltzing."

"I don't know how."

"I'll show you," Sam said.

"How do you know how to waltz?"

"Don't laugh, okay?" Sam felt her cheeks get warm.

"Okay."

"I had to learn for my debutante ball."

Lisa's mouth dropped open. "We are totally going to talk about that later." Her nose crinkled up as she smiled. "Okay, show me what to do."

Sam took Lisa's right hand in her left and then showed her how to do the waltzing box step. Lisa made a couple of mistakes early on, like trying to lead, but in no time, they were waltzing around the living room effortlessly. At her debutante ball, Sam waltzed with a couple of guys, but they moved awkwardly, not naturally the way Lisa did.

When the song ended, they sat down to let the newlyweds dance alone to their wedding song.

Aunt Fran turned off some lights. She leaned closer to Sam and whispered, "I'm creating atmosphere."

The couple's song ended, and William bent Evelyn backward and kissed her in true movie romance fashion. They were so in love. Like she was with Lisa. Aunt Fran started a round of clapping for the newlyweds.

Another slow song came on, and Lisa leaped to her feet, hand outstretched. Sam obliged, and they melded together on the dance floor. Sam sighed at the perfect fit. She felt safe in Lisa's arms. They had never slow danced like this before, and it was exquisite. Lisa nuzzled Sam's neck, and normally Sam would have been embarrassed at such a public display of affection, but they weren't exactly in public. She snuck a peek and saw that no one was paying them any attention. She closed her eyes and moaned quietly in Lisa's ear. Her body hummed as they moved. Out of the corner of her ear, she heard Evelyn whisper, "C'mon, let's give them privacy. Everybody back in the kitchen."

Sam loved Evelyn at that moment.

Aunt Fran gushed, "I told you they looked grown up, didn't I?"

Lisa must have realized they were alone because she pulled Sam closer and kissed her way along Sam's neck and jaw. Sam moaned when soft lips reached her own. She lost herself in the kiss, letting her body hum like the vibrato of her violin.

"You're so beautiful," Lisa murmured in between kisses.

"Same."

Lisa kissed her again and said, "I wish we could go to school dances together. I wish we could go to our proms together."

"Sam wants to. She really really wants to," Sam said, referring to herself in the third person. "But Samantha Rose can't."

"I know."

They danced for a while until Lisa whispered softly in Sam's ear, "I want to be alone with you."

"Me, too."

"If we leave now, we'll have plenty of time before I have to be home."

"We'll miss dessert," Sam said. "Evelyn's apple pie."

"Do you care?"

Sam shook her head so fast that it made Lisa laugh.

"We'll see them tomorrow anyway. C'mon," Lisa grabbed Sam's hand, "let's go say goodbye."

Chapter 9
Thirteen and Two-thirds

Sam sat on the bleachers with Lisa, Susie, and Marlee and watched the early morning semi-final playoff game between third-ranked Southbridge and second-ranked Elmhurst. After that, their own first-place team was scheduled to play the fourth-place Milford team. The winners from each game would meet in the finals. It was a perfect softball day with a brilliant blue sky and no clouds. The soft breeze kept the mid-80s temperature at bay. It was also a perfect day to have your girlfriend meet your parents.

Elmhurst had the bases loaded. The batter at the plate smashed a sizzling shot down the left field line that would score one, maybe two, runs.

"*Aay,*" Susie said, shaking her head. "Southbridge is getting killed."

"I thought their new pitcher was supposed to be good," Sam said. "We struggled against her last time."

"She *is* good," Marlee said. "But she only has a rise ball."

"Which she's not throwing well today," Lisa finished.

"Obviously," Sam said, "they don't stand a chance without Bree."

"Who is happily sitting in juvenile detention hall at this moment." Susie high-fived Sam and then grinned at Marlee.

"And, man oh man, she can stay there," Marlee added. "Getting stalked like that was really creepy."

Lisa nodded. "You had the emotional trauma from Bree, and Sam had the physical." She gestured toward Sam's black eye. She leaned in close and whispered, "Your black eye makes you look so butch."

"Shuddup." Sam pushed Lisa away good naturedly. "It's almost gone, anyway."

"Oh, geez. Look." Lisa pointed toward the parking lot. "The gang's all here."

William, Evelyn, Aunt Fran, and Aunt Margaret were making their way from the parking lot to the bleachers. Lisa's parents, two sisters, and brother were right behind them. Lisa waved frantically to them. Sam threw in her own waves as well.

"You have so many people coming to watch you play," Sam said. *And I have no one.*

As if reading Sam's mind, Lisa pointed toward a red Prius pulling into the parking lot. "Isn't that Helene's car?"

Sam craned her neck. "Yeah, it is."

"I didn't know she was coming today."

"Me neither." Helene usually went to Sam's high school games but rarely summer games. Alarm bells jangled. Did her presence have anything to do with her friends coming back to the house for the pool party later?

Coach Gellar bellowed for her East Valley Nor'easters to start warming up, so Sam didn't have a chance to wait for Helene and ask. Sam stood up and shouldered her softball bag. "I'll see you later," she said to Lisa.

Lisa nodded and picked up the overlarge duffel that held her mitt and catcher's equipment. "Ready, Marlee?"

Marlee nodded. She and Lisa lugged their equipment off the bleachers and headed for the cowpen behind left field to warm up. Sam and Susie headed in the other direction to warm up with the rest of the team in the grassy area between the parking lot and the right-field fence.

Sam and Susie led the team through their usual stretching routine, and then everybody paired up to throw. They'd take their laps around the field once Elmhurst finished trouncing Southbridge.

Sam and Susie threw the ball back and forth a few times, and then Sam said, "Hey, Sus, throw me some easy grounders. Okay?"

Susie nodded and tossed a slow roller. Sam charged the ball, keeping her head down all the way. She scooped it up easily and threw a bullet back to Susie.

"Make 'em a little harder." Sam backpedaled to her original spot and crouched low. This time she moved to her left to get the ball, but she did it without pulling out her head or getting tense. She tossed it back. "Harder now."

"You asked for it, *gringa*." Susie cocked her arm back and launched a hard grounder in Sam's direction.

"Head down," Sam murmured to herself. She moved her feet and got in front of the ball. It bounced into her glove, hitting the sweet pocket. She scooped it in and blew out a sigh of relief. She wasn't ball shy like Lisa said, not anymore. She wasn't going to pull her head out. Not ever again. She tossed the ball back to Susie, feeling confident until she remembered that Coach Gellar might not even start her in the first game. Or the second. Coach Gellar was not beyond making an example out of debutante Samantha Rose Payton.

Sam threw some high pops to Susie until Coach Gellar called them in for a team huddle. Lisa and Marlee were still in the cowpen, but Sam and the rest of her teammates formed a loose circle around their coach.

"Girls," Coach Gellar looked straight at Sam, "this is what we've worked for all summer. We've struggled through a few games, but we came out victorious in all of them. But not today." She paused and spread her laser beam glare around the circle. "Oh, we'll be victorious all right, but we're not going to struggle. We're going to show both teams and the people in the stands that East Valley has the best team in this league, this county, and the entire North Country."

"Yeah!" Abby punched a fist in the air.

"And we want them to keep on remembering that when the school season rolls around next spring." Coach Gellar put her hand in the middle. "Who's with me?"

A resounding cheer went up from Sam's teammates, but Sam didn't join in as heartily. It seemed rude to cheer for East Valley dominance when they'd be playing against Marlee and Lisa.

"Nor'easters on three," Coach Gellar said. "One, two, three!"

"Nor'easters!" the team shouted.

On the field, Southbridge made their last out of the summer. The Nor'easters hustled to get their gear and headed to the dugout.

"Sam," Coach Gellar grunted, "in my office." She pointed to a spot on the grass that was apparently her office.

Sam swallowed against the lump building in her throat. Now what? She reached down to pick up her bag.

Susie patted her on the back and whispered, *"buenas suerte, mi amiga."*

"Thanks." Sam shouldered her bag and hustled to her coach. She felt like a kindergartener getting in trouble for eating paste.

"Payton," Coach Gellar said, her laser beam eyes rooting Sam to the spot. "Why should I start you?"

It wasn't the question Sam was expecting. In fact, Sam wasn't expecting a question at all. She figured Coach Gellar was going to tell her she'd be sitting out the first game.

"'Cuz I'm a good second baseman." Sam tried not to make it sound like a question.

Coach Gellar laughed. "You weren't a good second baseman on Thursday. I had to put Miller in for you."

"I know. I was having a bad day. I'm good now. I'm going to keep my head down and make good throws, and—"

"What about Abby?"

What about her? Sam didn't have a chance to process the question.

"It would be nice if you two had a better rapport, relationship, bond. Middle infielders have to stick together. You two are the meat of the infield. First and third? Ah, they're just the potatoes."

Sam held her breath so she wouldn't burst out laughing. "I'll work on it."

"You do that." Coach Gellar whirled around and headed for the dugout. The meeting in her *office* was apparently over.

Sam opened the gate and dumped her bag just inside the fence. She sprinted to catch up to her teammates, running their laps around the field. She caught up to them at the final straightaway down the left field line. When she made it back to the dugout, Lisa, Susie, and Marlee surrounded her.

"You okay?" Lisa asked under her breath.

Sam nodded.

"You sure?"

"Yeah." *I think.*

"Okay, girls," Coach Gellar said, "here's the starting lineup. Jacobs in center, Payton at second—"

Sam stopped listening after she heard her name. It would have been embarrassing to ride the pine with Helene and Lisa's entire family there.

Sam and her friends watched the Milford team warm up on the field until Coach Gellar bellowed, "Infield, let's go," and then headed toward home plate for their own pre-game warmup.

Sam desperately wanted to run up to the bleachers and ask Helene if her parents had changed their minds about the pool party, but there was no smooth way to do it.

Mae, East Valley's first baseman, threw grounders to the infielders. Sam fielded hers cleanly and threw the ball back with authority each time. She and Abby turned a couple of practice double plays, and Sam felt good. With much relief, she even fielded Coach Gellar's hard-hit grounders without having to ask for more.

After their pre-game warmup, the Nor'easters stayed on the field as the home team. Marlee joined them and took her five warmup pitches.

"Comin' down," Lisa bellowed from behind the plate. Lisa caught Marlee's last practice pitch and rifled the ball to Abby, who covered second base. Abby caught it, made a sweeping tag at a fake runner, and then tossed the ball from her glove to Sam, who caught it with her bare hand. Sam pivoted and threw it to Keisha at third. Keisha whipped the ball across the infield to Mae, and then the infielders ran to the pitcher's circle to deliver the ball back to

Marlee.

After a quick cheer, Lisa balled a fist and gave Sam a light punch on her arm for encouragement before hustling back behind the plate. Sam ran to her second base position and raked the ground with her cleats until the umpire called for the first Milford batter.

"C'mon, Marlee," Sam called. "Just you and Lisa. Fire it in there." She pounded a fist in her glove, hoping she wouldn't mess up if the ball came to her.

"Stee-rike!" The umpire called enthusiastically.

"That's it, Marlee, two more," Sam yelled.

Marlee put her hands together. She raised both in the air and then launched herself and the pitch toward the plate in an explosion of power. The batter swung and launched the ball right back up the middle. Marlee reached to her left for the sizzling grounder but missed. Sam took a step in and instantly regretted it. The ball was too fast. She mistimed the bounce, and it hit off her wrist. She ignored the pain and scrambled after the ball. She threw it to Mae at first base, but too late. The runner was safe.

"Shit," Sam muttered. "What the frig is wrong with me?" She blew out a sigh and headed back toward her second base territory, terrified that Coach Gellar would yank her out of the game in front of everybody.

"Hey, Marlee," Abby called, "give us a second."

Marlee nodded and bent down to retie a shoe.

"Samantha Rose," Abby said, "don't be mad, okay? Coach wanted me to, uh, I mean, she—okay, this is what I do before every pitch. I picture a ball coming at me, and I scoop it up clean. I think, 'It won't hurt if it hits me.'"

"That's not exactly true." Sam displayed the red welt rising on her wrist.

"I know, but you have to psych yourself into getting in front of those hard ones." Abby headed back to her shortstop position. "Just try it, okay?"

Sam nodded and pounded her glove. Marlee put her hands together for the next pitch. Sam pictured a hard-hit grounder coming at her. She pictured scooping it up cleanly like she'd done with Susie before the game.

Marlee sent the pitch toward the plate. The batter swung and sent a searing line drive foul off the third baseline.

"You've got the steal," Abby said and cheated a few steps toward third.

Sam nodded and took a step closer to second. Sure enough, the runner on first took off on the next pitch.

"Going," Sam yelled to Lisa and headed to cover second base.

Lisa snagged Marlee's pitch and fired it toward second base from her knees.

The throw was right on target. Sam moved in position, and Lisa's bullet smacked in her glove. The runner slid feet first. Sam held her ground and put all her might into tagging the runner low and strong. The runner slid into the glove, and her momentum carried her across the bag knocking Sam over. Pain exploded in her cheekbone. She clutched her face with her free hand, trying to get the pain under control.

"Out!" the umpire yelled.

Thank God! Sam thought.

Abby rushed over. "Are you okay?"

"I don't know. You tell me." Sam pulled her hand away from her face.

"Shit," Abby said. "You've got a nasty welt under your eye. I think she got you with her knee. Are you trying to get another black eye?"

Sam chuckled in spite of the pulsing pain in her cheek. Her teammates, Lisa included, swarmed around her. Coach Gellar and the team trainer pushed their way through.

"Give us room, girls," the trainer said. Sam's teammates backed away. She said to Sam. "Look at me." Sam looked up. "Left, right, down. Okay, good. No damage to the eye," the trainer mumbled to herself. She felt around the cheekbone, and Sam tried hard not to wince at the mauling she was receiving. "You're fine. We'll get ice on that when the inning's over, okay?"

Sam nodded and stood up. She pulled the glove off her hand and brushed herself off. She tried to open her eye wide only to wince as the cheek protested. She felt her face; her cheek was already swelling.

"You okay to stay in the game?" Coach Gellar asked.

"I'm good."

Coach Gellar and the trainer headed back to the dugout. The trainer glanced back at Sam and said to the coach, "She's been taking a beating out there lately."

"No kidding. She's working on borrowed time."

Sam groaned. The trainer said something else, but they were too far away for Sam to make it out. She shot a glance at Abby, who was still standing on second base. "Didn't you say it wouldn't hurt?"

With a shrug and a grin, Abby backpedaled to her position.

Lisa stood in the pitcher's circle with Marlee. She mouthed to Sam, "Are you okay?"

Sam nodded and smiled to reassure Lisa. Thank God this was

the last day of summer softball. Otherwise, her mother would yank her off the team for sure.

Sam settled into her spot at second base and blew out a sigh. They were only in the top of the first inning. How would she ever make it through the next thirteen and two-thirds?

Chapter 10
Tougher Stuff

After their semi-final win over the Milford Cobras, Coach Gellar gave Sam and her teammates a short ten minutes to say hello to their families before taking on the Elmhurst Rage in the finals.

Sam ran up to Helene in the bleachers and blurted, "Is everything okay? Can they still come over?"

"Everything's fine, Samantha Rose." Helene patted Sam's arm in a calming manner. "I came to watch you play. That's all."

Sam sighed in relief and then pointed to the blue skies overhead. "You were right about the weather."

"Mmm." Helene tilted her head toward the August summer sun and closed her eyes for a moment. "It's a beautiful day, isn't it?" She opened her eyes, grabbed Sam's chin, and turned it to the side. "Honey, when will you learn to keep your face out of the way?"

"Sorry."

"Are you okay?"

"Yes." Sam reached up and felt her cheek. The swelling had receded slightly from the trainer's ice treatments between innings. "I'll live."

"Well, that's always a good thing. I'm going to watch about two innings of the next game and then head home to help your mother finish getting ready for your party."

"Thanks, Helene. You're the best." Sam grabbed Helene's hand and pulled her up. "C'mon, you have to meet Lisa's family before you go."

"That would be nice." Helene ran a hand over her hair, even though her usual blond ponytail looked fine and smooth as usual.

Lisa's parents stood up when Sam and Helene approached.

"Mr. and Mrs. Brown," Sam said to Lisa's parents, "this is Helene, my nanny."

"Nanny?" Lisa's mother looked confused.

Sam felt the blush creep up her cheeks. "Yeah, I still kind of have a nanny." She mumbled the last part of the sentence.

Helene laughed. "I'm more like a jack of all trades in the Payton household, but, yes, I did help take care of Samantha Rose when she was younger."

You still do, Sam thought.

"It's nice to meet you, Helene." Lisa's mother shook hands with her.

"Likewise."

Lisa's father smiled. "It's nice to meet somebody from Sam's camp finally."

Helene smiled graciously and shook the offered hand.

Lisa's mother reached out to give Sam a warm hug. She pulled back and examined Sam's bruised cheek in much the same way Helene had done. "Are you okay?"

"Yeah," Sam said. "I like to stop base runners with my face."

Lisa's mother chuckled. "You should rethink that strategy, Samantha Rose."

"I agree." Sam smiled.

"So," Lisa's mother turned to Helene, "tell me all about Samantha Rose as a baby. We've told her Lisa's baby stories, but she won't tell us any of hers."

"With pleasure." Helene made herself comfortable on the bleachers next to Lisa's mother.

"Oh, no." Sam faked a grimace, but inside she was smiling. "I'd better make a fast exit." She loved that Helene and Lisa's mother were getting to know each other. Bridget apparently wanted in on the action and climbed into Helene's lap. Helene didn't seem to think anything of it and simply readjusted Bridget into a more comfortable position. Sam flashed a grin at Helene.

"Sam, Lisa," Susie called from the dugout, "c'mon." She pointed to her wrist as if she were wearing a watch.

Sam hugged Helene over Bridget. "I love you."

"Love you, Samantha Rose."

"Wuv you, Samtha Wo," Bridget echoed.

"Thank you, Sweetpea. I love you, too." She gave Bridget a hug.

"Wish us luck," Lisa said to her tribe.

"Bye, everybody." Sam waved to Lisa's entire family and then reached for Lisa's hand. Remembering where she was, she pulled back at the last second.

They bounded down the bleacher steps and ran toward the dugout in time to hear that the starting lineup would be the same for the championship game.

The umpire asked the Nor'easters to take the field, and Sam sprinted out to her second base position. Luckily Marlee was still pitching well and struck out the first three Elmhurst batters she faced. Unfortunately, the Elmhurst pitcher also struck out everyone she faced that first inning, including Sam. Lisa came close to getting on base in the bottom of the second inning, but the Elmhurst left fielder made an amazing over-the-shoulder catch. By the top of the fourth, neither team had scored.

"C'mon, guys," Lisa encouraged as she squatted behind the plate to start the fourth inning.

"Yeah, c'mon, Nor'easters," Sam shouted from her second base position. "Throw it in there, Marlee."

The lead-off hitter for Elmhurst swatted Marlee's first pitch through the five-six gap between third and short. Marlee pounded her glove against her thigh, obviously agitated that the batter had gotten a hit. It was, after all, the first hit of the game for either team.

"Let's get two," Abby called to the infielders.

Sam nodded and crouched low. She had to guard against the bunt, a steal, a grounder, a pop, or a line drive. She was ready to bolt in any direction.

The batter squared around to bunt before Marlee released the ball.

"Watch the slap, Samantha Rose." Mae crept closer to the plate leaving first base unguarded.

Sam took a cheat step toward first. The batter put down a bunt which died in the middle of the infield. Sam sprinted to cover first base as both Mae and Keisha ran in from the corners to field the ball. Keisha got to it first.

"One, one, one," Sam called to Keisha. There was no way they'd get the runner out at second.

Keisha threw sidearm from her crouched position. Sam felt for the bag with her right foot, planted it, and stretched for Keisha's bullet.

"Out at first," the umpire yelled.

Sam yanked the ball out of her glove and ran toward the runner on second, who had rounded the base with a big lead. She wasn't going anywhere, though. Susie had snuck in from left field to cover third.

"Time," the umpire called.

Sam tossed the ball back to Marlee. "We've got this, Marlee. Just let 'em hit it."

Marlee worked the next batter to a full count but lost the battle and walked her to put runners on first and second with one out.

"Watch for the double steal," Lisa called to Keisha on third base. Keisha took a step closer to her base.

Unfortunately, Keisha moving closer to her base had put her out of reach for the grounder smashed to her left.

Sam groaned. Elmhurst had the bases loaded with only one out. All they needed was a long fly ball, and they could sacrifice in the first run of the game.

"Play's at home," Lisa called.

Sam tried to hide her smile. Lisa was an Amazon warrior at almost five-eleven. She looked formidable behind the plate with all her catcher's gear on. Sam loved the way Lisa caught Marlee's pitches in that huge catcher's mitt, how she threw the ball back, and how she splayed her big hand across her chest protector and adjusted it. She did it all with smoothness, grace, and what seemed like minimal effort.

Sam pounded her glove, trying to get herself to focus on the game instead of Lisa's long curves and strong hands.

The Elmhurst batter quickly got behind in the count with two strikes. She swung late on the next pitch and fouled it off the first base side of the field. Sam took a step closer to first, hoping she wouldn't get burned the way Keisha had gotten burned at third.

Lisa flashed the sign for a fastball. Marlee put her hands together for the 0-2 pitch. She reached both hands up and then shot the pitch toward home. The batter barely got a piece of it and sent a slow roller between Sam and Mae.

"I got it," Sam yelled to Mae and headed for the ball, but Mae either didn't hear or didn't think Sam could get it because she kept running for it, too. Sam scooped up the ball with both hands, leaped around her first baseman, and threw a line drive to Lisa at the plate. Somehow Sam landed on her feet.

"Out!" the home plate umpire yelled.

"Yes!" Sam pumped a fist.

"Sorry, Samantha Rose," Mae said. "I heard you call for it, but I thought I could get to it first. My bad."

"It's cool." Sam bumped gloves with Mae. "Let's just get out of this inning."

"You said it."

Of course, a bumbling play like that wouldn't be complete without Coach Gellar weighing in. "Do you two need hearing aids? Talk to each other out there, or somebody's coming out of this game."

Both Sam and Mae nodded that they understood. One could not ignore Coach Gellar when she spoke. Ever.

Elmhurst's cleanup hitter, their shortstop, stepped into the batter's box with the bases loaded. Luckily there were two outs and a force at every base. Marlee pitched two quick strikes but then missed with three rise balls in a row to fill up the count.

"Payoff pitch," Sam muttered under her breath. "C'mon, Marlee, ring her up!" She knew they were in trouble when Marlee hung a fat pitch down the middle of the plate.

The Elmhurst batter swung and sent a mighty blast into the left-center field gap. All four Elmhurst runners were set in motion, rounding the bases.

"There goes the freakin' merry-go-round," Sam muttered. She could only watch helplessly as Susie sprinted after the ball and grabbed it at the fence. She fired it to Abby, who relayed it to third. The batter slid, but the tag from Keisha wasn't even close. The batter was safe with a base-clearing triple. On one pitch, the Nor'easters were losing by a score of 3-0.

"Way to get it back in, Sus," Sam called out to left field. Susie was muttering, probably in Spanish, and probably with words that were illegal in most states.

On the next play, the runner on third must have been feeling cocky because she tried to steal home on a rare wild pitch from Marlee. Lisa got a lucky bounce off the backstop and shovel passed the ball to Marlee, covering the plate.

"Out!" the umpire yelled.

Sam leaped off the ground and then sprinted to the dugout. "Nice play, you guys."

Marlee rolled her eyes. "Sometimes that stupid rise ball gets away from me."

"It's all right." Lisa unbuckled her chest protector. "We got the out."

"Sam," Susie flew into the dugout from left field, "let's get those runs back. We lead off."

"Don't remind me." Sam grabbed her helmet and batting gloves from the cubby with her name on it and then threw her glove inside. She pulled her bat off the rack and headed to the on-deck circle with

Susie. Sam backed up a few steps and took her practice swings.

"Hey," Susie said, "guess who called me?"

"The president of Science Geeks Anonymous?"

"No, but that was funny."

Sam knew Susie was trying to distract her from the game. However, Susie's ploy wasn't working because Sam knew she was still at the center of Coach Gellar's radar. "Okay, who called?"

"Ronnie."

"Ronnie Alesi?"

Susie nodded. "He wants me to convince you to do the play."

"Sounds like something Ronnie would do." The umpire called for Sam's presence in the batter's box. On the way to the plate, she looked over her shoulder and bugged her eyes out at Susie. She had no idea if she was going to try out for the play or not. She wasn't naïve enough to think the part of the fiddler would be handed to her. She would have to audition. She wanted to earn the part anyway.

"Hmm," Sam said out loud as she dug her cleats into the batter's box. *Maybe I do want to audition for the part.* "Hmm," she said again. *Maybe I can be distracted.*

Sam pulled her bat back and got ready for the first pitch of her second at-bat of the game. The pitch was on the way. Fastball. Inside. Way inside. Sam turned to dodge it but couldn't get out of the way in time. It hit her square in the back. She reached behind with her left hand and rubbed the spot.

"Take your base." The home plate umpire pointed toward first base.

"Gladly," Sam muttered and headed up the line.

"You okay?" Susie asked on her way to the plate.

"Yeah. It just stings a little." Sam threw her bat toward the dugout and jogged the rest of the way to first.

Sam stretched her back and checked Coach Gellar for the signs. A hit-away sign for Susie, but nothing for her. She hoped Susie would get on base. They desperately needed to score. Losing the championship game would suck because Coach Gellar would hold a grudge and take it out on them in the spring season. No, something had to happen. Right away.

Sam made a decision standing on first base, one that could completely backfire, but she didn't care. She was in the Coach Gellar doghouse anyway, so why not chance it? She had good speed. She could make it.

The Elmhurst pitcher put her hands together for the pitch. Sam rocked back. The pitcher circled her arm, and Sam shifted her weight forward. Sam exploded off the base as the pitcher released the ball toward home plate. She had one goal—second base. Her teammates were yelling. The Elmhurst players were yelling. She had no idea where the ball was, but it didn't matter. She was on her way. The Elmhurst shortstop straddled the base, glove extended. Sam threw her arms back and slid. The shortstop tagged her on the thigh.

"Safe!" the umpire in the field yelled, throwing both arms out to the side.

"Yes!" Sam smacked the ground and bounded up to her feet. She turned to face center field, secretly smiling at the cheers she heard. She brushed the dirt off her sliders before turning around to sneak a peek at Coach Gellar.

Coach Gellar stood in the third-base coach's box with both hands on her hips. The non-smile on her face told Sam all she needed to know. She was still in the doghouse, but she didn't care.

She'd taken a chance, and it had paid off. She was in scoring position with no outs and her team down by three runs.

Susie stepped into the batter's box for her next pitch and smacked a single up the middle. Sam sprinted to third base but was stopped by Coach Gellar.

"No outs, Samantha Rose," Coach Gellar said with a detached and businesslike tone. "No heroics. Let the batters get you in." Coach Gellar never did like players doing things she hadn't authorized.

Sam nodded. With no outs, it was a better strategy to see if Lisa or Marlee or possibly Abby could hit her in to score than to do something foolish like trying to steal home.

Lisa stepped into the batter's box with runners on first and third. Coach Gellar flashed the steal sign to Susie. Susie took off on the first pitch. The catcher caught the ball and leaped to her feet. She faked the throw to second and then rifled the ball to third, obviously hoping to catch Sam leaning. Sam got back to the base easily.

"Way to go, Sus," Sam called to Susie on second base.

"You, too, *gringa*."

Lisa stepped back into the batter's box. She trailed one foot outside and read the signs from Coach Gellar. Once Coach Gellar looked away, Lisa shifted her gaze to Sam on third base. The smile in her eyes almost melted Sam to her toes. Sam smiled back. Big. She couldn't help it. Sensing Coach Gellar watching her, Sam coughed into her fist and focused on the Elmhurst pitcher.

Lisa could put a hurt on anybody with her bat, and that at-bat was no exception. She smacked a single into the left-center field gap, and Sam easily scored the first Nor'easter run of the game. Coach Gellar held Susie up at third, much to the dismay of the people in the stands, most of whom were related to Lisa. Sam high-fived Marlee, who was heading to the plate for her turn at bat. As the fans continued to boo, Sam tried not to laugh. They didn't realize that booing would do no good. Disapproval never fazed Coach Gellar. If anything, it made her dig her heels in more.

"Nice job, Samantha Rose." Abby high-fived her from the on-deck circle.

"Thanks, Abby. Get a hit."

"That's the plan."

Sam chuckled. Abby was another one. She was confident in everything she did, but she was different than Coach. If Abby messed up, she admitted it. Coach never did. Of course, Coach probably thought she never messed up.

Sam laughed out loud at the thought. She put her helmet and batting gloves back in her cubby and watched Marlee walk on four pitches to load the bases. Abby stepped up to the plate with no outs.

"Ducks, Abby," Keisha yelled from the on-deck circle. "Ducks on the pond."

Abby worked the pitcher to a 3-1 count.

"A walk's a run, Abby," Sam yelled.

A big fat meatball of a pitch headed for Abby's bat. She sent it down the right-field line.

"Go, Abby, go," Sam called to her. "We've got our own merry-go-round now." Sam squealed and watched her friends run around the bases.

Susie scored easily. Lisa turned on the speed, rounding third, and scored to tie the game up 3-3. Coach Gellar held Marlee up at third to the accompaniment of more boos from the fans. Abby motored in to second base with a two-run stand-up double.

Sam and her teammates mobbed Susie and Lisa when they got back into the dugout.

Keisha got up to bat and sent a pop fly to the right fielder, sacrificing herself so Marlee could score the go-ahead run. Two more quick outs followed, and at the end of the fourth inning, the Nor'easters were ahead by a score of 4-3. During the fifth and sixth innings, the scoring drought was back, and neither team scored any runs. Heading into the top of the seventh inning, all the Nor'easters had to do was keep Elmhurst from scoring and the championship would be theirs.

The Elmhurst shortstop had other plans and led off the inning with a double to left-center field. With one swing, Elmhurst had the tying run in scoring position.

Sam's stomach clenched. Close games always made her nervous.

The next batter put down a bunt. Mae ran in and fielded the ball cleanly. She threw it to Sam, covering first base.

"Out at first," the umpire yelled.

The runner who had been on second advanced to third on the play. With only one out, she was dangerously close to scoring and tying up the game.

Sam tossed the ball back to Marlee. "C'mon, Marlee, let's get the next one."

With one out and the tying run on third base, the next batter dug in at the plate. She swung at the first pitch and sent a high pop toward shallow right field over Sam's head.

"Shit," Sam muttered. She turned and ran after the ball like a Buffalo Bills wide receiver. It was just out of her reach, and the right fielder was nowhere to be seen. The damn runner on third was going to score and tie the game. Sam knew what she had to do. If she missed, it didn't matter because the ball would fall in for a hit anyway. She leaped. The resounding thwack of the ball hitting her glove made her rejoice. For a split second. She hit the ground hard, hip first, then shoulder. She used her momentum and rolled, miraculously hanging on to the ball.

"Third, third, third," Mae yelled. "She didn't tag up."

Sam leaped to her feet. The runner that had been on third was scrambling back to the base. Sam rifled the ball to Keisha, who caught it on one hop. Sam held her breath for the umpire's call.

"Out!" The umpire yelled. "Ball game!" He threw both hands in the air.

Sam leaped and punched a fist in the air. She then covered her face with both hands. She couldn't help the tears streaming down her cheeks as relief poured out of her. Her teammates were on her in a flash. They had just won the summer league championship game.

"*Magnifica*, Sam." Susie wrapped her in a bear hug and twirled her around.

The rest of Sam's teammates chanted the Sports Center "da-da-dat" theme after congratulating her.

"Way to go, Samantha Rose," Abby patted her on the back. "That was freakin' awesome." She headed to the high-five line.

"Thanks, Abby," Sam called after her.

"Oh, man, Two." Marlee gave Sam a relieved hug. "That was an amazing catch. I owe you an ice cream sundae with sprinkles, a cherry, and everything."

"Awesome, P," Sam said. "You pitched two great games yourself."

"Thanks. I think I'm ready to relax in somebody's pool now." Marlee winked at Sam, and then she and Susie headed for the high-

106

five line.

"Oh, my God," Lisa gushed. "I want to go make babies with you right now."

"What?" Sam screeched in laughter and whipped her head around to make sure no one heard.

"Ronnie was right." Lisa raised a suggestive eyebrow. "You *are* butch."

"Shuddup." Sam nudged Lisa with her shoulder. They made their way to high-five the other team. Sam's body protested, but she ignored her new bruises.

After the line, Sam held the dugout door open and let Lisa enter first. Coach Gellar was just inside, putting her scorebook away. Coach Gellar, not one for hugs, patted Sam on one shoulder. "Way to hang in there, kid. You're made of tougher stuff than I thought."

Chapter 11
She Didn't Care

The front door to the mansion opened before Sam's key touched the lock.

"Welcome, girls." Sam's mother opened the door wide. "Please come in." Her sweeping gesture invited them into the overlarge foyer.

Sam let Lisa, Susie, and Marlee enter first. Each carried a bag with a bathing suit and a change of clothes inside. Their footsteps echoed on the marble floor. Sam closed the door behind them.

Her mother leaned toward Sam for a quick hug. Sam played along, even though they never hugged. She made sure her battered cheek was turned away. Her mother wore casual salmon-colored slacks and a thin floral cardigan over a white tank top. As always, she looked pristine.

"Mother, you know Susie."

"Yes." Sam's mother turned to Susie and nodded. "It's nice to see you again, dear."

"Likewise," Susie said.

"This is Marlee," Sam continued. "She's that awesome pitcher I was telling you about. She and Lisa go to Clarksonville High School."

"Nice to meet you, Mrs. Payton," Marlee said.

Sam's mother nodded. "Yes. It's nice to meet Sam's friends."

"And this is Lisa," Sam continued, "our catcher. Well, she *was* our catcher, but now she's not because the season's over." Sam shut up because she was starting to ramble.

"It's nice to meet you," Sam's mother said to Lisa. "We're having lunch on the pool deck. I'm sure you're starving after your match." She turned and headed toward the back of the house.

When her mother's back was to them, Sam blew out a nervous sigh. Lisa patted her on the back for reassurance, but Sam could tell that Lisa was just as nervous as she was.

"Go ahead, you guys." Sam gestured for her friends to go first.

"Did you girls win your contest?" Sam's mother looked back at them.

"Yes," Lisa answered. "Sam made an amazing catch in the last inning to win the game."

"That's nice." Sam's mother said without much emotion. She turned back around.

Lisa paused at an oil painting hanging in the hallway. She smirked back at Sam. It was Sam's debutante portrait. In the portrait, Sam wore a white gown with pearls that contrasted nicely with her tanned skin, even though the ball had been in January on her sixteenth birthday. Her hair had been pinned up into a low loose bun with a few tendrils falling gracefully against her neck.

"You look like a bride," Lisa whispered.

Sam grunted and nudged her along.

Sam's jaw dropped open when she saw the elaborate lunch spread on the pool deck. Two caterers in cooking whites stood behind tables laden with cold cuts and cheeses, bags of chips, and a mind-boggling assortment of breads. A cooler overflowing with drinks sat next to the table. There was enough food to feed an army.

"Mother," Sam said, "did you do all of this?"

Her mother put her hand to her neck. "Do you like it, dear?"

"Of course, I do. Thank you so much."

"Yes, thank you," Lisa added. "It looks wonderful."

"I'm glad you're all pleased." Sam's mother gestured toward several chaise lounges. "You may place your things there. Steve and—" She looked at the nametag pinned to one of the server's shirts. "Steve and Jarvis will take your orders. Have as much as you want, girls."

"You don't have to ask me twice," Susie said and gave her order to Steve, the older of the two servers.

Once the girls had their sandwiches, chips, and drinks, they sat at one of the concrete poolside tables. Although it was late in the afternoon by this time, the August sun was still intense, and they needed the oversized umbrella to keep them in the shade.

"Oh, man," Marlee said, "this is awesome. I'm starving." She took a big bite of her turkey sandwich and then rolled her eyes heavenward as if in rapture. "Mmm, so good."

"I hope we won't have to wait an hour to go swimming." Susie took an equally big bite.

"House rules say swim whenever you want." Sam looked toward the pool. "Nobody else swims in it anyway."

"Your family doesn't go in the pool?" Lisa asked.

"Helene does laps sometimes, but the rest of us are too busy with other stuff."

Lisa leaned toward Sam. "I like your mom. She's nice."

"Thanks." Sam felt her cheeks get warm. "Hey, how does my face look?"

Susie recoiled. "*Aay*, don't scare us with that thing."

"Ha ha, Sus." Sam turned her cheek toward Lisa.

"It's still a little swollen, but you should be okay. I'd keep dodging your mom if you can."

"Yeah, I think I will."

They ate heartily, including Sam, who kept waiting for her mother to give her the evil eye about her huge roast beef sandwich, but she never did. She kept a respectful distance away from their table.

Once lunch was devoured, Sam directed her friends toward the pool house to change.

"This is a pool house?" Lisa asked. "It looks like a log cabin. I love the detail." She ran a hand along the birch welcome sign.

"My dad wanted an Adirondack theme."

"That's so cool," Marlee said.

"Susie, you can change in there." Sam pointed to the private changing room on the left. "Marlee, in there." She pointed to the other. "Lisa and I'll hang in the rocking chairs that no one ever sits in either."

"Will do." Marlee entered the right-side changing room.

Sam's mother wandered over. Luckily, Sam was able to keep the injured side of her face pointed away. "Samantha Rose, dear, Helene left your bathing suit and cover-up on the right side."

"Thanks, Mother. She told me she was going to do that. I'll be sure to thank her later."

Sam's mother nodded and turned to go, but Lisa stood up. Sam's nerves jangled. What was Lisa going to do?

"Mrs. Payton?" Lisa said.

Sam's mother turned around. "Yes, dear?"

"I wanted to tell you how lovely your roses are. Those are *Comte de Chambord* roses around the fountain out front, aren't they?"

"Yes, they are." Sam's mother seemed impressed.

"They're outstanding. I don't know how you get them to bloom so heartily."

Sam covered a smile with her hand. She could tell her mother was eating up the attention.

Before Sam's mother could respond, Lisa pointed to a trellis covered with roses near the tennis courts. "Are those Don Juan climbers?"

Sam's mother nodded. "They are."

"How in the world do you get them to do so well up here in zone four? My mother has tried and tried to grow them, but she gave up and planted lilacs instead. I can't wait to tell her about these."

"Would you like to see more of the flower gardens?" Sam's mother asked.

"I'd love that." Lisa fell into step with Sam's mother.

Sam wasn't sure if she should get up and walk with them but decided it might be easier to hide her face if she stayed seated. Lisa seemed to be handling herself okay without her.

Lisa walked with Sam's mother around the gardens surrounding the pool and tennis courts for several long agonizing minutes. Sam overheard them talking about flowers, ground cover, fertilizer, watering schedules, winter regimes, and a dozen other things Sam didn't comprehend. She was in awe, actually. She had no idea her mother knew so much about her own gardens. She always figured the gardening staff took care of everything while her mother took the credit.

"Hmm," Sam said out loud.

"Hmm, what, *muchacha*?" Susie had come out of the pool house.

"That." She nodded toward Lisa and her mother, squatting to examine a low-growing plant.

"*Aay, magnifica.*" Susie shook both fists in the air in victory. "That's a great sign." She sat in Lisa's abandoned rocker.

"It is at that." Sam nodded.

"What's a great sign?" Marlee asked as she emerged from the pool house.

Both Sam and Susie pointed toward Lisa and Sam's mother, heading to another section of the garden. Apparently, Lisa was getting the full tour.

"See? It might not be that hard to, you know, come out to your parents." Marlee whispered the last five words.

"Yeah, I don't know about that." Sam shrugged. "Hey, why don't you guys go in the pool? I'll wait for Lisa."

Susie didn't need to be told twice. She dropped her bag on the concrete deck and took a running leap. She landed in the water cannonball style, sending a tidal wave onto the deck. When she surfaced, she said, "C'mon, Marlee. It's awesome." She floated on her back with a huge smile on her face.

Sam laughed as Marlee made her way to the ladder and slowly, inch-by-inch, eased herself into the cool water. In some ways, Susie and Marlee were very different.

At long last, Lisa walked back. Sam's mother had gone to have a sandwich made by the caterers.

"Thank you," Sam said.

Lisa blew out a sigh. "I think that went well. Your mom is an amazing gardener. We have to get our moms together so that they can compare notes."

"Someday," Sam agreed. "C'mon, let's change." *And change the subject, too.*

Sam and Lisa changed in the pool house and met back on the porch. Lisa wore a light blue one-piece bathing suit that fit her perfectly. Sam tried not to stare at Lisa's curves and long legs, but it was hard not to drool over her firm, athletic body. She didn't have to ask what her own white bikini was doing to Lisa. One look at Lisa's melting expression told her everything.

They joined Susie and Marlee in the pool and playfully splashed around for a while. Once they were cooled off sufficiently, they claimed four of the chaise lounges and sunned themselves. Sam closed her eyes and, after a while, could have sworn she heard Susie snoring lightly.

"Did you win the second game?" Helene said.

Sam opened her eyes. "Yes, we did." She adjusted the back of the chaise into a sitting position.

"Sam made a diving catch to end the game," Lisa said.

"I'm sorry I missed it." Helene frowned. "That'll teach me to leave early." She looked back at Sam. "You didn't hurt yourself again, did you?"

Sam laughed and reached up to touch her cheek. "Nope. Not that time."

"Thank goodness."

Helene turned to Marlee and Susie. "I hope you girls saved room for dessert."

"Ooh," Marlee said. "Always."

"This is Marlee." Sam gestured to Marlee on the last chaise.

Helene walked over and put her hand out. "Sam's told me so

much about you. It's nice to meet you in person finally."

Marlee shook Helene's hand and then shot Sam a sidelong glance. "Good things, I hope?"

"Always," Sam said with a laugh.

"A little birdy told me that someone out here is bonkers for flan." Helene looked straight at Susie.

Susie sat bolt upright. "No way. Did you make flan? *Dios mio*, I am so moving in."

Helene laughed. "I'll bring it out in about fifteen minutes, okay?"

"Yum," Marlee said with a grin.

Helene headed back toward the house but then turned around. "Sam? Your father just got home from playing golf. He said he'd come out in a minute."

"Thanks, Helene."

True to Helene's word, Sam's father walked out a few minutes later. He still had on his pink Ralph Lauren golf shirt and white pants. His skin was tanned from playing golf and tennis all summer. He ran a hand through his boyish blond hair and strode toward Sam and her friends.

Sam started to stand up, but her father put a hand out. "Don't get up, girls. I came out to say hello and see how your party was going."

"We're fine, Daddy. Let me introduce you. You know Susie. And this is my friend Marlee."

"Hello." Sam's father nodded at Marlee and Susie.

"Hi, Mr. Payton," Susie said.

"Hi," Marlee echoed.

"And you remember my friend Lisa." *Friend. What a cop-out.*

Sam's heart was pounding in her chest, and with good reason. Her father had almost caught them in bed together.

"Nice to meet you again, Mr. Payton," Lisa said.

"Thank you. It's nice to meet you girls, too. I hope you're enjoying yourselves." He glanced at the sandwich spread. "I think I'll go get a roast beef sandwich." He waggled his eyebrows and headed toward the catering table.

Sam let out a slow breath. "Well, that was short and sweet."

"For a second contact," Lisa said, "it went okay."

Sam nodded and took a breath to calm her pounding heart. Her throat felt dry. She needed water. "Anybody need another drink?"

"Sure," Marlee said. "How about a Coke?"

"You got it. Anybody else?"

"No, thanks," Lisa said. Susie shook her head.

"Be right back." Sam got up and put on her cover-up. There's no sense getting Steve and Travis worked up any more than they probably already were with four teenage girls sunning themselves in bathing suits.

Sam's father ate his sandwich heartily at a stone table near the door to the house. Sam's mother sat down next to him. They were speaking in low tones, but Sam could just make out their words from her vantage point at the drinks cooler.

"She doesn't have many friends," her mother insisted. "We should let her do this, Gerald. Dr. Boyle says—"

"I don't give a flip what Dr. Boyle says," Sam's father interrupted, the irritation in his voice obvious.

Sam took her time at the cooler, hoping to hear what her mother wanted him to let her do.

"They're nice girls," her mother continued. "See the strikingly pretty girl with the long dark braid?"

"Lisa."

"Yes. She knows first aid. She has three younger siblings, for goodness' sake, so if anyone got hurt, she could help them."

Sam's father didn't respond. He simply took another bite of his sandwich.

Sam's mother sat back and folded her arms. "What if Helene stayed with them?"

Sam took a quick breath. *The lake house. They must be talking about the lake house. C'mon, Daddy, let us go.* Sam reached for a cup and filled it with ice, one slow cube at a time.

Sam's father dabbed at the corners of his mouth with a napkin. "Can they all swim?"

"Yes. I've watched them all afternoon. They're all good swimmers."

Sam could feel her father's eyes on her. He took a deep breath. "All right. I guess it will be okay." He stood up. "Let's go tell them."

Sam's eyes flew open wide. She scurried back to her chaise lounge with Marlee's Coke and a cup of ice. She tried to appear nonchalant as she handed them to Marlee. She'd completely forgotten to get water for herself, but she didn't care. Her parents were headed right for them.

"Girls?" Sam's father said. "Sam's mother and I would like to offer you the use of our lake house over Labor Day weekend. How does that sound?"

"Really, Daddy?" Sam asked calmly, even though she wanted to jump and yell her head off. "We can go?"

He nodded. "Sure. Mother says you can all swim."

Sam smiled at how quickly her friends nodded in agreement.

"Well, good." He turned to Sam. "We'll have Helene call their parents to make sure it's okay."

Ahh, ever the businessman, Sam thought. She wouldn't be surprised if he made them sign waivers, too.

"Thanks, Daddy. We'll be safe."

"I know you will." He turned to go.

Sam's mother hesitated a brief moment and then grinned. "This is so exciting, Samantha Rose. We'll make a shopping list for Helene tonight." She turned away, the grin still big on her face.

"*Impresionante, muchacha,*" Susie said, her eyebrows raised high. "How'd you pull that one off?"

Sam shrugged. She had no idea. And she didn't care.

Chapter 12
The Lake House

Sam sat on the top step outside the mansion, trying not to be nervous about the long weekend ahead. Waiting five whole days had been pure torture. All week, she expected her father to call her into his study and tell her he'd changed his mind, but he hadn't, thank God. Sam tapped her foot and looked past the meticulous flower gardens and the manicured lawns toward the eastern white pines surrounding the front gate. Even though they lived in one of the biggest towns in the North Country of New York State, it was oddly quiet. It was so quiet that Sam could hear the bees buzzing in the flowers and the crows cawing in the pines.

Helene came out the front door and sat down. She cradled the remote control that would open the gate once Marlee, Susie, and Lisa pulled up in Marlee's van.

"Are you excited?" Helene said.

"Oh, my God, yes. Thanks for coming with us. There's no way Daddy would've let us go without you *chaperoning*." Sam put air quotes around the word chaperoning.

"I think your parents realize you're not a child anymore."

"I wish."

"Having your friends over Saturday opened their eyes, I think. I know your mother was more than impressed with Lisa."

"Eee," Sam squealed. "Too bad I can't tell them about me."

"You'll know when it's time for that, honey." Helene patted Sam on the knee.

Yeah, like never. Sam cleared her throat. "Where did they go this weekend, anyway?"

"Syracuse. A Republican fund-raising gala. A thousand dollars a plate."

Sam shook her head. "My parents are conservative Republicans. How am I ever going to come out to them?"

Helene shrugged and stared toward the front gate. She had a faraway look on her face.

Sam watched her nanny out of the corner of her eye. If her parents didn't think she was a child anymore, did that mean Helene was leaving them soon? Leaving her? Was she at least going to Switzerland with them over Christmas break?

"Helene?"

"Hmm?" Helene turned her head slightly.

"Are you going—"

Before she could get the question out, the buzzer to the front gate rang in the house.

"There they are." Helene pressed the button on the remote control to open the gate. She stood up and headed toward her Prius.

Sam also stood up, her stomach fluttering at the thought of spending a long weekend, not exactly alone, but with Lisa.

"Oh, honey," Helene said, "what were you saying?"

"Nothing." Sam waved her hand in dismissal. "I'll ask you later."

"You sure?"

"Yeah, yeah." I just want to know when you're leaving me.

Marlee pulled her van around the circular drive and stopped in front of the granite steps. Lisa slid open the side door.

"Your chariot, my dear." Lisa smiled and slid over on the seat to make room. Lisa's devilish grin threatened to melt Sam to the core.

Sam couldn't help the smile bursting from her. She grinned at Lisa and then tore her eyes away to say hello to Marlee and Susie. She was about to hop into the van but had second thoughts.

"Hang on a second, you guys." Sam walked to Helene's car. Helene was putting on her seatbelt. "Are you sure you're okay driving an hour and a half by yourself? I feel bad."

"I'll be fine." Helene pointed to her massive purse on the passenger seat. "Somewhere in there, I've got the *Fiddler on the Roof* soundtrack."

Sam's jaw dropped open. "How did you know?"

Helene narrowed her eyes. "I have my sources."

"Who?"

Helene patted Sam on the arm. "Susie."

"That little sneak." Sam turned around and pointed an accusing finger in Susie's direction. Susie held up her hands innocently. Sam turned back around to face Helene. "I'm still not sure if I'm trying out for the play."

"Of course, you are." Helene grinned mischievously.

"C'mon, *muchacha*," Susie called from the van, "we're burning daylight. You're the one who wanted to get there before dark."

Sam headed toward the van and wagged her finger at Susie. "You're in big trouble." She hopped in the backseat of the van and slid the door closed. "Why is everybody so sure I'm going to try out for that stupid play?"

"Because you are, baby," Lisa said with a grin.

"Yeah," Sam laughed, "maybe I am." Sam wished she could hug Lisa but didn't want the security cameras to record them. "Hey, Marlee?"

"What's up, Two?"

"I know how to get there, but it'll be easier if you just follow Helene, okay?"

"You got it." Marlee put the van in drive and followed Helene's lead car down the Payton driveway.

"I missed you," Sam said low to Lisa.

"Me, too."

"You know I wanted to come over yesterday, but Mother and I had to do that grand opening at the new hair salon."

"I can't believe people pay your family to make appearances," Lisa said. "It's kind of weird."

"I know, but they don't really pay us. They gave us coupons for free haircuts, hoping we'll come back. We won't, but Mother says it's our community service obligation to go to grand openings like that."

"To help the poor and downtrodden, right, *muchacha*?" Susie butted in.

"Yeah, something like that." Sam rolled her eyes and felt her cheeks burning. It was embarrassing being paraded around East Valley like some kind of celebrity when she hadn't earned it.

"Hey guys, guess what I did yesterday?" Susie didn't wait for anyone to guess and said, "I set up a lab in the science center. Professor Harwood said I know more about rocks than most college students. I laid out all kinds of rocks on these long lab tables. There was quartz, calcite, gypsum, hematite, pyrite—that's fool's gold, sulfur, and—"

"Sus," Sam interrupted, "you're a rockhound. I bet you're going to tell us what kind of rocks we have at the lake, won't you?"

"Without a doubt."

Marlee chuckled. "Welcome to my world."

Sam laughed and sat back against the bench seat. She turned toward Lisa, and her heart did a flip-flop. Even though Lisa's smile hadn't been specifically for her, it was an amazing sight. Sam desperately wanted to put her arm around her but didn't dare. Not inside the Clarksonville County limits anyway. She settled for holding her hand instead.

"Oh, and guess what else?" Susie said. "I checked into that queer group. The Rainbow Council."

"Yeah?" Sam said. "What'd you find out?"

"They have a pride festival in October." Susie lowered her voice as if the forest might overhear. "They're having carnival games, face painting, gay movies, and speakers and stuff. They're having a band in the quad that night, too. I think."

"Sounds like fun," Marlee said.

Sam wasn't sure what to think. There was no way she could go to an event like that.

"The flyer said the theme was gay marriage." Susie grinned.

Marlee used her fist as a makeshift microphone. "Gay marriage—now legal in a state near you."

"And Washington D.C., too," Susie added.

"Geez," Lisa said, "that's so awesome. You know? To be able to get married. Legally. No hiding."

Sam grinned at Lisa. God, to be able to have a life with Lisa, legally sanctioned by the state they lived in, to have children like Aunt Fran and Aunt Margaret, to say that Lisa Ann Brown was her wife. Her wife!

"Sam," Lisa squeezed her hand tight, "where'd you go?

"Somewhere nice." Sam took a slow breath. "Somewhere really nice."

"Okay, get this," Susie said. "There's this National Coming Out Day on October eleventh every year. And it's not only in the United States. A lot of countries join us in the celebration."

"Why October eleventh?" Sam asked.

"Back in history, there was some big gay pride march on Washington on that date."

"When was that?" Marlee asked.

"Late eighties, I think."

"They've had this Coming Out day every year since then?" Lisa said. "How come we've never heard of it?"

"I don't know, but we're supposed to wear rainbows or something that shows your pride. I don't have anything like that, but maybe we could buy something at the festival. Do you guys want to go?"

"Not me." Sam shook her head. "You know I can't be seen anywhere near a place like that." Sam felt, rather than saw, Lisa deflate. "But you guys should go. Text me pictures and stuff. It'll be like I'm there."

"It won't be the same," Marlee said, "but we understand why you can't go, right guys?" She looked at Lisa in the rearview mirror.

"Yup," Lisa said, tight-lipped.

Sam looked at Lisa's hand in hers. "I'm sorry, baby. Maybe I can go with you when I'm in college. Maybe by then, I'll be out to my parents. I just can't right now."

"*Dios mio, muchachas,*" Susie said. "It's getting heavy in here, so let me change the subject and tell you what I'm cooking us for dinner tonight."

Leave it to Susie to gauge the situation and lighten the mood. They passed the first part of their journey listening to Susie describe the meals she was going to make for them. Flan apparently played a big part in the plan.

The sun was fairly low in the sky when Marlee pulled the van alongside Helene's car in the driveway of the Payton Family lake house. Sam smiled as her friends oohed and aahed over the three-story house with its wrap-around porch and big picture windows. Lisa especially liked the outdoor fireplace overlooking the lake.

"C'mon, everybody." Sam leaped out of the van the moment Marlee put the gearshift in park. "We're just in time." She beckoned for her friends to follow her past the canoe and kayak rack down the sloping lawn leading to the lake shore.

"Sam," Lisa said, "your house is beautiful." Her face softened when she looked at the lake. She reached for Sam's hand and squeezed. Sam squeezed back but then let go. You never knew who was watching.

"I'm glad we got here in time. I wanted you guys to see the sunset." Sam glanced over her shoulder. "Are you coming, Helene?"

"I'm trying to keep up. You girls are twenty years younger than I am, remember?"

"*Dios mio*, I see why you wanted us here before dark," Susie said.

"The sunsets are incredible." Sam was happy that Mother Nature's outstanding beauty accentuated their first moments at the lake house. Yellows and oranges topped the trees on the far side of the lake.

"Sunsets are weird," Susie said.

"Let me field this one," Marlee said to Sam, Lisa, and Helene. She turned to Susie. "How so?"

"The sun's not actually moving. The earth is, but we can't feel it."

Marlee put her arms out and stumbled as if she'd lost her balance.

Sam and Lisa snickered. Helene smiled.

"*Aay*, shuddup, you guys," Susie said.

"Hey, Susie. Marlee." Sam pulled out her iPhone. "Let me take your picture. Turn around, and I'll get the sunset behind you."

"Cool." Marlee moved closer and linked arms with Susie. They both grinned at the camera phone.

"Okay, girls," Sam moved to get the now red and orange sky in the background behind her friends, "say 'East Valley Rules!'"

"No way, man." Marlee frowned but had a twinkle in her eye. "If I remember correctly, we beat you the last time we played. Or did you guys conveniently forget that?"

"Are you kidding? Coach Gellar won't let us forget for a minute." Susie rolled her eyes. "We'll say 'cheese,' so I don't end up getting divorced tonight." She flashed a lopsided grin at Marlee.

Sam took a few more pictures and then handed her phone to Susie, who took photos of Sam and Lisa.

Helene put her hand out for Sam's phone. "Okay, all four together." She motioned with her hands for them to squeeze together. After taking a few pictures, she held the phone out for Sam to take back, but Lisa grabbed it instead.

"Sam and Helene now. Hurry before the pretty colors disappear."

Sam put her arm around her nanny and smiled. Lisa snapped a

couple of pictures and started to hand it back. "Wait," Sam said, "take one more, okay?" She glanced at Helene. "Rabbit ears?"

Helene chuckled. "Of course."

Sam spread two fingers behind Helene's head, and Helene did the same to her. Helene chuckled, which made Sam chuckle, too, and it wasn't long before everyone was giggling.

"Your parents would be appalled at our behavior." Helene gasped, trying to catch her breath.

"Who cares?" Sam blew out a sigh. "They'll never see these pictures, anyway."

Lisa kept taking pictures until Helene said, "Okay, girls, let's get the cars unpacked. The mosquitoes are attacking."

Reluctantly Sam and the others followed Helene back up the sloping lawn to the driveway. Within minutes they had the van and Helene's car unpacked. The suitcases were stacked in the front hall, and the grocery bags were on the kitchen counter.

"Sam," Helene said, "why don't you get the girls situated upstairs while I put these groceries away."

"Okay." Sam grabbed her bag and directed her friends to grab theirs. Sam only needed one small bag since she already had a lot of clothes in her room. She slung it over her shoulder and helped Susie with her massive suitcase.

"What have you got in here, Sus?" Sam lifted the back while Susie pulled it from the front.

"I brought my igneous rock collection," Susie said with a straight face.

Sam let her end of the suitcase drop. "You did not." She whipped her head around toward Marlee. "Tell me she didn't."

Marlee rolled her eyes. "You never know with this one."

"*Aay, muchacha*, I didn't bring my rocks. I just need, you know, things."

Sam sighed dramatically and picked up her end of the suitcase again. After several minutes, the slow-moving parade finally made it up the stairs.

"You two are in this room right here." Sam pointed to the room at the top of the stairs. "You're right above Mother and Daddy's bedroom, but you'll have complete privacy since they're not here."

"Thanks, Sam." Marlee opened the door and carried her bags into the room. Susie dragged her mammoth suitcase through the doorway by herself. They closed the door behind them.

Sam turned to Lisa. "Okay, our room is way at the other end of the hallway. Unfortunately, we're right above Helene's room, so, uh, you know."

"Gotcha." Lisa nodded. "She might be able to hear us. C'mon. Hurry up. I need to kiss you."

"Ooh, c'mon." Sam broke into a run.

Once they got Lisa's suitcase and Sam's bag into the room, Lisa shut the oak door behind them and pushed Sam against it. She moved to within inches of Sam without touching her.

Sam's breathing quickened. "Oh, my God, you are such a tease."

Lisa smiled devilishly and leaned closer but still didn't make contact. Sam felt Lisa's breath on her lips.

Sam couldn't take it anymore. With a moan, she pulled Lisa to her. Their lips met in a fury of need. Sam wrapped her arms around Lisa's back and was about to move her hands lower when Helene called for her.

"Sam?"

"Bad timing, Helene," Sam muttered. Reluctantly she pulled

away from Lisa and opened the door to her bedroom. "Yes?" she called down the stairs.

"Come on down for a minute."

"Okay, be there in a sec." Sam turned to Lisa. "Why don't you unpack? You can put stuff in my dresser. Just move my clothes over."

"Okay, but when you come back, I want to pick up right where we left off."

There was no mistaking the gleam in Lisa's eye. Sam's stomach flipped. "I'll," she cleared her throat and tried again, "I'll be fast."

Sam raced out the door and down the stairs.

"What's up, Helene?" Sam figured her nanny needed help with her suitcases, so she headed to the front hall. "Do you want help with these?" She picked up the bigger of the two.

"I do, actually," Helene said. "You can put them back in my car."

"What?" Sam put the suitcase down.

"I'm not staying here with you girls."

"What do you mean?"

"I mean that *mon petit hibou* is all grown up and deserves this weekend with her friends without her nanny ruining the fun. I have a reservation at the Seagull Inn up the road. Your parents don't know about this new arrangement, so don't spill the beans, okay? I'll call you later on tonight to make sure you're all right."

"Okay," Sam said tentatively. As much as her insides were doing double and triple happy dances, she was confused. "Are you sure this is okay?" Sam thought about how big the house was. She didn't know anything about the hot water heater or the central air conditioner or what to do if something went wrong.

"Honey," Helene cupped Sam's chin. "I see the worry in your eyes. You'll be okay. You and your friends can solve any problem that comes up. And you can always call me. I'll be two miles away. Okay?"

Still stunned, Sam nodded.

Helene pulled Sam into a hug. "It's about time somebody treated you like you could think for yourself."

Sam hugged her nanny back, trying to wrap her mind around the amazing turn her weekend had taken. "Uh, Helene?"

"Mmm?"

"You're suffocating me."

Helene laughed and kissed Sam on the forehead. When she pulled back, Sam saw a gleam of tears in her nanny's eyes. Without another word, Helene grabbed both of her suitcases and headed out the door.

Not quite sure what was happening, Sam watched the door close. She raced to the window and watched Helene drive away.

Chapter 13
Alone at Last

Sam rinsed the last plate and put it in the drying rack. Lisa wiped the countertop, rinsed out the rag, and dried her hands on the dishtowel draped over Sam's shoulder.

"I like doing dishes with you," Sam said, grabbing Lisa's hands.

"Me, too."

Sam pulled Lisa closer and looked through the open doorway into the living room. Satisfied that Susie and Marlee were out of eyeshot, she wrapped her arms around Lisa's waist. Lisa snuggled into Sam's embrace.

"You know what else I like?" Sam said.

"What?"

"You."

"Get a room, you two," Susie called from the living room.

"Shuddup, Sus." Sam laid her head on Lisa's shoulder and whispered, "I didn't think they could hear us."

Lisa smirked. "It doesn't matter because we actually have a room." She looked up at the ceiling toward Sam's room.

"Mmm." Sam squeezed Lisa tighter. "I love you."

"Same."

Sam, still holding Lisa's hand, led her into the living room. Susie and Marlee were sitting so close together on the couch that

Marlee was practically in Susie's lap.

"Look who's talking," Sam said. "You're the ones who need to get a room."

Susie grinned. "Thanks to you, we have one."

"You're very welcome."

Lisa sat on the carpet with her back against the loveseat and patted the spot next to her. Sam put a finger up to indicate she'd sit in a minute. She turned the dimmer switch down, lowered the lights in the room, put the gas fireplace key in its slot, and turned it. With a flick of a switch on the wall, the fireplace burst into soft yellow and blue flames.

"That's nice," Lisa said.

Sam's heart warmed at Lisa's come-hither smile. "Oops, wait," Sam said. "I forgot the most important thing. I'll be right back." She ran back into the kitchen and threw open the refrigerator door. She rifled through the groceries on the bottom shelf and found the bag she had stashed way in the back after Helene left. She pulled out her prize, hid it behind her back, and headed into the living room.

"Guess what I have." She held the bag out in front of her.

"Is that what I think it is?" Lisa asked, her eyes getting big.

Sam nodded and pulled the bag off. "If you thought it was a bottle of white zinfandel, then you'd be correct."

"Ooh, Sam. I don't know." Susie gestured toward Marlee.

"Oh, my God," Sam said. "Marlee, I'm so sorry. I totally forgot about…" *the drunk driver that killed your father.* "I'm an idiot. I'm sorry."

"No, it's okay," Marlee said. "Nobody's driving. Right?"

Sam shook her head.

"It's only one bottle, so it's not like we're going to get piss drunk." Marlee looked at Susie. "Are we?"

Susie shook her head. "It'll be okay, *mi vida*. I promise." She looked back up at Sam. "Let's go for it."

"Are you sure, you guys? Because we don't have to."

"No, let's do it," Marlee said. "I'd like to try it, actually, to see what all the fuss is about."

"Okay." Sam handed the unopened bottle to Lisa and ran back into the kitchen for a corkscrew and four of the biggest wine glasses she could find. Once the wine was evenly distributed, she sat on the carpet next to Lisa and held up her glass. "A toast." The others raised their glasses. "To good friends."

"To good friends," Lisa, Susie, and Marlee echoed.

Sam took a sip of her wine and turned to Lisa. "Have you ever had wine before?"

"Once or twice, like, at Thanksgiving or Christmas dinner, but just a sip, not a whole glass like this."

"Blah," Marlee said after taking a sip. "It tastes like grape juice gone bad. This is an acquired taste, isn't it?"

"Yeah, I guess it is." Sam chuckled. "My parents sometimes let me have an entire glass with dinner. I got this from our wine cellar." She picked up the nearly empty bottle.

"I hope it wasn't an expensive one," Lisa said. "Will they miss it?"

"Nah, they have a few cases of this kind. I think it's the cheap stuff they keep for unimportant company."

Lisa took another sip. "It's not that bad, I guess, but I wouldn't know a good wine from a bad one."

"Me, neither," Sam agreed.

"It's a waste of perfectly good grapes," Marlee said and took another sip.

Sam clinked glasses with Lisa, and at the precise moment she put the glass to her lips, the cell phone rang in her pocket. She deftly held on to the wine glass with one hand and pulled the phone out of her pocket with the other. She read the caller ID. "How does she always know?" She handed her glass to Lisa, stood up, and headed toward the kitchen. "Hi, Helene."

"How's everything going?"

"Great. Susie made dinner. It was awesome. Chicken and rice, but you're supposed to call it by some Spanish name. And Lisa and I did the dishes."

"It sounds like you're having a good time."

"I am. We all are. Thanks for letting us stay here without you. Ooh, sorry. That sounded bad. I didn't mean it that way."

"Honey, it's fine. It's what I wanted for you." There was something wistful in Helene's voice.

"Are you okay? Is the Seagull Inn as glamorous as it sounds?"

"I'm fine. Don't spare a thought for me, okay? Have fun with your friends this weekend. Be safe."

"We will."

"Make sure you turn off the fireplace before you go to bed."

"How did you—"

"Nanny's know all. Didn't you know that?"

"Ain't that the truth." Sam grunted. "I'll make sure it's off. And I'll check the doors and windows to make sure they're locked."

"That's my girl." Helene yawned. "Okay, I'm off to bed. I know you'll be busy with the girls tomorrow but call me sometime. Maybe before five? I'm taking myself out to the glamorous Village Inn for dinner tomorrow night."

"No, you're not," Sam said. "You're coming here, and we're cooking for you. You've cooked for me my entire life, so it's only fair that I have Susie cook for you."

Helene's laugh was music to Sam's ears. "I can't argue with that logic. What time do you want me?"

"I don't know. Uh, let's see, we should be done canoeing and stuff by late afternoon, I guess. How about six-ish? Is that okay?"

There was silence on the other end of the phone.

"Helene, are you still there?"

"Yes, honey. I was thinking how grown-up you are."

"Well, quit thinking and get to bed. You have a dinner date with us tomorrow and need your rest."

"Goodnight, honey. Don't forget about the fireplace."

"I won't. Goodnight." Sam felt a pang of something she couldn't quite identify. Sadness? Regret? Loneliness? "Helene? Are you still there?"

There was no answer. She'd hung up.

"I love you," Sam said softly and then powered off her phone. Taking a deep breath, she tossed the phone onto the kitchen counter. She wandered back to the living room and checked to make sure the door and windows were locked tight.

"You'll have to give me the recipe," Lisa was saying to Susie.

"*Arroz con pollo* is easy to make. The secret is in the spices. Sometime before we leave, I'll tell you how the Torres family makes it. Remind me later."

Lisa nodded. "Okay."

"Don't talk about leaving." Marlee held Susie tighter. "We just got here." She nuzzled Susie's neck.

Sam turned away from the couple, wanting to give them

privacy. She sat down next to Lisa and pulled her close. "I'm so glad your parents let you come for the weekend." She took her wine glass back from Lisa and took a big gulp.

"They trust me. They trust you, too." Lisa took a sip of wine and grinned at Sam over the top of her glass. "Maybe they shouldn't have, eh?"

"Maybe not." Sam drained her glass, and Lisa did the same.

"Phew, this is going right to my head." Lisa set her empty glass on the carpet.

"Are you okay?"

Lisa nodded. "My nose feels kind of funny."

Sam leaned forward and kissed Lisa's nose gently. She was about to sit back against the couch when Lisa grabbed the front of Sam's shirt and pulled her closer. Sam let herself get lost in the kiss, forgetting that she was in her parents' lake house and that her friends were only a few feet away.

When the scorching kiss ended, Lisa pushed Sam playfully away and said, "That oughta hold you."

Sam blew out a sigh and fanned herself. She couldn't help the grin spreading on her face. She snuck a peek at Susie and Marlee. They were occupied in pretty much the same manner that she and Lisa had just been, except Marlee was now sitting completely in Susie's lap. Sam nodded her head toward them.

Lisa smiled. "They're so cute."

Marlee broke off the kiss and whispered loudly into Susie's ear, "You know what I want to do to you next?"

"What?" Susie said, a blush creeping across her face.

"I want to rip off your—"

"Shh, shh, shush." Susie put a hand over Marlee's mouth to keep her from finishing the sentence.

Sam and Lisa laughed. Susie did, too, but it was obvious she was embarrassed.

"Uh, guys," Susie said, "I think we're gonna take this party upstairs."

"Okay, we'll see you in the morning," Sam said.

"Goodnight, girls." Marlee slid off of Susie's lap and stood up. She grabbed Susie's hand and yanked her toward the stairs.

Susie glanced back over her shoulder. "I think the wine is working."

Sam waved goodnight to her best friend. "Lisa and I'll make breakfast."

Susie nodded and let herself be dragged up the stairs by an impatient Marlee.

"Ahh," Sam snuggled into Lisa, "alone at last."

"Mmm, this is nice." Lisa twirled her hand to indicate the living room. "Someday, I want something like this. A romantic cozy house on a lake with a fireplace and, I don't know, everything."

"We will. Someday we will." Sam laid her head on Lisa's shoulder and nuzzled her neck.

"Mmm," Lisa murmured. "That feels good."

Sam stroked Lisa's braid. "May I?"

Lisa nodded.

Sam pulled off the small band holding the end of Lisa's braid together and slowly undid the three strands. "I love the way you smell."

Lisa moved her hair to one side, presenting her neck.

Sam obliged and trailed a series of kisses from Lisa's collarbone to her ear and back again. She felt Lisa's body respond, mirroring her own desire. Sam trailed her fingertips along the top of Lisa's polo shirt. The top two buttons were already undone, so Sam undid the third. She caressed Lisa's smooth skin along the shirt line and then moved lower to the enticing skin of Lisa's cleavage.

Lisa leaned her head back against the loveseat, eyes closed, breathing deep. The arousal in her features was intoxicating. A wave of desire hit Sam like a line drive.

"You're so beautiful," Sam said, barely above a whisper. She watched Lisa's eyes flutter open.

Lisa reached out to caress Sam's cheek. Sam should have been nervous, but for some reason, she wasn't. She was moments away from taking Lisa up the stairs and finally being completely alone with her. Maybe it was the wine. Maybe it was the cozy surroundings. Maybe, just maybe, it was because she loved Lisa soul deep.

Sam brushed her lips gently over Lisa's.

Lisa groaned. "Don't tease."

Sam couldn't stand it any longer. "Come on." She stood up and reached for Lisa's hands, pulling her up gently.

Lisa stood, and they locked eyes, searching each other's souls wordlessly. Sam's breathing quickened.

"Yes," Lisa whispered and leaned down to sear Sam with another smoldering kiss.

Sam broke away breathless. She took the briefest of moments to catch her breath and led the way up the stairs to her room.

Chapter 14
I Lied

Sam woke to Lisa snuggling behind her. They both lay on their sides, Lisa's front to Sam's back. Skin on skin felt amazing. Sam wriggled backward to feel more of Lisa against her.

"Mmm," Lisa moaned. "You feel so good. I could stay like this forever."

"Me, too." Sam reached for the hand at the end of the arm wrapped around her and pulled it to her lips. She kissed the fingertips gently. "I really, really like this hand. It did some incredible things last night." She kissed the palm.

"Mmm, you've got one that I really like, too."

Sam rolled over so she could see Lisa in the morning light. Her heart melted. Lisa was so pretty, even first thing in the morning.

"Good morning," Sam whispered.

"Morning." Lisa's smile melted Sam. Sam decided she could get used to waking up next to her every day.

"You know what?" Sam asked.

"What?"

"I lied."

"About what?"

"About the best sound I ever heard."

"Hmm?" Lisa sounded confused.

Sam grinned and felt herself blushing. "Last night, when you, uh, when you cried out as you, uh—"

"Oh, geez." Lisa's eyes grew wide. She pulled the sheet over her head. "Was I loud?" She peeked out with one eye.

"No, no, no, but it was music. The best music I've ever heard in my entire life. It's officially the number one best sound I've ever heard."

Lisa peeked out from behind the sheet. "I liked it when you, too, uh, you know, last night."

Sam laughed. "Believe me. I did, too."

Lisa ran her fingers lightly over Sam's lips. "Last night was amazing."

"Mmm." A delicious ribbon of desire shot through Sam. "Let's stay in bed. All day."

"I wish we could, but somebody promised to make breakfast for her friends."

Sam groaned. "I did, didn't I?" She rolled and flopped on her back. "Why, oh, why did I do that?"

"Because you're an awesome friend and an awesome host."

"They can wait, can't they?" Sam pulled Lisa on top of her and groaned when she heard someone stomping on the stairs. "Sounds like they're up already."

"Sam?" Susie knocked lightly on the bedroom door. "*Aay*, I'm sorry to bother you guys, but the fireplace is on. What should I do?"

"Shit," Sam mumbled into Lisa's shoulder as they sat up. "Hang on," she called to Susie. "I'll be right out."

"Susie, do you smell gas?" Lisa pulled the sheet up to cover herself.

"No, but the flames are kind of sputtering."

"Okay, I'm coming." Sam leaped out of the bed, self-conscious about her nakedness in the light of day, but she didn't have time to worry about it. She threw on a pair of shorts and a t-shirt and gave Lisa a quick kiss, lamenting the fact that she had to leave. "I'll be right back. Don't move a muscle."

Lisa's smile lit up her whole face. "I'm not going anywhere. Yell if you need me, though."

"Oh, I need you, but probably not for the fireplace." Sam smiled and hustled out the door.

On the way down the hallway and down the stairs, Sam berated herself. Helene told her to do one thing. Turn off the damn fireplace. And did she? No. She hadn't thought about it once. Why in the world did Helene say she was grown up? No wonder her father didn't think she could handle the lake house on her own.

Sam ran to the sputtering fireplace and threw in the key. Susie and Marlee hovered behind her. She twisted the key and turned off the gas, and the flames died out completely. She sniffed the air for the smell of gas and couldn't detect anything. The ceramic fireplace logs and metal grate radiated way more heat than usual. Thankfully nothing was burned or melted.

Sam sat back on her heels and closed her eyes for a second, trying not to imagine what could have happened if the house had filled up with gas. "I think it's okay. I'm such an idiot."

"Nah," Susie said. "Any one of us could have forgotten."

"Thanks, Sus." Sam stood up and stretched her neck from side to side, trying to release the tension. "What time is it, anyway?"

"Nine."

"Nine?" Sam's eyes bugged out. "Holy crap. I can't believe we slept so late."

"We just got up, too." Susie gestured to her pajamas. "I came down to get Marlee some cold water."

"Headache?"

Susie nodded.

"Do you need a Tylenol or something?"

"Maybe, but we'll try hydrating first.

"Why don't you go back upstairs for a while? I'll call you when breakfast is ready."

"Thanks, *gringa*." Susie bolted back up the stairs.

Sam squatted and checked over the fireplace one last time to make sure everything was truly okay. Satisfied that it was, she stood up and looked at the ceiling overhead. A warm feeling overtook her as she thought of Lisa, still in the bed, waiting for her. With one last check of the now-cooling fireplace, she took the stairs two at a time. The hall bathroom door was closed, and she heard the distinct sounds of Marlee and Susie getting ready to shower together. Sam flung open the door to her bedroom, slammed it shut, and launched herself on top of Lisa.

"Oof," Lisa grunted as Sam landed. She wrapped her arms around her girlfriend. "Everything okay downstairs?"

Sam kissed Lisa's forehead, nose, cheeks, chin, and finally, her soft lips. "Yup. I'm an idiot for leaving it on, but everything seems okay." Sam rolled over on her side. "I have an idea."

"Mmm?"

"Shower?" Sam pointed to her bathroom *en suite*.

"Together?"

"Is that okay?" In a rush, Sam realized she might have overstepped. Lisa was a whole year younger than she was. Maybe it was too much.

Lisa nodded shyly as a healthy red blush crept up her neck.

Sam breathed an inner sigh of relief and sat up. She put out her hand.

~~~

Sam set the batter for her Supersonic Strawberry Supreme Pancakes on the countertop. She stood hip to hip with Lisa, who was cutting up the last of the strawberries. Sam pulled out the cast iron skillet, the one Helene taught her how to make pancakes with, and set it on the stovetop. She turned the knob to light the burner, but nothing happened. Perplexed, she turned the knob off and then on again. Nothing.

"Maybe the pilot light went out," Lisa suggested.

A wave of panic shot through Sam. This was exactly the kind of thing she was afraid of. She didn't know anything about pilot lights or other mechanical things like that.

"Baby?" Lisa said gently. "It's okay. I'll check it out. You look like a deer caught in the headlights."

Sam nodded. "I don't know what to look for."

"Here, I'll teach you. I'm usually my dad's assistant when he fixes things around the house. I'm the go-fer."

"Gopher?"

Lisa chuckled. "I fetch things. I go fer this and go fer that. A go-fer."

Sam laughed. "Well, I guess I'll be your go-fer then."

"Okay. The first thing you can go fer is matches. I saw a box in the pantry." Lisa pointed behind her.

"Got it." Sam flung open the pantry doors. She searched high and low without finding them, and just as her panic rose again, Lisa told her where they were.

"Right there. On the top shelf to the left. You probably can't see them with your height disadvantage."

"Oh, no, you didn't." Sam tried to sound offended but knew she wasn't pulling it off. She jumped and snagged the box of matches from the top shelf. "I never knew those were there."

"Okay, first we take off these burner tops." Lisa set them on the counter. "Then we lift the lid to the stove. Here," Lisa showed Sam where to put her fingers, "help me lift."

Try as they might, they couldn't get the lid to lift up. "Hang on." Lisa twisted one of the knobs. "Oh, geez. Do you hear that clicking sound?"

Sam nodded.

"That means it has an electronic ignition."

Sam raised her eyebrows. She had no idea what that meant, which must have been obvious.

"It means there's no pilot light."

"So why isn't the stove lighting?"

"I'm not sure." Lisa opened the oven door and took a look. "There's nothing to see in here."

Sam heard Susie and Marlee's bedroom door open and knew they'd be downstairs any second.

"Shit!" Sam hit her forehead with her palm. "I left the damn fireplace running all night, and the gas ran out. Oh, my God. Now, what do we do?"

Lisa stood up and shrugged.

"Wait, wait, wait," Sam said. "I have an idea. Help me grab everything. They'll be down here any second." They gathered the breakfast supplies, and Sam led the way to the outside deck.

"We'll cook the pancakes on Daddy's grill out here. Hopefully, it has propane, and I can figure out how to use it."

Sam led the way to the grill on the wrap-around deck. The house was built into a hill, so the kitchen and living room were on the first floor in the front of the house, but they were on the second floor in the back overlooking the lake.

Sam turned the propane gas tank on like she'd seen her father do and then opened the top to the grill. The grate looked fairly clean, but it didn't matter because she was going to use the iron skillet.

"Shoot." Sam turned to Lisa. "Can you run back inside for the oil spray?"

"Sure thing."

"Oh, and the whipped cream," Sam called after her. "Don't forget the whipped cream."

"That's the best part." Lisa smiled and headed back into the kitchen.

It wasn't long before Lisa came back out with Susie and Marlee in tow carrying the breakfast fixings they had forgotten. Lisa handed Sam the oil spray while Susie and Marlee set the table.

"Two, this is so awesome," Marlee said. "Look at this view. And the sky. Crystal blue. Those are cumulous clouds, right Susie?"

Susie nodded. "I'm going to make you into a meteorologist yet."

Sam smiled. Her friends were having a good time. At least she could relax about that. Well, she could relax until she had to call Helene later and tell her about leaving the stupid fireplace on all night. That was going to suck.

"Hey," Lisa said, "let me take drink orders while Chef Sam

works on breakfast. Your choices are orange juice, coke, and water."

"OJ for me," Marlee said.

"Me, too," Susie said.

"Me, three," Sam called without turning around.

"Okay, four OJs it is." Lisa headed back into the house.

"So, Sam," Susie asked playfully, "why are you making pancakes out here?"

Sam glanced over her shoulder at her friends. It was time to fess up. "We ran out of gas because, like an idiot, I left the fireplace on." It was hard to admit she'd messed up, but it was the truth.

"*Aay*, that's why we ran out of hot water in the shower this morning," Susie said.

"We ran out, too," Lisa added. She set a carton of orange juice and four empty glasses on the table.

Sam whirled around with a plate of hot pancakes. "First round is ready." She set them on the table. "Maple syrup is optional, but you must use whipped cream."

"These look awesome, Two," Marlee said with a grin.

"Thanks, P. I hope they're good. I've never made pancakes on a barbecue grill before."

"A toast." Susie raised her glass of orange juice. Everyone else raised theirs. "To Sam."

"Why?" Sam put her glass down, but Susie reached under her arm to raise it again.

"Don't interrupt." Susie cleared her throat. "To our amazing friend Sam who made this fantastic weekend possible. Even if we have no gas in the house for showering or cooking, and even if I now have to try and figure out how to cook enchiladas on a barbecue grill." Susie playfully muttered the last bit partly under her breath, earning a smack on the arm from Sam.

"Did I mention that I invited Helene over for dinner?" Sam grinned wide.

Susie rolled her eyes skyward and muttered something unintelligible under her breath. "*Aay*, don't worry. I can do it. Nobody panic."

"Thanks, Sus. Sorry to spring that on you."

"Hey, we have to finish our toast." Marlee held her glass up higher. "To Sam!"

The four friends clinked glasses.

"Sam, somebody's pulling into the driveway." Lisa pointed around the corner of the house, where they could just see the edge of the driveway.

"Helene?" Sam's heart dropped. She put her juice glass down and headed to the edge of the deck. She was relieved when it wasn't Helene's car, but she was also confused by the Suburban Gas truck idling in the driveway. She turned around. "Did any of you guys call the gas company?"

"No," came the simultaneous answer from all three at the table.

"Gas company? Are you serious?" Lisa joined Sam at the edge of the deck.

"Helene," Sam said. "She must have called. She must have known I'd screw it all up." Sam couldn't help the tears that stung her eyes. She still needed a nanny.

The driver stepped out of the truck and consulted a clipboard. He looked up at Sam on the deck. "Excuse me, miss. Are you Helene Bouchard?"

"Close enough." Sam headed down the steps.

"I'm sorry, Miss. We were supposed to get here yesterday

afternoon to fill ya up."

"You were supposed to come yesterday?" The tank must have been low to begin with. Maybe running out of gas wasn't completely her fault.

"Yeah. The holiday weekend has been crazy busy. We couldn't squeeze ya in, but we made it first thing this morning."

"Thank you. The tank's around back." Sam pointed.

"Okay," he held up his clipboard and a pen. "Just need yer signature right here."

"Sure." Sam signed the work order on his clipboard and then sighed in relief. She headed back up the stairs to a waiting Lisa. She smiled at Lisa's easy grin.

"So, we're off the hook, eh?"

Sam nodded, happy that everything was going to be okay. They would have hot water for showers, Susie would be able to cook Helene's favorite enchilada dinner in the actual kitchen, and, best of all, Helene would never ever have to know she'd left the fireplace on all night.

They headed back to the table, but something dawned on Sam. "Wait, did you say, 'we're off the hook?' Lisa, this was *my* fault. Using up all the gas is on me, not you."

"I was as much to blame for not turning off the fireplace as you were."

"You're sweet, but it was my responsibility."

"But I'm here to back you up, baby." Lisa wagged a playful finger at Sam. "Don't forget that. Ever."

"I won't forget." A calm warmth spread through Sam as they went back to sit at the breakfast table. Is that what having a girlfriend was like? Having somebody on your side no matter what?

A partner in crime? A co-conspirator? If so, she liked it.

Chapter 15
Not a Chance

Late afternoon sun glistened off the lake. Sam stretched as she lay on the imported Shorea chaise lounge and soaked up the warm rays of summer. School would be starting in four days. The time to lie out or to hear the slap of her friends' kayak paddles on the lake would soon be over. She squinted against the sun to watch Marlee and Susie race their kayaks against each other. Susie was ahead, but not by much.

Sam snuck a peek at Lisa, lying inches away on the chaise next to her. Her face looked relaxed and content. Sam couldn't believe how lucky she was that Lisa, so perfect and amazing, was her girlfriend. Everything about Lisa was flawless. She was tall and had the perfect silhouette, the perfect proportions, even lying on a lounge chair. Lisa's eyes were closed, but Sam pictured the baby browns behind the lids and sighed softly.

As if sensing Sam's gaze, Lisa's eyes opened. The smile that took over Lisa's face made Sam's heart melt.

"Hi, baby," Lisa said in a sleepy voice. "I think I dozed off." She reached both arms up and stretched.

"We didn't get much sleep last night."

Lisa's cheeks tinged red.

"Did you know that I cut softball practice once?" Sam's own

cheeks got warm.

"You did?"

"Yeah. I went to watch you play," Sam said. "You guys had a home game. I was so in love with you, Lisa. I couldn't wait one more day to see you."

"When was this?" Lisa rolled on her side to face Sam.

"You didn't even know me then. It was the season before last when I was in tenth grade."

"And I was in ninth."

Sam nodded. "I only had my permit, but I convinced my driving teacher to let me drive all the way to Clarksonville High School. I made him sit through the whole game, and then I drove us back."

"How in the world did you get him to do that?"

"I gave him three hundred dollars, and I didn't care because I had to see you. I wanted to talk to you so bad, but I didn't know what to say. I was petrified."

"Petrified? Of me?"

Sam nodded. "What was I going to say? Like, 'Hi, I'm your stalker from East Valley. Can I take you out sometime?'"

Lisa chuckled. "Well, I'm glad you worked up the nerve. Remember that time me and Marlee and Jeri came to your night game in East Valley?"

"Of course, I do. I almost hyper-ventilated when I saw you walk up. I remember when Marlee introduced us, and I shook your hand through the fence."

"And I didn't let go. I got lost in the vortex of your blue-gray eyes. I couldn't decide if they were blue or gray."

Sam laughed. "I think it depends on my mood. My heart was pounding. I was sure you could hear it."

"But you seemed so confident. Remember the first time you invited yourself to my house?"

"Sorry, that was kind of ballsy."

"No, no, no. One of us had to get things moving. I feel bad that I don't have a car. It sucks that I only have a permit."

"I don't mind driving to Clarksonville, you know. I get to see you, and it gets me out of that big house."

"I'll have my license on my birthday in February. So, in five months, I'll be able to drive to your house."

Sam's nerves spiked at the meaning behind Lisa's sentence. Lisa would be driving to the mansion, where her parents would see who picked her up, and then they would know. She kept the smile on her face, hoping her face hadn't betrayed her momentary panic. She sat up in the lounge chair, pulling the back upright. Lisa did the same.

"Hey," Sam said, "I just realized something. I'm turning eighteen in January, but you'll still be sixteen for another month. Is it, like, legal for us to be together then? Could I get in trouble for being with a minor?"

"I don't know. Are we in trouble now? We're both minors now, but you're older." Lisa blushed to the roots of her dark hair.

"I don't know," Sam said. "Is that illegal? You know? For two minors to do what we did last night?"

"I have no idea, and you know what? It's nobody's business what we do, anyway." The anger in Lisa's voice was surprising.

"True." But Sam had to be careful. Her parents told her countless horror stories about people suing their family for all kinds of trumped-up things. Could this be one of those things? Would Lisa's family ever—

"Sam!"

Sam was jolted out of her thoughts.

"You were going somewhere dark. I could tell." The worried look on Lisa's face softened. "You know what?"

"What?"

"We are going to be uber-careful and not let anyone know we were, uh, intimate." Lisa's tone was reassuring.

"Okay." Sam relaxed a little. She hadn't realized how tense her shoulders had become. "Remember when you didn't know I was the East Valley debutante Samantha Rose Payton? Remember when you thought I was some random softball chick from East Valley High School?"

"Yeah." Lisa looked pensive for a moment. "How come you go to public school anyway? Why aren't you at some hobnobbing private school?"

"I went to private school up through eighth grade. St. Mary Catholic in East Valley, but they don't have a high school."

"Are you Catholic?"

"No, we're Presbyterian."

"Me, too."

"Cool." Sam smiled at Lisa. One more thing in common. "St. Mary's was the only non-public school in East Valley. Of course, Mother and Daddy wanted to send me to a boarding school in Switzerland, but I started getting bad migraines at the end of eighth grade."

"You did?"

Sam melted at the concerned expression on Lisa's face. "Yeah. Dr. Boyle thought they were brought on by anxiety. He thought it would be better if I stayed home and went to East Valley High School."

"You've talked about Dr. Boyle before. He's a psychiatrist, right?"

Sam nodded. "Don't worry. I'm not crazy."

Lisa's expression softened. "Do you still have migraines?"

"Not as often."

"That's good. I'm glad you stayed in Clarksonville County, 'cuz if you hadn't, I never would have met that pretty softball chick from East Valley."

Sam felt herself blush.

"And don't think you're getting out of telling me about this whole debutante thing."

Sam rolled her eyes. "Don't worry. My parents have a DVD of my coming out ball."

Lisa snickered. "That's what it's called? 'Coming out'?"

Sam nodded. She looked down for a moment. "So, are you okay with all this?" She gestured around her.

Lisa nodded. "As long as you and Helene and your parents know I'm not some—"

"Gold digger?" Sam suggested.

"Yeah, I'm not a gold digger."

"I know you're not. And you know what? There might not be any gold to dig once my parents find out I'm a big old queer."

"Do you really think they'll disown you?"

Sam shrugged. She had no idea, but the risks were too great to even think about.

Lisa's eyes narrowed. "You told me one time you wanted your parents to know you were in love."

"I know, but..." Sam looked away.

"Hey, you know what? It doesn't matter. Before I knew about

the Payton fortune, I totally pictured us in a three-bedroom Cape Cod house. You know, like William and Evelyn's? We'd mow the yard together, do the laundry, raise babies."

"That sounds nice."

"You totally didn't blink at the babies part."

"I would be honored to have babies with you."

"I'm going to keep you," Lisa said. "No, no," she put a hand up to the sky, "you can't change my mind. I'm keeping you, and that's that."

"That's been my plan since tenth grade."

Laughter from the shoreline diverted their attention. Marlee had somehow gotten her kayak wedged between two boulders.

"Oh, geez," Lisa said. "It looks like my fearless pitcher has gotten herself stuck."

Susie was trying to help Marlee but ended up splashing her with lake water, which caused them both to howl with laughter.

Sam shook her head. "I don't know how they had any energy to go back out after we canoed the entire lake this morning."

"Me, neither."

Sam stood up. "C'mon, let's go help. I think it's time to start dinner anyway."

~~~

"Out of my kitchen." Susie pointed toward the doorway with a wooden spoon.

"Okay, okay. We're going." Sam set the last fork on the table. She and Marlee headed to the living room, leaving Susie and Lisa to finish making the enchiladas, rice, and refried beans.

"Hey, Sus," Sam called, "don't forget about the flan. You promised Helene."

"*Aay*," Susie grumbled, "it's already made, dork. Now keep your voice out of my kitchen, too."

"Whatever," Sam called back and then laughed with Marlee. "Have you ever had Susie's flan?"

"Yeah, it's so good. I'd never had it before I met Susie, but there are a lot of things I'd never done before I met her." Marlee sat on the couch, a red blush creeping up her neck accentuating the large hickey there.

Sam grinned at her friend and flopped on the other side of the couch. "You guys make a great couple."

"Thanks. So do you and Lisa. You know, now that my mom and Susie's parents know about us, it's so much easier. We can be ourselves around them, more natural." Marlee shrugged. "I hated sneaking around and hiding stuff from my mom. You know? Not being able to talk to her?"

"Yeah," Sam sighed, "believe me. I know the feeling." Sam's heart almost stopped when she spotted the impaled cork and corkscrew lying on the carpet. She leaped off the couch and snatched it up. "Yeesh. I'm glad I saw this. Helene will be here any minute."

"Good catch."

Sam pulled the cork off, stashed it in her pocket, and rushed the corkscrew into the kitchen. Luckily, Susie's back was to her, so Sam wordlessly handed the utensil to Lisa and pantomimed that she wanted Lisa to wash it and put it back in the drawer next to the sink. Lisa nodded her understanding. Just as Sam was leaving, Susie turned around. Both Sam and Lisa froze.

"Out," Susie bellowed, this time pointing with a potholder.

Sam scurried out the door and then burst out laughing. "She is so mean."

"Cooking is serious business for her," Marlee said. "She should be a chef."

"Nah, if she became a chef, she'd open up a geology-themed restaurant, and we simply must save the world from that."

Marlee laughed and smacked Sam playfully on the leg. "You're so funny."

"Why, thanks."

"You know, it's great that you're out to Helene."

"Yeah, she's pretty cool," Sam said. "It'd feel weird hiding Lisa from her. I've known Helene my whole life."

"You've known your parents your whole life, too." Marlee fixed an unwavering gaze on Sam.

Sam was taken aback by Marlee's forwardness. "Did they put you up to this?" She nodded her head toward the kitchen.

"Not Lisa."

"Susie then."

Marlee shrugged and nodded. "She's worried about you, that's all. I am, too, Two."

"Ha. You said tutu."

Marlee snorted. "I did, didn't I?"

Sam jumped when the doorbell rang. She bolted off the couch, surprised that Helene had rung the bell.

"Right on time, Helene," Sam called and flung the door open. Her jaw hit the floor when she saw her parents standing on the doorstep. "Mother? Daddy? What brings you here?" She stepped back to let them in. Her heart was racing.

Sam's mother pulled her in for a stiff hug. "We were on our way home from Syracuse—"

"And since we were driving right by, we decided to see how my Kitten was doing," Sam's father finished.

"Daddy," Sam groaned, "don't call me that in front of company." Sam could only wonder what Marlee thought about her father referring to her as 'Kitten.'

"Everybody knows you're still my kitten." He tousled her hair and then gave her a warm hug.

"Where's Rolando? Didn't he drive you?"

"He'll be back. He went to gas up the car back in town. Where's Helene? Her car isn't out front."

Sam swallowed against the lump lodged in her throat. She recognized his no-nonsense tone. He knew Helene wasn't at the house. Sam was screwed. She'd never been good at lying, and he knew it. When he found out Helene had stayed in a motel, leaving them alone, she'd get fired for sure and probably shipped back to Montréal that night, and then Sam would get shipped off to a Swiss boarding school.

"She, um, she…" Sam glanced over her shoulder at Marlee as if searching for answers telepathically, but nothing came to her.

"Samantha Rose?" Her father folded his arms. "I asked you a question."

"Yes, sir. Helene is, uh—"

"Helene is right here," Helene said, coming through the front door. She held up a full Price Chopper bag. "I had to run out to the store for a few things." She walked right past Sam's parents toward the kitchen. "This is a nice surprise. Will you be staying for dinner? The girls cooked, and I think there's plenty." She paused at the kitchen doorway.

Sam blew out a slow sigh of relief.

"Well, that's up to the girls, I think." Sam's mother said and put a hand to her throat. "We simply came by to see how you were fairing."

"Mother, please stay."

"All right then, it's settled," Sam's father said to Helene.

"Great. I'll inform the cooks and put these things away." Helene turned on her heels and went into the kitchen.

Sam turned to Marlee and tried to keep the panic from her expression. "Mother, Daddy, you remember Marlee, the pitcher from my summer team?"

"Nice to see you again, young lady," Sam's father said. "Are you enjoying your weekend?"

"Yes, sir. Very much. Thank you both so much for letting us stay here. Your house is amazing. The view is spectacular. The sunset last night was incredible."

Susie saved the day by bursting out of the kitchen at that moment. "Mr. and Mrs. Payton, I thought I heard you out here. Please stay and have dinner with us. *Aay*, this is awkward. I'm inviting you to stay for dinner in your own house."

Leave it to Susie to diffuse the situation. Sam loved Susie at that moment.

Sam's mother chuckled. "We'd be delighted to stay. Won't we, Gerald?"

"Yes, thank you for the invitation."

Lisa poked her head out of the kitchen doorway. "Two more for dinner then?"

Susie nodded.

"Okay, I'll set two more places." Lisa hurried back into the kitchen.

"Everything is ready to go on the table," Susie said. "Come in and sit down. Sam, maybe you can find out what everybody wants to drink."

"Okay."

Sam followed her parents into the kitchen and got them settled at the table. As she took the drink orders, she thought of all the things her parents could have walked in on, and her heart sped up again. She reached in the cupboard for one last glass, and Helene sidled up beside her.

"Breathe, Samantha Rose, breathe," Helene whispered.

Sam nodded and took a deep breath to calm her shaky nerves. She filled the last glass with water and set it in front of her own plate. She sat down between her parents.

Since the baking pan was too hot to pass, Susie dished out the enchiladas individually. The rice, refried beans, sour cream, and Mexican cheese were passed from person to person around the table. The scene reminded Sam of dinner at Lisa's house. This was what a real family dinner was supposed to look like. She took another calming breath before digging in, and just as she got the first forkful to her mouth, she felt her mother's disapproving glare. Sam cleared her throat and put the fork down. She pushed the food around on her plate for a while and then took the barest of bites. Her mother nodded approvingly. Sam hated herself for doing it, but what choice did she have? Hopefully, there would be leftovers she could snarf down after her parents left. Wait. They were leaving, weren't they? She stifled a groan. What if they wanted to stay the night?

Amid the chatter and the clatter of plates and utensils, Sam's father said, "So, Helene, what have you and the girls been up to today?"

Sam marveled at how easily Helene's lies came. Sam wondered if she would ever learn to lie as effortlessly. Lisa flashed Sam a nervous smile. Sam grimaced back. At the beginning of the summer, Sam had thought she wanted her parents to know that she'd fallen in love. Now she wasn't so sure. Her father had the power to make unpleasant things go away, which for him could mean Lisa. Sam firmly decided once and for all that was not a chance she was willing to take.

Chapter 16
A Cold Day in Hell

Sam pulled her violin out of its case and rosined the bow. She tuned the strings by ear and then mindlessly played scales waiting for her last class of the day to start. It was the first day of school, and she was more than ready for it to be over. At least she had gotten to hang out with Susie at lunch and then in their AP Environmental Science class directly after, so she hadn't been totally alone all day. It sucked that she couldn't see Lisa after school. Although Sam agreed when Lisa suggested that the first week of school would be too hectic for them to hang out, she had been lying big time. What she really wanted to do was race to Clarksonville as soon as her Strings class was over, but she had to respect Lisa's wishes and simply count down the minutes until she would see her on Saturday.

Since Mr. Auerbach was busy talking to a couple of students near his desk, and it didn't look like the class would be starting anytime soon, Sam laid the violin in her lap and closed her eyes. Part of her was aware of the other students milling about the room, but most of her was thinking about the amazing weekend at the lake. Her parents hadn't stayed long after dinner that Saturday night. In fact, they left right after Susie's flan.

Sam had shut and locked the front door after her parents left, and then she blew out a long sigh of relief before heading back to the kitchen. She was surprised to see one lone place setting on the table. Helene, Marlee, and Susie smiled at her when she walked in. They looked guilty like they were hiding something, and Sam thought for sure they were about to play some kind of trick on her, but then Lisa pulled a plate of hot enchiladas out of the microwave and gestured for her to sit.

"Oh, my God. Thank you." Sam picked up the clean fork someone had put at her place setting. "I thought I was going to starve to death."

"This was Lisa's idea," Helene said.

Sam looked up. "You did this?"

Lisa nodded, a tinge of red creeping up her cheeks.

Sitting in the noisy classroom, Sam remembered another time later that Saturday night when Lisa's cheeks had tinged red. Sam could almost feel the touch of Lisa's lips on her face, the back of her neck, and other new delicious places. She wanted to sigh at the memory but held back. They had spent another amazing night together, totally not sleeping, but too soon, way too soon, the weekend was over.

Sunday morning, alone in Sam's room at the lake house, they said their private goodbyes to each other, mainly because they wouldn't be able to say goodbye to each other properly when Marlee dropped Sam off at the mansion. Sam had snuggled into Lisa's strong arms and kissed her as if they would never see each other again.

When they broke off the kiss, Sam was surprised that Lisa had tears in her eyes.

"Why are you crying?"

"Because it's getting harder and harder to leave you."

Sam's breath caught in her throat. "I wish we didn't have to go back to school."

Sam's eyes flew open when someone jostled her from the side.

"You are so caught," Ronnie Alesi said with a grin.

Sam sat up in the chair and cleared her throat. "What are you talking about, Ronnie?"

"It's Ronald."

Sam rolled her eyes.

"I saw that shit-eating grin on your face."

"Shuddup, Ronnie."

"You're in love, dearie. I can tell." He leaned in closer and whispered, "And she is gorgeous. Like an Indian princess with that long braid."

"Ronnie," Sam said exasperated, "you don't know what you're talking about." She didn't like denying her relationship with Lisa, but she couldn't come out of the closet yet. There was absolutely no way she could come out, especially not to Ronnie, who was the king of coming out. Talking to him would make her guilty by association.

Ronnie leaned back, the smug smile still on his face. "One day, you'll admit it, Samantha Rose, but I'll leave you alone for now." He stood up and headed to the rack that held his double bass.

A tap, tap, tap on the music stand in the front of the classroom got Sam's attention. Mr. Auerbach was dressed in his usual brown tweed suit and a wrinkled white shirt and bowtie, askew as usual. His flat brown hair fell into his eyes, and he brushed it away like he would a thousand more times during the class period.

"You guys know the drill," Mr. Auerbach said. "Instruments out and tuned. Rosin the bows if you need to and get pencils for taking notes on the sheet music. And that means you, Mr. Alesi. Pencil. Not pen."

"*Moi?*" Ronnie said with a splayed hand to his chest, looking hurt by their teacher's insinuation.

"Yes. Especially you." Mr. Auerbach wagged a finger at Ronnie, but his smile betrayed the fact that he was teasing.

Sam picked up her violin and waited for the pianist to give them their notes for tuning.

"Samantha Rose," Mr. Auerbach said, "may I see you at my desk for a moment?"

"Sure." Sam set her violin down gently on the chair.

Before Sam made it up to the front of the classroom, Mr. Auerbach blurted, "I have exciting news."

"What's up?" Sam always loved the twinkle in his eye when he got excited about something.

"Mrs. Dickens has an exciting part for you in the school musical."

"Ronnie told me about it."

His face lit up. "Isn't it exciting? *Fiddler on the Roof.* It's yours for the taking, Samantha Rose. It's yours for the taking."

"I don't know. Musical theater isn't my thing."

"Music is music. Anytime you get a chance to play, grab it and savor it like a fine wine."

She hid a smile behind her hand.

His cheeks turned red as if he realized his faux pas. "Oh, you know what I mean. At least tell me you'll think about it."

Sam bobbed her head from side to side, weighing her options. "I guess." The truth was, she still hadn't decided what to do.

"Good. There's a meeting this afternoon in the theater for

everybody interested in the play. Actors, musicians, stagehands. Everybody. Mrs. Dickens wants you there especially. I told her I'd take care of it."

"I played in the pit last year."

"Ah, but being up on stage is quite different. I think you'll be good at it. Go to the meeting. Don't say no yet."

Sam shrugged noncommittally. Maybe she could go to one meeting. She wasn't seeing Lisa until Saturday anyway.

~~~

Sam sat at her desk in the living room of her suite with her precalculus book opened in front of her. She had a third of her mind on the math, a third on the *Fiddler on the Roof* meeting earlier that afternoon, and the final third on her watch. She had six agonizingly long minutes to go until eight o'clock, and she could call Lisa. Her mind wandered back to the meeting after school in the theater. All those kids, they were so free. Some were singing, others were reciting lines from the play, and a few were dancing in the aisles. Ronnie made her sit with him and his friends. Alivia especially beamed when Sam sat down next to her. It was exciting, kind of like softball, but different.

Mrs. Dickens outlined the play for the assembled crowd. She talked about auditioning times and rehearsal schedules, but Sam's ears perked up when Mrs. Dickens spoke about the fiddler. "The role of the fiddler," she looked at Sam, "is metaphorical. Picture the fiddler straddling a pitched roof, left foot on one slope, right foot on the other. A precarious position, indeed. He is a metaphor for life which constantly pulls us back and forth, first one way and then another." She glanced around at the assembled students. "Tevye, the male lead in the play," she looked at Ronnie, who was the shoo-in for the role according to Alivia, "tries hard to cling to the traditions of his people, but the world is changing so fast that he struggles to keep his balance—like our fiddler. Every time the fiddler appears on stage, it is because Tevye is facing conflict." Mrs. Dickens looked back at Sam. "The play opens with this symbol of struggle, the fiddler perched high on the roof." She pointed toward the stage, high in the air.

Sam's eyes widened at the implication. She would be the first one on the stage—the first one everyone saw.

After the brief meeting, Mrs. Dickens handed out scripts to those auditioning for acting parts and sheet music to the musicians. Sam thumbed through the sheet music and then, later, when she got home, showed the sheet music to Helene. Helene said a couple of the fiddler pieces looked challenging, but Sam had always been able to master complex music in the past, so why would this be any different? Sam had agreed. She could do it, but did she want to? That was the big question. Did she want to be up on the stage in front of everybody? Perched high on top of the set? Would her parents even let her do it? She didn't mention a word to either of them at dinner. She'd tell them the next day. Maybe.

With firm resolve, Sam went back to her homework. She finished another problem and checked the time. She had one more minute until she could call Lisa. Ah, what the hell? It was close enough. She slammed her math book shut and picked up her cell phone.

She activated voice dialing and said, "Lisa."

Within seconds Lisa answered. "Hi, baby. I miss you."

"Same, same, same. Me, too." Sam walked to the couch and flung herself on it. "How was school?"

"Good, but geez, I'm tired. I've got way too much homework already."

"I know. Me, too, and I'm a senior. Seniors aren't supposed to have homework, are they?"

Lisa laughed. "At least Julie's in my Algebra Two class."

"Your first baseman?"

"Yeah, you remember her. She's the one that wanted to double date with us last spring."

"I can't."

"I know."

Pain flittered across Sam's heart at the sound of Lisa's resigned voice. "Baby, you know I'll do anything for you, but I can't do this. Not right now. If anybody finds out about us, I'm toast. You and me? Toast."

"Because your parents will find out."

"Yeah." An awkward silence grew between them, and Sam scrambled around her brain for something to fill it. "Speaking of the three musketeers, how are they?"

Lisa laughed. "We weren't speaking of them, but they're fine. Lynnie loves her new teacher and has already started her book report. Guess which book?"

"One of the Harry Potters."

"Good guess, but no. She's doing one of those books from the *Dragonriders of Pern* series you gave her."

"Anne McCaffrey. Cool. I knew she'd like them. I'll have to find more like that for her."

While Lisa talked about her siblings, Sam leaped off the couch

168

and scoured her floor-to-ceiling bookshelves for something else Lynnie might like. She smiled when she found *Another Fine Myth* by Robert Lynn Asprin. Lynnie would love the story about the magician's apprentice who teamed up with a demon. Sam tossed the book on her desk and plopped back on the couch.

"How does Lawrence Jr. like first grade so far?" Sam asked.

"He likes it. He said recess was awesome because they were allowed to play basketball. Bridget was cranky, though."

"How come?"

Lisa chuckled. "Because we all got on the school bus this morning and left her home alone."

"Oh, no. Poor Sweetpea." Sam smiled as she pictured the feisty three-year-old.

"Yeah, she's been clingy ever since I got home today. She has no understanding of homework."

"I wish I was there with you and your family."

"I wish you were here, too. Or I was there." Something softened in Lisa's voice. "I don't know how I'll handle not seeing you every day. I miss you so much."

"Me, too." Sam's voice caught in her throat. She hoped Lisa hadn't heard it. Up until that moment, Sam hadn't realized how lonely she was. "Hey, you know what?"

"What?"

"I think I might try out for the musical."

"Seriously?"

"Yup." Sam grinned at the excitement in Lisa's voice. "I went to the meeting they had after school. Mrs. Dickens gave me the sheet music."

"I've never heard you play, but I know you'll be awesome. So, you're really going to do it?"

"Maybe." Sam glanced back at the sheet music on the stand behind her. "I think so."

"I can't wait. And the kids, they're going to love seeing you on stage."

"Oh, God. Don't make me nervous."

"Sorry."

Sam smiled at the grin she heard in Lisa's words. "I wish I could kiss you right now."

"Mmm. Same," Lisa said. "What, Mom? Hang on, Sam."

Sam heard the sound of Lisa's hand covering the phone and a blurred conversation in the background.

"Okay, Mom," Lisa's voice came back loud and clear. "Hey, Sam?"

"Yeah?"

"My mom needs me to help Lawrence Jr. with his homework. And then I have to finish mine. So, uh…"

"You have to go. I know. I have homework, too."

"The lake weekend was amazing, Sam. I'll never forget it."

"Me neither." Sam didn't want to hang up, so she listened to the sound of Lisa breathing.

"Baby?" Lisa said.

"Yeah?"

"I'll text you tomorrow during school, okay?"

"Okay."

"And I'll talk to you tomorrow night? Same time?"

"Yup, and I'll see you on Saturday. Morning. Sunrise."

Lisa laughed. Sam smiled at the sound. It had become one of her top ten favorite sounds in the whole world.

"Okay. Yes, yes, Lawrence Jr., I'm coming." Lisa sighed into the phone. "Sam?"

"Yeah?"

"It wasn't my idea."

"What wasn't?"

"Not seeing you on school nights."

"It wasn't?" Sam swallowed against the lump forming in her throat.

"Nope. My parents thought it was best for now."

"That sucks."

"I know. And Sam?"

"Yeah?"

"I love you."

"Same." *More.*

Sam ended the call and glanced at her math book. She knew she should finish the assignment, but she was way too antsy. She pushed the chair back and looked toward the sheet music on the stand. Why not? It wouldn't hurt to try some of the pieces.

She stood up, closed the door to her suite, and pulled the Stradivarius out of the locked cabinet. After tuning up and rosining, she opened the sheet music book to a song called *Tradition*.

She took a deep breath and warmed up with some scales. Once her fingers were loose, she studied the first few measures and then worked her way through them.

Sam wondered how often the fiddler appeared on stage. Was it a small part or a big part? She'd have to ask Mrs. Dickens. *If* she decided to try out, that is.

Who was she kidding? She was going to try out.

Sam worked out some of the tricky spots in the piece,

thoroughly enjoying the challenge. Satisfied with the start she'd made on *Tradition*, she turned to the next piece and worked out the phrasing for *Matchmaker*. Once she got the feel for the song, she flung her bow across the strings and danced around the room, picturing herself on stage. She was so engrossed in the music that she didn't notice the door to her suite opening until her mother was in the room. Sam pulled the bow away from the strings and froze. She snuck a guilty glance at the sheet music.

"Samantha Rose," her mother asked, hand on hip, "what is that you're playing? It's familiar, but I can't place it."

"Just some sheet music Mr. Auerbach got for me." She hated lying, but she hadn't been ready for the question.

"What is it?"

"It's called *Matchmaker*."

"He's making quite a departure from the classical pieces you usually play." The disapproval was icy in her voice.

Sam felt bad instantly. She couldn't let Mr. Auerbach take the fall for her cowardice. "Well, uh, actually, he suggested I get the music from Mrs. Dickens."

"Who is this Mrs. Dickens?"

"Uh," was all Sam could manage. She walked over and placed her violin back in its case, her mind racing to find an answer. Her parents would never approve of her participating in musical theater as an actor. They hadn't liked when she'd played in the pit orchestra the year before. Her mother called it "music for the masses." It wasn't for serious classical music connoisseurs like the well-to-do Paytons from East Valley, New York.

"Samantha Rose? I'm waiting." Her mother folded her arms. The fact that her mother was even in her suite was weird and awkward. Her mother never came to this wing of the house.

"Mrs. Dickens is the drama teacher."

"Drama? Don't tell me you're in a musical theater class."

"No, no, of course not. We got our music in Strings today, though. We're doing the *String Sonata in D minor*." Sam hoped it would distract her mother from the original question.

"Vivaldi?"

Sam nodded and almost blew out a sigh of relief. "We're also doing Tartini's *String Sonata in D major*. Mr. Auerbach gave the quintet some music today, too."

"Good." Her mother nodded, seeming pleased.

"Ronnie's excited. The piece has a big part for him."

"He's that cute boy who plays the double bass?"

Sam nodded.

"Is he a close friend of yours?"

Sam did her best not to roll her eyes. Her parents had no clue, absolutely no clue whatsoever. "He's a friend, Mother, just a friend."

Her mother nodded and didn't press it. "Well, how about you? Are you excited for your last year of high school?"

Sam couldn't help wondering what her mother was up to. She rarely asked questions about school. "Uh, yes, I guess. Susie and I have a class together."

"That's nice."

Sam wasn't sure if she should invite her mother to sit down. It felt weird to do that, so Sam simply sat at her desk and reopened her math book. Maybe her mother would get the hint.

Her mother broke the silence first. "You and I need to go shopping."

"We do?"

"Of course. We simply must have new outfits for Switzerland. Don't you think? Saks is calling me."

"In Manhattan?"

Her mother nodded.

"That would be nice, Mother."

Whenever her mother had her shopping whims, Sam was powerless. They'd probably do what they had done in the past. They would fly down to the city on a Friday evening, shop all day Saturday and Sunday, eat at expensive restaurants – or push their food around – and then fly back on Monday. That would stink because she wouldn't be able to see Lisa for an entire weekend.

"When would you like to go to New York, Mother?"

"Soon, I suppose. I'll have Daddy reserve the jet for us. Let's stay at the Ritz Carlton again. We'll get a room overlooking Central Park."

"Central Park was beautiful last spring." Sam secretly wished she could take Lisa along but knew that would never happen. Not in a million years.

Her mother smiled, obviously satisfied with their plans. "You still need to renew your passport for Switzerland, don't you?"

Sam nodded.

"I thought so. I'll remind Helene you need to get that done right away."

Sam wondered, not for the first time if Helene would be going with them to Europe this time. She'd gone every other time before, but something felt different this year. Helene hadn't talked about the trip at all.

Sam picked up her pencil, hoping her mother would let her get back to her homework.

"Now tell me. What does this Mrs. Dickens have to do with your classical music training?"

Damn. Not off the hook. "Uh…"

Her mother strode to the music stand and picked up the open book of sheet music. She closed the pages and looked at the cover. "*Fiddler on the Roof*?" She held the sheet music in front of her. "Samantha Rose, are you playing in the orchestra pit for another one of those musicals?"

"No." Sam hung her head. It wasn't exactly a lie, but it wasn't exactly the truth either. "Well, maybe. I don't know yet." Her mother's glare bored into her soul. There was no way out of it. She had to say something. "Actually, I might do the pit again." That was definitely a lie, but it was far better than the truth.

The shocked look on her mother's face made Sam cringe. She was obviously trying to process the unthinkable. She waved the book of sheet music in the air. "Drivel, Samantha Rose. This is nonsense. I wish you wouldn't do this."

"I didn't tell them I'd do it yet," Sam mumbled.

"Your talents should not be wasted on this. You're a classically trained musician."

Sam pretended to study the open math book on her desk.

"Samantha Rose? I'm confused here."

Sam looked up. "Mother, I thought it would be fun. Like softball is fun. I—"

"Ahh," her mother said with understanding, "this was Dr. Boyle's idea, wasn't it? Like that softball." Dr. Boyle was the be-all-end-all of child psychologists. Her mother didn't make a parenting move without his approval. "I will speak with him immediately." Her mother's face hardened. "I don't know what has gotten into his

175

head." She shook her head in disgust. "I'm going to leave you to your studies." She dropped the distasteful sheet music back on the stand.

"Okay, Mother. Thank you. Good night." Sam waited until the door closed and then laid her head on her math book. She wasn't sure what had just happened. Poor Dr. Boyle wasn't going to know what hit him when her mother called. Sam's mother had been calling him for advice since forever. With a sigh, Sam went back to her homework. Maybe things would be better in the morning. She grunted. Yeah, right. It would be a cold day in hell when her mother would let her have anything to do with musical theater.

Chapter 17
Mazel Tov

Mrs. Dickens beckoned Sam onto the stage. "Are you ready, Samantha Rose?" She peered over her reading glasses.

Sam nodded and took her violin out of its case. It was Friday afternoon, and it was her turn to audition.

"Good luck," Ronnie called to her as she headed up the steps.

"Break a leg," Alivia added.

Sam flashed them an uneasy grin. She couldn't believe how nervous she was.

"I'm sorry to make you wait until the end of the rehearsal, but I figured it would be easier for you to audition with only a few people around."

"Thank you." Sam smiled at the drama teacher and then took a calming breath. She always got nervous before performances, but this was different. This was an audition for an on-the-stage acting part. Her parents didn't even know she was trying out.

"Alivia," Mrs. Dickens called, "would you get a music stand for Samantha Rose?"

"I don't need one," Sam said.

"Don't you need the sheet music?"

"No, I have my audition music memorized."

The look of surprise on Mrs. Dickens' face was priceless. She probably never expected Sam to memorize the *Prologue* and *Tradition* in only three days.

"Okay, then. Start whenever you're ready." Mrs. Dickens nodded at Sam.

Sam checked her tuning and then struck her ready pose. The melody was deceivingly simple at first, becoming increasingly intricate as it went. She transitioned from the *Prologue* into *Tradition* seamlessly and was secretly pleased. As she played, she pictured the *Fiddler on the Roof* movie she had downloaded onto her iPad and felt the excitement of the imaginary characters around her. The song grew in intensity, and she flung her bow across the strings. She was aware of Ronnie and Alivia quietly singing along, but all that mattered were the soulful notes she pulled out of her instrument. She was prepared to keep playing, but Mrs. Dickens put a hand up for her to stop. Her other hand went to her chest, and at first, Sam thought she was having trouble breathing or something, but then she realized Mrs. Dickens had been moved by Sam's playing.

"You are amazing, Samantha Rose, truly amazing. Mr. Auerbach knows what he's talking about."

"Thank you." Sam's cheeks warmed at the praise.

Ronnie and Alivia leaped to their feet and gave Sam a two-person standing ovation. "Brava," they both called.

Sam bowed her head to them slightly, a little embarrassed.

"Samantha Rose," Mrs. Dickens said, "the part of the fiddler is yours if you want it."

Sam's stomach jumped. Why did it feel like a giant octopus was squeezing the life out of her? Under Mrs. Dickens's expectant gaze,

Sam found herself saying, "I'd love to play the part of the fiddler."

"*Mazel tov*," Mrs. Dickens said. At Sam's confused expression, Mrs. Dickens added, "That basically means congratulations or best wishes."

"Oh. Thanks."

"So," Mrs. Dickens brushed a lock of her graying hair off her face and said, "by next Friday's rehearsal, I will need my male lead," she looked at Ronnie, "and my fiddler to block out the scene after the *To Life* number in the tavern. This is the scene where the Russian constable tells Tevye he has been ordered to have a *pogram*—an aggressive demonstration of looting and rioting against the Jews. The constable needs to have the *pogram* to prove to his superiors he has done his duty."

"That's barbaric." Sam frowned.

"Every great story has tension, Samantha Rose. This play is not only about the tension between the Jews and non-Jews, but also about the tension between traditional values and the ever-changing values in an evolving world. Tevye knows he has to bend, but he's never sure how far."

"I get that," Sam said. And she did, especially because she was trying to figure out how far to bend in her own life.

"You are the fiddler, the one who symbolizes Tevye's struggle."

Sam nodded.

"Can I count on you two having this short scene worked out by next Friday?"

Sam and Ronnie both nodded.

~~~

The first week of senior year had dragged a little, but after spending most of the weekend with Lisa, Sam had the lift she needed to get through the second week. She filled her free time learning the music for the play. Even though her parents didn't know the truth, her mother had reinstated Sam's Tuesday afternoon sessions with Dr. Boyle. Sam was bummed because she hadn't been to a session with Dr. Boyle in over a year and thought that part of her life was over. She wanted to protest because the sessions would be in direct conflict with play rehearsals, but she knew better. She shut herself up and, as usual, said, "Yes, Mother." Sam rarely disobeyed her parents, but if they denied her the opportunity to play her violin in the musical, she just might have to.

Ah, who was she kidding? She'd never get up the nerve to defy them.

Having made it through the second week of school, Sam sat in the theater and watched the actors read through the *To Life* scene. She and Ronnie were scheduled to run through their scene for Mrs. Dickens immediately following. Ronnie was perfect for the lead role of Tevye, and Karl was great as Lazer Wolf, the wealthy butcher of Anatevka. Sam knew Mrs. Dickens thought she was right for the part of the fiddler, but she was nervous. This would be her debut in front of the entire cast and crew, and her stomach was doing flip-flops. The only thing that had ever made her more nervous was when she had talked to Lisa for the first time. Sam knew she could play the music but was petrified about the whole acting in front of everybody part. Maybe she would suck at it, and Mrs. Dickens would have to politely tell her to take a hike.

Her cell phone chimed in her hand. It was a text from Lisa.

LISA: On the school bus. Heading home.

SAM: In the auditorium. Getting nervous.

LISA: LOL. Can I call?

SAM: No, Sorry. Going on stage soon.

Sam wished she could sneak into the lobby and talk to Lisa for a while, it might help slow her racing pulse, but she couldn't risk it. Mrs. Dickens could call her up to the stage at any time.

LISA: Good luck!

SAM: Break a leg!

LISA: ?

SAM: It's bad luck to wish an actor good luck.

LISA: Geez! Sorry. Break a leg! :)

SAM: Thanks! You too! jk

LISA: One broken hand was enough! I <3 you!

Sam snuck a peek on the stage. They were wrapping things up. She thumbed in a quick last text.

SAM: I heart you too! Got to go. Talk tonight?

LISA: Yes! SEE you tomorrow?

SAM: YYYYYYYYY!

Saturday was quickly becoming Sam's favorite day of the week. She remembered that Helene was taking her to the East Valley Post Office the next morning to get her passport renewed, so she added to her last text.

SAM: See you after Post Office and lunch with Helene.

LISA: Okay! Love you! ttfn

SAM: ta ta!

Sam slid the phone into her back pocket. She took a deep breath. Texting with Lisa had happily distracted her a little.

Mrs. Dickens gave the actors on stage some notes and then turned to look for Sam. "Ah, there you are, my dear. Come on up." She checked something off her ever-present clipboard and whirled her ample girth around toward Ronnie. "Okay, you two. Let's see what you've come up with."

Sam reached for her violin and was about to stand up when a girl seated a couple of rows behind her spoke.

"Rich bitch," the girl with the long blond hair said to her friend sitting next to her. "Her rich daddy probably made us do *Fiddler on the Roof* so his princess could get the lead part." She snapped her gum as if to emphasize her point.

Sam hated how people judged her without knowing her. She'd like to say it didn't bother her anymore, but it did. It always did.

Blondie's friend laughed. "She probably sucks, too."

"But Mrs. Dickens will let her stay anyway because *Daddy* bought her the part."

Sam almost burst out laughing. If they only knew the truth. Her father would kill her if he knew she was going to be on stage doing musical theater. Of course, she probably wouldn't be doing musical theater ever again once he found out. Sam rolled her eyes and pushed the unpleasant thoughts aside. With new resolve, she hopped up the stairs to the stage.

Both Sam and Ronnie had the last period of the day free, and so for four straight days, they bolted from their Strings class to the empty theater and blocked out their short scene.

Mrs. Dickens headed down the stage stairs, leaning on Karl's outstretched arm. She turned back to Ronnie. "So, you'll start the scene with your appeal to God, asking why he's made your life so hard. Do you two want to run through your marks without the violin first?"

Ronnie, looking smug, simply shook his head.

"Okay then. Have at it." Mrs. Dickens reached for the whistle on the lanyard around her neck and blew it. All motion stopped in the theater. It was an earsplitting way to get the students' attention, but it was effective.

Sam checked the tuning on her violin, nodded to Ronnie, and headed into the wings, stage right. Ronnie turned away from Sam and said his lines.

"*L'Chaim*," Ronnie finished his plea to God and raised an imaginary bottle in salute. He swayed drunkenly across the stage toward Sam.

That was Sam's cue. She played the first phrase of *If I Were a Rich Man* offstage and then jumped onto the stage. She grinned at Ronnie. He stopped in his tracks, surprised by her sudden appearance in front of him.

God, he's good. Sam kept the grin plastered on her face. In their four days working together, Ronnie taught her a lot of things about stage direction, like not turning her back to the audience. So far, so good.

Ronnie raised one dramatic eyebrow but basically ignored her and walked away. Sam ran after him while playing the second phrase of the song and then leaped in front of him again and was amazed she hit her mark. She was also amazed at how quiet the entire cast and crew were. Maybe they were feeling the symbolism of the moment. Ronnie had explained to Sam that this was a pivotal moment in the play when Tevye had no other choice but to deal with the fiddler blocking his path. The fiddler, representing change, could not be ignored.

After a slow nod from Ronnie, Sam picked up the tune where she had left off. She walked a close circle around him, playing all the while. He shrugged as if resigned to his fate, and they danced together in the middle of the stage. Sam increased the pace of the tune to match the frenetic pace of their dancing. Finally, they spun in fast circles, Sam playing frantically as she led them off the stage.

Sam jerked the bow across the strings one last time, and then she and Ronnie threw their arms around each other and laughed.

The auditorium burst into applause.

"C'mon," Ronnie said, grabbing her arm, "your first curtain call."

Sam let Ronnie drag her back onto the stage. The entire cast and crew were on their feet, applauding. Ronnie took a bow and then stage-pointed at Sam. Sam felt a blush fill her whole face as she bowed quickly and then rolled her eyes at Ronnie.

"*Brava!*" Alivia and Karl called.

Sam smiled at them and was surprised to see Blondie's friend on her feet clapping. Blondie, however, sat sullenly in her seat.

Oh, well, you can't win 'em all, Sam thought.

Mrs. Dickens nodded at her, and Sam smiled. Mrs. Dickens reached for her whistle, and Sam threw her fingers in her ears. Groans filled the auditorium as the shrill whistle pierced the air.

"Seats, everyone." Mrs. Dickens gestured to the auditorium seats in front of her. "It's time for the final notes of the day."

Sam and Ronnie, and the few crew members headed for the seats.

Mrs. Dickens nodded at Sam and Ronnie again. "You two have amazing chemistry on stage. Nice performance, both of you, and I don't have much in the way of notes for you, except that we're going to have to do something with that long hair."

Sam reached up and touched her head. She must have had a stricken expression because Mrs. Dickens laughed. "A hat, dear, that's all I meant. Some kind of hat you can tuck your hair under. But you're going to have to grow a beard and mustache. Can you get that done by opening night?"

Sam's eyes grew wide. She shook her head vigorously. The cast and crew laughed.

Ronnie patted her on the knee and whispered, "See? I told you we were going to make you butch."

"Shuddup, Ronnie."

"Ronald."

Sam was about to smack him on the leg when her cell phone rang.

Mrs. Dickens threw her a scathing look.

"Sorry," Sam choked out. She dug into her back pocket and silenced the ringer. The name on the screen made the breath catch in her throat. Gerald Payton. She sunk lower into the auditorium seat. Her father never called her. Ever. Why was he calling now? Oh, God. He must have figured out she was at the rehearsal. She placed the now-silenced cell phone on her thigh and held her head up high, remembering she was a Payton who had been trained to show no emotion. It looked like she would be keeping that appointment with Dr. Boyle on Tuesdays, after all.

Chapter 18
Passport to Hell

The bell on the door jingled as Sam and Helene left the diner. Sam held the door open for her nanny to pass through.

"I love their Reubens." Helene grinned at Sam.

"Best in town." Sam linked her arm through Helene's.

"Best in the whole North Country. I hope your parents don't find out we had lunch here."

A middle-aged man wearing a Buffalo Sabres t-shirt headed toward them on his way into the diner.

"Montréal Canadiens," Sam murmured loud enough for him to hear. "Stanley Cup champs." She hid a smile when he scowled at her on his way past.

Helene snickered. "Don't taunt the natives. Even though Montréal does have the best hockey team in the world, I'm pretty sure your family owns this diner, and we don't want to ruffle any feathers."

Sam nodded. She wasn't sure when she had adopted the Montréal Canadiens as her favorite hockey team, but it probably had something to do with the fact that it was Helene's favorite team. They had watched countless games together in Helene's apartment. And they'd always drink Canada Dry ginger ale in honor of the

Canadian-based team.

They headed toward Helene's Prius at the far end of the busy parking lot. Apparently, the East Valley Diner was a hotspot for hungry Saturday shoppers.

"Thanks for taking me to get my passport. I don't know why you had to go with me. I'm a big girl now. I could have done it all by my wittle self." Sam was teasing, but she was confused, too. Did her parents think she wasn't capable of bringing her birth certificate down to the post office and getting her passport renewed on her own?

"You're still a minor, so your parents wanted me to go with you." Helene hit a button on her key, causing the Prius to chirp as it unlocked the doors.

"I guess." Sam opened the passenger door and got in. "So, what did you and old Mr. Donahue talk about when I was getting my picture taken? I saw you two whispering like little schoolgirls."

"You caught me," Helene teased. "I'm having a scandalous affair with the postmaster." She placed her enormous purse in the backseat and then buckled her seat belt.

Sam buckled her seat belt as Helene started the car. "It's been a long time since we've hung out like this."

"Yes, it has. You've been so busy these days." Helene eased the car out of the parking lot onto CR 62. "Pre-season starts in two weeks."

"Already?"

Helene nodded. "The Dallas Stars are the first victims."

"Let me know when the game is, and I'll be at your door before the first puck is dropped." Sam wondered if Lisa liked ice hockey.

"Will do. So, tell me more about the play at school."

"It's a blast. It's only been two weeks, but I feel like I belong somewhere. Besides softball, that is."

Helene flashed Sam a sympathetic smile. "I've been waiting a long time to hear you say that."

"Say what?"

"That you belong somewhere."

"You have?" Sam didn't like the idea that Helene had been worried about her.

"Sure. You haven't exactly been happy these past few years, have you?"

Sam hung her head and picked at an imaginary thread on her jeans. "I didn't realize it was so obvious."

"Well, maybe not to everyone."

"Like Mother and Daddy."

"They're busy people." Helene shrugged.

"Did you know that both Mother and Daddy are making me see Dr. Boyle on Tuesdays again?"

"Whatever for?"

"They're both upset because they think I'm playing in the pit again. They think I'm becoming a *commoner*. Daddy even called me in the middle of rehearsal last week." Sam rolled her eyes.

"It may just be that you did something independently. You didn't run it by them first."

"Maybe."

"But Samantha Rose," Helene admonished, "why haven't you told them you're actually *in* the play?" Helene took her eyes off the road for a moment to fix Sam with a questioning look.

Sam wasn't sure how to answer the question, so she flashed Helene the cheesiest grin she could muster.

Helene couldn't help but laugh. "I can't wait for the fallout from this one. But you know what I think?"

"What?"

"Ever since you've been with Lisa, you're more willing to put yourself out there and try new things. You've been a lot more confident lately."

Sam burst out laughing. "No way. I couldn't even tell them I was auditioning for a play."

"Ah, but that's the thing. You auditioned. Last year's Samantha Rose wouldn't have gone anywhere near that auditorium."

Sam looked out the car window at the shops in the main part of downtown. "You know what?" she said with a sigh. "I think you're right."

"And if I'm not mistaken, you'll be heading for Clarksonville to see Lisa two minutes after we get home?"

"Yup. Just as long as it takes me to leap out of your car into mine." Sam felt her cheeks get warm at the thought of seeing Lisa. Having to wait an entire week sucked. Something had to change soon, or she would lose her mind. She glanced at the cell phone clutched in her hand. She wanted to text Lisa so bad but didn't want to while spending time with Helene. Helene would think it was rude. Sam would text Lisa as soon as she was in her own car and on her way to Clarksonville.

Helene eased the car into the turning lane at the stoplight. She often took St. Regis Road home from downtown East Valley instead of staying on CR 62. She said she liked the peaceful back roads better. A lot of Amish families lived on that route, which was why Sam avoided it. She got nervous sharing the road with the horse and buggies. The only time she took St. Regis Road was to get to

Raymond Road, where she and Lisa sometimes went to be alone.

"So, honey, you haven't told me what colleges you're applying to."

Sam rolled her eyes. "That's because I don't know yet. I'm applying to Wellesley, of course."

"Your mother's alma mater."

"Mm hmm. But Mother hasn't told me the others."

"Samantha Rose," Helene admonished again, "what about your newfound confidence? Tell your mother where you want to go. It's not her decision, you know. It's yours."

Sam was so surprised by the anger in Helene's voice that she was at a loss for words.

"Tell me. Where do you, Samantha Rose Payton, want to go to college?"

"I've never thought about it."

"What do you want to study?" The light turned green, and Helene headed west on St. Regis Road.

"I think Daddy wants me to study business so that I can take over the family finances when the time comes."

"But what do *you* want to study?"

"Mother wants me to continue my music."

"And you?"

Sam looked out the car window at the acres of corn ripe for September harvesting. She had absolutely no answer for Helene. She'd never allowed herself to entertain the idea of having a choice in where she went to college or what she majored in. She had never thought about what she would do as a career, either, or if she would even have one.

"Samantha Rose?"

"Lisa's mother says I'm good with kids."

Helene nodded. "She told me that, too."

"She did? When?"

"At your last softball game. You introduced us, remember?"

"Right. What else did you two talk about?"

"Oh, no. That's privileged information." Helene chuckled. "So, do you think you'd like to do something with children?"

"Maybe. Mother wants me to join the Junior League after college, so I'll need to do a service project for that. I thought about helping schools with their music departments. I could give free music lessons, donate violins, or maybe sponsor concerts for the kids. I don't know. Something like that."

Sam was suddenly overtaken by uncertainty about what was ahead for her. In a flash, she understood why Susie and Marlee got anxious when they talked about college. It was all so unclear.

"So, you have one community service project figured out for after college, but what do you want to do with the rest of your life? What do you want to do for a career? Manage the family finances like your father?"

"Not really." To be fair, she didn't know what was involved with running the family businesses but dealing with the endless spreadsheets and legal documents she'd seen on her father's desk didn't sound like an exciting way to spend the rest of her life.

"Then what do you want to do?"

"You can be mighty pushy for a nanny," Sam protested.

Helene chuckled and said, "It's my job."

Sam let herself get lost in thought as they traveled the lonely back road toward the mansion. The early afternoon sunlight did nothing to warm her new worries. No one had ever asked her what she wanted. It was unfamiliar territory.

"Lisa said I'd make a good teacher."

"Why's that?"

"Because I'm patient with her brother and sisters."

"So, how about that?" Helene said.

"What? Be a teacher?"

"Why not? You could be a music teacher."

"Oh, God. Can you imagine?"

"I can."

"Mother and Daddy would die. They'd never allow it."

"Just like they won't allow you to play softball or act in a play or be with Lisa."

"They don't know I'm doing two of those things."

"Not yet."

"Helene, you're not going to tell them, are you?" Sam's pulse sped up.

"Of course not, but they're going to find out one way or another, Samantha Rose. They always do."

They traveled along in silence for a while until Helene said, "Honey, all I ask is that you truly think about what you want to do with the rest of your life. I don't want you to have any regrets, okay?"

"Okay."

Helene slowed down and edged the car away from the shoulder as they passed an Amish family in a buggy. Sam laughed when she saw the kids in the back eating Cheetos out of a Wal-Mart bag. Her thoughts became more serious when she wondered what Helene meant by regrets. Did Helene have regrets? She had sacrificed nearly eighteen years of her life living with Sam and her family. Sam snuck a peek at Helene out of the corner of her eye. The subtle strands of gray in Helene's blond hair and the tired look on her face made Sam worry. Was Helene going to move out? Was she going to get married? Have a family of her own? They crested the hill leading down to the intersection with Raymond Road. The pleasant memories of taking Lisa to the isolated farm road on Raymond Road couldn't break through her new worries about Helene.

Sam blurted, "Helene, are you going to Switzerland with us?"

Helene's silence was all the answer Sam needed. After a few agonizing moments, Helene finally said, "No."

"Why not?"

"Honey, you don't need me anymore."

"Yes, I do," Sam pleaded. Her heart squeezed in her chest. Her worst fears were coming true. She blinked back tears as she looked at her nanny. Or was she looking at her ex-nanny?

"C'mon, you're a couple of months away from turning eighteen. I don't think your parents want to foot the bill for me to vacation in the Swiss Alps."

"They said you can't go with us?"

"No, it was by mutual agreement. There wasn't much discussion about it."

"Are you leaving? Are you moving out?"

"Samantha Rose—"

"Helene!" Sam screeched as a pickup truck barreled straight for them.

The squeal of tires filled the air. Sam braced for the impact she knew was coming. The sickening sound of metal on metal exploded in her ears. The airbags deployed with such force that she barely registered the sound of breaking glass. She grabbed the dashboard and hung on as the car spun around and around. In a heart-stopping moment, the car leaned precariously on one side, two wheels in the air.

"No, no, no, no, no," Sam pleaded to the universe and braced herself for the car to roll over. She only remembered to breathe when the car fell back on all four wheels and rolled to a standstill.

Sam took a shallow breath and braced herself against the dashboard with trembling arms. She tried to make sense of what had just happened. The pickup had rammed them at full speed. It ran the red light.

Dazed, she reached a shaky hand to the pulsing pain in her forehead. Her head was wet. She wiped at it a couple of times until she realized in horror that the wetness was blood. She put both hands up to her head. An open gash just above her eyebrow was oozing blood down her face and into her eyes. She tried without much success to wipe it away. She quickly scanned the rest of her body and was relieved to discover that she was okay.

The quiet in the car became deafening, and in a rush, Sam realized Helene wasn't moving. Sam turned her head, afraid of what she would see. Helene lay slumped over the steering wheel, eyes closed.

"No, no, no, no, no, Helene." Sam placed a shaking hand on Helene's arm and shook her. "Helene! Wake up, wake up, wake up."

When she got no response, Sam shook Helene so hard that she fell back from the steering wheel and came to rest against the driver's door. In a panic, Sam scrambled for her door handle. She couldn't breathe. She had to get out of the car. Once out, she took in the scene in one thunderous moment. The pickup truck, engine still running, was in a ditch on the side of Raymond Road. Helene's car was facing the wrong way on St. Regis Road with smoke pouring out of the engine.

"Oh, God," Sam said in a panic. Is the car on fire? As she raced to the crumpled driver's side door, she realized the smoke was just steam pouring out of the radiator. She yanked on the door handle. It didn't budge. She jerked the handle a dozen more times, trying to tear the door off its hinges. In a partial moment of clarity, she realized Helene's door was locked. She reached in through the broken window and flicked the electronic unlock switch up without daring to look at Helene. A satisfying click let her know she had succeeded. She grabbed the handle and pulled. The door didn't move. She tried again and again.

A roaring wave of panic rushed through her.

"Help me!" Sam screamed to the universe. "Somebody, please help me!"

Chapter 19
I'll Never Forgive Myself

The emergency room doctor stepped back and put a hand on his hip. His gray hair and furrowed brow revealed years of scowling at uncooperative patients. "Young lady, if you don't keep still, I'll end up stitching that eye shut."

Sam knew he was trying to put her at ease with humor, but she didn't care. "Where's Helene? They said she woke up in the ambulance, but is she okay? Where did they take her?"

The doctor sighed and turned to his assistant. "Would you please see what happened to the other accident victim?" He turned to Sam. "What's the name?"

"Bouchard. Helene Bouchard."

"I'm on it." The assistant opened the front curtain of the emergency room cubicle and headed toward the bustling nurses' station. Sam craned her neck, hoping to see or hear something, anything, about Helene.

The doctor felt the area above Sam's left eye. "Still numb?"

"Yes."

"May I finish now?" His kind face was patient.

"Yes, but can you make it fast?" Sam urged. Trying to relax was impossible because her mind kept racing back to the accident. When she couldn't get Helene's door open, she ran back around the car to

197

get her cell phone. She lost her mind when she couldn't find it right away. After a frenzied glance in the back seat, she spotted it. She punched in 911 and told the operator what had happened. The operator told her an ambulance had been dispatched, and within minutes, Sam heard the reassuring sound of sirens in the distance. The operator asked Sam if Helene was breathing. The question just about sent Sam into oblivion, but she held strong and put her hand near Helene's mouth. Panic rose in her throat when she didn't feel anything. She put her hand closer, and relief washed over her when she felt a shallow puff of air hit her hand. It seemed like a lifetime, but the ambulance and a fire truck finally arrived. Aside from allowing the paramedics to clean and bandage the cut on her forehead, Sam refused to let them touch her again until Helene was taken care of. Sam gritted her teeth as they placed a collar around Helene's neck and pulled her out of the passenger side of the car on a backboard. She forgot to breathe when they loaded Helene's unconscious body into the ambulance.

"I need you to relax," the doctor said, forcing Sam back to the present.

"Sorry."

After forever, the doctor stepped back. "You're all done."

She looked up as if seeing him for the first time. "Thank you," she said genuinely. "I'm sorry. I'm distracted."

"I know," he said gently. "Stay right here. I'll see if your parents have arrived yet. You said they were coming from Watertown?"

Sam nodded. "It'll take them a while to get here. Can you find out about Helene?" As an afterthought, she added, "And the guy in the pickup truck, too?"

"Yes, I'll see about them both." He scribbled something on the chart and stuck the pen in the front pocket of his white lab coat. "Now, you stay here. Stay awake. I'm fairly certain you don't have a concussion, but we don't want to take any chances." He closed the front curtain behind him.

Sam called out for him to open it back up, but he either didn't hear or chose not to hear. She leaped off the examining table, regretting the fast movement. A wave of dizziness overcame her. She held onto the table until it passed and then snuck a peek through the curtains to the nurses' station.

One of the older nurses spotted her. "Get back in there."

"Do you know anything about Helene? Helene Bouchard?"

By then, the nurse was at the cubicle. "I called upstairs. They'll let us know as soon as they know something, but for now, you need to sit in here and wait for your parents."

Sam sat down hard on the lone plastic chair in the cubicle. Exhaustion and frustration claimed all her energy. The nurse left her alone, and Sam took a couple of slow deep breaths to calm her nerves. With renewed strength, she pulled out her cell phone and called Lisa.

"Hey, baby," Lisa said, "are you on your way?"

"No."

"No?"

Sam tried to stop herself from crying but couldn't help it. "We got into an accident," she squeaked out.

"Oh, my God. Are you okay?"

"Yes."

"Helene?"

"I don't know." Sam's voice caught in her throat. "They won't tell me anything."

"Where are you?"

"East Valley Hospital."

"I'll be right there."

"How? You can't drive."

"I don't know. I'll figure it out." Lisa's voice sounded determined.

Sam wanted to tell Lisa to stay home, that there was nothing she could do, but the truth was she wanted Lisa there. She needed Lisa by her side, so she simply said, "Okay."

"Baby?" Lisa's voice had softened.

"Yeah?"

"Are you sure you're okay?"

"I got some stitches over my eye."

Lisa's sharp intake of breath made Sam realize how serious her injuries might be.

"How many?"

"I don't know."

"Baby, I don't know how, but I'll get there as fast as I can, okay?"

"Okay."

"Stay strong, and know I'll be wrapping you in my arms soon. Think about that, okay?"

"Okay."

Lisa blew out a sigh on the other end. "I love you. Never forget that."

"Same."

Sam hung up with Lisa and then maneuvered the chair so she could lean her head back against the cabinet. God, she was exhausted.

She wanted to doze off, but the nurses kept coming in and telling her to stay awake. After forever, she heard her mother's voice in the nurses' station. A glance at her cell phone told her it had been about an hour since the doctor left.

Sam got up and flung the curtain open. "Mother, I'm here."

Her mother looked up from the nurse's station. Her expression changed from one of worry to one of horror. "Samantha Rose, are you all right?" Sam's mother was on her in a flash; Sam's father was one step behind. The tears in his eyes surprised Sam. He was usually so composed.

Her mother wrapped Sam in a tight hug. Sam patted her mother on the back, trying to reassure her, and was alarmed at her bony thinness.

Once her mother let go, she directed Sam back to the plastic chair. She examined the stitches above Sam's eye closely. "The nurse said you had four stitches."

"Four? That's not too bad." Sam tried to soft-pedal her injury. Her mother never did react well in stressful situations.

"Oh, Samantha Rose. I'm glad you weren't seriously hurt." Her mother pulled Sam back into another quick hug and then surveyed the stitches again.

Sam was surprised by her mother's sudden affection. She was not a hugger. "I'm okay, Mother."

"How did this happen, Samantha Rose?" Her father's voice had an edge to it, and Sam felt like a little girl caught with her hand in the cookie jar. Her father had a knack for making her feel chastised no matter what the situation. He stood with his hands on his hips as she relayed the details of the accident.

"Where's the driver of this pickup truck?" Her father's tone was all business.

"The paramedics insisted he get checked out at the hospital, so he must be here somewhere. He was walking around after the accident."

"Besides you, were there any witnesses?"

"Yes, an Amish family," Sam said. "I heard the father tell the paramedics that they had just topped the hill on St. Regis Road when it happened. He saw the whole thing and said the traffic light was green for us. Helene didn't do anything wrong."

"Mm hmm," was all her father said.

If life wasn't bad enough for the pickup driver, it was about to get infinitely worse. No one crossed Gerald Payton or damaged his possessions without paying a serious price.

A tense silence filled the examining room. Sam stared at the old-fashioned green and white linoleum floor. Thank God the doctor finally came back.

He walked over and offered his hand to Sam's father. "Dr. Wisniewski."

Sam's father shook his hand. "Gerald Payton. This is my wife, Mimi."

He nodded at Sam's mother. "It's nice to meet you, Mrs. Payton."

"How's our Samantha Rose?"

"She'll be fine," Dr. Wisneiwski said. "Four stitches. She was an extremely lucky young lady."

"How's Helene?" Sam blurted as she approached.

"Helene is conscious and fairly lucid. She suffered a concussion and some minor bruising. They're taking her in for a CT scan now. She doesn't remember the accident."

"What's a CT scan?"

Before the doctor could answer, Lisa stepped into the examining room. "A CT scan is a CAT scan."

Sam couldn't help the smile that burst from her face. Lisa had made it there in record time. Sam tried to turn the volume down on her smile, but it was hard.

"Yes." Dr. Wisneiwski looked surprised that someone else had joined them.

"It checks for brain injuries," Lisa continued. "Like bleeding in the brain, right?"

"Yes, exactly. They're hoping the CT scan will rule out more serious injuries."

"Will they read the scan right away?" Lisa asked.

"They'll give Miss Bouchard the very best care."

Although Sam was comforted by Lisa's take-charge energy, Sam didn't want to hear about bleeding brains, especially when the brain they were referring to was Helene's.

"They asked me all kinds of questions about Helene in the ambulance," Sam said. "I didn't know if she was allergic to anything, and I didn't know if she'd had a concussion before. Has she?" Sam looked from her mother to her father.

Her father shrugged. "Not in the eighteen years since she's lived with us. Before that, I'm not sure."

"Daddy, why don't we know these things about Helene?" Sam heard the panicked edge in her own voice.

"Kitten, calm down."

"When can I see her?" Sam asked the doctor, ignoring her father.

"How did I know you were going to ask that?" The doctor tried for a reassuring smile, but Sam wasn't interested. "She's been admitted upstairs, and as soon as they're done with the scan, they'll settle her in a room—"

"The best room," Sam interrupted. "Daddy, make sure they put her in the best private room." She sent a pleading look to her father, not bothering to hide her tears.

"Yes, of course." Her father put a reassuring arm around her. Sam let herself be comforted.

"Who do I talk to about getting Helene a private room?" Sam's father asked the doctor.

"Someone at the nurses' station can help you." He pointed with his chin. "I've let them know upstairs that Helene has family waiting for her. That stairwell," he pointed with his chin again, "will take you straight to the second-floor waiting room."

"Thank you, doctor," Sam's father said.

"Now, as far as this young lady is concerned, I'd like her to come back in about five or six days to get those stitches removed." He turned toward Sam, "Make sure you keep your hands away from the stitches. We don't want to risk infection, especially so close to your eye. You can shower but try not to soak the stitches. No baths. No swimming."

"Okay." Sam nodded. "Thank you. How's the pickup truck driver?"

"He's fine. Only minor cuts and a few bruises." The doctor handed business cards to Sam's mother and father. "Call if you have any questions."

Once Dr. Wisneiwski left, Sam turned to her parents. "Let's go upstairs."

"Kitten," Sam's father said in the ultra-calm voice that Sam hated, "we can handle it from here. Why don't you go home?"

"No!"

"You've been through a lot. I'll see what's happening with Helene."

"I'm staying." Sam folded her arms in front of her.

With a resigned sigh, her father nodded. "Okay, go on upstairs. I'll arrange for the private room, and then I'm going to find the driver of the pickup truck."

The serious look Sam's father exchanged with Sam's mother made Sam more than a little nervous for the pickup truck driver. Her father headed to the nurses' station.

"Samantha Rose, go on upstairs without me," Sam's mother said. She whispered, "I need to make sure your father doesn't kill that driver." Her tone was somewhat serious.

"Thanks, Mother."

"You okay, *gringa*?" Susie said.

Sam jumped. She hadn't seen Susie and Marlee come in.

"I'm okay, I guess."

"Four stitches," Lisa said as they headed for the stairwell.

Susie hugged Sam. "Your face was scary enough without adding stitches to it."

"Ha, ha. Very funny."

"Where are we going?" Susie asked.

"To find out about Helene." Sam pushed the door open to the stairwell.

Lisa filled them in on Helene's concussion and impending CAT scan as they made their way up the stairs. Sam stopped on the first landing of the secluded stairwell.

Marlee gave Sam a quick hug and then moved out of the way for

Lisa. Lisa wrapped Sam up in her strong arms. Sam wanted to stay locked in Lisa's embrace forever, but her parents were somewhere nearby, and she stiffened up.

Lisa let go. She checked the stitches above Sam's eye. "Are you okay, baby? You look like Frankenstein."

Sam laughed. "Thanks a lot. How'd you get here so fast?"

"My mom drove me to Marlee's, and then Susie picked me and Marlee up there. Susie was at the college setting up labs or something."

"And then Susie broke the land speed record getting here," Marlee said with a grin. "Two, your eye's getting puffy."

Sam reached up, but Lisa grabbed her wrist gently. "Don't touch."

"You're right. Sorry." Sam nodded. "I think my cell phone knocked me for a wallop."

"Were you driving?" Marlee asked quietly as they continued their trek up the stairs.

Sam shook her head and relayed the story as they went. She glossed over her panic about not being able to wake up Helene.

Once situated in the much smaller but somehow cozy waiting room on the second floor, Sam's mother joined them briefly and then went to the nurses' station to inquire about Helene. With Sam's mother away, Lisa placed her hand over Sam's. A nurse walked by, and Lisa pulled her hand away. Sam sighed in frustration. She hated being so far in the closet that her own girlfriend couldn't give her comfort.

Lisa took a closer look at the stitches. "That doctor did a great job. Nice and even."

"I hope you won't have a scar," Marlee said.

"I don't care about that," Sam said. And she didn't. All she cared about was Helene.

"Did you lose consciousness?" Susie asked

"Nah, I remember every scary detail." Sam felt a rush of tears as she relived the accident. She hid her face in her hands.

Lisa put her arm around Sam and held her close. Sam let her. She didn't care if her mother or those nurses saw them. She needed her friends. She needed Lisa. Lisa rubbed Sam's back until Sam got herself back under control.

When Sam pulled her hands away from her face, she had to laugh because Marlee was holding a box of tissues inches from her face. "Thanks." She took a tissue and blew her nose. She took another and wiped at her eyes, careful not to touch the new stitches. "You guys are the best."

Lisa's hand was still on her back. Sam sat forward, and Lisa seemed to take the hint and pulled away.

"You know what?" Sam said to Lisa.

"What?"

"That might have been you."

"Where? What do you mean?"

"Those paramedics. That might have been you driving the ambulance or checking to make sure I was okay, or…" Tears choked her throat closed for a moment as she thought about the firefighters pulling Helene out of the car. "I'll never forgive myself if something happens to her."

Lisa's hand was on her back again. "You can't blame yourself. It was an accident."

"If my stupid passport didn't need to be renewed, this never would have happened."

Susie put a calm and reassuring hand solidly on her shoulder. Marlee held the tissues out with a steady hand. Sam snagged a couple more, grateful for her amazing friends.

"Thanks, you guys." Sam dabbed at her nose. She looked into Lisa's familiar light brown eyes and melted at the love and concern she saw there. Sam had built a pretty tough outer shell over the years, learning not to need anyone, but she understood something at that moment. She needed Helene. She also needed the love and comfort that Lisa gave her and the love of her friends. She watched her mother talking quietly with one of the nurses and realized with a start that she needed her parents, too.

Chapter 20
Helene Frances Bouchard

"Love you." Helene squeezed Sam's hand. Her eyes were closed.

"I love you, too, Helene." Sam tried to keep the emotion out of her voice but found it difficult. "You have to be better in two weeks, you know. Our favorite hockey team needs you." Helene didn't respond. She must have fallen asleep again. Sam gently kissed Helene's hand and sat down in the quasi-comfortable chair that had become her second home in Helene's spacious hospital room.

Sam blinked back tears and smiled at the long windowsill filled with flowers from Susie and Marlee, Lisa and her family, Sam's parents, Rolando and his wife, Mrs. Worthington, Mrs. Tardelli, and lots of other people. Sam, of course, trumped them all by having six bouquets sent. She breathed in the flowery fragrance, grateful Helene had so many fans.

The night before, Sam hadn't wanted to leave Helene alone in the hospital when visiting hours ended, especially since Helene had woken up, and they had talked for a few minutes. Helene hadn't remembered a thing about the accident and seemed more concerned about Sam's stitches than her own concussion. Typical of Helene, but this time Sam was going to play the role of nanny and take care of her.

Sam took another look at Helene in the bed. It was the day after the accident. And even though the early afternoon sunlight crept up to the bottom of the bed, making the room feel peaceful and cozy, Sam wished she could say Helene looked peaceful. She did not. The pain medication the nurse had given Helene must not be working well enough. The nurse told Sam that Helene's body was recovering from the impact of the pickup truck.

Sam pulled out her phone and scrolled through the happy pictures of her and Helene at the lake house. She blew out a sigh and said a silent prayer for Helene's recovery to a God she hadn't talked to in a long time.

A quiet knock on the door made Sam's heart soar. It was Lisa. It had to be. The door opened, and Lisa, Susie, and Marlee walked in.

"How's Helene today?" Lisa asked in a whisper. She flew over to Sam and gave her a quick hello kiss. She wrapped her in a snuggly hug.

"The doctor said she's going to sleep a lot while she recovers," Sam whispered back.

Lisa let go of Sam and reached for the medical chart tucked in a box on the end of the bed. She scanned the entries.

Susie gave Sam a quick hug and asked in a quiet voice, "How long does she have to stay here?"

"The CAT scan showed there wasn't any bleeding on her brain or anything like that," Sam said.

"Thank God for that, eh?" Lisa blew out a sigh and stashed the chart back in the box. "There isn't much on here. Everything's recorded electronically, I guess."

"She has a severe concussion and needs rest, so they're going to play it by ear. Three or four days at least." Sam gestured for her friends to sit in the chairs Susie and Marlee had snagged from the hallway the night before. "Lisa, you should go to medical school. You love this stuff."

"Me? Medical school?" Lisa got a faraway look on her face as if she'd never thought of it. "That's going to be expensive, but I guess I could get a student loan or a scholarship or something."

That's going to be expensive, but I guess I could get a student loan or a scholarship or something."

"Yeah, and your bio-dad gave your mom enough money to take a big chunk out of your undergrad costs."

Marlee gave Sam the envelope she had been holding. "It's a get-well card for Helene from me and my mom."

"Thanks, Marlee. That's sweet." Sam put the unopened card on the table next to Helene's bed.

"Oh, geez," Lisa said. "I forgot the cards in the van. The three musketeers made a whole bunch of get-well cards for you and Helene before we went to church this morning."

"We'll go get them," Susie said. "C'mon, Marlee, let's give the lovebirds some alone time."

Sam felt her cheeks get warm. It wasn't like she and Lisa were going to get down and dirty right there in Helene's hospital room, but it was kind of nice to have Lisa all to herself for a while.

"How about I call the three musketeers later? Let them know I'm okay."

"That's so thoughtful of you," Lisa said. Her loving smile made Sam get warm all over. Lisa pulled her chair closer. "You're so nice to think of them. When you do stuff like that, it makes me want to marry you."

"Ahh," Sam said, "do you know that we can legally get married right now?"

"Right now? How? We're both underage."

"I looked it up. We'd need written permission from both sets of parents, though."

Lisa laughed. "And you'd be able to get that really easy, eh?"

Sam rolled her eyes. "Not in this lifetime."

"What's the age we don't need our parents' permission?"

"Eighteen."

Lisa nodded slowly as if scheming. "Guess we'll cross that bridge when we get to it."

"Do you want to cross that bridge with me?" Sam asked shyly.

Lisa stood up and pulled Sam out of the chair. She swallowed Sam in her arms and seared her with a steamy kiss. When she let go, Sam was delightfully dizzy. She stumbled backward and sat down hard.

Lisa shot Sam a suggestive look. "Does that answer your question?"

"I'll say." Sam nodded slowly and fanned herself. Sam snuck a peek at Helene. She was still sleeping soundly, but her face looked more relaxed this time. The pain meds were probably kicking in big time. "For now, we'll have to make do with celebrating our four-month anniversary."

"On Wednesday."

Sam nodded. "I'll pick you up after play practice, okay?"

"Dinner at D'Amico's?"

"Maybe." Sam had actually reserved a table at *Le Grande Bistro*, a high-end restaurant in Southbridge, but wanted to surprise Lisa.

"Did you ever look up the answer to that other question we had?" Lisa sat back down.

"What other—"

"You know." Lisa blushed. "When you turn eighteen, and I'm still sixteen. Will you be in trouble if we, you know?"

"Oh, *that* question." Sam leaned closer and said in low tones, "Yes, we will be in trouble then because we're in trouble right now. Well, I am anyway."

Lisa's eyes grew wide. "Why?"

"You're not seventeen yet. It turns out that we'll be legal once you turn seventeen."

"Even though at seventeen, I'll still be underage?"

Sam nodded. "The website said anybody under seventeen years old is incapable of giving consent to, you know, have, uh, intimate relations." Sam blushed at the last two whispered words.

"Oh, I'm more than capable of consenting." Lisa waggled her eyebrows.

"Believe me, I know."

The door opened wide, and Susie and Marlee rushed back in. Marlee held up the plastic grocery bag filled with crayon-drawn get-well cards from Lisa's brother and sisters and handed it to Sam.

"Thanks, you guys," Sam said, genuinely grateful to finally have sincere friends in her life.

"Look at your cards later," Susie said. "Move your chair over here. Marlee and I found something quite interesting in the lobby." She held up a pamphlet.

Sam couldn't believe what she was seeing. "*STDs and You*? Why do you have that?"

"Just get over here," Susie hissed through gritted teeth.

Sam shook her head but did as bidden. "What is so exciting about STDs?"

213

"Shuddup. I'm giving you guys a quiz."

Sam rolled her eyes dramatically and then snuck a peek back at Helene, who was still sleeping soundly. "Okay, but we can't wake up Helene."

"*Sí, claro, gringa.* So, I assume you guys took Health in ninth grade, like me and Sam did, right?"

Lisa and Marlee nodded.

"Let's see how good your memories are. Name some STDs."

"Syphilis," Marlee said with a snap of her fingers.

"Yes."

"Gonorrhea," Lisa offered.

"Good. What else?"

The room was stock still. The only sounds that could be heard were the quiet noises of the medical staff moving in the hallway outside Helene's room.

"See," Susie said, "it's not an easy quiz."

"Wait, now," Sam said, "I remember something weird about warts, you know, down there."

"Oh, yeah," Marlee said. "Can you imagine how awkward that would be?"

"Uh, how about herpes?" Lisa said.

"Bingo!" Susie whispered enthusiastically. "But there are a couple of biggies you haven't said yet."

After a few moments of wracking their brains, Susie let them off the hook. "HIV is an STD."

"Yeah, I guess it would be," Sam said. "Any exchange of bodily fluids, right?"

"Right. Hepatitis B, too." Susie added. "*Aay, mierda.* Check this out. It says one in every five Americans has an STD."

Marlee's jaw dropped open. "One in five?"

Susie nodded. "Twenty percent."

"Oh, man. There are five people in this room right now. That means one of us could have an STD. Holy crap."

Sam's eyes grew wide. "Wait a sec. Are we counted in that one in five? Do *lesbians* have the same risk?" She whispered the word lesbians, still not comfortable saying the word out loud. "I thought we were immune to that stuff."

"I think we're at risk with any kind of exchange of bodily fluids," Susie said, "but I really don't know. And if your school is like ours, they only talked about hetero sex. Am I right?"

Sam and Lisa added their nods to Marlee's.

"They do their best to scare us into abstinence in ninth grade," Marlee said. "But, seriously, what STDs do *we* have to worry about?" Marlee asked the question before Sam could.

Susie shrugged. "I have no idea. Sam, give me that fancy phone of yours, and I'll look it up."

"No way," Sam said. "You're not looking that up with my phone. What if my parents saw it?"

"True that." Susie nodded.

"I use the school computers in the library for that kind of research." Sam winked at Lisa.

"Check this out, you guys." Marlee grabbed the pamphlet from Susie's hand. "It says here you can lower your chance of getting STDs by using a latex male condom or, get this, a female condom."

"*Aay*, a female condom?" Susie asked. "You made that up."

"I did not. See?" Marlee pointed to the pamphlet.

"I've never heard of a female condom. Have you guys?" Susie asked.

Sam and Lisa shook their heads. "Get back to us after you do your research, Sus," Sam said.

"Why me?"

"'Cuz you're the one who brought that stupid pamphlet in here," Sam said.

"Okay, whatever. I'll use a computer at the college because my mother will have a heart attack if she finds out I'm researching anything about sex."

"Can I read the get-well cards now?" Sam stood up.

"*Sí, claro*. Class dismissed." Susie grinned.

Sam moved her chair back next to Helene's bed. She leaned down and kissed the back of Helene's hand. Sam sat in the chair and smiled as she picked through the pile of hand-drawn get-well cards. They had also made cards for Helene, which was sweet because they had only met her once at a softball game, but they'd also made some for Sam. Bridget had drawn a picture of Sam with purple hair sticking straight up in the air. Lawrence Jr. drew a couple of transformers destroying a city, and Lynnie had written a get-well poem under the flowers she had drawn.

"Hey, you guys," Sam said. "Let's hang these on the wall where Helene can see them."

"Good idea," Lisa said. Sam handed her the cards.

"Do we have any tape?" Lisa looked around the room.

"They probably have some at the nurses' station." Susie stood up.

"Wait, wait," Sam said with a laugh. "Have you ever seen Helene's purse? It's enormous. I'll bet she has some." At Lisa's doubtful expression, Sam said, "I'm serious. She keeps everything in there."

Sam went to the cupboard on the other side of the bed and pulled out Helene's purse.

"Oh, man," Marlee said, "that thing could hold a bowling ball."

"Told ya." Sam walked back to her chair and placed the heavy bag on her lap. Rifling through it, she found what she was searching for. "Here you go." Sam handed a roll of scotch tape to Lisa.

"That's incredible." Lisa shook her head in disbelief. She stood up, and she, Susie, and Marlee hung the cards on the painted cinderblock wall.

Sam, meanwhile, stumbled upon her birth certificate in Helene's purse that they'd needed to renew her passport. For some reason, she had never seen it before. Now was her chance. She pulled the folded certificate out of the yellowing envelope and silently read her name and date of birth.

"Phoenix," Sam mumbled, confirming her place of birth. "Gerald Fitzpatrick Payton." She smiled at her father's aristocratic middle name. "Helene Frances Bouchard." In confusion, Sam's eyes darted back over the spot where the mother's name was supposed to be. "Helene?" Sam couldn't make herself move. Was she reading it right? Where was her mother's name? Sam scanned the document frantically looking for the words Miriam Lily Payton. She couldn't find them. She went back to the entry for the mother's name. It hadn't changed. *Helene Frances Bouchard.*

Sam looked at the injured woman lying in the bed. Scenes of her life with Helene flashed through her head. Helene bandaging a scraped knee, teaching her to read music, explaining the rules of ice hockey. "Helene took care of me like a…" Sam's vision blurred, and the room got dark as she slid from the chair. The last thing she heard before she hit the floor was her own voice saying, "mother."

Chapter 21
Sleepdriving

The noise level in the cafeteria rose steadily as students filed in for lunch. Mrs. Sherman, Sam's fourth-period ethics teacher, had let the class out early, and Sam sat alone at the lunch table she shared with Susie, Abby, and Rachel. Most of the time she bought her lunch, but she wasn't hungry today and didn't have the strength to get up and navigate the lengthening line. She should have been hungry since she hadn't eaten anything since the day before when she'd finished Helene's soup at the hospital. That was back when Helene was her nanny and not her...

Sam couldn't finish the thought. She couldn't even think the word. It was too surreal.

"Hey, *muchacha*," Susie tossed her paper lunch bag on the table, "how are you feeling?"

"I'm okay."

"You scared the crap out of us yesterday."

"Sorry."

"*Mierda*, we turned around, and you were out cold on the floor. What happened?"

"I told you; I don't know." Sam shrugged. "I think I freaked out about the accident and Helene being hurt." *Pick one. It won't be the real reason, anyway.*

Susie nodded. "Let me know if you feel faint again. Okay, *gringa*?"

Sam smiled in spite of herself. "I will." It was nice having friends who cared about her. While Susie got busy eating her sandwich, Sam stared back into nothingness.

The day before, when she woke up after fainting in Helene's hospital room, she shoved the obnoxious smelling salts away from her nose. Once she'd recovered enough of her senses, she remembered. She kept her panic under wraps and assured everyone, especially Lisa, that she was okay. With relief, she spotted the birth certificate under the chair and was pretty sure no one had seen it. Her friends had been too busy fussing over her. The secret was safe.

The medical staff ran Sam through some quick tests and determined that she was okay. They said her fainting probably had to do with the shock of the accident. She was in shock, yes, but not from the accident. Later, after Lisa, Susie, and Marlee left, Sam snatched the birth certificate from under the chair and read it over and over again. No matter how long she stared at it, the information didn't change. Sam snuck a peek at Helene, taking in her blond hair, remembering when people said they looked like mother and daughter. Sam had always found that amusing.

Not so much anymore.

"Sam?" Susie put a gentle hand on her forearm. "You okay?"

"Yeah." Sam blinked away the disturbing thoughts.

"You had a faraway look on your face."

"I'm okay." Sam groaned. Ronnie was heading right for their lunch table.

"Girlfriend," Ronnie squealed, pulling her back to the present, "what happened to your face? Rumors are flying."

"Easy, Ronnie," Susie warned.

Ronnie, usually one for a witty comeback, stayed silent. He sat on the other side of Sam. "Seriously, Samantha Rose, what happened?"

"She was in a bad car accident on Saturday," Susie answered before Sam could.

Abby and Rachel arrived at that moment and sat in their usual spots at the table.

"Oh, my God, Sam," Abby said. "Susie told us you were in an accident. Are you all right?"

Sam felt so numb inside she wanted to shake her head and then go to sleep forever. Instead, she simply nodded.

"How many stitches?" Rachel asked.

"Four."

A few of Sam's softball teammates and people from the play came over to form a crowd around the table. Bad news traveled fast, apparently.

Ronnie put a gentle hand on her forearm. "Was everyone else okay?"

Sam had been dreading that question. Flashbacks of the accident raced through her brain. The pickup crashing into them, the paramedics pulling Helene out of the car, the birth certificate telling Sam her entire life had been a lie. Her eyes filled up with tears before she could stop them.

Susie answered when Sam couldn't. "The driver of the car has a pretty serious concussion. She's still in the hospital."

Sam nodded. It was all she had strength for. She stared at the edge of the graffiti-covered tabletop.

"Hey, everybody," Susie said, taking charge, "I think Sam needs a little room, okay? She's still in shock from the accident."

In less than a minute, the curious onlookers gave Sam their well-wishes and moved away. Even Abby and Rachel moved to another table. Susie and Ronnie were the only ones left. Ronnie's hand still rested on her forearm. Sam didn't mind. Somehow it was comforting.

Once the crowd dispersed, Sam turned to Ronnie. "Can you tell Mrs. Dickens I won't be at rehearsal this afternoon?"

"Sure," Ronnie said. He squeezed her forearm and then sat back. "Should I text you later and let you know what we worked on?"

Sam nodded and pulled out her phone. "Let me text you now, so you'll have my number." He rattled off his cell phone number, and she texted him a smiley face. She then saved his number in her contact list. "You can't give my number out to anyone. Okay, Ronnie? My father will kill me, and then he'll kill you."

He nodded, and for once in his life, looked serious.

"Are you going to the hospital right after school?" Susie asked.

Sam thought about Helene lying in the hospital all by herself without family or anyone to care about her. She stood up abruptly. "No, I'm going right now."

"Right now?" Susie looked confused. "You're cutting classes?"

"I guess so." Sam turned to Ronnie again. "Can you tell Mr. Auerbach why I'm missing Strings?"

"You got it." Ronnie nodded.

"*Aay*, Sam," Susie teased. "Are you sure you want to miss AP Enviro? We're learning about the demise of Easter Island today."

Sam smiled, knowing Susie was trying to cheer her up. "You'll get the notes for me, right?"

"*Sí, claro.*"

Sam nodded and took a deep breath. "Thanks, guys. I'll see you tomorrow." She headed toward the back door of the cafeteria, the one that led directly to the senior parking lot.

~~~

Sam pulled into the hospital lot and found a spot near the entrance. She sat in her car, the engine still idling, unable to move. Memories raced through her mind. Memories of Helene teaching her how to ride a bike in the circular driveway, fixing her soup and a sandwich after her mother made her pick at her dinner, listening to Sam complain about her parents.

"Parents," Sam said. "I have three parents." *Daddy is my father. Helene is my ...* "Helene is my mother," she said out loud, testing to see how it sounded. Her brain still couldn't make sense of it.

Sam wondered about the woman she'd been calling Mother for eighteen years. "Mother didn't give birth to me," she said. *Who is Mother?* Panic rose in her chest. She took several deep breaths and focused on the hood ornament of the Cadillac parked directly in front of her. After a moment, she was back under control. She had almost mastered the Payton ability to deny all emotion, but this recent twist in her life was proving too big to deny.

She looked up at the hospital building toward Helene's window. She couldn't do it. Knowing what she knew, she couldn't face Helene. Not yet. Feeling lost, she closed her eyes for a moment and then pulled her cell phone out of her pocket.

Someone, presumably one of the nurses at the desk in Helene's wing, answered on the second ring.

"Hi, this is Samantha Rose Payton. I wanted to check up on

Helene Bouchard in room 305."

"Ah, yes," the cheery voice answered. "This is Naomi. Are you feeling better today?"

"Much better. Thanks for the smelling salts yesterday."

"Not a problem. You gave everyone quite a scare."

"I know. I just needed a good night's sleep." Sam's shoulders tensed up at the lie. "How's Helene today?"

"She's making an excellent recovery. She ate most of her soup with a good appetite."

"Excellent," Sam said. "Please tell her that I, uh, that I'm pleased."

"Should I tell her you're coming to visit?"

"Uh," Sam hesitated, "I'll surprise her later." Sam wasn't sure when *later* would be. "Thanks for your help, Naomi."

"You're welcome, Samantha Rose. Oops, that's someone's call bell. I gotta go."

"Okay, thank you." Sam clicked off her phone and slid it back into her pocket.

Not sure where she was headed, she pulled out of the parking space and exited the lot on a side street instead of heading directly back onto C.R. 62. She drove without paying much attention to where she was going. It was like she was sleepwalking. *More like sleepdriving,* she thought with a chuckle. She wasn't asleep, but she wasn't awake, either. She was nothing.

She couldn't face Helene. Not yet. Helene didn't know she knew. Her parents didn't know she knew. How had they kept such an enormous secret for eighteen years? Thank God she had been able to avoid eye contact with her parents when she got home from the hospital the night before. She had sprinted up the stairs to her

223

wing of the house, yelling, "Goodnight" as she went. She closed the door to her room and, in a rare move, locked both the outside door to her suite and the inside door to her bedroom. She wasn't sure if she was trying to lock everyone and everything out or if she was trying to lock herself in. She lay on her bed and stared at the ceiling in her dark room for hours. She had obviously fallen asleep at some point during the night because her alarm woke her up for school. She had slept in her clothes.

Sam drove along in the intense quiet of the neighborhoods near the hospital. She drove until she found herself on the street where Lisa's bio-dad William and his wife Evelyn lived. *Am I going to be calling Daddy my bio-dad from now on? Is Helene my bio-mom?* Sam groaned.

Not knowing why, she pulled into William and Evelyn's driveway and parked her car. She headed to the front door. After one ring of the bell, Evelyn opened the door.

"Samantha Rose," Evelyn said with surprise, "what brings you here? C'mon in." She stepped aside to let Sam in the house. "Oh, honey, what happened to your eye?" She grimaced at Sam's stitches.

"Car accident. I'm okay. I'm sorry to bother you, Evelyn," Sam started. She swallowed against the lump forming in her throat. The tears she thought she had under control eased down her cheeks. She didn't bother wiping them away.

"Oh, dear," Evelyn said. "You're upset. Come in, come in. Sit down." She led the way toward the kitchen table.

Sam took one step toward the kitchen and stopped. In the car, she had ignored the familiar pressure in her neck and shoulders that signaled an impending migraine. The pressure was becoming much more insistent. "Evelyn, I'm sorry. Can I lie down for a minute? I don't feel well."

"Of course, dear. C'mon." Evelyn led the way down a hallway to a sunny back bedroom. "This is the guest room. You can lie down here." She motioned to the queen-sized bed.

As Sam sat on the bed, the pressure in her head increased. With a grunt, she tried to take off her shoes. She didn't want to ruin Evelyn's pretty comforter.

"Here," Evelyn said, "let me help you, poor thing."

Sam nodded once. The energy drained out of her as the pounding in her head increased. "Do you have something for migraines?"

"I have aspirin. That's about it."

Sam groaned. "That won't touch it."

"Okay," Evelyn said, "let me get you settled, and I'll see what else we have."

Sam lay on her side and let Evelyn, a woman she'd only met a few times, place a thin crocheted blanket over her. Sam closed her eyes against the pain exploding in her head with each beat of her heart. She tried to relax her tense neck and shoulders with little success.

After forever, Evelyn came back. "I'm sorry, Samantha Rose. All I have is the aspirin. Should I call someone to come get you?"

"No," Sam said quickly. "I'll be okay." The last thing she wanted was to see her parents.

"I'll call William then. I'll see if he can leave work and can get something for your migraine at Kinney's. Okay?"

"Okay."

"Can I get you some water?"

"No," Sam blurted so fast it made her nauseous. "Bucket." She took a couple of shallow breaths. "Hurry."

"Oh, gosh," Evelyn scurried around the room and finally came up with a plastic trash can. She held it near Sam's head.

Sam raised her head slightly and grabbed the can with both hands. "Sorry." She dry heaved into the trash can. Nothing more than spittle came out. Her head pounded. She heaved again and again but had nothing to give despite her stomach's best efforts. Sam closed her eyes and held her breath as another wave of nausea hit. That time she rode the wave but didn't heave. She took that as a good sign and laid her head back down on the pillow. "Sorry."

"It's okay, dear. You're obviously sick." Evelyn yanked several tissues from the box on the bedside stand and wiped at Sam's mouth. Sam sensed Evelyn's rising panic. "The trash can's right here on the floor if you need it. Let me call William."

"Dark," Sam muttered. "Please." The bright, cheery room was more than she could bear.

The sound of the blinds closing soon followed.

Sam relaxed a micron after the room got dark. Her entire existence consisted of riding each wave of pain in her head and breathing slowly to keep the nausea at bay.

"Sam," a male voice asked gently, "are you awake?"

Sam groaned. Where was she? She must have fallen asleep. Miraculously, the migraine pounding in her head had downgraded from a category five to a category three.

"It's William. Are you awake enough to hear me?"

"Yes." She fluttered her eyes open but pressed them shut again when her head pounded. "What time is it?"

"A little after two. Evelyn says you've been sleeping for over an hour."

Sam opened her eyes again and took in William's tall frame in the dark room. "Sorry."

"I bought Excedrin Migraine. The pharmacist at Kinney's said it was good. Do you want to take some now?"

"Yes, please." Sam took a deep breath, grateful she didn't seem to be as nauseous anymore.

He set a glass of water on the bedside stand and opened the bottle. She held out a shaky hand for the tablets. William put two in her hand.

"Get the bucket ready," Evelyn said from where she was leaning against the doorjamb. Sam would have laughed if she'd had the strength.

Sam put the pills in her mouth and then took the water glass William handed her. He reached down and picked up the bucket, ready to launch it in her direction if necessary.

Sam sat up and swallowed the pills with minimal water and then handed the glass back to him. She couldn't focus on the bedside stand long enough to put it down by herself. She kept her head up for a moment to see if the pills would stay down. When they did, she lay back down and closed her eyes. "Thanks." After a quiet moment, she added, "Sorry."

The doorbell rang, and Evelyn said, "Who could that be?"

After a moment, Evelyn came back into the room. "Samantha Rose, a man in a black suit is at the door. He said his name is Rolando."

Rolando? Sam groaned. How had he found her?

"There's a black Town Car in the street," Evelyn added.

"Did you call my father?" Sam heard the weakness in her own voice.

"No," Evelyn said. "We don't have your parents' number. Should I let Rolando in?"

"Yes."

After a moment, Rolando was in the room. "How are you, Miss?"

"Been better. How'd you find me?"

Rolando hesitated for a moment, looking down at the floor. He looked up at her. "I shouldn't tell you this, Miss, but I think it's time you knew." He reached into the pocket of his suit jacket and showed her his cell phone. "Your father tracks you with the GPS on your phone. He knows when you're at school, at softball, when you go to that pretty girl's house in Clarksonville, and when you go to the yacht. He knows where you are at all times."

Despite the pounding in her head, Sam's eyes opened wide. Her father had been spying on her. Her father knew her every move.

"He even knows you've come here to these nice people's house. He had them checked out, you know."

Sam couldn't believe what she was hearing. "Why are you telling me this, Rolando?"

"As I said, I thought you should know. But, Miss?"

"Yes?"

"I will go to my grave denying I ever told you. I can't lose this job." He lowered his gaze.

"Don't worry, Rolando. The Paytons are amazingly good at keeping secrets." *All kinds of secrets.* She took a slow breath, amazed her migraine had downgraded further to a category two.

Rolando cleared his throat. "Your father is waiting for you in the car. He would like you to come home now."

Sam's head pulsed. "I can't. Tell him I have a migraine." *Which is true.* "I don't care. Tell him anything."

"Yes, Miss." Rolando turned to leave but then turned back. He reached into his pocket and pulled out a butterscotch candy. "Feel better," he said as he handed the candy to her.

Sam smiled at him. "Thank you, Rolando."

"You're welcome, miss." He turned and left the room.

Sam closed her eyes, hoping Rolando would drive her father back home, so she could be left in peace.

No such luck. Within minutes, Sam's father walked into the back bedroom. She could feel him fuming. William and Evelyn hovered, obviously unsure how to handle the situation.

Her father turned to them. "May I have a moment alone with my daughter, please?"

"Of course," William said. "We'll be in the kitchen." William ushered Evelyn out of the room and then closed the bedroom door behind him.

As soon as the door clicked shut, Sam's father advanced. He placed both hands on his hips. "Samantha Rose, do you mind telling me what's going on?" His voice boomed. "Why are you lying in the back bedroom in a house owned by a used-car salesman and a dental hygienist? Why are you not in school? Did you know that Madeleine Baxter called me directly? I must say, young lady, I'm unaccustomed to the school principal calling to tell me my daughter is AWOL from school."

Sam desperately wanted to close her eyes but didn't dare. Not when her father was on a rant. "I have a migraine," she said weakly. Her migraine was escalating back up to a category three. She had no choice, she had to close her eyes for a moment, or she would be sick again.

"You could have driven home. You could have gone to the school nurse. Hell, you were at the hospital. Why didn't you see a doctor there?"

Sam's eyes flew open. "How did you know I was at the hospital?" She wanted to see if her father would admit to spying on her.

"That, young lady, is beside the point."

Sam wanted to laugh but couldn't muster the courage or the energy. God, it was all so tragic. If only her father realized she knew the whole sordid truth about the birth certificate, maybe then he would leave her alone. Maybe the whole world would leave her alone. Maybe she should open her mouth and tell everyone the deep dark Payton Family secret. Surely the postmaster already knew because he had to examine her birth certificate. Her father had bought him off. Who else knew? Dr. Boyle. He had to know, didn't he? Rolando? Mrs. Tardelli, their cook? Her mother's gardening committee? Did they all know? Sam groaned.

"Kitten, look." Her father's voice softened from *forte* to *mezzo-forte* but was still commanding. "I know you're upset, but you're going to be fine. You can talk to Helene on the phone any time you want." Sam didn't understand what her father meant by calling Helene, but she didn't have a chance to process it when he added, "I want you to get up right now and come home with me. I'll send someone for your car later."

Sam stayed silent, trying to gather her thoughts. Anger churned deep in her gut, displacing the numbness she'd lived with for the past twenty-four hours. She wished she had the nerve to look her father dead in the eye and say, *Daddy, I read my birth certificate* or *Daddy, I know Helene is my birth mother,* but she didn't do either of those things. With a sigh, she sat up in the bed, put her shoes on, and followed him out the door like the good little girl she'd been trained to be.

Chapter 22
April Fools

Sam bolted out of the Town Car and ran into the house, refusing to let her father see her cry. Her mother looked stunned as Sam ran by and up the stairs to her suite. She slammed the door to her rooms, opened it, and slammed it again. Not that anyone cared. All they cared about was themselves and their secrets. That's why she hadn't bothered talking to her father as Rolando drove them the fifteen minutes home from William and Evelyn's. That was plenty of time to say nothing to each other. Her father didn't even seem to notice. It was as if she was something to be dealt with and, once handled, he could get back to more important things.

Sam grabbed the remote control lying on the arm of the couch and heaved it against the wall. The splintering plastic wasn't as satisfying as she'd hoped. She headed to her bedroom and slammed that door, too. Tears of frustration poured out of her as she flung herself onto the bed, her head pounding.

"No," she grunted to no one and pounded the bedspread once with her fist. *I will not cry.* She didn't want to give in to her emotions. If she did, her father would win. Win at what, she didn't know. Who was he anyway? Was he really her father, or was he just the man who provided the sperm? And who was Helene? Did she have an affair with her father and accidentally get pregnant? Did

Helene become something that needed to be dealt with, too? Had she threatened to sue? Is that why she was being sent away? *Was I an inconvenience? An accident? Oh, God,* Sam thought. *Mother. Where does she fit into all of this? She must have resented me all these years. Raising Helene's bastard child in her own house.*

A wave of nausea spiked through her. She bolted off the bed to the bathroom, but luckily the feeling passed. Ignoring the stitches above her eye, she checked out her reflection in the mirror. Her skin was pale, which made the dark circles under her eyes stand out more. She looked at her eyes. Yup, she definitely had her father's gray-blue eyes. Everyone said so. She turned her head and examined her profile. She gasped when she saw it. It was so obvious. She had Helene's profile, her nose, her chin. She even had Helene's dirty blond hair. Why had she never noticed before?

The clues had been there her whole life. She felt like the butt of a bad joke, and at any moment, someone would jump out and yell, "April fools," even though it was mid-September. Yeah, she had been a fool. She had been a fool to hide her emotions and be Mother and Daddy's perfect little princess. She wasn't even their real daughter. She wasn't anything. She had let them run her life for almost eighteen years and let them make her scared to be who she was. She had hidden her relationship with Lisa because of them.

"Ahhh!" she screamed and swept everything off the bathroom vanity onto the floor. The breaking glass made her head pound, but it was oh so satisfying. She gripped the edge of the vanity as angry tears rolled down her cheeks. She searched frantically for a happy place to go in her mind, but Helene's image kept coming up. She took a deep breath and thought about Lisa. She remembered their first kiss in the Clarksonville College dugout. There hadn't been another soul around. She remembered how Lisa's initial hesitation had turned into passion so quickly it had made Sam woozy.

She smiled at the memory, but the ever-increasing pounding in her head told her she needed to lie down. She splashed a little water on her face hoping that would make her feel better, but it didn't. Resigned, she lay back down on her bed. Before closing her eyes, she flipped open her phone and smiled when she saw that Ronnie had texted her. He said Mrs. Dickens hadn't planned to rehearse any of Sam's scenes that afternoon, anyway, so she was off the hook. Sam was about to text Lisa when there was a knock on the outside door to the suite.

At first, Sam figured it was Helene, but then her heart sank when she thought it could be her father. Shit, what did he want now? Couldn't her father leave her alone for two minutes?

He would let himself in anyway, so there was no reason to actually invite him in. Sam stashed her cell phone under the pillow and turned to face the wall.

"Samantha Rose, dear?"

The sound of her mother's voice surprised her. She opened her eyes and looked toward the door. "I'm in here, Mother."

"I have some soup for you." Her mother walked into the bedroom carrying a tray with a bowl of hot chicken and rice soup. It was Sam's favorite soup from childhood.

"You made this?"

Sam's mother nodded.

"All by yourself?"

Sam's mother smiled gently. "I'm not that inept in the kitchen, you know. And, yes, I opened the can all by myself. I brought you those favorite crackers you like, too." She set the tray on the bedside table, and Sam sat up. She moved over to make room for her mother to sit down on the edge of the bed.

"Oyster crackers. Thank you, Mother." Sam wasn't sure if she could handle food at the moment, afraid her stomach might recoil, but then it growled. "I guess I am kind of hungry." She ignored the pounding in her head and pulled the tray onto her lap. She ate one test spoonful. When it stayed down, she ate more heartily. She couldn't help thinking how ironic the whole scene was. Helene was the one who usually brought her a tray of food.

"How are you feeling?" Her mother asked tentatively. "Daddy said you're having migraines again."

"I'm okay." Sam shrugged. She wasn't used to having touchy-feely talks with her mother. *Actually,* one part of her brain thought, *I have had touchy-feely talks with my mother. My mother, whose name is Helene.* Sam groaned.

"Are you sure you're okay?"

"Yes, Mother." Sam sat up straight like the good debutante she was and added, "I'm a little tired. And I'm worried about Helene."

"Yes, I imagine you would be."

"I'll probably go see her later."

"I'll drive you," her mother said.

Something in her mother's voice made Sam take notice. "You don't have to, Mother."

"I just got off the phone with her, and she said she was up for company. I haven't been there since Saturday, so I should go."

Sam, all at once, realized how hard it was for her mother to watch Sam worry about the woman who had given birth to her husband's bastard child. No wonder her mother was so cold and stiff. A knot of sympathy tightened in Sam's chest, and she gave her mother a quick hug.

Her mother stood up abruptly as if thrown by the hug. She cleared her throat. "When shall we go?"

"I think I need a short nap. Is that okay? My migraine's almost gone, but I don't want it to come back."

"That sounds reasonable. I'll be downstairs reading. Come find me whenever you're ready."

"Thank you, Mother."

"We need to plan our New York weekend, too, don't we?"

"We do," Sam said. "We can talk about it on the way to the hospital."

Her mother nodded and turned to go.

"Mother?"

"Yes, dear?" Sam's mother turned around.

"I love you."

"Oh." Her mother put a hand to her throat. "Thank you. I love you, too." Her mother's cheeks turned a glorious shade of red. "I'll see you after your nap."

If her head hadn't hurt so much, Sam might have laughed when her mother practically bolted out the door.

~~~

"It's nice to see you're feeling better, Helene," Sam's mother said. She sat in the chair farthest from Helene in the hospital room.

"Any day now, I'm gonna bust out of this joint," Helene said with a laugh.

"Only when the doctor gives you the green light, okay?" Sam said. "Promise?"

"Promise."

Sam's mother stood up and smoothed down her skirt. "I'm going to wander the halls in search of a cup of tea. Can I get you two anything?"

"No thanks, Mother."

Helene shook her head. "Ooh, yesterday, I couldn't even do that with my head."

"Okay, then." Sam's mother locked her gaze onto Helene's and added, "I'm sure you two have a lot to talk about."

Helene nodded, and Sam wasn't sure what to make of the exchange.

Oh, God, Sam thought. Helene's going to tell me she's my mother. I'm not ready for this conversation. Even though I already know, I'm not ready.

"Are you okay, Samantha Rose?" Helene asked. "You look like you've seen a ghost."

Sam swallowed against the lump growing in her throat. "I'm okay."

Helene looked at her hands. "There's something I've needed to tell you for a while now. I wanted to tell you at the diner the other day, but we were having such a good time, I didn't want to ruin it."

"What's up?" Sam said past the growing lump in her throat. She tried to act natural, but how does one do that when a bomb was about to drop?

Helene took a slow breath and sighed, obviously trying to gather her thoughts. "I'm moving out."

Stunned, Sam fell back against the chair. That was not what she had been expecting to hear at that moment. "What?" she asked weakly. Her brain tried desperately to make sense of the words.

"Your parents and I came to an agreement a long time ago that when you turned eighteen, I would move out."

"I'm not eighteen yet."

"You will be soon." Helene's smile was tired and resigned. "You're a young woman now, and you don't need a nanny."

Sam couldn't help the tears streaming down her cheeks. She leaped out of the chair and grabbed Helene into a hug. She rested her head on Helene's chest like she'd done countless times as a child. "I need you, Helene." *I don't need a nanny; I need my mother.* Sam desperately wanted to say the words out loud, but they wouldn't come.

Helene rubbed Sam's back. "Shhh, *mon petite hibou.* At least we've had these eighteen years."

Sam continued to cry. "When are you leaving? Where are you going? Back to Canada?"

Helene nodded. "I'm going to live with my sister and her husband for a while. She has the baby coming and can use my help."

Sam picked her head up. "When?"

"I was going to move my things out when you and your parents were in Switzerland."

Sam stood up. "Were you going to tell me? Or was I going to come back and find you and all your stuff gone?"

"No, honey, that's why I'm telling you now. Your mother thought it was best I tell you as soon as possible."

That's why Mother drove me back here. So Helene could break my heart. Sam sat down hard on the chair. She rested her forehead on her fist and stared at the cheap linoleum floor. Her parents were trying to get rid of Helene. They were trying to get rid of the evidence. Maybe they had an eighteen-year contract, and it was expiring.

Sam looked up through a sheen of tears. "Will I ever see you again?" Her face scrunched up as she started to cry again.

"Of course, you will."

"Helene," Sam blurted, "I know. I know you're—" Agony closed her throat. She couldn't say the final words.

After a moment, Helene said, "Your father thought I'd told you earlier today. He thought that's why you ran to William and Evelyn's."

"Did you know he's been spying on me? He uses my cell phone to track me."

"I suspected, but no, I didn't know for sure." Helene pressed her lips together for a moment. "Why exactly did you skip your classes this afternoon?"

Ahh, Sam thought, *the million-dollar question.* "I didn't sleep well last night." *Because I kept freaking out over you being my mother.* "I got a migraine at school, so I left."

"But you didn't go home."

"Nope."

"Why not?"

"There was no one at home to take care of me." It was kind of a lie, but kind of the truth, too.

"Samantha Rose, you don't know William and Evelyn that well. I can only imagine what they're thinking."

"Helene," Sam grunted, "that's Mother's line. That's the code she lives by. You don't care what other people think, do you?" Or maybe she did. She probably had to. She'd had to keep the big dark Payton Family secret her whole adult life.

They sat in silence for a while until Sam said, "I'm going to miss you."

It was finally Helene's turn to cry.

Sam stood up and wrapped her arms around Helene gently. "I'll always love you, Helene. Always."

~~~

Sam calmly said goodnight to her parents as if her entire world hadn't been thrown by the events of the last few days and went up to her suite. She made sure the door to her wing was cracked open, as well as the door to her suite. This way, she would be able to hear when her parents went to bed. She'd learned that trick long ago when she wanted to sneak down to Helene's apartment at night without her parents finding out.

While she waited, she meticulously cleaned up the broken glass in her bathroom. Next time she'd take her anger out on something less breakable. Within the hour, she heard the unmistakable sounds of her parents making their way up the stairs to their suite. She waited ten more agonizing minutes to be sure they weren't going to come out, and then she tiptoed down the carpeted hallway to the dark stairwell. She froze when she heard a noise from her parents' rooms. She held her breath, praying no one would come out. Her prayers were answered, and after waiting another quiet moment, she padded down the stairs to the door leading to Helene's apartment. As expected, the door was locked, so Sam pulled out the key Helene had given her. Sam wasn't sure if her parents even knew she had a key to Helene's apartment.

Sam unlocked the door and let herself in. She cursed herself for not thinking about bringing a flashlight but then remembered she still had her cell phone in her pocket. She powered it on and used the light of the display to guide her way to Helene's bedroom. She wasn't exactly sure what she was looking for, but she needed to find more clues about who Helene was and how she'd gotten pregnant by her father eighteen years before.

She walked into Helene's usually neat bedroom, surprised by the disarray. Clothes were strewn all over the bed and chair. Half a dozen boxes were filled with clothes and knick-knacks and other things. Helene had been packing.

"You really are leaving me, aren't you?" Sam said to the empty room.

Sam had been devastated when she thought she'd lost Helene in the car accident, but now, seeing tangible proof that she truly was losing her, something snapped in her head. Losing Helene twice in one week and learning that both their lives had been a lie was one big cosmic April fool's joke.

Sam steeled her chin in true Payton fashion and didn't give in to her anger. Even though no one around her seemed to know how to tell the truth, Sam vowed right then and there that she was going to break that legacy. She was going to start telling the truth about everything.

She hit the message button on her cell phone and entered Susie's, Marlee's, and Lisa's names. "Screw it," Sam said out loud and added Ronnie's name to the list. She wrote, "I'm kicking down this closet door, ladies! Take me to that big old gay pride festival in October!"

With a determined grin, she hit the send button.

Chapter 23
Stealing Second

A month later, Sam pulled the Sebring into a parking spot and threw the gear shift into park. She sat for a moment with the engine idling, gathering up the courage to turn off the car and get out. She remembered the last time she sat in her idling car, wondering if she should get out. That had been in September, the day after she found out that Helene, her beloved nanny, was actually her biological mother.

Ever since she'd found out, Sam had lived alone with the secret. She hadn't told Susie. She hadn't told Marlee. She hadn't even told Lisa, and she told Lisa everything. The one thing she did tell her friends was that Helene was moving out at the end of the year, so naturally, they did their best to cheer her up on a regular basis. Friends were one thing, but the betrayers she lived with were another. She didn't tell her father or the woman she had called Mother for eighteen years that she knew about their secret. She didn't mention a thing to Helene and, in fact, barely spoke to her. And she certainly didn't tell Dr. Boyle when her mother forced her to keep the appointments with him. Sam had been to enough therapy sessions in her life to know she was staying in control of the situation by not telling anyone about the dirty little Payton family secret.

She and Dr. Boyle spent most of their sessions talking about Helene leaving, and Sam spoke honestly about the hole in her life it would create. They also spent some of the time talking about the play at school. He reassured her she could continue her role as the fiddler if that was what she wanted to do. He thought it was a healthy outlet for her, and he would reassure her parents it was okay for her to continue. And, much to Sam's relief, he was going to tell them that she had an actual actor-on-the-stage role in the play. At least one good thing would come out of the sessions.

Sam took a deep breath. She didn't want to think about life back at the mansion. She checked her pocket for her cell phone but then remembered. She'd left the stupid thing at home, so her father wouldn't know where she was.

She looked up at the innocent-looking brick building that housed the Clarksonville Community College auditorium. She closed her eyes for a minute, knowing that if she turned off the engine and got out of the car, her life would substantially change forever. It wasn't only her fear talking; people knew who she was. A lot of people. Once she stepped out of the car, everyone would know.

But no, she'd done enough hiding. Mother, Daddy, and sometimes Helene had told her what to be and how to act for far too long. She picked her hand up and reached to turn off the key in the ignition. Her hand stopped halfway to the key. With a pounding heart, she felt as if she were stealing second base—leaping off first base, adrenaline pumping, racing toward second, not knowing if she'd be called safe or out. But that was softball. This was life. Her life. And if going into that auditorium was a bad decision, then so be it. She'd take her chances.

Sam yanked the key out of the ignition, flung off her seat belt, and heaved open the door. She took a cleansing breath of the crisp October air and, with determined steps, made her way to the auditorium.

The lobby was blessedly empty, but the unmistakable sounds of an impassioned speech came from within the auditorium. What were the chances that she, someone virtually everybody in Clarksonville County knew, would be able to sneak into the auditorium and find her friends without anybody noticing? *Slim to none,* she thought as she steeled her nerves. She eased open the heavy door and groaned at the well-lit auditorium. It was packed. The woman at the podium looked to be somewhere in her mid-thirties and wore a tailored business suit. Her strawberry blond hair was pulled back in a bun. She took one look at Sam and faltered in her speech.

It seemed like every one of the over three hundred people in the auditorium turned to see who had made the speaker stop in mid-sentence. Sam was used to being recognized, but not like this. As cool as she could, she kept her head high, her back straight, and scanned the seats for Lisa. After a hundred years, the speaker cleared her throat and continued.

A micro-moment later, a small voice called, "Sam."

Sam whipped her head to the left and was relieved to spot Lisa, Susie, Marlee, and Ronnie waving to her from the middle of a row. She hoped the relief she felt wasn't screaming from her face. Lisa motioned to the saved empty seat next to her, and Sam couldn't get there fast enough. There it was. Lisa's smile. The smile that said everything was going to be okay. Sam smiled back and then nodded to Susie, Marlee, and Ronnie. Marlee's smile was sweet; Ronnie's and Susie's were smug. Ah, but who cared. She had broken through her fear and had the support of her amazing friends.

Susie leaned clear over Marlee and Lisa to whisper at Sam, "I thought you were going to chicken out."

"Me, too." Sam grimaced.

Susie whacked her on the arm for good measure and then slid back into her seat.

"I'm proud of you," Lisa whispered into Sam's ear.

"You are?"

Lisa nodded. "Big step." She smiled that awesome smile again and then turned her attention to the podium.

Sam took a slow breath to calm her thundering heart and snuck a peek around her. No one was staring at her anymore. They seemed to be riveted by the speaker.

"Don't let yourselves be victimized," the speaker boomed. "Don't be silenced. Let your voices be heard." She took a moment to scan the audience. "I've listened to countless gays and lesbians during my campaign, and my heart goes out to you. For years the LGBTQ community has hidden behind the fear of rejection, behind the fear of ostracization, but no more. You now have the right to marry in New York State."

The audience, Sam and her friends included, broke into thunderous applause. They leaped to their feet for a standing ovation as if the speaker had single-handedly passed the law herself.

She nodded with them until the applauders regained their seats. "But now we have a bigger fight. We have to push for federal recognition of your marriages."

Another round of thunderous applause erupted.

The speaker shook her head as if gathering her thoughts. "You know," her voice softened, "most people are ignorant about who you are. Look, I'm not making excuses, but people believe the stereotypes they see on TV—those carefully chosen media images of extreme behaviors. To be honest, people are scared. Did you know that anger is simply a manifestation of fear? Look, I can't imagine what it's like—living under a cloak of lies and deception, not being able to be who you truly are. You're not hurting anybody, are you?"

"No!" the audience boomed back.

"Is loving someone wrong?"

"No!"

"Hell, no!" the speaker said, and the audience burst into applause.

"Who is she?" Sam nodded toward the speaker with her chin. *I like her.*

"That's Asa Crete. She's the assembly member from our district. She's the only Democrat assembly member in the entire North Country."

"That's right. I remember her campaign." Sam also remembered how pissed her father had been when the Republican candidate he backed lost the election to Crete. Her father had dragged Sam to a few fund-raising events to show that his candidate had the support of the young people. Not that Sam supported the candidate in the least. In fact, she thought he was a puppet doing everything her father wanted.

"You weren't here when she started her speech," Lisa said. "She said she was straight but not narrow."

"Cool." Sam nodded and sat back.

"So," Assembly Member Crete continued, "remember this. Don't let anyone tell you how to live. Demand respect!" She pounded the podium. "The respect everybody deserves. No second class!" She pounded the podium one last time, and the audience leaped to its collective feet and cheered.

A chant of "No second class" rippled through the auditorium for several empowering moments.

Sam couldn't believe how good it felt to be among other people who were like her. It was amazing.

Assembly Member Crete thanked the crowd and sat down in the guest-of-honor seat on the stage. A man who looked to be in his forties got up behind the podium. Sam liked his rainbow tie-dyed "Got Pride?" t-shirt. He invited everyone to enjoy the rest of the day visiting the vendors, listening to the bands, and watching the film festival that would start in an hour.

Sam and her friends filed out of their row and followed the crowd to the quad. They moved off to the side to get away from the mass of people.

Sam hugged Ronnie first. He looked stylish in black pants and boots, a white linen shirt, and a tight leather jacket. He wore his hair spiked short and had broken out his Adam Lambert guyliner.

"Glad to see you finally kicked down that closet door, Samantha Rose."

"Kicked it down? No." Sam laughed. "It's more like opening it up a crack to see what's out here."

"I'm still proud of you."

"I'm proud of all of us. I'm glad you could meet us here, Ronnie."

"Well," Ronnie said. "I don't have any gay friends except you guys. But look at me, I'm a veritable lez-magnet."

Sam laughed and nudged him with her shoulder. She could tell he was nervous about the whole gay pride event, too.

"Hey, *gringa*," Susie said, "would you mind if Marlee and I held hands? Marlee thinks we shouldn't because it'll make you uncomfortable."

"Go for it, girls."

"Really?"

Sam nodded, and Susie reached for Marlee's hand.

"Yeah, you heard that speaker. 'No more hiding.'"

"This is huge for us, too." Marlee lifted Susie's hand in hers. "We've never held hands in public before."

"C'mon, let's check out these booths." Susie led the way toward the vendors in the quad.

Sam leaned against Lisa and whispered, "Do you want to hold hands, too?"

"We shouldn't."

"Why not?" Sam was ready for that step, but Samantha Rose most definitely wasn't.

Lisa's cheeks turned the cutest shade of pink. "Let's not out you before your time, eh? You haven't even told your parents yet."

Sam nodded, more than a little relieved, and fell into step with Lisa and Ronnie, following the trail Susie and Marlee blazed through the crowd.

"Hey, Sus," Sam called, "hang on." She stepped up to the Rainbow Council's Youth Alliance booth.

An older woman with short dark hair handed Sam a pamphlet. Lisa looked over Sam's shoulder as she opened it.

"The Youth Alliance meets every other Tuesday right here on campus," the woman said. "We're meeting this Tuesday. Feel free to join us."

"Thank you." Sam was about to move away when a guy with

purple spiked hair sidled up to the table. He looked like he was their age, but Sam didn't recognize him from East Valley High School.

"Lord, the rumors are true. It is you. Samantha Rose Payton, you have to go to our next YA meeting. It would be so cool if you joined us." He fanned himself as if he were a southern belle. "I can't believe you're here. Is this your girlfriend?" He leaned closer to Lisa and said, "You should come, too. Everyone is welcome. Bring all your friends." The sweep of his hand included Susie, Marlee, and Ronnie. He leaned closer to Sam and whispered out of the side of his mouth, "And you must introduce me to this gorgeous creature." He flashed Ronnie a devilish smile.

By this time, Sam had gone from flustered to amused. "Seeing as I don't know your name, you'll have to introduce yourself."

"Where are my manners?" He bowed in front of Ronnie. "My name, sir, is Jordan Saunders."

"Pleased to make your acquaintance. My name is Ronald Alesi."

Sam exchanged a smile with her friends. "They were made for each other," she whispered.

"Ronald, I can show you around if you like." Without waiting for a response from Ronnie, Jordan turned to the woman behind the table. "Anne, you don't need me for a while, do you?" He shook his head emphatically as if hypnotizing her to agree with him.

"Go. Have fun," Anne said.

"You girls don't mind?" Ronnie pleaded to Sam with his eyes. It was obvious he was intrigued by the spiky-haired Jordan.

"Go. Have fun," Sam echoed.

Ronnie mouthed, "Thank you," and took off with Jordan.

"See, girls?" Anne said. "There goes proof positive that you're not alone. There are people you can talk to who've been through what you're going through." She pointed to a phone number on the back of the pamphlet. "That's our hotline number if anybody needs help. We're all in this boat together."

"Thanks," Sam said.

"Yes, thank you," Lisa added.

They turned away from the booth and headed back into the crowds.

"Ooh, funnel cake," Marlee said with glee. "C'mon, girls."

They followed the heady smell of fried dough and powdered sugar. The funnel cake cart sat in the middle of a myriad of other food carts, and Marlee decreed it was time to eat. After lunch, with shared funnel cakes for dessert, Sam patted her stomach and groaned. "Funnel cakes always sound like a good idea—"

"But so aren't," Marlee finished Sam's sentence. She looked a little green. "Next time, guys, turn me toward the broccoli cart."

"You don't like broccoli," Susie said.

"Exactly." Marlee held her stomach and groaned.

"C'mon," Sam said, "we have a whole 'nother section of booths to check out." Sam led the way underneath a giant rainbow balloon arch.

"Speaking of checking out," Susie said, "you've got some fans checking you out, Sam." She nodded her head toward a group of women taking pictures of Sam with their cell phones.

Sam turned away. "God, I hate that. Can't they just leave me alone?"

"You said it might be like this," Lisa said, "but I had no idea. It's crazy."

"I'm sorry, you guys." Sam turned away from another bunch of people taking pictures.

"Hey, look," Susie said. "This booth will cheer you up."

"Oh, hell no, Sus." Sam laughed. Leave it to Susie to find the Safe Sex booth.

"Okay, chicken." Susie pulled Marlee along by the hand. "We'll check it out and get back to you."

Marlee grimaced over her shoulder with a "help me" plea on her face.

Sam and Lisa laughed, and then Sam guided Lisa toward a vendor that sold pride souvenirs. Sam wanted to get Lisa something. They looked at earrings and necklaces, but Lisa didn't seem enamored by anything, so they meandered toward a section that had rings.

Sam wanted to hold hands with Lisa but couldn't bring herself to do it. She was jealous of everyone who felt free enough to hold hands or walk with their arms wrapped around each other. It was pathetic, really. If she couldn't bring herself to hold hands with Lisa when they were surrounded by gay people, when would she ever be able to?

"Do you see anything you like?" Sam asked, changing the subject in her head.

"You know you don't have to buy me things all the time, baby."

"I know. I just like to."

"How about these?" Lisa tried on an inexpensive mood ring.

"A mood ring?" Sam couldn't help the smile creeping up her face.

"Yeah, let's each get one, and then we can think of each other every time we look at them." Lisa smiled at Sam sweetly.

Sam couldn't speak past the emotion in her throat, so she simply nodded. There were so many thoughts tumbling through her head. She wanted to say to Lisa, right there at the pride festival where everyone could hear, *You've changed my life. You fill my heart like I never thought anyone could, and I'm ashamed that I still lie about your existence.*

Sam flicked a tear away, wishing she had the nerve to voice what she felt. She left Lisa thumbing through some pamphlets and went to pay for the rings.

"Samantha Rose," a male voice called.

Thinking it was Ronnie, Sam looked up but cursed herself for doing it. A photographer from the Clarksonville Courier snapped her picture. A reporter was right behind him with a tape recorder and a microphone.

Chapter 24
I'm Still Me

Sam's phone sat propped up on her desk. She had it set on speakerphone as she rosined her violin bow. Opening night for the school play was only five weeks away, and she wanted to practice a few of the songs after she hung up with Lisa.

"I had such a great day yesterday," Sam said.

"Me, too," Lisa purred. "I'm looking at my new ring right now."

Sam put the bow down and held up her left hand. "Me, too. It's black."

"Sorry."

"That's okay. Talking to you will make it green again. Or does blue mean you're in love?"

"I don't remember." Lisa laughed. "I can't find the paper."

"I've got mine. Hang on." Sam put her bow down and reached into her top desk drawer. She pulled out a bunch of pamphlets she'd gotten from the festival. She rifled through them and found the slip of paper with the list of mood ring colors. "Here it is. Blue means love. Black means anxious, and green means mixed emotions."

"Mine's blue right now," Lisa said.

"Aww, that's nice." Sam laughed when she noticed another pamphlet sitting on top of the stack.

"Why are you laughing?"

"I'm looking at the pamphlet Susie got for us yesterday. 'Guarding Against STDs: Lesbian Edition.'"

"You kept that?"

"I didn't mean to. I forgot they were in my jacket pocket when I got home. I don't know how Susie had the nerve to go to that booth in the first place."

"She was a woman on a mission, eh?"

"Yeah." Sam scanned the pamphlet. "At least this one tells us about the risks for two girls gettin' it on."

"Sam!"

"Does that embarrass you?"

"A little."

"Sorry. You want to talk about something else?"

Lisa was quiet for a moment and then whispered, "I never heard of dental dams before."

"Me neither."

"How would you get them? Ask your dentist? I don't think so."

Sam chuckled. "According to Susie, it's just a piece of latex. I guess you could get latex gloves and cut them into squares, right?"

"Or cut up a male condom, maybe," Lisa said. "And how about those pouchy female condom thingies she showed us in those pictures? They were fascinating."

"Yeah, hetero women can be in control of their own bodies now, you know? If they don't want to take birth control or whatever."

"Yeah," Lisa said.

There was an odd silence on Lisa's end for a moment which made Sam worry. "Lisa?"

"Hmm?"

"Are you worried about, you know, what we did at the lake

house?" Sam hoped Lisa wasn't having regrets about the two amazing nights they'd spent together.

"No." It was only one word, but Lisa didn't sound one hundred percent sure.

"It sounds like there's a 'but' coming."

"I think it's good to know about these things. To be safe. I mean, we should know all the options."

"Yeah, it *is* good to know because I plan to be with you for a long, long time." Sam smiled inside and out.

"Same."

They were quiet for a moment until Lisa said, "I have news."

"News?"

"Remember how I emailed Coach Greer about maybe applying to Rockville University next year to play softball?"

"Yeah."

"She emailed me back this morning."

"What did she say?"

"She hoped I'd be back at camp next summer—"

"Without a broken hand this time," Sam said.

"Exactly." Lisa chuckled.

"And, hopefully, without Tara anywhere nearby."

"She graduated," Lisa said. "And shouldn't be anywhere near Rockville next summer or ever again."

"Here's hoping," Sam said, keeping her tone light. She had no wish for Lisa to be anywhere near her ex-girlfriend ever again.

"Yeah, right?" Lisa said. "Anyway, Coach Greer said she was counting on me to apply to Rockville and play ball for her."

"Really? That's so cool."

"That's not all she said."

"What else?"

"Full-ride," Lisa gushed.

"Scholarship?"

"Yeah."

"No freakin' way!" Sam squealed. "Lisa, that's amazing. I'm so happy for you."

"Thanks. It kind of takes the pressure off my family. She said it was too soon to bank on the scholarship, but she hoped to keep a spot open for me when the time comes."

"That is so awesome. We have to celebrate." Sam was quiet before adding, "My parents want me to go to Wellesley College in Massachusetts. It's a women's college."

"They still have those?"

"Mm hmm. Mother—" Sam choked on the word. "Um, she went to Wellesley and wants me to go there, too. I'd be a legacy or something."

"What does that mean?"

"It means you're the child of someone who went to that school."

"Do you want to go to Wellesley? Massachusetts is kind of far away."

"I know," Sam said.

"If you don't go there, where would you want to go?"

"Why does everybody keep asking me that?"

"Duh?"

"Because it's *my* life?" Sam sighed and picked up the pile of pamphlets. She tucked the STD pamphlet in the middle of the stack and shoved them toward the back of the drawer.

"You know they have a music department at Rockville," Lisa said. "Supposedly a good one."

"Yeah, I know. I went there for the All-State Orchestra Festival last year. It's an award-winning department, according to them, anyway."

"Mm hmm," Lisa said. "They have a pre-med program there, too."

"Pre-med?" Sam sat straight up in her desk chair. "No way! You're seriously thinking about becoming a doctor?"

"Maybe. I don't know. You were the one who said I'd be good at it."

"And you totally would be."

"Sam, if you went to Rockville with me, we could play softball on the same team. For three years anyway. We could live in the same dorm, too."

"Whoa, that would be totally awesome." Sam chuckled. "Oh, my God. I just said, 'totally awesome.' The debutante has morphed into a surfer dudette."

Lisa laughed, and Sam loved the sound of it. She also loved that Lisa was planning their future together.

"Ah, it's a nice dream, baby," Sam said, "but I don't think my parents will let me go to Rockville."

"I know." Lisa sighed into the phone. "So, has there been any fallout from those stupid reporters yet?"

"Nah, not yet."

"They were so aggressive."

"No kidding, but I think we handled them okay. Don't you?"

"By running away?" Lisa laughed.

"Yeah, good thing we could run faster than they could. They never did find us in the dark film festival."

"It took a while for Susie and Marlee to find us, too."

"But they did after you texted them twelve times," Sam said.

"You know, I can't believe you forgot your phone at home like that. You must have been nervous yesterday."

"Yeah," Sam said. *Something like that.* "It's nerve-wracking waiting for your parents to explode."

"Are your parents really gonna freak out?" Lisa's voice softened.

"Probably. And if they do, I want to say happy fifth anniversary to you now."

"Thanks, baby, but it's not until Friday."

"I may not be here." Sam seriously wouldn't put it past her parents to box her up and send her to a Swiss boarding school.

"Don't say stuff like that."

"I'm sorry. I guess it's just that I'm not too hopeful about their reaction."

"Sam?"

"Hmm?"

"Remember that no matter what happens, you're made of tougher stuff than you think. Coach Gellar told you that."

"If you say so."

As if on cue, the intercom on her desk sprang to life. "Samantha Rose," her father bellowed. "Get down here right now."

Sam lunged for the talk button on the intercom. "Yes, sir. Be right down." She released the button and tried to dislodge her heart that had jumped into her throat. She held the phone away from the intercom as if her father could still hear her and whispered to Lisa, "The proverbial shit is hitting the fan as we speak. I have to go. Wish me luck."

"Oh, geez. Good luck," Lisa whispered back. "Call me when it's over. I love you, baby."

"Same."

Sam hung up with Lisa and tucked her cell phone into her jeans pocket. She tried to breathe to calm her nerves, but it didn't help. She was on the verge of hyperventilating. She didn't run down the stairs to the main floor, but she didn't exactly stroll either. It was best not to keep Gerald Payton waiting. Once on the main floor, she followed the sound of her father's pacing and stopped in the doorway of his study. As expected, her mother was sitting in one of the two tufted-back leather chairs. Sam was surprised to see that she'd been crying. The sight disarmed Sam enough that she jumped when her father spoke.

"What is the meaning of this young lady?" Her father held up the local section of the Sunday Clarksonville Courier.

Sam swallowed hard. At least Lisa wasn't in the half-page photo. Sam, on the other hand, had been caught red-handed. Rainbow flags and gay-sloganed t-shirts surrounded her in the photo. She couldn't claim someone had photoshopped them in. She thought about saying she was only there to support a friend, but that would be selling out. Something shifted inside. She was tired of hiding who she was.

"Samantha Rose?" Her father's face was turning bright red. "I'm waiting for an answer."

Before Sam could answer, her mother blurted, "Why are you associating with those kinds of people?"

Those kinds of people? Sam was so stunned by the question that she couldn't formulate a response.

Sam's mother must have taken her silence as some kind of answer because she put shaking hands over her face and cried again.

Her father slapped the newspaper on his desk. "Sit," he

commanded and pointed to the empty leather chair. Sam did as she was told. "Are you like those people?"

He can't say the word either. The word is gay, *Daddy! Gay!* she shouted in her mind. *And, yes, I am.* See? Her life was already changing because she'd gotten out of her damned car and gone to the pride festival.

"I'm waiting."

Sam wanted to say she was more than *like* those people because she *was* one of those people. She couldn't figure out how to say the words, so she simply nodded.

"This is the last thing I expected from you. What in God's name makes you believe you're this way?"

This way? "I just am." Her voice sounded weak and mousy to her own ears, but at least she'd had the courage to say the words.

"This can't be true," Sam's mother said. "It's not like you to defy us like this."

"Defy you?" Sam was confused.

"It's those softball friends of yours," Sam's mother continued. "They did this to you. They brainwashed you."

Sam burst out laughing. She couldn't help it.

"That's it, young lady," her father said. "You're grounded. No car. No friends. Rolando will drive you to school and back. You can stay for those blasted play rehearsals, but then he will drive you straight home."

"Straight," Sam murmured to herself with a chuckle.

"Give me your phone." Her father held out his hand.

Sam reached into her pocket and pulled out her phone. "Are you sure you want to take this?" *You won't be able to track my movements if you do.* She held the phone just out of reach. Her heart was pounding. She had never ever defied her father like that. She waved her phone from side to side, taunting him.

His eyes flamed in anger at her defiance. "Phone. Now."

"Whatever." Sam dropped the phone into her father's outstretched hand.

"What made you this way?" Sam's mother asked. She dabbed at the corner of her eyes with a tissue.

"It's not a disease, you know," Sam said calmly. She took a breath to find her resolve. "Maybe you should ask what it's been like for me all these years—growing up different. Hiding who I am. Some people even say it's genetic."

"Well, you didn't get it from me," her mother said.

A month before, Sam would've thought the statement was uttered out of sheer arrogance, but she knew better. She knew the family secret now. If it truly was a genetic thing, then Sam's mother was right. Sam couldn't have "gotten it" from her.

Sam cleared her throat and said, "I don't know how to make you understand this, make you understand *me*." Her nerves jangled underneath her calm exterior. "I'm sorry if I'm a disappointment to you both, but this is who I am." An odd sort of peace was taking over her as she spoke. Maybe it was that 'tougher stuff' Lisa insisted she had. She decided to go for broke. "I've never been attracted to boys. Ever." She paused for a moment taking in her parents, who looked both confused and angry. She decided to go for broke. "Perhaps if either of you had been present during my childhood, you would have realized that."

"Don't speak to your mother that way," her father roared.

Sam leaped to her feet and roared right back, "She's not my mother, and you know it."

There was a gasp behind her. Helene stood in the doorway, eyes wide, a hand over her mouth.

Sam held her ground and stared down at her father. Denial flickered across his face, but then his shoulders slumped. He sighed in defeat. Sam remained rooted to the spot, hands balled into fists, mouth firm.

Her father sat down hard in the leather chair that Sam had just vacated. He looked down at his hands, obviously unnerved. Sam's mother pleaded with her eyes for him to do something, anything that would make this horrible situation go away.

The ticking of the antique grandfather clock grew as loud as the silence.

Sam broke the quiet first. "You all lied to me for eighteen years, and I lied to you about who I really am. I can't live this way anymore. I'm sick of the lies."

"Samantha Rose," her father said softly. "C'mon, Kitten. You're in shock."

"No, I was in shock a month ago when I saw my birth certificate, but not now. I don't know how to prove to you that, even though I'm in love with a girl, I'm still me. Just me. Same old me. Except—" Sam looked at Helene in the doorway. "Except now I'm not sure who any of you are." Sam bolted past Helene and ran up the stairs to her suite, locking every door behind her as she went.

Chapter 25
Mother and Daughter

Mondays had never been one of Sam's favorite days, but the Monday after the pride festival was turning out to be the worst in the history of Mondays. Everyone at East Valley High School had apparently seen the picture in the Clarksonville Courier or had heard about it.

The bell rang, ending her fourth-period ethics class, and before she could stand up, Ryan Dunham was by her side, trapping her in the desk. He was standing so close to her that the hem of his varsity letterman's jacket touched her shoulder.

"Go out with me, Samantha Rose." Ryan put both hands on his hips. "I can be a real man for you." His friends laughed behind him.

"Move," Sam said quietly.

"C'mon, one date."

Out of the corner of her eye, Sam saw Mrs. Sherman conspicuously ignoring what was going on at Sam's desk. Apparently, teachers didn't always know how to stand up to bullies either.

"Back off, Ryan. You're being an idiot." Using all her pent-up anger, Sam put both hands on his chest and shoved him out of the way. He stumbled backward into a desk in the adjacent row.

"Ooh," Ryan's friends taunted.

Sam bolted out of her chair, grabbing her backpack as she went. She paused long enough to send her teacher a what-the-hell glare and then headed into the crowded hallway, where she met up with more jeers and taunts from other classmates.

"Look! It's the 'gina diner!" some creep said with a laugh as he passed by.

"What a dyke!" a junior girl goaded.

"She hasn't even denied it," another junior girl added. "Can you imagine?"

All morning, she heard the words *dyke, lezzie, rug-muncher,* and a host of others thrown at her. Even classmates that had been friendly in the past took the opportunity to knock her down. Sam didn't let any of them see that their arrows hit the mark. Where was that tougher stuff Lisa and Coach Geller said she had?

She steeled herself in true Payton style and blazed a lonely trail to the cafeteria. She locked eyes with Susie, her lifeline, and ignored the rest of the world.

She wasn't sure what to make of the crowd at her lunch table, but she forged on since they looked like friends, not foes. Abby sat at the table next to her new boyfriend, Pete. Rachel was in her usual seat. Ronnie, Alivia, and Karl sat at the table, too. Sam wasn't expecting them to be there, but she'd take it. She threw her backpack on the floor and fell into a chair, exhausted.

"How are you holding up?" Susie asked.

"People suck," Sam said. She rested her chin on her fist. She was so tired. If she had her car at school, she would have been long gone.

"Welcome to my world," Ronnie said. "These jerks around here are ignorant, you know? Just like that speaker said on Saturday. Hey world, we're here. We're queer. Get over it already."

"I can't believe how mean they are," Sam said. She looked at Abby, Pete, and Rachel. "Thanks for the support, you guys, but you don't have to hang here if you don't want to. I'm the new pariah if you hadn't noticed."

"We're your friends," Abby said. "And your teammates. We're not abandoning you at the first sign of trouble."

"Here, here," Karl said, and the others at the table echoed. "Tell them to get lives."

"Thanks, guys." Sam touched Karl's letterman's jacket. "At least not all jocks are jerks."

"Thanks." Karl's cheeks tinged red, and Alivia smiled at him.

"You know," Abby continued, "I always wondered why you didn't have a boyfriend. I thought maybe the guys around here were intimidated by your family name."

"That's probably true, too," Sam said with a chuckle.

"And Lisa," Abby continued, "is she your…"

"Yes." Sam nodded.

"Ah, so many things make sense now." Abby nodded and then added, "You two make a great couple."

"Thanks." Sam felt her cheeks get warm. "God, what a nightmare this is. I didn't want to come out of the closet in such a grand fashion." She closed her eyes for a moment wishing she could be somewhere else.

"You know, Sam," Abby said, "I think people are reacting this way because you were so far above the rest of us."

"I never—"

"I know, but let me finish. Your parents are like the king and queen of the North Country."

"Payton Valley, you mean?" Sam couldn't help her sarcastic

tone, even though she knew Abby was just trying to help.

Abby nodded. "Yeah, something like that. But right or wrong, you've been untouchable, better than everybody else, above reproach."

Sam frowned.

"In their eyes, I mean," Abby was quick to add. "We know you're cool, right guys?"

Heads around the table nodded.

"And now we find out you're as human as the rest of us mere mortals." Abby grinned, letting Sam know she was on her side.

"What she means is," Ronnie said, "the mighty have fallen, and these ignorant assholes see you as an equal or, let's be honest, less than equal."

"I've never—"

Susie's hand on her arm silenced her. "We know, *gringa*. You're vulnerable right now. They're going in for the kill. All of us at this table agree that you're an awesome person. We're all here to help you. We're here for each other, okay?"

"Has anyone bothered *you* today?" Sam asked Susie, hoping she hadn't taken heat by being her friend.

"Not too much. I'm okay. Don't worry about me." Susie squeezed Sam's arm gently and then pulled her cell phone out of her pocket. "Now, in about three minutes, this phone is going to ring, and it's going to be for you."

"Lisa?" Sam's eyes grew wide.

Susie nodded. "She has lunch now, too."

"You're the best."

"I know," Susie said. "I texted Marlee and Lisa this morning after you told me what happened with your parents."

Except nobody knows all the sordid details, Sam thought. "Thanks, Sus."

"Hey, what're friends for? Right, guys?"

"Absolutely," Alivia said. "We're here for you, Samantha Rose."

"I don't think Samantha Rose exists anymore, so call me Sam from now on, okay?"

"Okay," Alivia said.

Rachel cleared her throat and said, "How about we declare an official moratorium on the name Samantha Rose, and only those that are true friends get to call you Sam?"

"I'm all for it. Thanks, guys." Sam blinked back tears. She hadn't been expecting such unconditional support.

"Since there's absolutely no privacy at this school," Susie held up her car keys, "you're going to go sit in my car and talk to your girlfriend until the bell rings to end lunch. Okay?"

"Thanks, Sus." Sam stood up. "Thanks, everybody." She blew out a sigh, shut her ears, and headed toward the side door of the cafeteria.

~~~

Sam waited until her parents went to bed and then snuck down the stairs to Helene's apartment. This time Helene was home. She knocked lightly on the door, almost hoping Helene wouldn't answer. The door opened within seconds.

"I was hoping you'd come by." Helene opened the door wide enough for Sam to enter.

"Sorry it took me a whole day. Well, a whole month, actually."

Helene closed the door behind them and led the way to the

kitchen. She gestured for Sam to sit at the table. "Canada Dry or tea?" Her own freshly made cup of tea sat steeping on the counter.

"Tea, please."

"The usual?"

Sam nodded and then, without warning, started to cry. A month's worth of torment flooded out of her.

A familiar arm went around her shoulders. "Shh, shh," Helene pulled her close.

Sam let herself be comforted until she ran out of tears. "Sorry."

Helene brushed the hair away from Sam's face. "I have so much to tell you."

"Not yet, okay? I don't think I'm quite ready."

"Me neither." Helene laughed, which made Sam smile. "Let me get your tea." Helene stood up and pulled out a box of Sleepytime tea. "Five lumps?"

Sam nodded.

"We haven't done this in a while."

"We've both been busy." And now you're leaving me.

Helene poured the hot water from the tea kettle into a cup and put a tea bag in. She set it down in front of Sam and pushed the box of sugar cubes and a spoon toward her. Sam shook out five cubes and dunked them in her cup. She couldn't help thinking it might be the last time she and Helene shared their stolen nighttime ritual.

"How was school today?"

"Pfft." Sam wiped at her eyes, willing herself not to cry again. "They're a bunch of jerks."

"Rough, huh?"

Sam nodded.

"That's not how I wanted things to go for you."

"Helene, will I ever see you again?" Sam looked at her teacup, not wanting to make eye contact.

"Yes. Of course, you will, but you won't be able to cross the border by yourself until you're eighteen."

"Unless a parent accompanies me." Sam looked up shyly.

Helene's smile softened. "When did you find out?"

"A month ago. When you were in the hospital. I was looking for something in that duffel bag you call a purse."

"And you found your birth certificate. That's why you fainted."

Sam nodded.

"Do your friends know?"

Sam shook her head. "I couldn't bring myself to tell them. I was in shock. I still am." Sam sipped her tea as silence overtook the room. She set her cup down gently and asked, "Are you really my mother?"

Helene nodded.

Sam swallowed against the growing lump in her throat. Her insides quivered. She didn't want to ask the question but had to. "How?" She fixed her gaze on the teacup.

Helene stood up and faced the sink, her back to Sam. "Your parents should be telling you this."

"Helene, c'mon. For eighteen years, you made me think you were simply my kind and loving nanny, and now I find out you're my mother, and you can't tell me how?"

Helene's head drooped. She, too, bore a heavy burden. She turned around slowly and leaned back against the sink. "Your parents found me in Montréal."

"Found you?"

"Your mother couldn't have children—"

269

"She must have been devastated." Sam felt bad for the woman she had called Mother for eighteen years.

"I think she was. That's why they looked for a surrogate."

"And that was you." *So, it wasn't an accident. I wasn't an accident.* "How did they find you exactly?"

Helene sat again. Both cups of tea went untouched. "I was eighteen and had moved out on my own. My mother—"

"My grandmother?"

"Yes, I guess so. She died a few years ago."

"I'm sorry, Helene. I didn't know."

"Thank you."

"And your father?"

Helene frowned. "My father left us right after my sister Chantal was born. I guess he wasn't too keen on being a family man. He drank himself to death a few years later."

"You never talked about your family before. I feel stupid that I never asked about them."

"You did ask. When you were little, but I never gave you many details. You stopped asking after a while. So, anyway, my mother was having trouble raising the two of us in the small town where we lived, so as soon as I could, I moved to the big city."

"Montréal."

"Yes. I rented a room from two girls who had a three-bedroom apartment. I got a job waitressing and sent as much money to my mother as I could spare. That whole apartment thing didn't work out. The other two always *forgot* to pay their share of the rent." Helene made air quotes around the word forgot.

"And I bet they weren't as neat as you are either."

"No, they weren't." Helene chuckled. "I moved into a studio

apartment on my own. My waitressing job paid for the rent and not much else. Luckily Vinny, the restaurant owner, took pity on me and let me eat for free, but there wasn't a lot of money left over to pay bills after I sent money home. I had to choose between paying the electric or the water bill."

As Sam listened to Helene tell the tale of her difficult early adult life, she felt guilty about the riches she took for granted. She took in Helene's blond hair, and minus the streaks of gray, it was the same color as hers. And Helene's facial features—they were so much like her own. Sam realized with a start that her life could have been incredibly different. It was a sobering thought. She took a sip of her now cooling tea, not really tasting the sugary concoction.

"After a while," Helene continued, "I knew I had to do something. Then one day, a regular customer of mine made me an offer."

"Daddy?"

"No, it was someone that worked for him."

"Oh." Sam wondered how much money Helene's surrogate services had been worth but figured that was one of life's questions she was better off not knowing the answer to. "He told you about becoming a surrogate mother?"

Helene nodded. "Except it's illegal in the Province of Québec."

"How about in New York?"

"It's illegal here, too."

Sam's eyes grew wide. She wasn't legally born.

"Your father has wide influence, Samantha Rose. You know that. What your father wants, your father gets."

"But doesn't everybody think Mother is my biological mother?"

Helene nodded slowly.

"How did you guys pull that one off? And why are you still here after eighteen years? Why did they keep you around? I don't mean to be blunt, but my father easily rids himself of potential problems. And I'm not sure I want to know, but how did you get pregnant in the first place?"

"Whoa, slow down with the questions. You always were such an inquisitive child." Helene laughed and got up. She went to the cupboard and pulled out a box of shortbread cookies.

"Ooh, my favorite."

"I know. We need sustenance because I think we're going to be here for a while. More tea?"

Sam shook her head, and Helene sat back down.

"Okay." Helene opened the box of cookies. "Let me try to answer your questions. You've earned that right."

"Start at the beginning. Wherever that is." As perverse as it sounded, Sam enjoyed their exchange. She was going to miss Helene fiercely when she went back to Montréal. When her insides had finally stopped shaking, she reached for a cookie, amazed she could eat anything at all.

"Oh, my God," Sam blurted. "I just realized. I'm half Canadian. That's why I like hockey so much."

Helene burst out laughing. Sam chuckled, too, glad she was able to ease a little of the tension.

Sam blew out a sigh once she caught her breath from laughing. Her thoughts turned serious again. "Helene?"

"Mmm?"

"I got my music from you, didn't I?"

Helene nodded. "I've always thought so."

"That makes sense. Neither Mother nor Daddy has much

musical ability."

They sat quietly for a moment, each lost in thought, until Helene cleared her throat. "Your parents told everyone around here that they were off on an extended vacation while your mother was *pregnant*." She made air quotes around the word pregnant. "They were hiding out in Phoenix."

"So, I really was born there?"

"Mm hmm."

"Were my parents there for nine whole months?"

"No, about six or seven. They brought me here to the US when I began my second trimester with you. We lived in a gorgeous Adobe house in an old part of Phoenix. Your father accompanied me to all the prenatal doctor appointments. He was so excited when he learned you were a girl."

"He was?"

Helene nodded. "When the time came for you to be born, your mother stayed in the house while he took me to the hospital."

"So, no one ever realized you were a surrogate. Maybe they thought you were his, uh, his…" She couldn't say the word mistress out loud.

Helene nodded. "They knew we weren't married. And he was twenty years older, so, yes, they might have thought that."

"But why Phoenix?"

"You know how small towns like East Valley are."

"I found that out today. No secrets."

"They knew they couldn't get away with faking your mother's pregnancy here. I think your father made a big donation to some hospital fund or something. That way, he had an *in* with a doctor in Phoenix."

"Which bought the doctor's silence." Sam recognized it as something her father might do. "The doctor didn't have all the facts, did he?"

"Nope. For some reason, your father never tried to get the birth certificate altered. Maybe he didn't want to push his luck."

"Or maybe he thought he could keep it hidden from me my whole life."

"He did for eighteen years," Helene said.

"You all did."

Helene's cheeks tinged red.

"Was I a difficult pregnancy?"

"Not the pregnancy."

Oh, my God, Sam thought as a wave of dizziness washed over her. *She really is my mother.* "You had trouble giving birth?"

Helene nodded. "But you're getting ahead of our story."

"It is *our* story, isn't it?" Sam took a deep breath to keep her frayed nerves in line. "This is so surreal, Helene. I never dreamed I'd be sitting here talking to you about this."

Helene reached across the table and gave Sam's hand an affectionate squeeze. She cleared her throat, obviously trying to keep her emotions at bay. She stood up. "I have something for you." She went into the adjoining living room and rifled through one of the boxes she'd been packing. After a minute, she pulled out what looked like a scrapbook. She also reached into her mammoth purse and pulled out a plastic shopping bag.

"First of all," Helene said, "I'm hoping your parents will come around at some point, but in the meanwhile…" Helene held out the shopping bag for Sam to take.

Sam opened the bag and looked in. "Two smartphones?"

"One for you and one for Lisa. Maybe Susie can deliver Lisa's the next time she goes to Clarksonville."

Sam threw her arms around Helene and hugged her. "Oh, my God. Thank you so much. I didn't know what I was going to do without my phone. Lisa's my rock."

"I know. One day I hope your parents see it, too. I got the plan with lots of texting minutes and the feature where you can see each other when you talk. I made sure of that."

"This is so cool. Lisa's going to flip. I will pay you back as soon as I get off restrictions."

"No need. It's my gift to you and Lisa. Now all you have to do, young lady, is not get caught using it."

"Helene?"

"Mmm?"

"Does Chantal know?"

Tears welled up in Helene's eyes as she shook her head. "No."

Sam's heart broke. "Your own sister doesn't know you have a child." God, Helene had sacrificed so much.

"It's okay." Helene grabbed a tissue and dabbed at the corner of her eyes.

"No, it's not," Sam said. "Helene?"

"Mmm?"

"Was it hard hearing me call her Mother?"

Helene looked down for a moment. "Yes." She sighed and then looked up. "I'm not going to lie, but anything was fine since I was allowed to be part of your life." Helene patted the thick book in her lap. "This is a scrapbook I've been putting together for you since the day I had you. I had one of the nurses take pictures of me holding you. I knew that I'd be leaving one day, and I wanted something to remember you by. I'm so happy that I can give you this, so you'll remember me, too."

"I will always remember you, Helene. And when I turn eighteen, I'll be keeping the road to Montréal hot." Helene held the scrapbook out for Sam to take, but Sam put a hand out to stop her. "I have an idea."

"What's that?"

"How about we meet back here every night, and you show me a few pages at a time. That way, we can relive my childhood together, but this time..." Sam cleared her throat as emotion choked her up. "But this time, we'll relive it as mother and daughter. Okay?" The last word got caught in her throat as she started crying.

Helene nodded as the tears rolled down her own cheeks. Sam was the one who supplied the comforting arm that time.

Chapter 26
Can I Call You Mom?

Sam stared at her reflection in the lighted makeup mirror. She had already applied a light foundation but was waiting for Alivia to make her way down the row of performers to finish the job. It was the second Friday in November, the play's opening night, and Sam was doing her best to keep her nerves under control. Not only was this her first performance as an actual actor on a stage, but it was the first time she would see Lisa in the flesh in over a month. Having a long-distance relationship using only smartphones wasn't fun, although it had lessened the separation somewhat. They had even managed to use the phones to study together for Sam's SATs and Lisa's PSATs. With any luck, they could find a way to be together for their six-month anniversary on Monday. Not being together for their five-month celebration still weighed heavily on Sam's mind. Sam wasn't hopeful, though. Her father hadn't given any signs of ungrounding her.

Sam touched the mood ring on her hand. It was green, indicating mixed emotions, but Sam smiled anyway. It would turn happy blue the moment she saw Lisa. Oh, God. Lisa would be in the audience. So close. Lisa's family would be there, too, William and Evelyn included. Sam's anxiety ratcheted up a notch. Susie and Marlee were coming, and even Sam's parents would be there—a minor miracle.

Alivia smiled at Sam as she moved closer. "I'll be with you as soon as I'm done with Karl."

"Ha," Sam said with a devilish grin, "the way I've seen you two look at each other, you won't ever be done with him." Sam waggled her eyebrows at Alivia and then reached over and smacked Karl on the arm. Alivia and Karl had become an item shortly after the trouble started for Sam at school.

Sam wouldn't say the month since her public outing had flown by because it certainly hadn't, but at least school had become more bearable. With her friends backing her up, the taunts lessened after the first week. In fact, many of her other classmates found their voices and were friendly and supportive toward her. Every day she found things to look forward to — lunch with her friends, play rehearsals, phone calls with Lisa, and nightly chats with Helene. Sometimes after she left Helene's apartment and went back to her suite, there would be a text from Lisa waiting for her. Those nights were the best. There was no way her father could stop Lisa from attending the public performances, especially when Lisa planned to be at all four—Friday night, both on Saturday, and the last one on Sunday.

Alivia tapped Karl on the top of his head when she finished making him up and then sent him a smoldering smile. Sam grinned. She knew the feeling.

"Are you ready, fiddler?" Alivia swiveled Sam around in her seat.

"Yes, Golde."

Alivia was already in costume for her role as Golde, Tevye's wife. "Let's finish getting your makeup on, and then we'll get your hair tucked under your cap so that it won't come out, okay?"

"And then you have to put your own makeup on."

"Yep. There's plenty of time." Alivia put her fingertips on Sam's chin and moved Sam's head to the left. She brushed a finger along Sam's eyebrow. "I love this little scar from your car accident. It's kind of sexy."

Sam felt her cheeks get warm. Was Alivia flirting with her? No way. She was straight. And besides, she had Karl.

Alivia leaned closer and applied the stage makeup to Sam's cheeks, nose, and forehead. Alivia's femaleness, so close, made Sam realize how much she missed Lisa. When Alivia turned to put the makeup away, Sam brushed a tear back. She hadn't known how lonely she had been.

Alivia turned around. "Okay, let's lose the ring."

Sam looked at the mood ring on her finger and frowned. She didn't want to take it off. She wanted to see it turn happy blue, but Alivia was right. Fiddlers in the town of Anatevka didn't wear mood rings. She tugged it off and tucked it into her pants pocket.

"Are you upset that Mrs. Dickens decided not to have you wear a beard and mustache?" Alivia asked.

Sam chuckled. "Nah, I think it's probably better given my, uh, recent foray into marginalization."

"An interesting choice of words. I can see why you and Ronnie feel pushed to the margins of society. The mainstream population isn't quite ready for you guys. Maybe one day."

"I hope it's in my lifetime."

Alivia smiled and nodded thoughtfully. She patted Sam on the shoulder. "Okay, let's turn you into a fiddler, shall we?" She tacked Sam's ponytail up on her head with about a thousand bobby pins.

Sam's head felt heavy. "Hand me your cap."

Sam reached out and grabbed the dark cap hanging off the edge of the mirror.

Alivia plunked the cap on Sam's head, and bobby pinned it fast. "Shake your head."

Sam shook her head vigorously, and the cap didn't move. "Feels good."

Alivia tapped her on the shoulder. "You, oh fiddler, are all set."

Ronnie came bopping into the green room at that moment. "Whoa, look at you," he said to Sam.

Sam stood up and smoothed down her long black coat, complete with tails. She made sure the prayer shawl stuck out underneath the vest.

Ronnie grabbed her hand and twirled her around. "You are so butch. Your girlfriend is going to cream when she sees you."

"Ronnie!" Sam smacked him in the chest. She glared at him for a moment and then teased back. "Nice beard. Couldn't grow one on your own, eh?"

Ronnie made a face and then said, "C'mon." He grabbed her hand and led her through the maze of hallways. They weaved their way around stored sets and stagehands until they were in the wings of the stage. Ronnie moved the heavy velvet curtain an inch. "You can see who's here. Look," he gushed, making room for Sam to look out, "there's Jordan."

"Where?"

"One, two, three, fourth row."

"I see him."

"Isn't he cute?" Ronnie swooned. "It'll be one month for us on the morrow."

"Happy anniversary."

"Thanks." Ronnie was obviously head over heels. There seemed to be a lot of that going around.

Sam scanned the audience but couldn't find Lisa.

"Don't worry," Ronnie said. "She'll be here. It's still early."

"Am I that transparent?"

Ronnie nodded. "I'm going back for vocal warmups. Don't stay here too long."

"I won't. Thanks, Ronnie."

He was gone before she'd finished saying his name.

Looking out over the filling auditorium, she watched Helene come in and find a seat in the center section. *That's my mother,* Sam thought, remembering all the softball games, violin recitals, and orchestra concerts Helene had faithfully attended throughout Sam's childhood. Her other parents had only attended a smattering of them. She remembered when she and Helene diligently watched every NHL playoff game leading up to the Montréal Canadiens winning the Stanley Cup. She'd never shared anything like that with her other parents. A lot of things were starting to make sense in her head.

Sam thought it was ironic that they had been bonding more ever since she found out Helene was leaving. Just about every night since her public outing, Sam had gone to Helene's apartment, and together they looked through the scrapbook or watched hockey games on Helene's TV.

That very first night, though, Sam got answers to many of her questions. They had moved from Helene's kitchen to the couch in the living room, the teacups forgotten on the kitchen table.

Helene tucked her feet under her at the same time Sam did.

They laughed, and Sam said, "I think we're more alike than I ever realized."

"You may be right."

"So," Sam started, "how exactly did you get, uh…" Sam felt her cheeks get warm.

"By artificial insemination. In Montréal." The red tinge on Helene's cheeks spread.

"Oh."

Helene laughed. "I think you were bound and determined to be born because I conceived you on the first try."

"That's good." Sam was relieved to hear that because it had taken Lisa's Aunt Fran several tries before she got pregnant. "But you said my birth was hard?"

"You were my first child, my only child, of course, but it took you twenty hours to be born. I was so exhausted and weak that I had to stay in the hospital for an extra few days. Once they released me, I still wasn't strong enough to go back to Montréal."

"Is that when my parents invited you to live here?"

"No, actually, we stayed in the adobe house in Phoenix for another month. That was when, and I don't mean to be disrespectful, but that was when your mother discovered she wasn't the nurturing type. Your parents thought her motherly instincts would kick in after a while, but they never did. Every time you cried, neither she nor your father could get you to settle down. I finally asked if I could try."

"I bet that was hard for Mother," Sam said.

"Incredibly, but your parents were at their wit's end. You quieted down when I held you."

"I did?"

Helene nodded.

"I must have known who my real mother was."

"Your parents extended my contract—"

"Contract?" Sam interrupted, mortified by the term.

"Don't delude yourself, Samantha Rose. Your father is all about the bottom line."

"Like on financial spreadsheets?"

Helene nodded. "My surrogacy started as a business arrangement, but after your father extended my contract a half-dozen times, he decided I should remain with you until you went to boarding school in Switzerland when you turned fourteen."

"And then I didn't go because of my migraines."

"Exactly. So, my contract was renegotiated again, and they wanted me to stay until you turned eighteen. I knew I had been handed an amazing gift, so I grabbed it, even if it meant I was contract-bound to never admit to anyone I was your biological mother."

"That must have been incredibly hard."

"If it meant I could keep you, then the secret was easy." Helene sighed and added, "It was difficult when I was left out of things, though."

"Family meals." Sam had always hated when Helene wasn't invited to sit down and eat with them.

"Yes. And birthdays. Christmas mornings were always the worst."

Sam smiled. "So that's why Santa made two stops at the mansion? One in the main house and one here?"

Helene nodded. "I could never compete with the gifts your parents gave you, but at least I usually had part of Christmas day with you." She pointed to the scrapbook and squeezed Sam's forearm gently. "I've got pictures of all our Christmases together. Tomorrow night we'll start on page one, okay?"

"Okay."

"For now, I think you should head on to bed."

"Awww," Sam whined and pretended to kick her feet on the couch like she'd done as a child.

"That's my grown-up girl." Helene laughed and rolled her eyes.

Sam wanted to ask something but wasn't sure how to phrase it, so she simply blurted, "Can I call you *Mom*?"

Helene pursed her lips. "I would love that more than anything…"

"But?"

"But I think you should continue to call me Helene or your nanny, and you should call your mother *Mother*, the way you always have."

"Okay."

"This way, you won't slip up in front of someone. We should wait for my name change until after you and your parents mend some fences."

"They don't listen when I talk to them."

"I can't promise they'll come around, but it might be easier when I'm gone."

At that point, Sam tried not to get more depressed than she already was. "I'm going to miss you, Helene." They stood up and shared a healing hug.

"Oh, *mon petit hibou*, I'm going to miss you so much." Helene kissed Sam on the forehead. She swallowed hard and then took a deep breath. "Okay, little one. Bed for you." She wiped at her eyes when they broke apart.

Sam clutched the velvet curtain in the wings of the stage and smiled at the month-old memory. She watched Helene settle into her seat in the auditorium, jacket over her arm, playbill in hand, a bouquet of gerbera daisies resting in her lap. Susie and Marlee came in and sat behind Helene. Sam positively melted when she spotted Lisa, hair deliciously down, wearing the winter coat Sam had sent her from the Neiman Marcus website. Sam was pleased with how well the coat fit her. Even though Sam was housebound, she could still send her girlfriend presents. Bridget held Lisa's hand and led the family down Helene's row. Sam's heart swelled when Bridget released her sister's hand and ran to sit in Helene's lap. The surprised but happy smile on Helene's face somehow made Sam realize that life would go on and everything would be okay.

Someone tapped her shoulder. A stagehand gestured for her to get back to the green room. It was almost time for the play to start. Sam nodded and made her way back, disappointed that she hadn't seen her other parents yet.

After the group prayer, led eloquently by Ronnie, Sam worked her way onto the dimly lit stage and climbed up the stairs behind the scenes to the set roof. She sat on the fake stone chimney and let the stagehand clip her into the safety restraints.

"Snug?" The stagehand tugged on the restraints.

"Yup."

"Pretend that you're playing."

Sam moved around like she knew she would while playing. The restraints felt good and secure. During the dress rehearsals, Sam never once felt vertigo being up so high. She'd been on mountain tops in the Swiss Alps that were infinitely scarier than the set she was sitting on. Even though she had assured everybody she was perfectly safe, Helene and her parents would probably have a collective heart attack once the curtain opened.

Sam took a deep breath and made sure she was sitting on her mark as the orchestra in the pit tuned up. She joined them from atop the roof.

Mrs. Dickens' voice filled the auditorium. "The students and I are glad you could join us on this cold November night. I think I even heard a forecast for snow on Sunday." A few groans followed, and Mrs. Dickens chuckled. "That's life in the North Country, right?" She paused while people laughed and then added, "Now, if you could take a moment to turn off your cell phones, the cast and crew would greatly appreciate it." She paused for a moment and then said, "Please join me for East Valley High School's production of *Fiddler on the Roof*."

Sam heard the clapping and took a deep breath to calm her nerves. She waited for the stage manager's cue. He lowered his arm, and Sam played one long note. She was amazed at how good her instrument sounded through the auditorium speakers. The curtain opened as she played the introductory piece in the dark. A spotlight behind her came up, slowly simulating the sunrise. The backlighting kept Sam's features hidden from the audience, but she could see into the first few rows, including Lisa and Helene's row. She played as Ronnie came on stage as Tevye. The backlighting subtly moved to the front, illuminating both Ronnie's and Sam's faces. Sam was surprised she could still see the people in the first rows.

"Samtha!" Bridget yelled and pointed. "Wook, Weesa. Samtha!"

Several people chuckled at Lisa's three-year-old sister, and it was all Sam could do not to smile. She spotted Lisa's gaze riveted on her. Lisa put a hand over her heart and patted it a few times. Sam read the message loud and clear, wishing she had a way to signal back.

Sam was surprised to see Helene dabbing at the corner of her eyes with a wadded-up tissue. Before she lost it, too, Sam forced herself to focus her attention on Ronnie. He moved stage right, and beyond him, seated in the well-lit first row, were her parents. They were still wearing their coats, and they were not smiling.

Chapter 27
A Payton after All

Sam placed a hunk of Brie between two slices of French bread buttered on the outside. She lifted the lid of her mother's George Foreman grill and placed the sandwich inside. It wasn't the exact recipe Lisa had shown her, but the Payton household didn't stock American cheese and white bread. As she made a second sandwich for Helene, she thought about the play's last performance later on that day. Well, to be honest, her thoughts drifted to the wrap-up party at Ronnie's house after the play. She hoped her parents would let her go. Maybe then she could finally spend time with Lisa. Ronnie had helped sneak Lisa backstage after the Friday night performance and then again after both Saturday performances. With dozens of people milling around, Sam had to settle for giving Lisa a quick hug and small talk. She didn't want to upset anybody's sensibilities by dragging Lisa into a bathroom stall to kiss her properly. Especially not since her parents were waiting in the auditorium to take her home each time. Something had to give, though, and soon. A month was way too long and tortuous to let Lisa's lips stay unkissed.

Sam blew out a sigh and checked her sandwiches. "This wasn't what you had in mind, was it?" Sam mumbled. Not only was she referring to the sandwich recipe, but their budding relationship as well.

"Who are you talking to?"

Sam jumped when her mother spoke. "You startled me, Mother. I'm making lunch. Grilled Brie on French bread." *And I completely didn't answer your question.*

Sam's mother wore an expensive exercise outfit that Sam thought was better suited for a fashion runway than an actual workout. "It smells wonderful."

"Let me make a sandwich for you." Sam unwrapped the loaf of bread, knowing full well her mother would decline.

"No, I'm not hungry. Stefan will be here soon, and I was heading to the treadmill to get a head start." Stefan was Sam's mother's fitness trainer who got paid handsomely to come to the mansion three times a week and watch her mother walk on the treadmill and lift one-pound weights.

"Mother, you need to eat." As soon as the words were out, Sam wished she had phrased it differently. She tried again. "Would you like some chicken soup instead?"

"Oh, all right. A little soup won't hurt. Shall I get out two bowls?"

"You know what?" Sam said. "Can you get out four?"

"Four?"

"You, me, and Daddy are going to eat lunch with Helene today. Helene's leaving in less than a month, and at least here in the house we can stop pretending she's the hired help."

Sam's mother raised an eyebrow as if surprised by Sam's bold statement. She was silent for so long that Sam wasn't sure what to do. She decided to wait her mother out and quietly stirred the soup.

Her mother broke the silence. "I don't know if that's a good idea. Your father has a business meeting downtown today."

"On a Sunday?"

"You know what he always says."

"Business waits for no man," Sam imitated her father.

"Hey, who's making fun of me?" Her father stepped into the cavernous kitchen.

"Just me," Sam said.

He went to the refrigerator and pulled out a sparkling water.

"Hey, Daddy?"

"Yes, Kitten?"

"Can you get out three more waters?"

"Thirsty?"

Sam chuckled. "No, I'm hosting a lunch for you, Mother, and Helene. In fact, Helene will be here in a minute."

"I have a business—"

"Which can wait," Sam interrupted and then wondered who had taken over her body to make her interrupt her father like that. "You are having lunch with your family." Sam hoped she hadn't overstepped and gotten herself grounded until she was twenty-one. She pulled the loaf of bread back out of its sleeve and cut enough slices for more sandwiches. She was even going to make one for her mother, though it would probably go uneaten.

"Mother," her father said, "I believe our daughter has me wrapped around her little finger. Okay, then." He seemed amused when he turned to Sam. "What are you serving for lunch?"

"Soup and grilled cheese sandwiches."

"Where in the world did you learn to make grilled cheese sandwiches?" He stroked his chin.

Sam didn't meet her father's eyes when she said, "At my friend

Lisa's house." She groaned inside, ashamed of wimping out and reducing Lisa to just a friend.

Sam's mother, who had begun pulling china plates and bowls out of the sideboard, stood up at the mention of Lisa's name. "Is Lisa your close friend?"

"Yes." Sam wanted to say so much more but couldn't think of a way to say any of it. Her parents must have been trying to figure out which one of her friends at the pool party was her girlfriend or, as her mother put it, her 'close friend.' But then again, her father had tracked her through her phone and knew she spent a lot of time at Lisa's house. He'd probably checked out Lisa and her family the way he'd checked out William and Evelyn. The more she thought about that, the angrier she got. Her hands shook as she fussed with the sandwiches.

Her father cleared his throat. "We'd like to meet her again one of these days. Wouldn't we, Mother?"

"Yes, of course," Sam's mother said stiffly. "That would be fine."

The growing silence could definitely be described as awkward, so Sam's *tougher stuff* asserted itself, and she said, "Lisa does a lot of cooking for her family. She taught me how to make meatloaf and mashed potatoes."

"Well, well," her father said. "What do you think of that, Mother?"

"I think it will come in handy when she goes off to Wellesley."

"I suppose that's true," he said.

Sam checked the sandwiches on the grill as she tried to decide how far she could push her parents. If she ever hoped to see Lisa again, she needed to chill out, but, God, it felt good to talk about her, at least for a minute.

Sam stirred the soup, determined it was hot enough, and ladled equal portions into the four soup bowls her mother had lined up on a tray.

"Daddy, can you get the oyster crackers from the pantry?"

He looked lost for a moment, as if he didn't know where the pantry was.

Sam laughed and pointed to the walk-in pantry. "Middle shelf, right side."

"Ah." He walked over and pulled them out. "I didn't know where we kept them." He put the crackers on the tray with the soup bowls. "Speaking of college, I got an interesting call from your guidance counselor last week. She said you insisted on applying to Rockville University in Cayuga County."

"Rockville University?" Sam's mother asked.

"Mm hmm," Sam said calmly. She had hoped to have an acceptance letter in her hand before talking to her parents about Rockville. "You remember last year when I went to the All-State Orchestra Festival? That was at Rockville University."

Sam's mother's face brightened. "Gerald, the Wright School of Music is housed at Rockville. Isn't that right, Samantha Rose?"

Sam nodded.

"Does this mean…" her mother put a hand up to her throat and looked expectantly at Sam.

Sam nodded again. "Yes, Mother. You'll be happy to know I'm pretty sure I want to major in music."

"Very good." Sam's mother's mood lightened considerably until she added, "Wellesley has an excellent music department as well."

"I know, mother, but—"

"And they have one of those softball teams, too."

Sam almost laughed at the way her mother was trying to make her alma mater sound appealing.

"I'll tell you what, Mother. I'll give both schools equal consideration, okay?" *If I'm even given a choice, that is.*

Sam's mother nodded. "That sounds fair. Now, Samantha Rose, I don't want you to be angry with me."

"Why would I be angry with you, Mother?"

"I found some pamphlets in your room."

Sam's heart sank. Her mother had found that stupid STD pamphlet in her top desk drawer. Something in Sam's brain shifted. Wait. Her mother had been searching her room, invading her privacy.

Sam must have had a look of outrage on her face because her mother hastened to add, "It was only the one drawer, I promise. I don't usually snoop, but I was concerned about you." She paused for a moment as if trying to find the right words. "I found a pamphlet about a group called P-F-L-A-G."

"PFLAG? Parents, Families, and Friends of—"

"Lesbians and Gays," her father said the words slowly as if wary of their meaning. "I've looked into the group, and they're legit. I'm meeting one of their representatives in less than an hour."

Sam was stunned. "That's your business meeting?" His casual khakis, mauve button-down shirt, and loafers now made sense. Wearing such casual attire meant he didn't take the group too seriously; otherwise, he would be wearing a suit.

Her father held his lips closed and nodded. "I'm trying to figure out what my daughter has gotten herself into with this lifestyle choice."

I didn't choose it, Daddy. It chose me! She wanted to shout the words at him, but her father was on a roll, and it was best not to interrupt him.

"And," her father continued, "your mother and I will be accompanying you to your next session with Dr. Boyle on Tuesday." He clapped his hands together once. "Now that that's taken care of let's get this lunch thing going." Apparently, the discussion about Sam's *lifestyle choice* was finished. "Rolando should be here any minute."

"Did he get that tire fixed?" Sam's mother asked her father.

"Yes." Her father looked at Sam. "Rolando's car had a blowout on the way to your performance Friday night. That's why we were late."

"Ah," Sam said, "I saw you in the front row. You still had your coats on."

Her mother nodded. "We made it just as the curtain opened. We were so cold and miserable that we left our coats on for the entire first act. Rolando couldn't track down another car from the service, so we had to travel the rest of the way in a taxi. A filthy taxi! Can you believe it?"

It was all Sam could do to keep a straight face. Biting down a laugh, she said, "I wondered why Rolando took us home in a different car Friday night." Something dawned on Sam. "Wait, Daddy. Did you say Rolando was driving you today? Isn't he driving me to school for the play? I have to go right after lunch."

"Actually," her father said, "your mother and I have decided to loosen the reins. You're off restrictions. For now."

"Really? I can use my car?"

"Yes."

"Go anywhere I want?"

"Within reason."

Ahhh! Sam screamed in her head. *What does 'within reason' mean? Can I go to Lisa's or not?* Why did everything have a loophole in it? It was so annoying. Sam hid her frustration behind her patented Payton smile.

"Can I go to the wrap-up party at Ronnie's after the play later?"

Her father nodded and then reached into his pocket and handed her the cell phone he had confiscated over a month earlier. Sam held in a laugh; he was so transparent. He would be able to tell where she went.

"Your mother and I haven't finished thinking this one all the way through, Samantha Rose," her father said. "We have to analyze the risk potential your lifestyle choice might mean to the family." Apparently, the topic wasn't finished, and apparently, he thought she had a choice, and apparently, he was arrogant enough to believe he could change that choice.

Always the bottom line, Sam thought, like Helene said.

"What your father is trying to say is that we're not ignoring you or your situation," Sam's mother said.

My situation? Were they trying to decide if her *situation* could be fixed without incurring too much damage? Sam wanted to challenge her mother's choice of words but instead utilized her years of stoic Payton training and held her tongue. She'd have her say, but she'd wait until they were in the somewhat safe environment of Dr. Boyle's office. Dr. Boyle could referee when she unloaded on her parents. She'd tell them how it felt to discover her *situation* in early childhood, hide it from everyone, and see the anger and disapproval in her parents' eyes.

Even though Sam's parents had given her some freedom back, she knew not to trust it. Her father protected what was his at all costs. The pickup truck driver, the Clarksonville Courier reporter, and the photographer were all being sued by her father on her behalf, even though she wanted nothing to do with any of it. She had no choice like she'd had no choice in most things in her life.

"Yoo hoo," Helene called as she strode into the kitchen. "Oh, excuse me." She backed out as soon as she saw Sam with her parents. She must have sensed the tense air. "I didn't mean to intrude."

"Wait," Sam called. "Come back." *You're my lifeline right now.*

Helene reappeared in the doorway. "I hope I'm not disturbing anything."

Sam smiled. "You're fine, and you know what? I'm happy now because I have my whole family with me." She gave Helene a quick hug and said, "I'm the luckiest girl alive. I have a dad, and even better, I have two moms." *Let's not forget about this big Payton family secret, now, shall we?*

Sam's mother smiled, but it was the fake smile Sam had seen her hone over the years. Her father's expression remained neutral, but Helene's smile was genuine. Sam's smile was also fairly genuine, but behind it, she hoped her parents understood that she wasn't beyond blackmail. She was a Payton, after all.

Chapter 28
I Seriously Doubt That

The audience applauded as the curtain calls for the Sunday performance continued. Sam waited in the wings for her turn. The actors playing Tevye's daughters and their husbands ran onto the stage and bowed. Sam was two beats behind them. She stopped alone on center stage, tucked her violin and bow underneath her arm, and bowed. She grinned when she heard Lisa yell, "Way to go, Sam!" Sam moved over and joined the ever-growing cast to make way for Alivia.

Alivia ran out and curtsied, followed quickly by Ronnie, who bowed. The entire cast grabbed hands, although Alivia had to link arms with Sam because of the violin, and they made a group bow. They separated hands and collectively pointed toward the orchestra pit. The audience clapped louder if that was even possible. The cast pointed up to the lighting booth and then to Mrs. Dickens. Karl dragged her onto the stage and then presented her with a bouquet of roses produced from somewhere behind the assembled cast.

Mrs. Dickens clearly moved, took the flowers, nodded graciously to her cast, and then nodded to the audience, who had been clapping the entire time. Eventually, the cast closed ranks around Mrs. Dickens, and when the applause died down, she led them behind the curtain.

Mrs. Dickens came up to Sam and gave her a warm hug. "You were the best fiddler I've seen in that role in a long time, Miss Samantha Rose."

"Thank you," Sam said. "I had a lot of fun."

"I'm sorry you're a senior, and we didn't discover this talent of yours until now."

Although Sam had enjoyed the role, she doubted she would make musical theater part of her life, something her parents would be happy about, no doubt. She kept the thought to herself and continued to smile.

"I'll see you at the wrap-up party?" Mrs. Dickens asked.

"You bet."

"Good." Mrs. Dickens turned to talk to the stage manager.

"Amazing run, girls." Ronnie wrapped Sam and Alivia into one boisterous bear hug.

"You, too, Ronnie," Sam said. "You were born to be on the stage."

"Thanks." Ronnie smiled his million-dollar smile. "C'mon, girls," he linked arms with each of them. "Let's go out front and see our significant others."

"Hey," Karl protested good-naturedly, "what about me?"

"C'mon, honey," Alivia held her free arm out so Karl could link up with her.

The four of them skipped back onto the stage and then separated to find their respective friends and families in the audience.

Sam knew not to look for her parents. They had a commitment in Syracuse. She spotted Lisa waiting for her near the stage. Helene, Susie, and Marlee waited a few rows back. Sam made a beeline for

Lisa's open arms. Lisa whispered in Sam's ear, "I can't take my eyes off you in this sexy butch outfit."

"I'm so lucky I'm off restrictions." Sam felt a wave of desire run through her as they separated. "That coat looks amazing on you." Sam stroked Lisa's new coat hanging over her arm.

"You shouldn't have spent the money, baby, but I love it."

"Good." Sam raised an eyebrow suggestively. "I like pleasing you."

"Just wait 'til we're alone." Lisa handed Sam a single rose. "I wish it could have been a whole dozen, but…"

"I don't care. It's from you, and that's all I need. I miss you so much." *And I can't believe how much I want to kiss you right now.*

"Me, too, baby. Me, too."

Sam and Lisa walked toward Helene, Susie, and Marlee. Sam desperately wanted to hold hands with Lisa, something Alivia and Karl could do without the world staring at them but decided she didn't want to be judged. She reached her arms out and hugged Helene.

"I'm so proud of you," Helene said and squeezed.

"Thanks for coming to all the performances. It must have been boring for you."

"Not a chance," Helene said, tears filling her eyes.

"Helene, don't," Sam said. "You'll make me cry, too."

"She cried every time you appeared on stage," Susie said.

Sam laughed. "Was I that bad?"

"Not a chance. You're a Payton," Helene said.

And a Bouchard, too, Sam thought, but simply smiled.

"Two," Marlee said, "you were so good. I wish I could play an instrument like that."

"Put in about ten million hours of practice, and you will."

"Lynnie can't stop talking about you," Lisa said. "She wants to take violin lessons now."

"She does?"

Lisa nodded.

"I think I can help with that." Sam created a mental Christmas list. Item one—a violin for Lynnie.

"*Aay, gringa*," Susie said, "you were awesome. If I didn't know better, I'd think you grew up doing musical theater."

"Oh, God. Don't tell my parents that, okay?"

"Hey," Susie said, "did you ask Ronnie if it was okay for me and Marlee to go to the wrap-up party?"

"Yes. He wants you guys there. He doesn't want Jordan to feel all alone."

"You girls have fun at the party," Helene said. "I'm heading out." She turned to Lisa, Susie, and Marlee. "Take good care of her, okay?"

Sam turned away from the group and wiped at the sudden tears in her eyes. She knew Helene wasn't only referring to the wrap-up party, and by the sudden change in mood, her friends seemed to understand that, too. Both Sam and Helene were going to be devastated when Helene moved away.

Sam gave Helene another hug and watched her walk up the aisle toward the exit with a heavy heart.

Sam took a deep breath and blew out a sigh. "Okay, you guys, let me get changed, and then we can head over." She tossed her keys to Lisa. "I'll meet you at the Sebring in a few."

Sam raced backstage and removed her makeup in record speed. Before changing, she reached into her pants pocket and pulled out the mood ring she'd kept hidden during every performance. She carefully slid it on her finger, barely able to contain herself because she was finally going to be with Lisa. She changed clothes as fast as she could, threw on a coat, and raced to her car in the lot.

Sam nodded to Marlee and Susie in the van and yanked open her car door. Lisa's smile knocked the wind out of her.

"Oh, my God," Sam said, catching her breath, "you're a sight for sore eyes."

"I missed you, too, baby."

Sam looked at the people milling about the parking lot. "I want to kiss you, but there are way too many people around here."

"That's okay. It's only been thirty-five days, eighteen hours, and..." Lisa checked the time on her watch, "twelve minutes since the last time you kissed me, so what's another five minutes?"

"Thirty-five days? It seemed like thirty-five weeks." Sam couldn't help but smile at Lisa's cheesy grin. "Don't worry. I'll find a private spot near Ronnie's house, so I can kiss you properly before we go in, okay?"

"Hurry."

Sam started the car and headed toward Ronnie's house. Marlee and Susie were right behind them.

A thousand cars lined Ronnie's street, so Sam pulled the Sebring down a quiet side street. Marlee parked behind her.

Sam flung her seatbelt off and practically threw herself at Lisa. Their lips met in a fury of passion and promise. Sam ran her fingers through Lisa's long hair, and then, without warning, Sam started to cry. She pulled away and hid her face behind her hands.

"Oh, geez." Lisa pulled her close. Sam rested her head on Lisa's chest. "It's okay, baby. Why are you crying?" Lisa stroked Sam's back. "I'm right here, baby. What's wrong?"

"I missed you so much. I can't believe it's been over a month since I've seen you. We missed our five-month anniversary. God, I let them ruin my life." Sam sat up and searched Lisa's eyes. She saw the love she hoped to find there. "I can't believe how much I love you." Their lips met again.

Sam was ready to scrap the party and whisk Lisa away somewhere private as the kiss heated up. Her new plan was interrupted by a tap on the window.

"*Aay*, I hate to break up the reunion, *muchachas*, but it's cold out here." Susie stood outside the car with her arms wrapped around her. Marlee was doing mini jumping jacks to keep warm.

"Sorry, guys," Sam said. She turned to Lisa and gave her another quick kiss. "C'mon, let's get this wrap-up party wrapped up, so we can find a place to be alone."

They let themselves in the front door when nobody answered Sam's knock. The club music was so loud that obviously, no one had heard them.

Ronnie headed for them. "Hey, girls, drop your coats off somewhere in the back office." He pointed to a room beyond the bathroom. "Drinks and food are in the kitchen." He pointed toward the bright kitchen packed with cast and crew from the show. He leaned in closer. "And if you want special beverages, see Karl, and he'll hook you up discretely."

"Thanks, Ronnie," Sam said, "but I think we'll pass on the special beverages." Sam glanced at her friends and, by the relieved look on Marlee's face, knew she'd made the right decision. And besides, Mrs. Dickens and other teachers were there at the party.

"Okay, lightweights, enjoy yourselves." Ronnie turned to go but then turned back. "Don't worry about babysitting Jordan." He pointed to a corner of the living room where his new boyfriend held a group of underclassmen mesmerized with a story. "As you can see, he has an audience already, so you're off the hook."

"Okay, cool," Sam said. She turned to Lisa. "How *out* do you want to be?"

Lisa shrugged. "I'm cool with whatever you want to do, but it's up to you."

Sam lifted one eyebrow and flashed Lisa a devilish grin. She reached for Lisa's hand, squeezed it, and held on. Lisa nodded her approval. Sam smiled as a slight touch of crimson grew on Lisa's cheeks.

"C'mon, kids," Sam said, "let's get some food. I'm starving."

They headed to the kitchen and loaded up their plates. Susie found room for them to sit comfortably on the living room carpet.

Alivia sauntered by with Karl in tow. "Hello, girls," she said.

"Alivia," Sam gestured to Marlee, "this is Susie's girlfriend, Marlee. And this is my girlfriend, Lisa." Sam felt her cheeks get warm. It was the first time she had publicly acknowledged Lisa as her girlfriend. It felt good.

"Nice to meet you both," Alivia said. "This is my love-muffin, Karl."

Karl burst out laughing. "I've never been called a love-muffin before." He shook hands with Marlee and Lisa. "I remember you guys from Stewart's. Right before school started."

"Oh, yeah," Lisa said. "We weren't sure if you were dating Ronnie or Alivia."

Alivia shrieked with laughter. "That's a good one. Wait 'til Ronnie hears that. There he is." Ronnie was heading into the kitchen. "C'mon, Karl, let's go." Alivia reached for Karl's hand. She turned back and said over her shoulder, "It's nice to know Sam and Susie have nice girlfriends. Cute ones, too."

"Thanks," Lisa and Marlee said simultaneously, and everybody laughed.

As always, whenever the four of them got together, their conversation turned to softball. They predicted what the spring season would bring, which team would take the North Country trophy, and which team would qualify for the state playoffs. Naturally, all of their predictions included Clarksonville and East Valley high schools.

"You know," Sam said, "I hate that we play on different high school teams."

"Yeah," Marlee agreed, "that sucks."

"We can play together in college," Sam suggested. "Did you guys apply?"

"To Rockville?" Susie asked.

Sam nodded.

"Yep, we both did," Susie said.

"Yes!" Sam punched a fist in the air.

"Now, all we have to do is get in," Marlee said.

"*Aay*, no problem for you, *mi vida*." Susie nudged Marlee with her shoulder. "Did you know she applied to Cornell, too? She's such a brain."

Marlee blushed. "Susie wants to major in geology, and I could major in mechanical engineering or physics at Rockville. A lot of their graduates go on to work for prestigious engineering firms. And how amazing would it be to play on the same college team? All four of us?"

"Their softball team is great," Lisa said. "According to Coach Greer, that is. They even go to Florida for spring training."

There was something off in Lisa's tone. Sam leaned in closer. "What's the matter, baby? You don't seem that excited."

"I am."

"You don't sound it."

"You guys talking about college makes me remember that you're all seniors, and you'll be graduating and leaving me here."

Sam gave Lisa a quick hug. She wanted to hold Lisa longer, but she still wasn't comfortable showing affection in a crowd. "Okay, that does it. We're all deferring for a year."

At Susie and Marlee's startled expressions, Sam said, "I'm just kidding, but I wish there was a way you could graduate a year earlier."

Lisa shrugged. "I can't. I won't have enough credits."

"You looked into it?"

"I did." Lisa threw her hands up. "Ahh, whatever. I can't change reality. I'll just have to get a job, so I can buy a car and make regular trips to the Rockville campus to visit all my friends."

A brilliant idea formed in Sam's mind. Of course, she'd have to act fast. There was probably a time limit on how long she would be able to blackmail her parents. Sam decided that item number two on her mental Christmas list was to give the Sebring to Lisa. Sam was going to ask for a new car for Christmas anyway. Maybe a Lexus SUV, as long as it had room in the back to move around in and didn't look like a soccer mom minivan.

"Sam, you look like the cat that caught the canary," Susie said. "What's going on in that head of yours?"

"Nothing that involves you, Miss Missy," Sam teased.

"Ooh," Marlee taunted, "catfight."

"Actually, guys," Sam said, "I think it's time we made our rounds and then headed out of here."

"I'm with you on that," Lisa said. "Let's make this fast."

They left the party thirty minutes later and headed toward the side street where their cars were parked. They reached Marlee's van first.

"Sus?"

"Yeah?"

"Here." Sam slipped Susie her old phone and asked her to hang onto it until she picked it up at the end of the night. Sam gave her friends the briefest of explanations about her father's use of the GPS feature, and they were outraged at the invasion of privacy.

Susie tucked Sam's old phone into her pocket and patted it twice for safekeeping. It was better for Sam's father to think she had gone to Susie's house than to the secluded farm road on Raymond Road near the site of the car accident. Since the crash, Sam hadn't been back to the intersection, but she might have enough strength to face it with Lisa by her side.

"Hey," Marlee gushed, "isn't your six-month anniversary coming up?"

Sam nodded and reached for Lisa's hand. "Tomorrow."

"*Aay*, I don't know how you guys are going to top your four-month anniversary," Susie said. "Dinner at *Le Grande Bistro* in Southbridge? Fancy schmancy."

"I think they're gonna top it," Marlee said knowingly.

"We are?" Sam looked at Lisa. This was the first she'd heard of plans for their six-month celebration."

"But I'm sworn to secrecy," Marlee said.

Susie frowned at Marlee. "You're in on it?"

"Yep." Marlee held her lips tight together, indicating she would say no more on the matter. "Actually," she turned to Lisa for permission, "can I say?"

"Go ahead."

"My job," Marlee said to Sam, "is to pick you up and chauffeur you to William and Evelyn's tomorrow evening."

"Yeah?" Sam smiled at Lisa.

"I'm cooking for us." Lisa smiled back. "I'm sending William and Evelyn out to dinner and then to a movie. They have explicit instructions to stay away until I text them."

"This sounds like the answer to my prayers." Sam looked up in the sky and thanked the Gods.

"You're a lucky dog, Sam." Susie punched Sam lightly in the arm.

Sam grinned. "I can't wait. What's for dinner?"

Lisa wagged a finger. "You'll find out tomorrow."

Sam stuck out her lower lip. "Okay, fine. Hey, Sus?"

"Yeah?"

"We'll come by in about two hours. Okay?"

Susie nodded. "Sounds good. We'll be in my room."

"I can't believe your mother lets Marlee hang out in your room now."

"She's made a few surprise visits. Let me tell you."

"She never caught us doing anything, though," Marlee added with a wink. "The screen door to their mudroom squeaks really loudly, no matter how quietly she tries to open it. And I can move pretty fast when I have to."

Sam and Lisa laughed. "All right, you guys. We'll see you in a while. Have fun."

"We're going to have as much fun as you two," Susie teased.

"Oh, I seriously doubt that." Sam put her arm around Lisa, and they headed to the Sebring.

Chapter 29
I'll Take it from Here

"**H**ow did that make you feel, Samantha Rose?" Dr. Boyle asked.

"Good," Sam said. "I worked hard in the play, and it felt good when the audience clapped for me."

"No anxiety on stage?"

Sam shook her head. "Not really. I'm used to getting attention."

"That was positive attention," Sam's mother said from her seat on the couch. "Sometimes it's not."

Sam nodded. She knew her mother was trying to bring up the gay issue in a non-direct way, but Sam wasn't biting. She wanted someone to bring up the subject more directly, so she skirted the issue and said, "Like how people gawk at me because I'm a Payton? It's like I'm an alien or something."

Dr. Boyle didn't say anything. It was obvious he wanted Sam and her parents to keep the slow-moving ball rolling. Sam wasn't sure what was going to happen because her father sat stone-faced on his end of the couch, and her mother, so far, had only thrown out a sentence or two.

Dr. Boyle sat in one of the two leather chairs. His lemon-yellow sweater worn over a white button-down shirt, his thinning gray hair, khaki pants, and comfortable shoes gave him the look of a trustworthy grandfather. Not that Sam had ever met any of her grandparents. They were all dead, including those from Helene's branch of the family.

Sam squirmed in her seat. The squeaking leather was the only sound in the otherwise silent room. She twirled the mood ring around her finger. She wasn't surprised that it was jet black. Dr. Boyle would say touching the ring was Sam's attempt at comfort. He'd be right because thinking about Lisa was the only thing that was comforting at the moment.

Dr. Boyle adjusted his glasses and waited patiently. Sam knew from past experience that he could outwait anybody, so the four of them sat in stony silence.

Amazingly, Dr. Boyle caved in first. He cleared his throat. "Samantha Rose, you received a lot of attention from a photograph in the Clarksonville Courier recently. How did that make you feel?"

Finally, Sam thought. Leave it to Dr. Boyle to be the only one brave enough to bring up the elephant in the room.

"That wasn't cool."

"Why wasn't it cool?" Dr. Boyle asked.

"I wasn't ready."

"What weren't you ready for, Samantha Rose?" her mother asked.

Sam swallowed hard against the emotions bubbling up. She fought hard to keep her tears in control, but it was a losing battle. She put a hand up to hide her eyes.

No one moved to comfort her. It wasn't the Payton way. Keep your head up. Don't let them see you cry. You are the pinnacle to which all others seek. She didn't feel like a pinnacle at that moment.

Completely out of character, her mother laid what was meant to be a comforting hand on her arm.

Sam pulled away. "Don't try to console me, Mother. You and Daddy have a—what was that you called it on Sunday? Oh, yes, a *situation* on your hands. One that obviously needs controlling. *Situation*—that was the word you used wasn't it, Mother?"

"You're skating on thin ice, Samantha Rose," her father warned. His face flushed red.

Hey, Sam thought, *he finally speaks!* They'd been there for twenty minutes at that point.

Anger flashed in Her father's eyes when he added, "Do not disrespect your mother."

"Really?" Sam wiped at her tears so that she could see her father clearly. "You want to go there again?"

Her father appealed to Dr. Boyle, demanding he get a handle on the situation.

"No, no," Dr. Boyle said, putting a hand up. "This is good. We need these feelings to come out." He faced Sam. "Let's stick with the lesbian topic for now."

Sam's mother inhaled sharply.

"Mimi," Dr. Boyle said, "why did the word *lesbian* make you gasp?"

"It's such a hateful word." Her mother looked everywhere but at the people in the room.

"But the word applies to your daughter."

Sam's mother looked at her hands, mindlessly picking at her recent manicure. With a resigned sigh, she looked up at Sam. "I wish you had come to us sooner about this."

"What your mother is trying to say—"

"Daddy," Sam blurted, "let Mother speak for herself."

"Why am I the bad guy around here all of a sudden?" He sank back in the couch like a scolded little boy and sulked.

"Daddy, you're not the bad guy." Sam softened her voice. "I just feel like you never let people speak for themselves." *Like me.* "And all I want to do is make you both understand who I am. Somehow you and Mother missed all the clues."

Her father sat up taller. "What clues?" His voice had also softened.

"Like the fact that I never had any boys calling or coming over. How I had crushes on girls my whole life."

"We thought you'd outgrow that," Sam's mother said.

"You knew?"

Sam's mother nodded. "Of course, we did. And truly, we thought it was natural for a child to have crushes on her friends."

"It is natural, but I'm not a child anymore. And I haven't, as you say, outgrown it. I'm not going to. How in the world did you not know? We live in the same house." Sam was sure Dr. Boyle was cheering them on quietly in his head.

"Well," her mother said, "I think we got used to Helene taking care of you, and, as the years wore on, we grew more and more distant from you." She exchanged a glance with her husband. "That's something I regret now. We obviously don't know you as well as we should, and I think Helene realized it, too."

"Why didn't you send Helene away sooner? And don't say it was because you had that contract, Daddy." She said the word 'contract' with disgust. "We all know you can do anything you want."

Her father didn't respond. He simply gestured for Sam's mother to speak.

"You had bonded so well with Helene," Sam's mother

continued. "We didn't have the heart to send her away."

"So why are you sending her away now?" Too bad, Dr. Boyle, Sam thought. My mommy issues are coming up sooner than expected. Apparently, all the Payton family issues are intertwined.

"Helene is the one who wants to go," her father said quietly.

"What?" Sam sat back, stunned. "Why?" It didn't make sense.

"First of all, Samantha Rose," her mother said, "please know that she loves you very much. Don't ever forget that. It was a tough decision for her. She wants the three of us to spend more time with each other."

Sam mulled it over. "Helene would say something like that. She was always so selfless." And if she had told me it was her idea to leave, I would have begged her to stay. That's why she let me believe Mother and Daddy were kicking her out.

"She is a very kind person," her mother said. "She was more concerned about the stitches above your eye than her own concussion."

"I know." Sam reached up and touched the scar above her eye. "Mother, did you ever get jealous of Helene?"

Her mother took a deep breath and sighed. "Yes. She was so good with you. So much better than I could ever hope to be. I wish I could have—"

"Mother, it's okay. Remember on Sunday when I said I was lucky to have two moms?"

Her mother nodded.

"I meant it. The three of you raised me together. And I'm not going to lose Helene from my life because she's moving out. I hope you both understand that."

Her mother smiled. "I wouldn't have it any other way."

"Daddy?"

He nodded. "Like your mother said."

"Are we ever going to let people know who Helene really is?" *Sorry Dr. Boyle,* Sam thought, *you can go home now. I'll take it from here.*

"Did you tell your friends?" her father asked.

Sam shook her head.

"What about your special friend?" Sam's mother asked. "Did you tell her who Helene is?"

"She has a name, Mother." Sam didn't want to stir the pot now that she and her parents were communicating, but she needed to let them know she was done hiding, and they needed to respect that.

"You're right. I'm sorry. Lisa. Does she know?"

"No. I think it's the one and only thing I've kept from her. I mean, how in the world would I explain it?"

"Yes, I can see how that would be difficult." Her father looked lost in thought for a moment and then added, "I'd like to continue to keep this our secret. For as long as we can."

Sam nodded.

"Scandals like this can hurt the family businesses. And we've managed to keep this whopper quiet for—"

"Eighteen years," Sam finished. "Has Dr. Boyle known this whole time?"

Her father nodded.

Time was getting dangerously close to running out on their session, and there was no way she was going to let Dr. Boyle call time before she'd had her say. "I need you both to understand that I'm queer. I'm a lesbian. I know those words seem harsh, but it's not a phase. It's my reality." Sam turned toward her mother. "Mother, a

314

while back, you accused my friends of brainwashing me, but that's so far from the truth. I'm the one that pursued Lisa, you know. I love her—"

"You *think* you love her," her father interrupted.

"No, I *know* I love her, and I know with all my heart that she loves me." Sam couldn't read the fleeting expression crossing her mother's face. "Nobody twisted my arm. Believe me."

"Is this really what you want?" Her father shrugged.

"Daddy," Sam cried, "it's not..." She paused for a moment, trying to find the right words. "It's not something to *want* or *not want*. It just is. It's part of what makes me who I am. It's not something I came up with to annoy you. I'm not in the throes of teenage rebellion. I'm not doing this to hurt you. I, ahhh—" She tilted her head back and groaned. "I don't know how to make you understand." She sent a pleading look to Dr. Boyle, but he simply sat there, enjoying the show. She looked at her parents. "I'm happy. I'm truly happy for the first time in my life. When I'm with Lisa, it's like I finally found a reason for living." She looked from her mother's sympathetic face to her father's stoic one. "I hope you can accept me someday."

"We're afraid for you, Samantha Rose," Sam's mother said. "There's so much hatred out there."

Her father cleared his throat. "The Paytons are used to being in the spotlight. I know you haven't always liked it, but we're afraid that people will crush you because of your, uh, lifestyle—"

"It's not a lifestyle—"

"Okay, okay." Her father threw his hands up in a defensive gesture. "People may take the fact that you're dating a girl as permission to harass you."

Already been there, Daddy, Sam thought. She hadn't told her parents about the harassment she had received at school, and she doubted she ever would. The less they knew, the better.

"Kitten, I think your mother and I are slowly coming to terms with your, uh, news. The PFLAG group has been quite informative, actually." Sam's father turned to Sam's mother. "Mother, you should come with me to their next meeting. They said a lot of things that made sense." He turned back to Sam. "I'm just afraid that the rest of the world won't be as accepting of you."

Sam's mother reached over and rubbed Sam's arm. "I'm sure everything will be okay. You have a good head on your shoulders. And you know what?"

"What?"

"I like her. Your friend. Your *girlfriend.*" Her mother grinned. "There, I said it."

"That's good, Mother," Sam said. "You're making progress."

Sam's mother's smile grew. "Lisa is very pretty, and she seems sweet. We should count ourselves lucky, Gerald, that our baby met someone kind and nurturing. And she knows so much about gardening. Maybe we can have her over for dinner sometime. Would you like that, Samantha Rose?"

Sam nodded. She couldn't believe her ears. Were her parents supportive? Wait. She hadn't heard from her father.

"Daddy?"

"I'm still musing on all of this, Kitten. This was a mighty big bomb you dropped in our laps. I'm still trying to figure it all out." He sighed and then said, "I want to meet your friend's parents. I want to know what kind of people my daughter is associating with."

"I'm sure they'd like to meet you, too." The fact that he didn't say Lisa's name was not lost on her. He was clearly going to be the tougher sell, but at least he had opened the door a crack.

"I always pictured a son-in-law," he mused. "One that would take over the family business so your mother and I could travel more."

"Daddy, c'mon. That is so sexist."

"I know. I know. Nothing says my little girl can't run the business with, uh, with a significant other."

Sam laughed at the archaic expression. "But you know what?"

"What, honey?" her mother asked.

"Lisa wants to be a doctor." Sam almost burst out laughing when her mother's eyes grew wide.

"A doctor? Gerald," her mother gushed, "our baby is dating a doctor."

"Mother," Sam's father said with a laugh, "Lisa is not a doctor yet."

"Oh, don't ruin my moment."

Dr. Boyle chuckled and announced the end of the session. They had, in fact, gone over by ten minutes, which was a minor miracle because Dr. Boyle was a stickler about his sessions ending on time. He was almost obsessive-compulsive about it.

As Sam and her parents stood up to leave, Sam realized something. Her parents weren't having that much trouble with the fact that she was dating Lisa. Their trouble seemed to be more about how the rest of the world would perceive it and how their plans for Sam's life weren't coming together exactly as they had pictured.

"Thank you for your services, Doc." Sam's father shook Dr. Boyle's hand. "I guess you should keep Tuesdays set aside for the Payton Family for a while."

"Sounds like a fine idea. I'll put you on the schedule myself." He saw them to the door.

On the way down the elevator, Sam said, "Mother, let's go to New York like you planned. Would it be crazy to go the week of Thanksgiving?"

"Probably, but let's do it anyway." Her mother's smile reassured Sam that her family might actually be on the mend. "I thought you had forgotten."

"No. We've all been preoccupied, I think. Oh, and Daddy? I hope you can help me with a problem I'm going to have after Helene leaves."

"What's that?"

"I'm not going to have anybody to watch hockey games with. What do you think?"

"Hmm." He rubbed his chin. "I used to play, you know."

"I didn't know that."

"In prep school. I played junior varsity, and I was terrible. I couldn't skate backward." He laughed. "But I would be honored to watch hockey with my daughter. Who are we rooting for?"

"Montréal."

"Not the Sabres?"

"No, Daddy." The elevator doors opened, so she whispered the next part. "I'm half Canadian, don't forget." Sam's heart swelled when he burst out laughing.

She linked arms with her parents, and they headed for the Town Car.

After the brief car ride home, Sam ran up to her rooms and freshened up. She only had a few minutes before Marlee arrived to chauffeur her to William and Evelyn's house. A thrill ran through her, and she had the oddest feeling, one she almost didn't recognize. Hope.

With one last check in the bathroom mirror, Sam was ready to celebrate. She grabbed her Moncler peacoat from the couch where she'd tossed it and headed down the stairs to Helene's apartment.

Helene opened the door and smiled. "How did it go with Dr. Boyle?"

"Really well," Sam said.

Helene blew out a relieved sigh. "Thank goodness. I know you have to head out, but you'll give me some details later?"

"Absolutely."

Helene pulled Sam into a hug and whispered, "Happy anniversary, Sam. Give my best to Lisa."

"I will." The front doorbell chimed. "I gotta go."

"I know. Enjoy."

"I will." Sam hurried to answer the door.

Marlee's chauffeur's hat made Sam laugh. "Ready to go?"

Sam nodded, and they headed to Susie's house first to drop off Sam's old phone. There was no way in hell Sam was going to let her father ruin the special anniversary evening Lisa had planned for them. It was better for him to think she and her phone were at Susie's.

Marlee and Susie then chauffeured her to William and Evelyn's house. Sam waved goodbye to her friends and then knocked on the front door.

"Come on in," Lisa called from the kitchen.

Sam walked in to find her incredible girlfriend putting the finishing touches on a pasta primavera dinner she'd made herself. The low lighting, lit candles, and soft music set the romantic mood perfectly.

"Come in," Lisa said. She wore a deliciously low-cut blouse with a silver necklace that lay strategically against her chest. Her dark hair was pulled back into a loose ponytail and tacked up on her head.

"I love your hair that way."

"Thank you."

Sam moved closer to get a kiss, but Lisa put a finger to Sam's lips and whispered in her ear, "Soon."

A ribbon of desire spiraled through Sam's body.

"Sit."

Sam sat.

Lisa brought two plates filled with amazing food to the table, setting one in front of Sam and one on the far side of the table. Sam frowned. Lisa would be too far away; Sam wouldn't be able to touch her.

"Non-alcoholic," Lisa said as she set two glasses of sparkling cider on the table. "I don't want to cause any trouble for William and Evelyn."

"Good thinking." Sam didn't mind because being near Lisa was intoxicating enough.

Throughout the meal, the conversation was light. They mainly talked about Lisa's family and the shenanigans her brother and sisters were up to. Lisa never once asked about the therapy session, which was fine with Sam because she wanted to keep their six-month anniversary untainted by family drama. After dinner, Sam stacked their plates and stood up to put them in the sink. Lisa had cooked, so Sam figured she should do the dishes.

Lisa had other ideas, though. She took the plates from Sam, set them on the counter, and reached for Sam's hand. Wordlessly, she blew out the candles in the kitchen and led Sam through the living room and down the hall to the back bedroom. Ironically, it was the same bedroom where Sam had suffered from a migraine five weeks before.

While Sam waited in the center of the softly lit room, Lisa pushed play on the iPod Sam had gotten her, lit a few more candles, and then fixed Sam with a smoldering gaze. Inch by inch, Lisa made her way closer. Without speaking, she pressed her lips to Sam's and then trailed kisses along Sam's jawline, eventually moving on to feast on Sam's neck. Sam moaned and turned to putty. Kiss by kiss, Lisa undid the buttons on Sam's shirt.

When Sam tried to work at Lisa's clothing, Lisa pushed Sam's hands back gently and whispered in a husky voice, "I'll take it from here, okay?"

Sam dropped her hands to her sides and surrendered.

~~~ The End ~~~

Newsletter Signup

Sign up for Barbara L. Clanton's newsletter to stay on top of new (and revised) releases. She also likes to provide writing tips for newbie (or oldbie) writers and recommend books to read (other than her own, of course).

Sign Up on Barbara L. Clanton's Official Website:

www.BLClanton.com

About the Author
Barbara L. Clanton

Barbara L. Clanton is a native New Yorker who left those "New York minutes" for a slower-paced life in central Florida. While in middle and high schools, she played any sport she could find—softball, volleyball, basketball, and field hockey. During high school she could even be found in the upstairs gym  playing handball with her friends. She played softball at Princeton University and was the team captain during their Ivy-league champion senior year.

Her career has been spent teaching mathematics at college preparatory schools in both New York and Florida. She also coached softball and basketball in both states as well. She was inducted into the ASANA's (Amateur Sports Alliance of North America) Hall of Fame as an amateur softball player.

Somewhere in adulthood, she picked up a new hobby. "Dr. Barb" plays the bass guitar and has been in several pop-rock bands, playing such notable events as Gay Days Orlando.

When asked why she started writing, she said she was writing the books she wished she had in high school to help her make sense of her "differentness." Although the world is evolving, it's still not easy to come out to yourself or the world. She hopes her books will help.

Barbara L. Clanton's Website:
http://www.blclanton.com

Barbara L. Clanton's Instagram:
https://www.instagram.com/barbara.clanton14

Barbara L. Clanton's Facebook:
https://www.facebook.com/BassGuitarGirl

Barbara L. Clanton's Goodreads Page:
https://www.goodreads.com/author/show/3072442.Barbara_L_Clanton

Barbara L. Clanton's Author Page on Amazon:
https://www.amazon.com/Barbara-L-Clanton

Books by Barbara L. Clanton

THE CLARKSONVILLE SERIES (Young Adult)

The Clarksonville Series follows four high school girls in upstate New York as they maneuver the difficult process of coming out to themselves, each other, and their families. And it doesn't always go well. The four friends have a mutual love of softball which helps them bond and find love. Each book is from a different character's point of view, but all four main characters are present in each book. There are currently eight books in the series.

Out of Left Field: Marlee's Story
(Book One in the Clarksonville Series)

High school junior Marlee McAllister lives and breathes softball. She's the pitcher for the Clarksonville Cougars in the North Country of upstate New York. With the season opener approaching, Marlee and her best friend, Jeri D'Amico, go to scout their rivals, the East Valley Panthers. The Panthers' star pitcher, Christy Loveland, took the All-county pitching title the preceding year. It is a title Marlee covets. Marlee and Jeri settle in for the game, but as the Panthers take the field, Marlee finds herself staring at Susie Torres, the Panther left fielder.

For reasons Marlee doesn't understand, she's drawn to Susie. Over the next few weeks, Marlee and Susie will slowly act on their mutual attraction. But suddenly, Susie pulls away without explanation, and Marlee realizes it has to do with Christy. Susie won't explain the bond she and Christy share, but whatever it is, it threatens Marlee's burgeoning relationship with Susie.

Struggling to maintain her grades, dealing with the ever-increasing estrangement from her best friend Jeri, and handling the pressures of the All-county pitching competition, Marlee also has to confront the bittersweet realities of what it might mean to be gay.

ISBN: 978-1-953734-04-4 (eBook)
ISBN: 978-1-953734-16-7 (Paperback)

Tools of Ignorance: Lisa's Story
(Book Two in the Clarksonville Series)

Lisa Brown is the starting catcher for the Clarksonville Cougars High School softball team, and she has a major crush on her pitcher Marlee. Lisa continues to carry her torch for Marlee, even when Sam, a rival softball player, flirts sweetly. However, Lisa becomes more confused than ever when Tara, the first girl she ever kissed and the first girl who ever broke her heart, resurfaces. Since Marlee doesn't know Lisa's alive, should Lisa give up on her once and for all?

Sam seems to have secrets of her own, but Lisa wonders if she should overlook them and allow her fledging attraction to grow for the pretty blonde, or should she fan the tiny flame still burning in her heart for Tara? Lisa faces these problems and deals with society's tools of ignorance in her quest for love and acceptance.

ISBN: 978-1-953734-06-8 (eBook)
ISBN: 978-1-953734-17-4 (Paperback)

Going, Going, Gone: Susie's Story
(Book Three in the Clarksonville Series)

Susie Torres planned to spend most of the summer before her senior year of high school with her girlfriend, Marlee McAllister, but that's proving to be quite challenging. Marlee works at D'Amico's restaurant, and Susie babysits for Mrs. Johnson, her mother's boss. Susie hates the job because she not only works like a slave but almost gets paid like one. Susie is desperate to take her physical relationship with Marlee further, but she knows she has to go at Marlee's slower pace. Complicating things is the attention that a pretty blonde softball player from another team shows Marlee, and Susie falls into a funk when Marlee seems to enjoy it.

On top of that, nothing she does seems to be good enough for her summer softball coach. Frustrated with life, Susie accidentally, on purpose, comes out to her mother. It would be an understatement to say that her mother didn't take it well. Can Susie deal with a girlfriend whose head has possibly been turned by another, an employer who treats her like dirt, a coach who doesn't respect her, and a mother who tells her she is unnatural? Can she get her life back on track before senior year starts?

ISBN: 978-1-953734-05-1 (eBook)
ISBN: 978-1-953734-18-1 (Paperback)

Stealing Second: Sam's Story
(Book Four in the Clarksonville Series)

Samantha Rose Payton likes girls, but her parents don't know that. And Sam would like to keep it that way because her parents are ultra-conservative Republicans. They live in a mansion and have servants and chauffeurs. However, instead of playing the dutiful debutante who plays the violin and still has a nanny at age seventeen, Sam would rather watch ice hockey on TV and play second base on her summer softball team. Having to hide her relationship with her girlfriend, Lisa, from her parents is becoming an agonizing struggle. Not only are her friends pressuring her to come out to her parents, but they are also trying to convince her to attend a very public gay pride festival at the local college.

At least she has her nanny Helene to confide in, but for how much longer? Sam is acutely aware that the time for Helene to move on may be fast approaching. And if that isn't enough, Sam's summer softball coach gives her no end of grief after an error-filled game and isn't afraid of making an example out of her. Will Sam remain the perfect princess her parents expect? Will her beloved nanny leave her forever? Will her girlfriend get fed up about being kept hidden? Will her friends continue to pressure her about coming out? Will Coach Greer make her life miserable? All of these questions are answered in Stealing Second: Sam's Story.

ISBN: 978-1-953734-07-5 (eBook)
ISBN: 978-1-953734-19-8 (Paperback)

Out at Home
(Book Five in the Clarksonville Series)

Marlee McAllister just wants to fit in. She didn't know she didn't fit in until Kate and Rita - the prettiest girls in the senior class - pointed it out. Even Marlee's grandmother declared that Marlee's too old for "this tomboy nonsense." All the other girls at school have long hair except Marlee. All the other girls wear something other than jeans, a t-shirt, and sneakers to school every day. Except for Marlee. All the other girls fit in except Marlee.

Marlee decides to grow out her short hair, buy femmy girly clothes, and pretend she has a boyfriend named Ronnie. Really, though? She has the most amazing girlfriend in Susie Torres. Susie is everything Marlee hoped for - sweet, sexy, kind, athletic, pretty. And best of all? She loves Marlee as much as Marlee loves her. Although their parents know about their relationship, not many other people do.

Marlee is out at home but not to anyone else. And if anyone else finds out she's into girls, Kate and Rita especially, the entire school and her grandparents will know within a day. Life as she knows it will be over.

Out at Home is the story of Marlee McAllister's life-altering struggle to fit in.

ISBN: 978-1-953734-20-4 (eBook)
ISBN: 978-1-953734-24-2 (Paperback)

Tools of the Devil
(Book Six in the Clarksonville Series)

Seventeen-year-old Lisa Brown loved going to church. Oh sure, sometimes she'd rather sleep in, but she liked the calming and empowering strength of her faith. Sundays revitalized her spirit when she thanked God for the wonderful things in her life, like her loving family and amazing girlfriend, Samantha Rose. One day she hoped to marry Sam, have a house and yard, and have babies together. One day.

But then it happened. That fateful Sunday, the guest preacher stepped behind the pulpit and spoke four words that would change Lisa's world forever. "Homosexuality is a sin," he said. Had she heard him right? When her mother put a hand on her forearm, she knew she had. Every muscle in her body tensed, and she forgot to breathe. What was happening?

The church she'd been baptized in, grown up in, and wanted to get married in had, in one instant, turned against her. Still not quite believing what she'd heard, she mumbled, "Ignorance is a sin, Reverend." Never one to back down from a challenge, she scanned the congregation but didn't find a single soul who looked upset by his statement. On the contrary, many nodded in agreement. Under her breath, she muttered, "Game on, people. Game on."

ISBN: 978-1-953734-21-1 (eBook)
ISBN: 978-1-953734-25-9 (Paperback)

Going Under
(Book Seven in the Clarksonville Series)

Susie Torres is a second-semester senior with devoted friends and an amazing girlfriend in Marlee McAllister. Susie's father has the kind of job that takes him away from home on frequent business trips, but lately, his trips seem to be longer and more frequent. Tensions rise at home when Susie's mother challenges him about that. At first, Susie and her younger brother Miguel hide in her room when their parents' frequent squabbles elevate to out-and-out yelling matches. But as her parents' war escalates further, Susie finds other ways to escape the tension.

A fake ID becomes a clear and easy way to anesthetize herself with alcohol. Her crumbling home life becomes momentarily forgotten whenever she swims in a sea of peaceful drunken bliss. Unfortunately, Susie doesn't realize that she is alienating everyone around her with her attempts to cope with her parents' possible divorce. Including Marlee. Her best friend Sam tries to warn her that her excessive drinking is driving away all of her friends, but Sam's well-meaning advice isn't heard. Will Susie finally realize that it is her own actions that are making her life fall apart around her? That her new love of drinking is getting in the way of everything good in her life? That her amazingly patient girlfriend isn't going to put up with much more?

ISBN: 978-1-953734-22-8 (eBook)
ISBN: 978-1-953734-26-6 (Paperback)

Stealing Hope
(Book Eight in the Clarksonville Series)

Sam Payton is a high school senior with a bit of an identity crisis. Raised in a well-to-do family, she dutifully plays the role of Samantha Rose Payton, the wealthy debutante. Now, almost one full year into her life-changing relationship with Lisa Brown, Sam is hit with many life-challenging events. Her best friend, Susie Torres, struggles with alcohol addiction and a wrecked home life as her parents go through a bitter divorce, and Sam tries to help her friend keep her head above water. In another struggle, two friends cross the line between friendship and intimacy—a line that should not have been approached. Sam finds herself trying to make them see how incredibly egregious the transgressions are for all involved. And to top it all off, Sam's mother is diagnosed with a serious illness.

Through the love of her parents and her girlfriend, Sam navigates these challenges the best way she can, all while trying to fulfill everyone's varying expectations of her. Sam struggles to break free of the preconceived roles she seems to be bound by to figure out who she really is. It ultimately comes down to whether Sam can make everyone see that she is both a softball-playing ice-hockey-loving lesbian named Sam as well as a classically-music-trained debutante named Samantha Rose.

ISBN: 978-1-953734-23-5 (eBook)
ISBN: 978-1-953734-27-3 (Paperback)

THE WHICKETT SERIES (Young Adult)

Art for Art's Sake: Meredith's Story
(Book One in the Whickett Series)

High school senior Meredith Bedford is a social outcast. Her family recently moved from the Catskill Mountains to the sprawling suburbs of Albany, the capital of New York State. Shy and self-conscious about her acne scars, she stays to herself and tries to remain invisible. Her twelve-year-old brother, Mikey, has Down Syndrome, and she tries hard not to blame her troubles on him. Despite verbal and sometimes physical harassment, she survives because she has her art. She was selected to be part of the elite Advanced Placement art class and is quite good at capturing the emotions of her subjects in her portraits. Besides her family, art is the one thing that helps her cope with her outcast status.

One day, at a senior class meeting, she sees Dani Lassiter, president of the senior class and captain of the lacrosse team and knows that she must paint this enigmatic young woman. One class period later, Dani manipulates things to have Meredith as her partner for a history project. Meredith is suspicious of Dani's motives but takes a chance. And it pays off. Meredith slowly sheds her invisibility cloak and allows Dani in - a little at a time. They explore an old Victorian house for their history project and become close with Esther and Millie, the two older women who own the house and who've lived together for about forty years. But, when Dani reveals to Meredith that she is gay, Meredith simply can't deal with the news. How had she not known? What is it that won't allow her to come to terms with this unexpected news? Will Meredith control her own homophobia, or will she reject the one person who had taken a chance on her and made her feel human?

Dani's Story
(Book Two in the Whickett Series)

< Coming Soon >

THE GRASSE RIVER SERIES (Young Adult)

Quite an Undertaking: Devon's Story
(Book One in the Grasse River Series)

Devon Raines, a sixteen-year-old journalism nerd, was happily minding her own business when wham, her life was turned upside down. She struggled with grief when her grandmother died from a sudden heart attack. But it was at her grandmother's wake that she locked eyes with the most beautiful black girl she'd ever seen. No, Rebecca Washington was the most beautiful *girl* she'd ever seen, period. Would this beautiful dancer freak out if she knew Devon was gay and attracted?

Enter Jessie Crowler, Rebecca's basketball-playing best friend. Or were they only friends? Devon tried to hide her attraction for the ebony dancer, but would fate allow Rebecca to look her way? Would Jessie get in the way? Would the difference in skin color keep them apart? All this adds up to quite an undertaking in Devon's formerly quiet existence.

Rebecca's Story
(Book Two in the Grasse River Series)

< Coming Soon >

THE GIRLS' SPORTS SERIES (Children's Books Ages 9-12)

Bases Loaded

Sixth-grader Mackenzie Kelly's first love was soccer until her best friend talked her into playing summer softball. Now Mack is eager to be on her school's softball team and dreams of playing in the Olympics with her idol, Cat Osterman. But first, she needs to bring up her failing English grade to stay on the team. When she learns softball has been cut from the Olympics, she's determined somehow to get it back into the Olympic Games so she can fulfill her dream.

"I just wanted to let you know I received the book and I think it is FANTASTIC!"
– Jessica Mendoza, *US Olympic Softball Team*

ASIN: B00094IT3RK (eBook)
ISBN 978-1-934452-79-0 (Paperback)

Side Out

Seventh-grader Dina Jacobs feels like she's landed on another planet when her family moves from Long Island, New York to Indiana. She tries out for the seventh-grade volleyball team, and her new friend, Christine, introduces her to Olympic volleyball. Now Dina dreams of playing in the Olympics like her newfound idol, Logan Tom. Indiana doesn't seem so bad until Dina's Jewish faith crashes against her coach's win-at-all-costs attitude. Miserable, Dina is torn between staying true to her religious customs or putting them aside to play the game she loves.

ASIN: B005HM9CUU (eBook)
ISBN 978-1-934452-65-3 (Paperback)

Live, Love, Lacrosse

Addie Coleburn, fresh out of the sixth grade, is spending the summer at her grandmother's house in Syracuse with her mother and brother. Kimi Takahashi, a girl who lives up the street, invites Addie to go to the park and play lacrosse. Addie hasn't the first clue what lacrosse is and would rather sit on Grandma's front porch eating potato chips, drinking sodas, and reading books. But then again, spending the summer dealing with her younger brother isn't that appealing, either, so she goes to the park with Kimi. Within a week, she's hooked on lacrosse. She's overweight and can't keep up with the faster, stronger girls. She has to find a way to lose her excess weight quickly or risk getting cut from the team.

ASIN: B09GPYMHDK (eBook)
ISBN 978-1-943837-50-2 (Paperback)